the Necessary Marriage

Elisa Lodato grew up in London and read English at Pembroke College, Cambridge. After graduating she went to live in Japan, where she spent a year teaching, travelling, and learning to speak the language. On returning to the UK she spent many happy years working for Google before training to become an English teacher. Helping pupils to search for meaning in a text inspired Elisa to take up the pen and write her own. Her first novel *An Unremarkable Body* was longlisted for the Bath Novel Award 2016. Elisa lives in Gloucestershire with her husband and two children.

Also by Elisa Lodato

An Unremarkable Body

the Necessary Marriage

Elisa Lodato

WEIDENFELD & NICOLSON

First published in Great Britain in 2018
by Weidenfeld & Nicolson
an imprint of the Orion Publishing Group Ltd
Carmelite House, 50 Victoria Embankment
London EC4Y 0DZ

An Hachette UK Company

1 3 5 7 9 10 8 6 4 2

A CIP catalogue record for this book is
available from the British Library.

ISBN (Hardback) 978 1 4746 0637 0
ISBN (Export Trade Paperback) 978 1 4746 0638 7
ISBN (eBook) 978 1 4746 0640 0

Typeset by Input Data Services Ltd, Somerset

Printed and bound in Great Britain by Clays Ltd, Elcograf S.p.A.

MIX
Paper from
responsible sources
FSC® C104740

www.orionbooks.co.uk

For Jim

Prologue

Monday, 12 November 2001

Julia was teaching her first lesson of the day when the head teacher, a small, birdlike woman with hair that was too long and too yellow for her, came to knock on the glass panel of her classroom door. She looked up and smiled, despite her irritation. Another impromptu inspection dressed up as professional development.

'Please, come in,' she said, opening the door wide.

The girls in her class automatically stood up and chorused, 'Good morning, Mrs Southern.'

'Good morning, girls,' Mrs Southern returned with perfect equanimity. 'Miss Campbell, could I have a word with you outside, please?'

'Yes, of course,' Julia said. She put her whiteboard marker down on her desk and followed Mrs Southern out into the hallway. 'What is it?' she asked, as soon as the door was closed.

'We've just had an urgent message from your mother. She rang the office a few moments ago.'

'What's happened?'

'We're not sure. She said she had to speak to you. I'll finish off your lesson while you go downstairs. She left a number for you to contact her on.'

Preeti, the school secretary, looked up in quiet expectation of Julia. She pointed to a desk in the corner of the room, used by another part-time member of staff. 'You can use Mrs Lawson's desk. Dial nine for an outside line.'

'Where's the number? Mrs Southern said my mum left a number.'

'I've written it on the pad next to the phone. It's all over there.'

Julia sat down and lifted the receiver. She did exactly what she'd been told to do, noting as she dialled that it was an unfamiliar mobile number. Her mother answered on the second ring.

'Julia?'

'Yes. Are you OK?'

'It's Becca. She's had a dreadful accident.'

'Where? What happened?'

'I don't know all the details. The police came to find us this morning. They say she threw herself from a window.'

'Fucking hell.'

Preeti looked up from her desk, her nose wrinkling as she sniffed at the 'fuck' that lingered in the air.

'Listen to me. I'm on my way. Andrew's driving as fast as he can. This is his phone.'

'On your way? Where are you?'

'On the M4. We've been away. It doesn't matter. The point is, I need you to go to the hospital and be with your sister until I can get there.'

'I'm leaving now. What hospital?'

'Kingston. Phone me on this number when you know anything.'

'Will do.'

'Everything OK?' Preeti asked as soon as Julia put the phone down. She wanted to have something for Mrs Southern.

'No. I think my sister's tried to kill herself.'

Part I:

Jane and Leonard

It is given that as man and woman grow together in love and trust, they shall be united with one another in heart, body and mind.

The Marriage Service

Chapter 1

Jane Forster was seventeen when she first became aware of Leonard Campbell. He joined Hinchley Wood School for Girls as a deputy head in September 1974. Jane was one of twelve pupils in a small class of A-level students studying nineteenth-century British history. He was a tall, gentle man with absurdly full lips. His hair had already begun to thin on top, and his left hand was without a wedding ring. The space on his long white finger marked the beginning of an enquiry for Jane. It began with the delicate brown hairs that had sprouted in the empty space, free from precious metal and the cloying fingers of another.

It wasn't a crush or the start of an infatuation with an older man; it was much simpler than that. Leonard Campbell was her teacher. A new teacher. And he knew a lot. His eyes were small and wet in an expanse of pale, delicate skin.

He wore dark brown suits with shirt collars that sat – sharp and ready – on his lapels. His shoes were polished but well worn: he walked around the classroom as he spoke, distributing dates and reform acts like gifts, and when he walked past Jane, she took a deep breath and sometimes discerned the musky interior of a car and, other times, the scent of manufactured orange air freshener. As he approached her desk, she lowered her eyes to her book in order to glance sideways when he passed and inspect his hands and the watch that poked out of his shirt cuffs. It had a brown leather strap with a gold face. She liked the way it perched comfortably, unobtrusively on the soft hairs that grew as far as his wrist but no further, the watch marking not just the passing of time but the border between the private and public realms of his body.

She wanted to know about him: how often he washed his hair, how closely he trimmed his nails. She knew that she had gone beyond the initial interest her classmates had shown when he first walked into the room and wrote his name on the board, and in her effort to glean more, she decided to listen to what he was saying. She learned about the men and women who had tried – through legislation, literature and demonstrations – to create a more liberal, compassionate society. When they examined the revolutions of 1848, Jane felt her understanding grow and widen in a way that was almost painful. He smiled as he spoke, even when he was on his way back to the blackboard at the front of the room. It was as if he didn't need to see the faces of his pupils. He was confident that his words – like seeds thrown by a benevolent farmer – would grow and flourish where they fell. She grabbed at the wider reading, quickly noting down any novels or essays he suggested to the class.

In the November of her first term, Leonard noticed the copy of *Mary Barton* on her desk, her embroidered bookmark resting neatly at the midway point.

'Are you enjoying it?' he asked as he paused beside her.

She looked up and found the lump and line of his crotch waiting for her. 'Er, yes. Yes, sir. I am.'

'Good.' His smile disappeared, but he didn't. She felt his eyes on her as she returned to the questions she was answering in her notebook. The brown curtain of his groin remained in her peripheral vision.

'Let me know when you finish, Miss Forster.'

'Sir?'

'*Mary Barton*. Let me know when you finish. I have many more recommendations for you.'

'Yes, sir.'

He began lending her his own copies, bringing them with him to lessons so that he could place them – discreetly – on her desk. In one or two of the volumes he had highlighted certain passages for her attention.

And within this academic generosity Jane was able to peer more closely at the man – her teacher – Leonard Campbell. He looked as though he were squinting as he described Sir Robert Peel, a wealthy factory owner himself, his eyes widening as he outlined the principles of the legislation aimed at curtailing the number of hours young apprentices could work. Jane noticed how he held the middle two fingers of his left hand with his right, lengthening and pulling them straight as he built his argument that slow, progressive reform saved the country from bloody revolution. Jane watched how he handled his own body gently, pulling on his fingers as if for a word, a phrase that would add even greater cadence to his impression of the past, and as he did so, she imagined – for the briefest moment – how those fingers would feel were he to slip them inside her. The thought shocked her own body; she closed her eyes as she felt the rush of arousal drop and burst within her. She experienced it as an urgent need to go to the toilet. To release something that threatened to flow.

'Miss Forster. Are you OK?'

She opened her eyes. Leonard and the rest of the class were watching her and yet, even in the uncertainty that flooded the room, which could only be broken by her avowal that she was OK, she could not let go of the image of Leonard using his fingers to enter her.

'May I go to the toilet, please, sir?'

'Yes, of course.' Leonard dropped his hands to rest by his side.

If Jane was confused by the new feelings she had for her teacher, she was careful not to show it. Not because she feared being discovered but because she sensed that close study of the period and careful attention to Mr Campbell would unlock more moments like the afternoon with the fingers. She was interested in the interplay between learning and sex, listening to someone and being aroused by them, receiving a piece of their mind and then looking to their body for more, and she pursued it as she would have done any academic task.

The following January, when Leonard introduced the topic of the repeal of the Corn Laws, Jane picked up her pen, ready for careful study. He outlined key dates and principles, how the act split Peel's Conservative Party, and then he sat down at his desk and, clasping his hands together, rested his chin on his interlaced fingers and asked the class to consider hunger.

'What does it mean to you, Miss Barrow?' he asked the girl who sat behind Jane.

Brenda Barrow was a large, confident girl who'd given her virginity away as though it were an old school tie. Her breasts were so immense they simply occupied an area, a zone of maturity that attracted boys and gave the girls pause.

'It means to go without food.'

'Very good. And what kind of food could you go without?'

Brenda paused as though Leonard had failed to understand. She smiled down at her breasts and then, with an arched eyebrow, said, 'There are some things nobody can go without.'

'Be specific, Miss Barrow. If you were really hungry, what food would you crave?'

She sat up straight. 'I don't know.'

'Oh, come on! There must be something. Think, Barrow!'

'Sausages.' The word was out before she could reposition herself.

Leonard unclasped his hands and opened his arms in an attitude of democratic acceptance. 'Sausages. Anyone else?'

Jane put up her hand.

'Yes, Miss Forster?'

'Bread, sir.'

'Bread!' He clasped his hands back together and returned his head to its rest. 'Now tell me, Miss Forster, why bread?'

'Because it's the food of the masses, sir. It's cheap and filling. Factory workers spent a great proportion of their wages on bread in the 1840s.'

'Very good. And if bread is expensive . . . ?'

'Then workers apply pressure on employers to raise wages.'

'Excellent, Miss Forster. So you see, everyone, repeal of the Corn Laws had become an economic necessity. And it was called for by the emerging, newly powerful middle classes, who could see that keeping grain prices artificially high benefited only the land owners.'

Leonard turned to the board and wrote the key dates and names. His right arm was raised and vigorous in its scrawling, lifting his suit jacket just enough to reveal the very top of his thigh. With every head down, reproducing the words on the board, Jane closed her eyes and imagined standing just behind him. Not touching but close enough that when he turned round, his surprise would make him fall back against the blackboard. She thought of the mess it would make of his brown jacket, how – despite his protestations – she wouldn't move. She'd pull the stick of chalk from his fingers and, leaning across him, her breasts, so much smaller than Brenda's, finally making contact with his chest, write her own word on the board.

Chapter 2

Jane's interest continued to grow. She asked for further reading, wrote extra essays and waited around at the end of class with questions she hadn't thought to ask during the lesson. On a bright Monday morning, Leonard strode into the classroom purposefully and wrote the details of a lecture on at Central Hall, Westminster, the following Saturday, 7 June.

'It's not a school-sponsored excursion, as I only found out about it myself a few days ago, but I've contacted the event organisers and it seems the material will be uniquely suited to any student examining the rise of liberalism in the nineteenth century.' He smiled as he lifted his heels and forced his weight forwards. 'I myself will be on the steps outside the hall at ten a.m. sharp should any of you wish to join me.' Splaying his fingers open on the desk and deepening the lean, he looked hopefully at the blank faces before him.

Brenda Barrow came to find Jane at lunchtime to ask her if she was going.

'I'm not sure,' Jane said. She was sitting alone in the canteen, eating her sandwiches.

'I am.'

'You are?' she asked as Brenda sat down beside her.

'My mum and dad won't let me out of the house unless I'm going to the library or to study at someone's house. They'll lap this one up.'

'So you're not actually going?'

'Oh, I'm going. Going round to Gary's house.'

'Who's Gary?'

'Gary Stevens. You don't know Gary Stevens? He's Jamie's brother.'

'I don't know Gary or Jamie.'

'You need to come out with us a bit more. Get yourself a boyfriend.'

'No, thank you,' Jane said, shifting her chair a couple of inches to the right.

'Anyway, if anyone asks, can you tell them I went to the lecture with you?'

'I'm not sure I'm going.'

'Of course you are. You fancy him, don't you?'

'Who?'

'Mr Campbell. It's obvious. You're always watching him and trying to impress him.'

Jane looked down at her sandwich. The mouthful she'd bitten off when Brenda had appeared was still a mushy ball of cheese, bread and butter at the back of her throat. She felt too exposed to swallow.

'I'm not getting at you or nothing,' Brenda said quickly. 'And I think he likes you. Listen, it's not difficult. You've just got to make more of yourself. You know, a bit of lipstick, a tighter bra.' She focused her eyes on Jane's short brown hair. In an attitude of appalling tenderness, she lifted a few strands and let them fall as though Jane's hair could do nothing but drop back into place.

Jane pulled her hair back, away from Brenda's grasp, and

tried to smooth it down. 'I'll say you were with me if anyone asks.'

'Thanks, Jane. And listen, if you ever need anything – you know, any advice – I'm always here.'

Jane picked up her sandwich and chewed slowly in response.

She was standing on the steps outside the hall at nine thirty the following Saturday morning. She didn't want to risk being late and missing her opportunity to sit next to Mr Campbell. But as the minutes ticked past, she realised it would only be her waiting for him. He arrived twenty minutes later, wearing dark blue jeans with a brown belt, his face flushed from the brisk walk. His shirt was yellow with small blue spots, which, as he climbed the steps and got closer, she realised were in fact blue daisies. She looked down at his feet, embarrassed and elated that it was just the two of them, and noticed his shoes: the same brown brogues he wore to school every day. They looked strange underneath the flared cover of denim, as though the effort of weekend casual had been too much for his feet.

'Miss Forster. Good morning!'

'Good morning.'

'Is it just the two of us?'

'I think so.'

'Let's give it a few more minutes and then go inside. Did it take you long to get here?'

'No, not really. My dad gave me a lift to Hinchley Wood and I got the train to Waterloo.'

'Yes, I did the same. I must have been on the train behind.'

Jane nodded and pulled at her skirt. It had ridden up during the walk from Waterloo. Her new shoes – a pair of heeled Mary Janes with a small buckle nestled under the ankle – had dictated the outfit. She needed to wear tights in order to showcase her ankles, and the dark brown and red woollen skirt was the only one she owned, but now, in the June sunshine, she knew the heavy material had been a mistake.

The silence billowed beyond a few seconds and became harder to fill. Jane looked in her bag for a tissue, and Leonard raised his hand to his forehead in an exaggerated effort to see into the distance.

'I think we'll go in, shall we?'

'Yes, sir.'

'Please. It's a Saturday and we're not in school. Call me Leonard,' he smiled.

'Leonard,' Jane said, repeating the secret back to him.

Leonard's slender frame meant his thighs were comfortably contained by his seat, but at intervals during the lecture, he crossed his legs and once or twice she felt the top of his shoe rub gently against the nylon of her tights. She made notes whenever he did, following his handwriting and his thoughts, oblivious to the speaker she'd paid to listen to. At the interval, they went to the café, where Leonard bought tea and sticky buns to take away. They returned to their seats in the almost-empty auditorium and watched people come and go, clean their glasses, rearrange belongings and endlessly seize and relinquish seats. As Jane chewed her bun, she thought of how others might view them, nestled together at the back of the hall. It struck her that the age difference was less obvious because of the way they'd dressed that morning. Jane's skirt gave her an older, more formal appearance, and Leonard's jeans and stylish shirt spoke of a desire to appear younger than he actually was. The realisation made Jane more comfortable: she crossed her right leg over her left, angling her body towards him.

'Have you been to lectures here before?' Having finally mustered the courage to ask him a question, she'd fired it just as he took a big bite out of his bun. She looked down at her lap. 'Sorry.'

He swallowed uncomfortably and picked his cup of tea up from the floor. 'Sometimes,' he said, taking a gulp of tea and swallowing again. 'It depends. If it's something I'm interested in or happen to be teaching, I'll make an effort to come.'

She wanted to ask him if there was a girlfriend or companion who liked to come along, but as she looked around the deep, wide sphere of the hall, she saw that her interest in him would be too obvious. Like a noisy fart when all is silent and accounted for, she knew they'd never get over it.

'And you, Miss Forster? What are Saturday mornings usually taken up with?'

'Oh, I don't know,' she said, taking a sip of her tea and trying not to wince. She'd been too embarrassed to ask for sugar and now she was struggling to drink it. 'I help my mum and dad around the house, read, study, go shopping.'

'Is it just you at home? Do you have any brothers or sisters?'

'No, just me.'

'I see.' He waited a few seconds before taking another bite of his bun.

'I had a baby brother,' she said suddenly to the concert hall. 'But he died.'

Leonard stopped chewing and turned to her. 'I'm sorry.' His mouth was slightly open.

She smiled, dismissive. 'It was a long time ago. I don't even remember him. I was very young. My mum found him one

17

morning. He was five weeks old.' Then, because she'd never told anyone before, because it had always been her parents' story to tell, she felt the thud of the words, the painful wringing-out of what was true. And the tragedy that had always belonged to them suddenly moved her to tears. She felt the hall contract around them: the seats, the suspended silence closing in on this unlooked-for intimacy.

He pulled a white handkerchief from his pocket and passed it to her without speaking.

'Thank you.'

'How upsetting for you.'

'It's so strange,' Jane said, wiping her eyes and breathing in the faux-orange smell she had begun to associate with him. 'I've never told anyone before. It happened such a long time ago, when I was just three.'

Leonard nodded.

'I actually have no recollection of him. As a live baby, I mean. But my first memory is being passed from knee to knee in a church.'

'At the funeral?'

'I think so. And then quiet. So much quiet.'

'How do you mean?'

'My mum and dad. It felt like they just stopped talking – my dad especially. Of course, I understand why now, but I felt so confused by it. I wanted to share in the sad thing, but I didn't understand it enough to make the tears come. My dad just slept a lot – mostly on the sofa during the day. And once or twice . . .'

'Go on.'

'Once or twice – this must have been when I was a bit older, maybe four – I woke up to find him sitting on the floor beside my bed. He was cross-legged, just watching me sleep. And I can see now' – she blinked and the tears spilled down – 'I can see now that he was watching me sleep because he didn't want the same thing to happen to me.'

'He thought vigilance would stop another tragedy.'

She nodded. 'So when I think about being a child, being really small … well, I think of silence. My dad asleep, or if not asleep, then not talking but watching. I can't believe I'm telling you all this.'

'I'm so sorry.'

'No, I'm sorry. I shouldn't have said anything.' She tried to hand back his handkerchief.

'Keep it, please.'

She nodded as she spread the white square on her skirt. It was so thin and insubstantial compared to the thick, warm wool beneath it.

'Miss Forster, would you like to go for a walk after this? It strikes me we could take a stroll down to St James's Park and enjoy a little more of this June sunshine.'

Jane looked down at her new shoes. 'Yes,' and then, as if something was bothering her, 'You can call me Jane.'

They walked briskly through the London streets, waiting for the pavement to become grass. In the park, Jane began to touch her hair more often. She tucked it behind her ear as she spoke and used her hands to roll the points she made beyond her body. Leonard also began to relax. He told her how, in his early twenties, he'd endured a brief spell of insomnia. It was in the months after he'd graduated from Oxford, and what began as a general restlessness quickly morphed into an unnatural sensitivity to how sleep came to him each night. The doctor who treated him had recommended waking at five thirty in the morning. He told Jane how the unexpected freedom of having the morning to himself had given him the time to read: history books, novels, political essays, whatever he could get his hands on.

The disclosure, so trustingly given on that path in St James's Park, made Jane think back to Brenda Barrow's circumspect observation. Perhaps he did like her.

'I'd like to read more. To understand more.'

'And you will. You have your whole life ahead of you.' And with that reference to her life, how much of it was still unlived compared to his own, his steps slowed.

'Is something wrong?'

'Perhaps I could devise a reading list for you to read over the summer. Would that be helpful?'

'Yes, please.'

And just like that she was his student again.

Jane took more than usual care over her appearance the following Monday morning. She woke up early and ran a bath, attaching a shower hose to the taps in order to rinse her hair properly. In her bedroom, she unwrapped the new mascara she'd bought in Woolworths on her way back from London on Saturday. She held the wand close to her right eye and closed her lashes – so straight and virginal – over the black brush. She blinked rapidly until her vision cleared and she saw the older, more experienced version of her face. Her eyelashes clumped together made her look more serious, more attractive.

Peter Forster was reading the newspaper when she came down to breakfast. He poured her a cup of tea from the pot and stirred in a sugar.

'There you go. Get that down you.'

'Thanks. Where's Mum?'

'She's having a wash. Said there was no hot water.' He raised his eyebrows at Jane.

'Oh,' she said, touching her hair.

'You look very nice today. What have you done to yourself?'

'Nothing. Just washed my hair, that's all.'

'Well, you look lovely.'

'Thanks.'

She was buttering a slice of toast when her mother came into the kitchen, her hair bound in a towel on top of her head. The elaborate folds and sharp pull of her face made her look like a harsh and unforgiving empress.

'There was no hot water upstairs.'

'I know. Dad told me. Sorry.'

'You don't usually have a bath in the morning,' she said, bending her head to look down at her daughter. She pulled at the towel and began drying her thin, wet hair. 'What's all this? Make-up?'

'Eh?' Peter looked up.

'Jane's got mascara on,' she said to her husband.

'Mum.'

'Leave her, Jen.'

'I'm only saying. You look pretty. You look nice.'

'Thanks.'

Peter put down his newspaper. 'Shall I give you a lift to school? I'm going that way this morning.'

'Yes, please.'

'After you've had your breakfast,' her mother said, as Jane got up and walked towards the door.

'I'm not hungry.'

Leonard didn't seem to notice the effort she'd made that morning, or any of the days that followed. Jane felt that he'd made a decision not to speak to her directly. He avoided all eye contact and stopped placing books on her desk. At the end of June, panicked by the thought of six weeks without him and the promised reading list, Jane decided to wait around after the lesson. It was a carefully orchestrated approach and she saw, from the way Leonard sat back in his chair, that he had been readying himself for this moment.

'Sir?'

'Miss Forster. How can I help you?'

'When we went to the lecture together, you mentioned a reading list for the summer?'

'Ah yes. I've had rather a lot on my plate. Can I give it to you next week, perhaps?'

'Yes. Thank you.' But as she walked towards the door, she remembered her new eyelashes. The different – more alluring – girl she now saw in the mirror. She pushed the door shut, and in those few seconds between the door closing and Leonard looking up, she waited for a sign – a softness in the floor, a crack in the wall, something that might attest to the fact that this privacy with her teacher was fragile. And precious. She knew she had to take what she needed before the building fell.

'Mr Campbell, have I done something wrong?' She turned to face him, her back against the door.

'I'm sorry?'

The handle of the door was pressing into her lower back. It forced an s-shaped curve to her spine, one that sent her chin down to meet her rising chest.

'You haven't said a word to me since London.'

'Miss Forster, I hardly think—'

'Jane.'

'Excuse me?'

'You can call me Jane. And you said I could call you Leonard?' she said, her voice now a whisper.

'Jane.' He stood up and walked away from her, towards the large window on the other side of the room. Jane watched his retreating figure, how his jacket lifted and his trousers tightened across his backside as he put his hands in his pockets. 'It's inappropriate for you to call me Leonard. In school.'

'And if we're not in school? If we met up somewhere else?'

He turned. 'Is that something you'd like to do?'

'Yes.'

'You know what this would mean?'

She kept her eyes trained on his, not in assent or understanding, because in truth she didn't know what it meant.

The following week, Jane considered repeating the approach, waiting for the classroom to empty before seeking him out, but Leonard was one step ahead of her. As the lesson drew to an end, he said, pointedly, to her, 'Miss Forster, would you mind staying behind, please? I have those books for you.'

She stood up and packed her bag slowly. When the last of the stragglers disappeared into the hallway, she walked towards his desk.

'I thought you might enjoy this,' he said, handing her a copy of *Hard Times*. 'Dickens handles the topic of utilitarianism in relation to human happiness.'

'Utilitarianism. The greatest happiness of the greatest number?'

'That's right.' Leonard smiled at her. 'A key ideology in the Victorian period.'

'Thank you.'

'That's all right,' he said, continuing to smile at her. Jane put the book in her bag. 'Jane. I've been meaning to ask, if you're not busy . . . Perhaps you are. Do you work?'

'No, I don't.' She was mumbling, her heart pounding as she tried not to notice that he was holding his fingers again.

'If you're not busy over the summer holidays, if you wouldn't perhaps like to meet somewhere? We could discuss the reading and perhaps get to know one another a bit more.'

'Yes, I'd like that. That would be nice.'

'Perfect. Well, I've taken the liberty of writing my telephone number on the inside cover there. Please feel free to telephone me so we might arrange a time and place.'

'Yes. OK. Thank you. Leonard.'

She phoned him at the end of July and a week later found herself in the passenger seat of his car, looking at her reflection in the glass as Leonard, with sudden intimacy, reached behind for the back of her headrest, twisting his torso towards her so he could peer out of the back window. She smiled at herself, at how she was cheating the summer. Nobody knew she was out with her teacher, sitting beside him in his car.

'You're a very good driver.'

'Thank you,' he smiled, as he pulled up the handbrake.

She took his hand and put it on her knee. She felt her heart beat harder as she looked at him, willing him to move it up her skirt.

'Let me open the door for you,' he said, pulling his hand away.

The terrace outside the Roebuck pub was busy and all the benches were taken up by locals, who were practised in catching the late-afternoon sun. Jane, unprepared for an order of drinks in a pub, opted for a gin and fizzy orange. She'd seen her mother drink it at Christmas. They took their drinks out to the terrace and stood by the railings, looking down at the sweeping view of the Thames. Leonard sipped his pint of dark ale and became expansive in the warm sunlight. 'Richmond is a very wealthy pocket of London and you can see why. This view is unparalleled in London.' He turned to her and smiled.

'It's beautiful.'

'And of course, at the end of *Great Expectations*, Pip accompanies Estella to a house on Richmond Green, which is just over there,' he said, pointing away, down the hill.

'I haven't read *Great Expectations*.'

She'd seen bits of the film. A graveyard and a worn-out old woman confined by her house and her shattered dreams. She watched his right hand, the one holding his pint glass, and wondered whether her disavowal should have included a desire to read it, when quietly, and with great precision, he slid his glass across the railing to his left hand and put his right hand over hers. It was wet. She turned her hand round in order to interlace her fingers with his, and together they stayed like that, looking at the view, held back by the railing and all that lay unsaid.

After the second round of drinks, they walked down the hill and into the town centre, where Leonard had booked a table at a small Italian restaurant. He ordered a bottle of red wine and recommended the lasagne. Jane ate and drank what was put in front of her and found it all delicious: the rich bolognese sauce still bubbling in the dish, the red wine in her glass, Leonard across from her talking about performances at the Richmond Theatre he'd particularly enjoyed. She reached her hand across the tablecloth and hoped he'd take it again. She wanted his hand to reaffirm he'd chosen her.

'Am I the first girl you've ever brought here?'

'My first?'

'First, you know, girlfriend?'

'Is that what you are?'

'No. I don't know. It was silly. Ignore me.'

'I hoped we might eventually reach that understanding, but I didn't want to push you. Jane, this isn't something I've ever done before. With a student.'

'I know,' she nodded. 'I just like you. Very much.'

Leonard drove her home to Hinchley Wood at around eight thirty in the evening. As they neared her road, Jane suggested he drop her off a few houses away.

'Yes, of course,' he agreed.

'I'm not sure how my parents will feel about us spending time together like this.'

'I understand. It's a matter of some delicacy,' he said, turning off the engine.

'Thank you for a lovely evening.'

'It's I who should be thanking you. Should I stay in the car?'

'Yes, please,' and in an effort to soften the injunction, she leaned across and kissed his cheek. He bowed his head and smiled.

They continued meeting throughout August, their togetherness becoming more of an established fact between them, if nobody else. When September arrived, Jane resumed the role of pupil in Mr Campbell's class, but a diminished version, as though she'd become a cardboard cut-out of herself with room for someone – anyone – to put their face through the hole and pretend to be her. She'd already stepped back and away, waiting for Leonard to take her beyond the desks and chalk, the dusty window frames and scarred wood.

When Jane turned eighteen in September, she told her parents she was going out to a party with Brenda Barrow, but Leonard picked her up from Kingston Bus Station and drove her out to Egham, where he'd reserved a table at a fish restaurant. He ordered a bottle of champagne and together they toasted her ascent into adulthood. When he dropped her home, parking the car a few roads away, as had become his habit, Jane leaned across and kissed him on the mouth. She lingered there and, with gentle provocation, licked the inside of his top lip, pulling his mouth more firmly onto her own. He took a deep breath and put his hand on her hip, his thumb pressing – almost pinching – the flesh above the cradle of her pelvis.

She had never handled a man before. She knew they got hard when aroused but had no idea what that looked like. And as she kissed Leonard, she understood that looking was not the thing to do. With her left hand she reached out, as if blind, and as her fingers grazed the hardness, her body suddenly became aware of him as a man like any other. In her urgency, she pressed herself against him, and her fingers, as if responding to a private summons, set about trying to open his fly. She wanted to feel him, to take him in her hand and show him she knew what to do. But as she did so, she felt his face pull back from hers.

'I'm sorry. I can't do this.' His lips were wet from her own. 'Not yet. It would feel wrong.'

'It's OK,' Jane said, too embarrassed to do anything but face her bit of road. 'I understand.'

'It's not that I don't want to. It's just that you're still so young, and I'm, well . . .' He tried to laugh. 'I'm older than you.'

Jane continued looking ahead. 'I'm not as young as you think I am.'

'Please, Jane. I understand what you're saying. But I think we should take things slowly.'

They approached the business of secrecy at school with absolute efficiency and dedication. Jane told no one, and neither did Leonard. During the October half-term, he accompanied a lower-school trip to the Lake District. Once there, he took the opportunity to write her a letter.

Dear Jane,
We have arrived safely at Borrowdale and plan to set out early tomorrow morning for Wast Water. As I unpack my belongings and prepare for the evening ahead, I find myself thinking of you.

Our time together, both in and out of the classroom, has given me such pleasure and happiness that I hope, in time, we might make our relationship more public and – I'd like to add – accepted.

Jane, I hope you won't consider it indelicate of me if I refer to our little misunderstanding in the car on your birthday. It wasn't my intention to cause you any pain. Please understand that I hope for a complete and loving union with you in the future. But while our relationship remains a secret, I just don't feel it's right to take things in that direction. Yet. As I said to you in the car, you are still young and we have, I hope, plenty of time together.

I send you my best wishes and look forward to being reunited with you next week.

Love,
Leonard

She read the letter, penned in the same hand as the comments in the margins of her essays, with a thrill that continued to build upon itself, each sentence confirming what she had suspected. That he loved her. She felt pleased that she understood him, that it was because of her such gentle sentiments were expressed.

She put the letter down but then quickly lifted it to read again. The ink was irrefutable. It was there and there again, and his intentions were clear: he wanted to be with her. He would make love to her once her parents knew about them. Jane put the letter back in its envelope and walked downstairs. The lounge door was open; she could see her mother sitting in an armchair, threading hooks into some curtain tape she'd just sewn on. She couldn't see her father, but as she walked into the lounge, she heard the sound of his drill start up. He was standing on a chair, making a hole above the window for the new curtain rail. She stood in front of her mother, with her back to the window, and shouted, 'I think you should meet my teacher.'

'Why?' Her mother squinted, looking up. 'Peter! Pete, hang on.' She waved her hand at her husband's back. 'Jane's trying to say something. What's going on? What have you done?'

'Nothing.'

'So why does she want to see us?'

'He.'

'Why does *he* want to see us?'

'Because he likes me.'

'I'm very glad to hear it. Can't this wait until parents' evening?'

Peter began drilling again.

'Dad!'

'What?' He turned off the drill but kept the bit in the hole. 'What is it, Jane?'

'I want you to meet my teacher.'

'What's going on?'

Peter looked back at the hole in the plaster, his finger poised over the trigger as he heard Jane say, quietly and firmly, 'You need to meet him because we're together.'

'What do you mean, together?' Jennifer said, narrowing her eyes.

'He's my boyfriend.'

Chapter 3

'Is this some sort of joke?' Peter asked, getting down from the chair.

'He loves me,' Jane said, simply. She handed him the letter.

'What's this?'

'It's a letter from him.'

'Jen, are you hearing this?'

'What teacher is it?' Jane's mother asked, folding the curtains together so she could stand up and see the letter. 'It's not Mr Keary, is it? He's got three kids.'

'No.'

'Who is it, then?'

'Mr Campbell. Leonard Campbell. He's my history teacher.'

'I don't know him,' she said to her husband, who was still busy reading the letter.

'You wouldn't. He's the new deputy head.'

'The deputy head! You're telling me you've been seeing the deputy head! Pete?'

'Be quiet, will you? I'm trying to read this. "*I hope, in time, we might make our relationship more public and – I venture to add – accepted*." Bloody hell. And this is the deputy head?' He sat down.

'I'm eighteen. I can make my own decisions now.'

'You can't marry a married man!'

'He's not married. Mum was talking about someone else.' Jane stepped closer to her father.

'So he's not married, but how old is he? He can't be remotely close to you in age.'

'He's thirty-nine.'

She'd never seen her father's face swell with rage before. She was unprepared as he leaped from the chair, his chest suddenly inches from her face. She took a step back and bumped into her mother, who was also too close.

'He's an old man!'

'He's younger than you!'

'Only just! Jesus Christ.' He looked beyond his daughter for his wife. 'What are we going to do?'

'We're going to phone the school and complain about this teacher who's molesting our daughter.'

'He has done no such thing!' Jane turned from one to the other, a piggy in the middle. 'He's intelligent and thoughtful, and I'm an adult now. I can choose who I want to be with.'

'Go upstairs. I can't look at you right now. Me and your mum need to talk.'

That evening, Peter Forster sat with the letter Leonard Campbell had written to his daughter. He read it over and found within its lines a timid honesty that made him look up at his wife. She was sitting in the armchair, her lips pursed with grim determination as she pulled at the cord in the curtain tape, wrapping the strands round her fingers and yanking until they screamed yellow under the pressure.

He watched her for a while before looking back at the letter.

Jane was their only child. In the three years before Jacob was born, she was their first child, and for just five weeks, she was their eldest. And then afterwards she became their only. Cot death. Two flimsy little words – that's all the Forsters were given – to make sense of the incomprehensible. And they'd worked hard to roll them out, stretched and taut until they were virtually transparent, so that they might be pulled – like a perilous cover – across the black hole of their loss.

Peter looked up at his wife because, after the death of Jacob, he'd always looked to her for their reaction. That she had survived losing Jacob told him that he could too. 'Jen, I don't know what to do.'

She put the curtains down and removed the glasses from her face.

'This is my fault.'

'Pete.'

'After Jacob, I fell apart. I wasn't strong enough for her. For you.'

'So now it's our fault? After everything we've been through, we should blame ourselves for this?'

'I'm just saying isn't it worth considering? That maybe she's looking for a father figure. Someone she can rely on.'

'No. You were depressed. Jane knows she's loved. She knows she's always been loved.'

'He might love her too.'

'I'm sure he does,' she said quietly.

'She seems to be very taken with him.'

'She's a young girl. Of course she's taken with him.'

'But if this is what she wants, shouldn't we at least meet him?'

33

She rubbed her right eye with the back of her hand. 'It's either that or phone the police.'

Jane telephoned Leonard as soon as he returned from the Lake District. She told him her parents knew everything and that they were willing to meet him. It was agreed that he would come over for tea the following Saturday afternoon. Her mother, who'd been the more reluctant, spent the morning opening and closing her wardrobe, pulling dresses out and putting them back. Her father cleaned the downstairs toilet, bleaching the bowl and wiping the seat. They were curiously determined to put on a good show.

He arrived punctually at three o'clock with a small bunch of flowers for her mother. In the hallway, Jane stood back, observing the vigorous handshake, Leonard's broad smile, the creases round his eyes. The half-term had seen unusually sunny weather for October and his face had a golden hue that made him look handsome and healthy. And relaxed. She could see that he was happy and the realisation – that today he wasn't her teacher but her lover returned – made her greedy. She wanted to push her father aside and touch Leonard, grab him in a way that was unambiguous.

They sat in the lounge. Leonard was directed to take an armchair in front of the window where the new curtains hung. Jane and Peter sat on the two-seater sofa, while her mother busied herself about the coffee table. She poured the tea and cut a slice of cake, carrying both over to Leonard.

He took the cup and saucer gratefully but found himself disabled by his eager hands. 'May I?' he asked, turning his body towards the windowsill.

'Yes, pop your tea up there.'

'Thank you. This looks delicious, Mrs Forster.'

'It's only a Victoria sponge.'

Jennifer took her seat and resumed the cutting of the cake. She looked up at Peter, who had been following her movements and who now saw it was his turn to speak.

'Mr Campbell—'

'Leonard, please.'

'Leonard. I think it's probably a good idea to get straight to the point. I'm not one to beat about the bush.'

'I understand.'

'You are older than our daughter. And her teacher. Am I right?'

'Yes, Mr Forster, but if I might add—'

'You see, my wife and I, we think, given your position, this is inappropriate.'

'Mr Forster—'

'Please, let me finish,' he said, looking over at his wife. 'We've invited you here because Jane wanted us to meet you. And we accept she's no longer a child in the eyes of the law. But I mean … it can't be right, can it? You're her teacher. You're in a position of authority.'

'What my husband's trying to say, Mr Campbell, is that we feel, given the age gap, things will be too serious too soon. We'd like Jane to go to university next year, to have a life before she settles down.'

'I quite—'

'And in your letter you talk about having plenty of time together.'

'I didn't realise Jane had shown you the letter.' He glanced across at Jane, who sat looking down at her hands folded in her lap.

'I'm sure you didn't!'

'Jen, hang on.' Peter put his hand out in his wife's direction. 'Let the man speak.'

'Please rest assured, Mr and Mrs Forster, having a personal relationship with a student is not something I have ever done before. Jane is very important to me, and as I think I expressed in my letter, I should like to make my intentions perfectly clear. That they are honourable and reflect the great respect I feel for her and her family. Which is why I'm here. I don't wish to deceive anyone or to conduct our relationship in the shadows—'

'Any longer.'

'I'm sorry?'

'You don't wish to deceive us any longer, Leonard,' said Jennifer.

Peter turned to his daughter. 'And you? What are your thoughts on this?'

Jane looked down at her slice of cake, on its side. She pressed her index finger into the line of red and white that ran through the sponge. 'I want to be with Leonard,' she said, looking up at him.

One night the following January, Jane dreamed she couldn't find her history classroom anywhere. Every time she thought she'd found the right corridor, the door she was expecting had simply disappeared. She tried to find someone to ask, but there was no one around. As she walked back to the foyer, she found Leonard standing in the middle of the space in a three-piece suit. He was looking at his watch, and as she approached, he turned and walked the other way. She woke with a start and quickly put her hand to her chest, which was wet with sweat. As her breathing returned to normal, she looked at the clock on her bedside table. It was just after midnight, and she felt thirsty. She got out of bed and went downstairs, where she saw the lounge was lit by the face of Peter Sellers as Inspector Clouseau.

'What's this?'

'Hello. What are you still doing up?'

'Bad dream. Thought I'd come down and get a glass of water.'

'Sit down. I was about to get an apple anyway.'

'Thanks,' she said, sitting down on the sofa. The top of her nightie was damp. She held it out and away from her breasts while her father was in the kitchen.

He returned with a glass of water, a small paring knife and a red apple. Sinking heavily into the seat beside her, he pressed the knife into the skin under the stalk. With each movement the peel lifted and curled away, hanging perilously above the carpet. As he reached the stamen, he lifted the apple above the coffee table and allowed the long ribbon to drop to the surface. He cut the apple in half and then into quarters. Jane watched him, knowing he would offer her some as soon as he'd cut the triangle of core away.

'No, thanks.'

'So what did you dream about?' he asked, taking a bite of the piece he'd intended for her.

'Nothing. It was silly.'

'Can't have been that silly if it woke you up.'

'It's fine,' she said, sipping her water. 'I'd better get back to bed – I've got school in the morning.'

'You don't want to get into trouble with your teachers, do you?'

'What's that supposed to mean?'

'I want to talk to you, that's all. We don't talk anymore.'

'There's nothing to say. I know you and Mum don't want me to see him.'

'We've only ever wanted the best for you.'

'He's a good man. He's kind and loving. Like you.'

'What about boys your own age? Have you given up on them?'

'It really is just about his age, isn't it? If he was eighteen, you'd have no problem with him, would you?'

'I'd certainly feel happier if you were going out with someone your own age.'

'Why?'

'Because you'd do things at the same time. He'd be thinking about going off to university next year like you should be!'

'Not necessarily.'

Peter lifted a quarter of the apple from the table and put it back again. 'You should be with someone your own age.'

'Why?'

'Because then I wouldn't feel like this is my fault.' He looked to Peter Sellers, speaking with quiet animation to a room full of suspects. 'I know the house hasn't always been happy, but your mother and me, we did our best.'

'Dad—'

'You know we had no control over it. He was just gone. And that was it.'

'Please don't.'

'And I just couldn't get myself back together. I'm sorry. It's my fault, isn't it?' He looked at Jane, his eyes wet and pleading.

'No.' She was firm. 'This has nothing to do with you, with what happened.' And as if to prove the point, she picked up a small piece of apple. It had already started to brown at the edges.

Chapter 4

By the spring of 1976, Jennifer – fearful of her daughter's intractability – counselled Peter to accept the relationship. They stopped asking her about university and welcomed Leonard when he came to collect Jane.

On a Sunday evening in March – after a day of marking – Leonard took Jane to one of his favourite pubs in Berkshire. They arrived early and sat in a little nook beside an open fire. He ordered dinner for both of them and began telling Jane how the pub was used as a royal hunting lodge in the sixteenth century. Jane sipped her glass of red wine and listened. She met his explanations with nodding comprehension and the occasional question, all the time looking forward to the moment when he would take her hand in his. As if the riding habits of Henry VIII were just an elaborate preamble to their entwined fingers.

'You are quite beautiful tonight.'

She smiled and put the back of her hand to her cheek. 'Thank you. I think it's the fire. It's making my cheeks rosy.'

'Wine and a roaring fire will do that.'

'What else will do that?'

'A hearty meal! That's what. I'll go and see what's happened to our food.'

Later, during the drive back to Hinchley Wood, Jane put her hand on Leonard's leg. 'Let's go back to your place tonight.'

'I'm not sure your parents would approve of that.'

'Come on, Leonard. We've been together – how long? Eight months? And I've never been to your house.'

'It's not my house.'

'Do you live with someone? A housemate?'

'I wouldn't call her a housemate.'

'You're married.'

'No!' Leonard slowed for a roundabout. 'Nothing like that. I live with my mother.' He snuck a glance at Jane, as though – with these words – she would understand everything.

'You still live with your parents?'

'My mother. My father was killed in the war. The Second World War, I might add.'

'How old were you?'

'Five. I was three when he went away to fight and he died in 1941. So, like you, I know what it is to be an only child.'

'I'm sorry.'

'We coped. My mother was a very industrious woman. She cleaned in the day and worked as a seamstress in the evenings, and, together with my father's pension, managed to pay the rent, feed and clothe us both and eventually hire a tutor to help get me into Oxford. She was entirely devoted to obtaining the very best possible start for me.' He looked over at Jane for a response, but she stared resolutely at the road ahead. 'And now, in her seventies, she's my responsibility. So we live together in a small house not far from you.'

'That's why I've never been to your house.'

'I was waiting for the right time. To tell you about her.'

'You've had a long time to do it.'

40

'You've never asked to come back before.'

'I just thought you were too shy or, you know, gentlemanly to ask me.'

'Well, that is part of it. Your parents have come to accept our arrangement—'

'Arrangement!'

'Forgive me. Our relationship. And I didn't want to return their trust with deceit.'

'It's not deceitful for a couple to want to spend time together, alone.'

'I agree. But these things need to be handled carefully.'

'By "things" do you mean your mother?'

'Yes.'

'So I can't come back with you now?'

'Please, Jane. I need to prepare her. She doesn't like to be surprised.'

Leonard invited Jane to meet his mother on a warm, bright day in March. Their home was a small Victorian cottage on a narrow cul-de-sac on the edge of Hinchley Wood. The small front garden was paved over long ago and skirted by a low brick wall. Beside the front door was a honeysuckle plant in a pot, whose fragrant fronds were the only part of the garden to have remembered itself and proclaim the season. Jane took a deep breath as she stepped into the narrow, dark hallway and followed Leonard into the living room.

'Jane, I'd like you to meet my mother, Eileen Campbell.'

'Hello, Mrs Campbell,' Jane said, taken aback by the woman's blank expression.

Leonard kneeled down in front of his mother and took her small white hands in his. 'Tea?' he said, so close to her face he might kiss it.

Eileen squeezed his hands and made a smacking sound with her lips, opening and closing them in tight, quick bursts.

'I'll go and make some,' he said, rising to his feet. 'Jane, would you like to come with me?'

Jane looked at Eileen, uncertain about the propriety of the move, but the old woman's gaze had returned to the road. She followed Leonard into the small kitchen at the back of the house.

'Mother had a small stroke two years ago,' Leonard said as he filled the kettle at the tap. 'It was followed by another, more serious one that took her speech away.' He put the kettle on the stove and opened a drawer to extract a box of matches. Jane watched his long, adept fingers pull at a match and strike it against the coarse surface on the side of the box. She'd been watching him so closely that the flame, when it erupted, surprised her.

'She can't speak?'

'She can communicate. She squeezes my hand and makes that noise. I'm sorry,' he said, bending down to light the gas. 'She sounds rather like a fish gasping for breath.'

Jane didn't know what to say. The only words that came to mind were 'poor thing', but she felt too young to say them to an older man caring for his elderly mother. She felt too young for that house.

'Would you like tea?'

'Yes, please.'

Leonard spooned the sugar into her waiting cup and turned back to Jane. 'I know this is a lot. I should have warned you about the stroke. And about living with Mother. But I thought it would put you off. And I'm so pleased to have you here.' He took a step towards her and leaned down looking for her mouth with his, but the memory of Eileen's lip-smacking rose up before her and she turned her head away.

'Not here.'

'No. I'm sorry.'

'I don't want to make a bad impression.'

He turned back to the work surface and began pouring hot water into a teapot. 'You couldn't make a bad impression if you tried.'

They returned to the living room and Leonard carried the conversation. He translated everything Jane said into louder, more distinct words shouted not in his mother's ear but in her face. 'She likes to see the movement of my lips,' he said to Jane by way of explanation. 'She can understand what I'm saying if she watches my face and mouth.'

He held his mother's hand for most of the afternoon. Jane sat on the small sofa holding her cup of tea and watched the two of them. She thought of how Leonard had described her as 'industrious' and looked more closely at those small white hands, worn out and folded in her lap. And she became frightened by this vision of exhausted motherhood, where care and concern had led her brain to bleed into itself, removing all speech, replacing it with a monstrous, gaping helplessness.

'I think I'd better go,' Jane said, getting up and placing her empty cup carefully on the small trestle table at her side.

'No, please. Stay. I take Mother upstairs at seven and get her settled. You can stay down here – help yourself to the books – and then, when I come down, I can prepare something for us to eat.'

'OK. But let me do something while you're upstairs.'

Jane went into the kitchen and set to work, peeling potatoes and putting them on to boil. In the fridge, she found some sausages and began frying them in a pan. Leonard came down after twenty minutes and found her searching in the cupboard beside the stove.

'What are you looking for?'

'A masher. Do you have one?'

'On the hook over there,' he said, indicating the wall on the other side of the kitchen.

'Butter?' she said, already taking Leonard's assistance for granted.

'In here,' he said, opening the fridge.

He stood back to admire the push and pull of Jane's muscles, the relentless strength in her long, slim arms.

'Is she in bed?' she asked, as she took the butter from him.

Leonard nodded and smiled.

'What's funny?' she asked him.

'You and me. Cooking. I had a small insight of what it might be like to be married to you.'

She pulled the wax paper from the block of butter and smiled shyly. 'Knife?'

'Just in there,' he said, pulling a drawer gently towards them. 'Are you making gravy?'

'I wasn't planning to.'

'Are you mad?'

The happiness bubbled up inside so that her laugh sounded like a hiccup. She put her hand to her mouth in apology as he reached round her, touching her hip gently with his hand as he slid out a sharp knife. He began slicing an onion, dropping the shreds into the pan with the sausages, manoeuvring her aside so he could open a cupboard she was leaning against and extract a packet of Bisto. He mixed the powder with some hot water from the kettle and poured it over the sausages and onions.

'You make gravy with the sausages still in the pan?'

'Yes. You get the flavours of the meat that way. I build up the water slowly and then add a little salt and pepper. It's delicious.'

Jane stood back and leaned against the fridge. 'I had no idea you were a cook.'

He stretched his arms over the stove and wiggled his fingers in the manner of a magician. 'I believe the word you're looking for is "chef".' Jane had never seen him so relaxed and happy. On a whim she took a step towards him and put her arms around his waist. He let the wooden spoon drop into the pan and held her hands. 'You are quite precious to me.'

With Eileen in bed, Jane felt more free to peer at the books in the living room, many of which she recognised. There were a few photographs on show: one of a tall young man with a thin face holding a baby who, judging by the folds of fat, looked to be around six months in age.

'Is this you?' Jane asked as Leonard walked into the lounge.

'Yes. As you can see, I was rather chubby,' he laughed. 'That was my father. One of the few photographs we had taken together.' Leonard began drawing the curtains.

'Won't you sit down?'

'Thank you,' she said.

'Dinner will be ready in five minutes.'

They sat at the small round table in the back room and ate quietly. With each mouthful the end of the meal drew closer, and the question of what two people should do when they find themselves alone in a house together for the first time. They talked about school, teachers, Jane's other subjects, somehow managing to eat the food in front of them.

'Let me help you,' Jane said quickly as Leonard began gathering up the dishes.

'I won't hear of it. You've done enough. Would you like another glass of wine? I can light the fire if you're cold?'

Jane took her glass into the living room and waited for Leonard to join her. When he walked in, ten minutes later, she'd taken her shoes off and had tucked her legs under her on the sofa. His shirtsleeves were rolled up, revealing damp skin that flexed over his muscles. As she noted that he had taken his watch off, she remembered how she used to search for it when he walked past her in the classroom. Thinking of herself as a stranger, a student, aroused her; it made her want to reach for Mr Campbell and make him Leonard. With the curtains drawn and the fire lit, the room seemed smaller and more private. Looking at the walls lined with books, Jane felt as though she were on stage, the scene set so she could direct her own character to do anything she pleased.

They began kissing, gently at first and then more deeply. She pulled away from him and lowered her knees to the floor so that she could run her hands up his thighs. Leonard had his eyes closed, the lids creased and tense with the effort of relaxing. She fumbled for his belt and began pulling his zip down when he stood up quickly, knocking her back into the coffee table and unsettling the glass she'd placed there.

'Don't do that.'

'Do what?'

'That,' he said, turning away from her to do up his trousers. 'On your knees like that. I don't like it.'

'What's wrong? I just want to be closer to you.' She got up and stood behind him, her hands on his shoulder blades.

'Where did you learn to do that?'

'Leonard, what's the matter?'

'On your knees. I can't.'

'Why not?'

'Because it's not right.'

'I'm eighteen. And we're here, alone in your house. Isn't this what couples do?'

'When they're married, yes.' He walked away from her and sat back down. As though he'd called her up to the board to demonstrate something and had now finished.

She turned to face him. 'You want to wait until we're . . . until marriage?'

'I just think there are some things that should take place within the confines of a marriage. A sacred vow between two people.'

And as she looked at him sitting on the sofa, his knees higher than his hips, she understood. 'You're a virgin.'

He opened his mouth, as if he were about to give her a royal bollocking for her impertinence. But there was nobody there to sanction his authority, and the words were out.

Jane sat down beside him. She tried to take his hand, but he pulled it away. 'Leonard. It's OK if you are. I am too.'

'I can't.'

'Can't what?'

'I live with Mother. It's been very difficult for me to have a life outside of my obligations to her.'

'Not at university?'

He shook his head.

'It doesn't make a difference to me. We can just take it slowly.'

'Mother has always said she'll go into a care home if I marry. That was her will before the stroke, and it is certainly the case now.'

'Who looks after her during the day?' The practicalities of

Leonard's existence as teacher and carer were becoming more apparent to Jane, a course of insurmountable obstacles that demanded her attention the longer she stayed in his house.

'We pay a nurse to stop by in the morning and just before lunch. If I'm working late, they can usually scramble somebody to come and tend to her in the afternoon.'

'So your mum will only live in a home if you marry?'

Leonard nodded. 'That's what we agreed. I would keep the house and pay for her care in a residential home. She wants to see me married.'

She sat back and stared into the room, astonished by the turn her play had taken. Her gaze settled on his mother's cushion waiting patiently in her armchair.

'I think it's too soon.'

'I understand,' he said, turning to her. 'I never intended to propose this evening. I knew it would be too much, but your attentions rather forced the subject. I'm sorry.'

'I'd like to go home.'

They said very little to one another on the way back to the Forsters'. Eventually, Leonard cleared his throat. 'Jane, I'm sorry. I'm sorry this evening went so wrong. I don't know how to rescue it.'

She thought of the red wine and the cosy living room. She had wanted to know more about his body, how his hands might feel on her skin. She had wanted to see him: the hair that grew in places he never showed to anyone. And now he was withholding it from her.

'Why didn't you tell me?'

'Tell you what? That I'm inexperienced?'

'That you want to get married first.'

'It's a rather presumptuous thing to say to a person you've

only been involved with a short time.'

The words stung her. Made her feel childish. 'It's not fair to do that to someone. To surprise them like that.'

'I think that's a little rich.' His voice was low and knowing.

'What's rich?'

'Wouldn't you call showing your parents a private letter I sent to you a "surprise"?'

'That was completely different.'

'In what way was that different? I was unprepared for the fact that your parents had read it. Read it so well they could quote from it!'

'They're my parents. They deserve to know what's going on.'

'You play the child when it suits you. Other times, you act the grown-up wanting to fellate me while my mother sleeps upstairs. Which is it to be, Jane?'

'Stop the car. I want to get out.'

'Let me at least see you home.'

She was hot with anger and grabbed at the door handle, ready to get out while the car was still moving. He pulled over and she opened the door quickly. As she stepped onto the pavement, he thought about leaning across her seat to say something, but he could see she was already heaving her arm back to slam the door.

Chapter 5

Jane avoided her history lesson for the next two days, and when she returned the following Thursday, she made a point of turning round to speak to Brenda Barrow, who sat behind her, whenever possible. As she left the classroom, Leonard called her back: 'Miss Forster. If I might have a word, please?' She pretended she hadn't heard him and linked arms with Brenda, surprising everyone with her open affection.

Brenda looked at her quizzically. 'Mr Campbell wants to speak to you.'

'He can wait,' she said, and continued walking.

At lunchtime, Leonard found her sitting at one of the tables in a far corner of the library. Jane quickly gathered up her books when she saw him approach.

'Leave me alone.'

'Jane, I—'

But she was already walking away. He reached out and grabbed her arm, his fingers sharp.

'I'm talking to you!'

'Get your hands off me,' she hissed.

Leonard recoiled, as if he'd been stung. 'I'm sorry. I shouldn't have done that. I just want to talk to you.'

'I don't want to talk to you.'

'Why, Jane? What have I done?'

She looked at his eyes and then his mouth. At the lines that led downwards. For all his intelligence, he couldn't fathom what he'd done that was so wrong. As she looked at his pained, willing face, she realised she didn't understand what he'd done wrong either. It had suddenly been too much.

'I can't do this.'

'Can we at least talk? Come back to my house this afternoon, after school. Mother—'

'No.'

'Somewhere else, then. Please, at least tell me why.'

'I'm late for English,' she said, walking away.

The following Saturday evening, Jane went to a house party thrown by Brenda's boyfriend, Gary, and his brother, Jamie. In the car on the way there, Brenda explained that Gary and Jamie's dad had walked out when the boys were young. Their mother worked nights as a nurse at Kingston Hospital, so her sons often took the opportunity to have 'a few people round'.

Jane had expected more people – she counted twelve in the living room, small groups clustered against the wall, sitting on the sofa and three girls stranded in the middle of the room who looked as though they were waiting for the music to start. Brenda handed her jacket to Gary and prompted Jane to do the same. He threw them on a pile of other coats on the bottom stair before taking them through to the kitchen, where Jamie was leaning against the work surface, busy with bottles and plastic cups. He raised his head in appraisal at Jane, bringing it down in a nod of greeting as she stood uncomfortably in the hallway.

'What are you girls drinking?' Gary asked.

'I'll have a Martini and lemonade,' Brenda answered as she peered into the living room. 'Jane?'

'I'll have the same,' Jane said, folding her arms across her chest. She was wearing a long-sleeved, floral paisley dress. The pattern was bold, and the colours – a swirling design of red, blue and black – were sharp, but as she looked around her, she saw that the shirt-collar neckline was too high and demure for this party.

'Come on, I'll introduce you to everyone,' Brenda said, taking Jane by the hand and leading her into the lounge. She was wearing the Mary Jane heels she'd worn to the lecture with Leonard. They looked incongruous on the orange carpet, sinking into the shagpile as though they knew they were also out of their depth.

Brenda reached out to hug a girl Jane recognised from the lower sixth – called Pamela – and was about to introduce her when Jamie approached with Jane's Martini and lemonade.

'Where's mine?' Brenda looked at him sharply.

'Gary's got yours. Why don't you go and get it?'

'Charming. Will you be all right on your own?' she asked Jane.

'I'll look after her,' Jamie said, raising his cup to remind her she was still without a drink.

'What's your name, then?' Jamie asked. He was standing beside her, not facing her. Her only clue that the question was for her was his proximity and the absence of anyone else.

'Jane,' she said, taking a sip of her drink.

'You go to school with Brenda.' Jane wasn't sure if this was a question or a statement. She took another sip and began to see how the action of drinking substituted the need for anything else.

Jamie put his hand on the small of her back. 'Do you have a boyfriend?'

'No.'

'Careful,' Brenda shouted from the kitchen. 'She's banging the deputy head.'

'Oh my God, is that you?' Pamela turned to them, eyes wide.

'I'm not. I haven't.' She looked down at her drink.

'Take no notice, Jane,' Brenda said, spilling her drink as she walked back into the room.

'What's he like, then?' Pamela pressed.

'I don't know what you're talking about,' Jane said stiffly.

She felt Jamie watching her, making his mind up about something.

'Has he got a big knob?' Pamela asked, leaning in, her mouth large and leering, trying to hoover up the intimacy.

Before she knew what she was doing, Jane flicked her wrist – as though it had received a message her brain hadn't been privy to – and in the moment between the drink landing on Pamela's face and her eyes closing against the unexpected deluge, Jane knew she was alone. Brenda and Jamie stared helplessly as Pamela looked down at her dress and screamed, 'You cunt!' She pulled Jane's hair towards her, as if she only wanted her hair and if Jane's head happened to follow, then so be it. Jane – bent in half, with only the perspective of the shifting feet beneath her – was dragged over into a large lampshade that, until that moment, had been ignored, not even turned on, in the corner of the room. She dropped the empty cup and put her hands out to stop her fall, but her left shoulder crashed into the wall and the lamp toppled on top of her.

'Stop! For fuck's sake! My mum's gonna go mad,' Jamie

said, stepping between Pamela and the bent form of Jane, being led round the room like a dog on a lead.

Pamela's teeth were bared, her lips pulled back in a grimace so vicious that everybody except Jamie stood back. He tried to grab Pamela's wrists, loosening her grip on Jane. 'Let go,' he demanded – and with his direction that the fight should come to an end, Brenda and the other girls gathered round Pamela gingerly advising to 'let her go' and that 'she's not worth it.'

Jane tried to stand up, but her hair was still being tugged down by Pamela's rage. She felt Jamie's arms close around her torso, drawing her away. She was like an elastic band stretched to the limit of its resistance. Jane was about to scream when she felt another set of hands forcibly breaking the connection. She was pulled backwards and out of the room into the hallway, her heels scraping ruts through the shagpile.

Jamie continued pulling Jane as though she were a sack of coal, until his own heels were impeded by the bottom stair. He turned round enough to lower Jane gently onto the coats. She looked up at him, sharing her disbelief at all that had happened to her and now, by association, to him.

'Come on. Come with me,' he said, offering her his hand. It was about the same size as Leonard's. She remembered the wedding ring she'd searched for and her quiet satisfaction when he told her he wasn't married. As she felt herself hesitate before Jamie's kindness, Brenda emerged from the lounge, exhilarated by the violence she'd witnessed.

'Oh my God,' she whispered, stooping before Jane. 'You really gave it to her.'

Jane looked from Brenda to Jamie, unsure of the correct response. She could hear Pamela's voice gathering in fury, getting closer to the hallway. 'If she comes anywhere near me, I'll have her fucking eyes out.' Jane put fingers to where her scalp had been pulled.

'Do you hear me, bitch?' Pamela was out, her friends reluctantly and ineffectively holding her back. Brenda moved quickly out of the way, ready for round two, which – given Jane's cornering on the bottom step – would be over quickly.

Jamie stepped in front of Jane and pushed Pamela back into the lounge. 'Sit down and shut up. Or go home.'

Pamela was crying now, choking on huge repressed sobs.

Jamie was unmoved. 'I don't care. Once more and you're out.'

He returned to Jane on the bottom step and extended his hand. 'Come on. Come with me.' And because he spoke to her kindly, with gentle authority, and because he had rescued her from Pamela, she stood up and followed him.

In his room, he was quieter, less conspicuous with responsibility. He sat down on his bed and lit a cigarette, twisting round and reaching up to open the window. Jane watched his T-shirt ride up with the exertion, revealing a slim, flat stomach.

'Do you want one?' Jamie asked, proffering the packet to Jane, who hovered in the doorway.

She shook her head and stepped into the room, leaning back against the wall for a moment before allowing her muscles to relax so that she was able to slide down to the carpet.

'So are you, then?'

Jamie's voice was small and pinched – he was speaking at the top of an inhalation. She looked over at him, his ribs rising in effort, as he blew the smoke – and the question – out of the window.

'Am I what?'

'Are you shagging him? The teacher?'

'He's the deputy head.'

'I'll take that as a yes.'

She was tired. 'I'm not shagging him, but it's not for want of trying.'

He laughed as he turned and exhaled once more out of the window. She allowed her own shoulders to drop with the confession. When he saw her smile – for the first time that evening – Jamie, who'd been so careful to keep smoke from the room, stood up with his cigarette and joined her on the floor.

'So why can't you shag him? Don't know what to do?'

She nudged him in the ribs with her elbow and he pretended to fall sideways.

'Would you like me to give you some lessons? A course of six should do the trick.'

'I'm pleased my love life is a source of humour for you.'

'And Pamela. Don't forget Pamela. She also wanted to get to the root of the problem.'

'Oh God.' Jane lowered her face to her hands.

Jamie transferred his cigarette to his left hand and pulled Jane's arm so that one of her hands came away.

'She's jealous of you.'

'I don't think so.'

'You're prettier than she is. And cleverer. But that's not difficult. I've got underpants with more brain cells.'

Jane's gaze lifted with his hand each time he took a drag, looking for a clue to how this situation would end.

'She's jealous of you. And I'm jealous of your deputy

head. The one you can't quite manage to shag.'

He cleared a space because he wanted her. The simplicity of sitting next to Jamie, who put his cigarette down on the edge of his desk so he could lean over and kiss her, was suddenly so appealing.

They fell asleep spooning, exhausted by their frenzied petting of the night before. Her thighs were clamped together. She attempted to lift her right leg and break the connection but found herself constrained by Jamie's right hand, wearily thrown over her hip. She felt for her knickers, remembering how Jamie had tried to pull them off, his eyes locked on hers, daring her to say no, which she had, pulling her knees up and turning away from him onto her side. She had felt him slump behind her.

'I'm not ready.'

'It's OK,' he'd said, stroking her arm. 'We can't cover everything in lesson one.'

Disentangling herself now, Jane tiptoed out of the room and down the stairs. As she approached the bottom, she noticed the pile of coats had diminished but not gone. She found her own under the others, and as she pulled it on, she glanced inside the lounge. One of the girls who'd held Pamela back lay on the sofa facing the fireplace, and on the rug in front of her, in a brown sleeping bag, lay Brenda. She slept in an s-shape, her bottom pressing up against the zip. She looked like a heavy pupa, long gestated and unhappy in its inability to fly free.

Jane opened the front door and stepped outside. She took a deep breath and began walking, eager to replay the night before on her own. She was so eager to return to her own company that she forgot to close the door behind her.

*

Brenda and Gary had had a fight. Brenda told her all about it the following Monday. They were in the library trying to write an essay on the Chartists. Jane had read the words in her textbook several times, copying them into her notebook for greater emphasis, but she couldn't stop thinking of Leonard. How he explained things to her, how he helped her to reach an understanding beyond the page. Since the evening at his house, she felt that she'd stepped backwards in time to a place where it was difficult to absorb anything. A place that contained Brenda Barrow, who compounded the haze with her interminable account of an argument with Gary.

'Hmm.'

A working-class movement.

'And do you know what he said?'

'No.'

Six main aims.

'"Well, fuck off out of my bedroom, then" – and then he threw me a sleeping bag! As I was picking my clothes up off the floor.'

'Oh dear.'

No property qualification to become an MP.

'So?'

Jane looked up, frustrated that Brenda was still there.

'I've slept in Jamie's room before. He's usually out. But I couldn't because you were in there with him.'

'The Chartist movement ended without achieving its aims.'

'What?'

'We have an essay to write for next week.'

'I reckon Mr Campbell will let you off.'

'I don't want him to let me off.'

'How about Jamie, then? Did he pop your cherry?'

Brenda's words – so blithely spoken – gave the signal

for her brain to slip back to Saturday night. Jamie's body, naked except for his black underpants, on top of her, moving rhythmically to his own dry pleasure. She looked down at her textbook, at the photograph of the great Chartist meeting on Kennington Common in 1848, the figures so grey and numerous and *old* compared to Jamie. She felt suddenly embarrassed for him and his fruitless thrusting.

'No. Nothing happened. We just slept beside each other.'

'Oh, come on. He hasn't stopped asking about you. Wants to know when he's gonna see you again.'

Jane began copying down the names of the principal leaders of the movement.

'How about tomorrow night? Or next Saturday? We could all go to the cinema together. Double date?'

'I can't. I have an essay to write.'

She went to find Leonard after school, ostensibly to ask about the Chartists, but when she knocked on the door of his classroom, she noticed he wasn't alone. Miss Moreau, her French teacher, was sitting comfortably in the middle of the front row, her legs – in glossy, flesh-coloured stockings – crossed. She was smiling up at Leonard, who stood before the blackboard, playfully demonstrating some finer point with a piece of chalk, laughing at his own self-conscious pedagogy.

She was too surprised to feel jealous. If she hadn't already knocked, already committed herself, she'd have stepped away and run for the school gates, her books held tight to her chest. Miss Moreau looked up first, quick to replace her smile with something professional and enquiring.

'Yes? Come in!'

Jane pushed the door open as though it were made of

lead and slowly, reluctantly entered. Leonard stared at her in surprise.

'Mademoiselle? What can we do for you?'

Jane focused on Miss Moreau, on her short black hair and immaculately lined eyelids. Standing in the doorway with her bag on her shoulder, she had no answer for her.

Miss Moreau stood up and decided to fill the silence. 'Come back when you remember.'

'I want to speak to Mr Campbell.'

Miss Moreau turned to Leonard, amused. 'Monsieur Campbell?'

'Would you mind if we continued our conversation another time?' he asked, putting down the piece of chalk.

'Of course! Good night, Leonard,' she said, managing a tight smile at Jane as she walked out.

She didn't close the classroom door behind her, so Leonard was forced to wait until her footsteps receded before crossing the room to close it. Even after he'd secured their privacy, he didn't speak. He walked towards his desk and began packing his briefcase.

'I'm sorry,' she said.

'So am I.'

'I behaved badly.'

'Yes. You did.'

'Leonard, please forgive me.' She stepped towards him and reached for his right arm, which was resting on the top of his briefcase. She wanted to touch his hand but would settle for the sleeve of his suit instead. He pulled it back just in time.

'I think you should go home.'

'Please.' Her voice began to distort in her throat. 'I'm sorry.'

'It could never have worked. I'm too old for you.'

60

'I don't mind that,' she said, trying to swallow the rising tears.

'Well, that's very good of you. Not to mind. But my point is that you need to grow up. To stop behaving like a petulant child.'

'I'm sorry,' she said, crying openly now. He walked to the door and opened it wide. She wanted to say something. In her desperation she thought of the Chartists, but he was waiting for her to leave, and like a diligent pupil, she complied. She walked out hoping to be called back, but all she heard was the soft click of the closing door.

On the last day of the spring term, Jane walked out of school to find Jamie waiting in an old Escort on the other side of the road. He was wearing jeans and a slim-fitting red T-shirt, his hair damp and effortlessly stylish. He crossed over when he saw her.

'Hello, stranger. Long time no see.'

She felt a thrill at his approach. At how the other girls whispered and stared. 'I'm sorry I left without saying goodbye.'

He dug his hands into his pockets. She saw the outline of a packet of cigarettes in one of them. As she looked around, she noticed the front of Leonard's car emerge from behind the school building and begin rolling slowly towards them. In a few seconds they would be in his way.

'Where are you headed? Oh, mind,' he said, putting his arm around her waist and pulling her out of the way of Leonard's car. She looked up to see him staring at her through the windscreen. She wanted to raise her shoulders in answer, to say, 'You did this to me,' but it was too late. Leonard had returned his attention to the road and was driving past them.

'Was that him?'

'What?'

'The teacher.'

'Oh no. That's all finished.'

'Where are you going now?'

'The bus stop . . . Well, home.'

'I'll take you.'

'No. I have a bus pass. It's fine.'

'Please. Let me take you.'

She looked at the rear lights of Leonard's car, breaking before the junction, and then the orange blink of his intention to turn left towards Hinchley Wood. 'OK. Thanks.'

They sat and talked outside her house for over half an hour. His car was clean and smelled of him: aftershave he'd applied, the waxy stuff he used to shape his hair.

'So will you come out with me?'

'Where do you want to go?' she said, laughing.

'Oh, come on. Don't torture me. I really like you. Let me take you out somewhere. We can go on a double date with Brenda and Gary, if you like.'

'They've made up, then?'

'Eh?'

'The night of your party, she slept downstairs. Said Gary threw her out of his bedroom.'

'Oh, that. They fight all the time. And I mean all the time. I'm not sure what he sees in her, to be honest.'

'I can see one or two things.'

'Are you referring to her massive jugs?'

Jane laughed.

'What can I say? He's blinded by her breasts.'

'And you?'

'Barrow's not my type.'

She turned towards him.

'But you are,' he said, reaching out for her hand. He pulled her closer and kissed her quickly, picking up where they'd left off as though the union of his tongue and her mouth had been put on hold for three weeks. Jane pulled back after a minute, embarrassed by the sudden intimacy, and began gathering her bag and coat, nestled between her legs in the footwell.

'Let me take you out. Just the two of us,' he persisted.

'I'll think about it.'

Two days passed before he knocked on her door. Jennifer and Peter were out shopping, and Jane was upstairs in the bath, reading a novel. She got out and dried herself, pulled a towel round her and tiptoed downstairs, the imprint diminishing with each step.

'What are you doing here?'

'I wanted to ask if you're free to come out with me tonight. Are your mum and dad home?'

'Why?' She pulled the front door closer to her.

'I don't want to get you in trouble.'

'I wouldn't be in trouble. I'm allowed to go out with people.'

'Sorry. I just thought, what with the deputy head and all.'

'I told you. That's over.'

'Yeah. Sorry. So how about it? We could drive into Kingston tonight and have a drink somewhere along the river?'

She put her hand up to her hair, conscious of how flat her wet hair must look to Jamie. 'What time?'

'Could pick you up at seven?'

'OK.'

'Shall I come here?'

'No. I'll meet you at the end of the road.'

*

Jamie was four months into an apprenticeship at his dad's repair garage in Kingston. It didn't pay much, but enough to run his car, which he'd rebuilt himself from scrap metal, and go out when he wanted to. He took her to a pub in North Kingston, nowhere near the river, and chose a table outside, in what turned out to be the rear car park, the seating area sectioned off by a few plant pots.

'What about you? What do you want to do?' he asked her.

'My mum and dad want me to go to university.'

'What do you want?'

She shrugged and looked down into her shandy. 'I might apply next year. I like history and English, so either of those. I don't know really.' *Leonard*, she thought. *I want Leonard.*

'Do you read a lot, then?'

'Yes,' she nodded. 'That's what I was doing when you called round earlier. I was reading Charlotte Brontë in the bath.'

He leaned in, his breath tainted by the lager he was drinking. 'I wanted to come back upstairs and get in with you.'

She tried to smile as his fingers rounded her knee and moved up the inside of her thigh. Then, involuntarily, as though a button had been pressed, she felt the same wet loosening Leonard had inspired that morning in his classroom.

'My mum's working nights this week,' he said.

This time she didn't demur when Jamie tried to pull her knickers down. She wanted him inside her. She wanted rid of her virginity and the purity that had given Leonard pause. *Fuck Leonard*, she thought as Jamie pushed through and into her. She remembered his words, how he'd called her a petulant child, as Jamie began moving backwards and forwards inside her. When it was over, Jamie pulled out carefully, keeping tight hold of the condom.

'Are you OK? I didn't hurt you, did I?'

'No,' she said, turning onto her side, so she didn't have to look at the semen, the physical evidence of her own spent virginity. 'It didn't hurt.'

'Hang on – let me get rid of this.' He left the room, and while he was out, she tried not to hear the sound of the toilet seat being lifted or the flush that preceded Jamie's return a few minutes later.

She felt the mattress sag under his weight as he moved in to spoon her.

'Was it too soon?'

'No. It's OK.' And then, 'It was fine. Thank you.'

She tried with Jamie. She wanted to use him to efface the sense of failure and loss she experienced whenever she thought of Leonard. And she found herself thinking of Leonard a lot. There were echoes of him in Jamie: the way he drove, the loose change in his pockets, the dark pubs he chose for their dates. He tried hard to impress her, not knowing the first impression had already been made by somebody else and it was deep. So deep he couldn't touch the sides.

The final straw came in May when Jamie invited her to see a film at the Odeon with Gary and Brenda. When Jane arrived, she saw that Jamie had already bought the tickets and a large container of popcorn. Brenda was excited, linking arms with her as they walked through the double doors into the darkened auditorium. The four of them proceeded up the central aisle of steps to the back row.

'What are we seeing?' Jane whispered to Jamie.

He was mumbling as he arranged his drink and popcorn at his feet. She heard the words '*Taxi Driver*'.

'That's the new Martin Scorsese film. I've heard it's very violent.'

'It's an eighteen, but that's because of the nudity. There's no violence.'

Jane looked to Brenda on her right and saw her hand was already busy in Gary's lap. 'They didn't waste much time,' Jane whispered.

Jamie leaned across Jane and slapped Brenda on the arm. 'Save it for later, you two.'

'Fuck off,' came Gary's muffled response.

'Do you want to move?' Jamie asked.

Jane was just about to say she'd rather enjoy Scorsese without the accompanying score of Gary's orgasm, but the opening sequence of the film had begun playing. The jaunty singing and image of black cabs manically circling London made her turn to Jamie.

'What's this?'

'It was Gary's idea. *Adventures of a Taxi Driver.*'

'I thought you said *Taxi Driver.*'

'Eh?' Jamie's eyes were glued to the screen and a blonde who was struggling to get her clothes off fast enough for the cockney taxi driver. 'Oh, it's just a bit of fun.'

'It's not my idea of fun.'

'What's that?' He turned to her. 'We can go and see your one another time if you like. But this is good. Hey, Gal,' he said, leaning across Jane and Brenda, and tapping his brother on the knee. 'This is funny. Watch this.'

'You've seen this before?'

'Yeah. I came earlier in the week. Look who comes in now!' He began laughing loudly.

Jane sat back in her seat and watched Jamie watching the film. She heard him laugh again and knew that with every minute that ticked by she was moving further and further away from Leonard. She couldn't bear the darkness, the wet fingers, the sweet, sticky smell of popcorn any longer. She stood up and walked quickly down the stairs towards the exit.

'Where are you going?' Jamie was behind her as she pushed the doors open and walked out into the dimly lit hallway.

'I'm going home. That's not my kind of film.'

'I'm sorry. I shouldn't have listened to Gary. We'll do something else.'

'No, I don't want to do anything else.' She turned to face him, keen to end it, to be out in the daylight, certain at last about what she wanted. 'I'm not right for you. I can see that now. Please forgive me.'

'Because of a stupid film? I said I was sorry.'

'It's not just the film.'

'It's because I'm not him, isn't it?'

But she was too eager to get out of the cinema to answer his question. Her run towards the exit should have been answer enough.

But it wasn't. Jamie waited outside the school gates for her, sent messages via Brenda, hand-posted letters through her front door and finally, exasperated by her silence, walked into school and waited in the foyer for her to emerge at the end of the day. Leonard, who had been in the staffroom checking his pigeonhole, walked past to see Jane having a heated conversation with the young man he'd seen her with on the last day of term. He'd been careful to avoid her, speaking to her in a professional capacity only, and always with someone else close by. But watching Jane being pulled so violently was intolerable.

'What in God's name are you doing? Who are you?'

When she heard Leonard's voice, she felt panic rise up in her. Not for herself but for Leonard. She knew he would do all he could to help her, even if that meant revealing his attachment to her. 'Let go!' she pleaded, desperate now to be free of Jamie.

'Take your hands off her immediately,' Leonard said, putting his hand over Jamie's and attempting to prise his fingers from Jane.

The school secretary, who'd been watching the scene unfold, got up from her desk and walked briskly round them and into the staffroom.

'I just want to talk to her.'

'This is neither the time nor the place,' Leonard said, moving his hand up and onto Jamie's wrist, squeezing the bones so hard Jamie's fingers loosened their grip.

'Is this him?' Jamie shouted, as Jane pulled her hand away. There was a malice in his eyes she'd never seen before. 'The one you wanted to shag?'

Leonard stepped back. 'What did you say?'

'You're the one she wanted to shag but couldn't.' He rubbed his wrist where Leonard had gripped it and smiled, victorious in his discovery.

Three male teachers followed the secretary into the foyer and surrounded the small group. 'You OK, Len? What's going on?'

'She wanted to fuck you but couldn't. So she fucked me instead!'

The teachers circled Jamie and pulled him, kicking and swearing, out of the building, while Jane and Leonard stood – still and separate – as statues. Neither one daring to look at or speak to the other.

*

68

She was waiting in his classroom later that afternoon when he returned from his meeting with the headmaster. He expressed no surprise at seeing her there, seated at her usual desk, her hands folded in front of her. He closed the door and walked to his chair at the front of the room.

'I'm so sorry.'

'Yes, you've said that before.'

'He wouldn't take no for an answer.'

'And you said no, did you?'

'I don't know what to say.'

'Perhaps you don't know what to say because you didn't say no?'

In tone and pitch, they might have conducted their exchange with every member of the class in their seats. Leonard's measured questions and Jane's faltering responses – to a distracted ear – might have presented itself as the to-ing and fro-ing of a teacher seeking clarification from his pupil. Perhaps he told himself the point, the idea he wanted to tease out, was for Jane's benefit. So that he might outline a powerful lesson she'd never forget: that she should never have opened her legs to someone whose youth and innocence made him heroic in a way he could only observe. But he'd tried to pull this boy from her and he knew, as he sat at his desk and questioned the only pupil in the room, that the lesson was all his. He hadn't been brave enough to take what Jane had offered him.

'Are they going to fire you?'

'No.'

'He's not my boyfriend.'

'I don't care who he is.'

'Leonard, please.' She stood up and approached his desk.

'Stay where you are.'

'Please forgive me. I didn't know what I wanted.'

He looked down at his hands and made a decision. 'And do you know now?'

'Yes. I want to be with you.'

'Jane—'

'I know you don't want anything to do with me anymore. Especially now, after all this, but I want you to know. I love you. I want you more now than ever.'

The words, when they came, were just a whisper. 'It's my fault. All of this is my fault.'

She took another step towards him, emboldened by the way he swivelled his chair to meet her approach. She kneeled before him – slowly and solemnly – and took his hand in hers. Her tears fell gently, deliberately onto the back of his hand. He pushed the chair back and joined her on his knees. And in the silence of the classroom, sheltered by the deep oak desk, they held each other close.

Chapter 6

They were married in July 1976 at Weybridge Registry Office a week after school broke up for the summer holidays. Her parents and Eileen Campbell were the only guests. They set off for Dorset in Leonard's car a few hours later.

That evening, after dinner in their small guesthouse, Jane ran a bath in the shared bathroom at the end of the corridor. Lowering herself into the water, she looked at the thin gold band on her left hand – comfortable in its new permanence – still surprised to be Leonard's wife.

She got out of the bath and dried her feet, her calves, her upper thighs and patted the hair between her legs. She looked at herself in the small mirror above the sink, standing on tiptoe in a futile attempt to see her pubic hair reflected back to her. Sex with Jamie had been rushed. There had been no opportunity or desire to look and observe, just the urgent smashing of their body parts together. But this was her honeymoon, the first night of her marriage, and she wanted to prepare herself by trying to see what Leonard would see. She practised smiling in the mirror, checking that her teeth were clean and food-free, then brushed her hair and applied moisturiser, rubbing her cheeks vigorously to encourage a flush. She pulled her white silk nightie on over her head and watched as her nipples rose up at the thin material. With the new dressing gown her mother had bought tied tightly round her, she tiptoed back to their bedroom. Leonard was already in bed, wearing light blue flannel pyjamas, reading a book. He hadn't even brushed his teeth.

They'd agreed that afternoon in the classroom never to speak of Jamie again. Leonard knew his wife was not a virgin and he'd come to accept the fact as the price he would have to pay for a life with her.

'My darling.' He looked up and smiled at her, moving over to the other side of the bed and inviting her to take his place. The mattress was dented and warm where he'd been, the pillows still propped up against the headboard.

She took her dressing gown off and slid in next to him.

'I'm so pleased we're here,' he said, reaching out to touch her hip.

'Me too,' she said, moving towards him.

He leaned over her to turn off the lamp on the bedside table and in the darkness got on top of her and began kissing her mouth. His pelvic bones were hard and sharp and grated against her own. She opened her legs in an effort to accommodate his weight, but Leonard had already reached down to fumble with his pyjama bottoms. After waiting so long, it seemed he couldn't wait any longer. It was the determined dash of someone who knows they have to take a running jump.

'Are you OK?' he asked, suddenly more aware of her.

'Let's just take it slowly.' She felt his face press against hers in agreement, his nose resting upon her cheekbone so that he might manoeuvre himself inside. His first thrust was accompanied by a gasp so frightening she thought he'd been knifed in the back.

In the darkness of the bedroom, their union sanctioned by rings and a shared surname, Leonard couldn't slow. He made love to her in the only way he knew how – by constantly reinforcing the point, repeating over and over his contention that their flesh become one. That to have his wife was to hold her.

She lay beneath him in her white nightie, taken aback and impassive. His orgasm brought to a juddering halt what Jane had spent so long looking forward to. He'd raced ahead to the pleasure of understanding and didn't consider for a moment if the girl beneath him had got anywhere close.

Jane looked up at the ceiling as Leonard climbed off her. He pulled his pyjama bottoms back on and lay on his back beside his new wife. When he reached out for her hand, she allowed it to be held.

'That was wonderful.'

She said nothing. Her limited experience amounted to the same disappointing conclusion: that sex wasn't something to be enjoyed. She understood, as she lifted her hips so that she could pull her nightie down behind her, that if it was a duty, then it was better to do it with someone you loved. She closed her eyes and tried not to sniff as the tears swelled beyond her eyelids. But she needn't have worried. Leonard was already asleep and snoring quietly beside her.

Chapter 7

The curtains were insubstantial before the sun's rays, and when Jane awoke at dawn, she knew that the room would soon be flooded with light. But she was too exhausted to do anything other than return to sleep, and when she woke several hours later, she saw that the portent had been fulfilled. Their bedroom was almost white with the searing imperative of a new day. She looked beside her for Leonard, but he wasn't there, and in those hazy few seconds she was unsurprised, as though in making love to her the night before, he had somehow extinguished himself. She propped herself up on her elbow and found a folded piece of paper on his pillow.

My darling,
  I've gone to get buns and tea. I couldn't bear to wake you – you looked so peaceful. I'll be back soon.
  Lx

She smiled as she refolded the paper and then remembered the bones of his face, pressed hard against her own the night before. Courtesy after coitus. Perhaps this was marriage. The sun had come to remind her it was time to leave the night behind.

Leonard returned twenty minutes later with a brown paper bag in his left hand and two takeaway cups of tea held together in his right. 'To revive you,' he said, offering his hand to her so she could take one.

'Remind me?'

'Well ... revive and remind.' He pulled the covers back and hoisted his legs into bed.

'Leonard! You've got your shoes on.'

'Oh. So I have,' he said, returning them to the carpet and showing her his back. 'Would you prefer I take them off?' He twisted so that she might see his raised eyebrow.

'Yes! You can't wear shoes to bed.'

He bent down to untie his laces. 'I just can't wait to be beside my wife again,' he said, wiggling his toes as he returned his socked feet to the bed. 'Are you happy now?'

'Yes.'

'And have you remembered?'

'Remembered what?'

'Why the buns and tea are significant?'

'We ate buns in the lecture hall.'

'Still my best pupil. And now my best wife.'

'I like to think I'm your *only* wife.'

'Yes, of course. You're quite right. I've forgotten about all the others,' he said, kissing her lightly on the end of her nose.

'You promised me buns. And tea. Take care you don't neglect your best wife.'

They spent the morning in Lyme Regis, wandering in and out of shops. At around one thirty, Leonard felt his stomach twist with hunger just as Jane walked towards a display of silver jewellery in a small gift-shop window.

'What is it?' she asked when he didn't follow her.

'I always forget what I'm going to say.'

'When you're with me?'

'Yes. I was about to say something, but . . . no. It's quite gone.'

She placed her hand gently on his upper arm. 'I'm hungry. How about you?'

He nodded.

'Come on, then. Let's go and grab a bench on the Cobb.'

'But what about these pretty things? Would you like me to buy you something? Earrings, perhaps?'

'Cod and chips. And a view of the Cobb. That's all I want right now.'

They hovered near an old couple on a bench who looked as though they were preparing to leave. Jane sat down and pushed her handbag along the slats to occupy the bench while Leonard went to buy food. She looked at the people who walked along the sand, the families who had come to this place to be together. She'd never even heard of Lyme Regis before. Never travelled so far by car with anyone. And yet she found herself, the morning after her wedding, sitting on a bench with the wind in her hair waiting for her husband to return with lunch for them both. She allowed her eyes to rest on the horizon and took a deep breath. At some point, she'd feel his return in her peripheral vision. They'd huddle together and take turns at picking the salty, greasy chips. They'd get thirsty and long for privacy, returning to the boarding house to make love again. This time slowly, with the daylight and heavy lunch tempering their movements. But not yet. None of it had happened yet. She stared at the horizon in this place she'd never been to and waited for marriage to happen to her.

Eileen continued to live with them until the following September, when a place became available at a local residential home. A month later, Jane discovered she was pregnant. Their first child, a daughter, came to them quickly, and as soon as Becca had burrowed into the lining of her mother's womb, she was all pull.

In those early weeks Jane could become hungry so suddenly that she was almost always too late to eat. The nausea was upon her before she could grab at a biscuit. As she vomited into the toilet, her stomach throwing up her lack of appetite as a rebuke, she felt her insides had been conquered by a force that would never be sated. In February 1977, as she moved into the second trimester of pregnancy, Jane began to feel as though her pelvis no longer belonged to her body. It moved with a flexibility she didn't recognise and sent a radiating pain down her inner thighs and round to her buttocks.

She had not intended to become housebound. But she hadn't made any other plans either. The silence descended on her each morning after Leonard had left for work. He was affectionate and solicitous in his departure, leaning down to kiss her gently on the cheek and asking her if she had all she needed for the day. He was generous, making his bank accounts available to her and topping up a small tin on the kitchen windowsill with ready cash in the event of an emergency. But there was nothing for Jane to spend money on: she had no friends, no job and nowhere – aside from her parents' house – to go.

Walking was difficult: her ligaments had loosened prematurely, in anticipation of labour, and every movement that wasn't about birthing – just walking down the stairs or shifting her weight on the sofa – felt like an extravagance.

Jennifer called in each morning to observe her daughter in her new home.

'Have you thought about distance learning?' Jennifer had just found a cushion to place on a small trestle table. She lifted Jane's ankles and tried to arrange them on the cushion, but the movement sent a sudden shooting pain up through Jane's left hamstring. She cried out suddenly.

'Jane, you need to go and see a doctor. You can't go the whole pregnancy like this.'

'I'm OK. It's better when my feet are on the floor. Like this,' she said, arranging her feet hip-distance apart. She was sitting in Eileen's old armchair.

Jennifer took a seat on the sofa and began to pour the tea she'd made for them. 'I'm just saying. You're a clever girl and could have done so much . . .'

'And I still can. Having a baby isn't going to stop me from reading.'

'Well, yes. But it's going to be hard. And most girls your age are either starting university or going out to work.' She poured too much milk in Jane's cup and stirred quickly, hoping Jane wouldn't notice the unsatisfactory colour.

'I can't work. I can hardly move.'

'I know. That's why I said distance. You can do that nowadays. Do the reading at home, write your essay and then send it off. I'd send it off for you.' Jennifer poured a tiny drop of milk into her own tea before swapping the cups quickly, taking the too-milky one from her daughter.

Jane saw only what was offered to her and began to sip.

'I'm thinking of you. It's not good being shut up in here all day on your own.'

'Leonard comes home as early as he can.'

'But still, Jane. You're young.' Jennifer lifted her own cup, ready for Jane's protest. 'I know, I know – you're going to tell me that has nothing to do with this. But you are young. And one day you might turn round and wonder what happened to you. A mother before you'd finished being a girl yourself.'

'I chose Leonard. We chose each other.'

'And I'm happy for you. I just don't want you to look back and regret anything.'

'And studying for some distance course is going to prevent that?'

'It'll keep your mind busy. Leave you no time to dwell.'

'I'm not dwelling.'

'Well, good. I've got a brochure here in my bag.'

The course her mother had found was called 'An Introduction to Modern Nineteenth- and Twentieth-Century Literature'.

'Exactly the period you like,' Jennifer said as Jane flicked through the booklet.

'When does it finish?'

'You can do it in terms. So this one runs from April to June. I think the last essay is due at the end of May.'

'The baby is due in June.'

'Well, that's perfect, isn't it? You can get another qualification under your belt.'

Jane thought of her aching hips. How she was keeping them steady to stop the pain that swirled in the synovial fluid. She didn't want any more under her belt. But as she looked through the course outline, she began to recognise titles of novels she'd always wanted to read. *Anna Karenina* was on there, as well as *Madame Bovary*. They were part of a unit on the fallen woman in nineteenth-century novels.

'When do I need to have registered?'

'Oh, I'll do all that,' Jennifer said, reaching for the booklet.

'It's OK. I can ask Leonard to look into it this evening.'

'No, no. Your dad and I want to pay for this. It'll be our treat.'

'Strange sort of treat,' Jane said as she sipped her tea. But she was smiling at the thought of those novels. Perhaps Leonard could drive her to a bookshop at the weekend.

Jennifer sat back and sipped her own tea, wincing at the milky brew.

Jane was unprepared for Tolstoy. His prose was old, established, printed on thin paper, and yet he took her. From the first paragraph she forgot all about her essay title and the white space of her notepad where she'd planned to make notes. There was no fallen woman in the pages she read. Only a beautiful woman, full of life and love. She read the Levin sections through patiently, a necessary respite before she could sink back into Anna.

Leonard watched his wife's absorption and felt a lightening of his own. She seemed to forget about her pelvic pain and the discomfort of carrying his child. He tried to talk to her about the revolutionary nature of Tolstoy's farming principles, that Levin was a character tasked with voicing the fundamental insecurity of Russia's landed elite in the nineteenth century, but Jane cared nothing for extraneous noise. She cared only for Anna – her heart broke for the lost woman. And when Anna's fall came, Jane hacked the emotion up from her lungs, allowing the tears and phlegm to flow. As the baby moved within her, kicking gently to claim her body and draw her attention back, Jane put her hand on her stomach and felt not just the movement of her child but the movement of longing. It didn't matter that Anna's life had ended. What mattered is that she had lived it so fully.

Leonard bought her a copy of *War and Peace*, but too stirred up by Anna, she found she couldn't care for Natasha Rostova in the same way. Leonard hovered, placing dates and battles before her as he would a cup of tea and a biscuit.

Jane resisted the urge to raise her hand and swat his voice away; it buzzed so persistently. And just like a fly, Leonard maintained a safe distance, aware that Jane was growing bigger with child and absorption. His whisperings were gently didactic, an overture loaded with nostalgia, but for Jane they spoke of a period that had already passed.

She never wrote a single essay. The course outline had been all she needed to begin an enquiry, and what she found was unbearable. The desire Leonard had awakened that first morning he walked into her classroom was universal. Everyone felt it. The need to connect with another human being. To have part of you awakened by the attentions of another. To have and to hold. To touch and to take. But her own decision to take Leonard at his first offering had weighed her down. To this armchair. To this child.

Rebecca Ann Campbell was born in June 1977. Labour was long and painful and bloody, the midwife remarking how 'This baby doesn't want to be born' to Jane, whose face was purple with effort. Jane remembered those words in the weeks that followed, when her daughter wouldn't be consoled unless she was in her mother's arms, pulling on the muscles of her neck and upper body, her cries drawing the milk to her heavily engorged breasts. She wanted to be held constantly, gripped by a mother who she felt was incontrovertibly hers. She wanted to suck her fingers and smear Jane's face with saliva. She wanted kisses and hair, snot and blood.

And in those quiet hours, as Leonard snored peacefully in bed beside her, Jane became afraid: afraid her daughter would never let go again. She didn't understand why Becca always needed so much. Motherhood made her uncomfortable, as though she were disintegrating and Becca was biting off great chunks, but it was never enough. She felt she'd go on and on, pulling and tearing until there was nothing left. And as Jane tried to conserve and pull back, Becca became even more greedy for her.

She could never hope to articulate these feelings to Leonard. Their courtship was a different time and a different relationship to this one. There was no classroom to frame their interaction, no textbooks in which their fingers might meet beneath the same word. She didn't have the language, nor did Leonard have the ears for it. He'd given Jane all that he felt was required of him: a home, a domestic allowance and now a child. And Jane did not want to voice her doubts about Becca. She didn't want to make her difference an established topic of conversation. Real.

And so she marched on and continued with her great task. When Becca was approaching her second birthday, Jane discovered she was pregnant again and wished only for two things: that her child be a boy and nothing like Becca. Only one of her wishes was fulfilled. Julia was nothing like her older sister. She was a quiet, watchful and self-sufficient baby from early on.

Jennifer and Peter Forster had maintained an attitude of conciliatory acceptance in the years following their daughter's marriage, and when Julia was born, they were on hand to help. Peter drove his wife to Jane's and then set about finding a comfortable armchair from which he might read the paper or drink a cup of tea made for him by one of the busy women.

His role was to facilitate his wife's administering of support to their daughter. And not to make himself a nuisance.

When Julia was just a week old, newly home and fussing at Jane's breast, Jennifer tried to suggest Becca sit on her granddad's lap for a story. She became tyrannical in her fury, stamping over to Jane's side and clinging to her thigh, her arm, even pulling at the baby in her arms in an attempt to dislodge the soft, warm lump that was suddenly everywhere and everything.

Becca's misery hurt Jane deeply. She knew Becca felt betrayed by the birth of her baby sister, and as she sat feeding Julia while Jennifer tried to put Becca to bed, she allowed herself to cry. The tears and sudden let-down reflex in her breasts were all one with her difficult new existence. She felt herself draining away – that by becoming a mother she was emptying herself. When Becca was finally asleep, Jennifer came downstairs and held Julia, while Jane busied herself in the kitchen.

'It does get easier,' she said, swaying her granddaughter from side to side until Julia closed her eyes.

'It can't get much harder,' Jane said quietly, opening the fridge to pull out a shepherd's pie her mother had brought over earlier in the day.

'This is the worst bit. That needs about forty-five minutes on one eighty.'

Jane nodded as she bent down to turn on the oven.

'You're tired; you've got a new baby and a demanding toddler.'

'Demanding,' Jane repeated flatly. It was neither agreement nor denial.

'She's a real mummy's girl, that one.'

'She's cross with me for having another baby.'

'She'll get over it and soon she'll have no memory of it having ever been otherwise.'

'Everybody keeps saying that.' Jane looked up at her mother, exasperated. 'She'll forget; she'll be grateful for a sibling. It doesn't help me, though, does it? I'm still the one who has to listen to her crying. I'm the one she won't forgive. Her little heart breaking.' A sob escaped from Jane as she finally said the things that hurt her most.

'Jane,' Jennifer said, walking over to her daughter and reaching out with her free hand to wipe away the tears. 'Every woman who has more than one child goes through this. It's difficult. Becca's had all of you to herself and now she's got to share you. I know' – Jennifer anticipated Jane's objection – 'it's difficult now, but you've got to let time pass. And before you know it, Becca will love Julia as much as you love both of them.'

Jane looked at her mother, swaying her granddaughter. She looked at the deep lines round her eyes and mouth, and thought about the baby her mother had lost.

'Oh, Mum. What you must have gone through.'

And as if the warm weight on her shoulder dictated it, Jennifer permitted her own tears to appear. She nodded as she felt Jane pull her close, their heads meeting over the sleeping baby.

Chapter 8

When Julia was just sixteen weeks, she began sleeping through the night. Jane was completely unprepared for the uninterrupted hours of rest. It was an unlooked-for abundance that gathered itself – as a great weight – on her chest. She woke to breasts that had hardened at the sight of the sleeping baby. But the sleep – instead of refreshing – intoxicated Jane. She woke feeling groggy and uncertain, not entirely sure she'd enjoyed what had just gone and if it would come again. But Julia was steadfast in her determination to go without milk in the night and so when Jane woke from a second night of undisturbed sleep, her breasts softening in their stance, she began to think Julia was the reward for Becca: a docile, easy baby delivered in recompense for the toddler who could never have enough.

It was around this time Becca began waking in the night. Her dreams were sometimes so frightening she'd wake up screaming. One night, Leonard found her huddled in the corner of her room, her knees tucked up inside her nightie.

'I don't want to go back to sleep,' she cried.

'Come on.' He pulled the covers of her bed back, but she wouldn't move. He crouched down and held out his hand.

'You won't have the same dream again. I'm sure the next one will be a nice one.'

'I don't want any dreams.'

'Well, that too. Come on, Becca – you need to go back to bed. I have work in the morning.'

She stared at his hand before allowing herself to be pulled up. Her thighs, Leonard noticed, were still soft and fat; her calves – just beginning to define themselves – were fuzzed over with a light smattering of hair. He watched his little girl curl up before him and felt his heart cramp with an indefinable suffering. For him and for her, knowing that they must surely be parted one day. As he drew the blanket over her small body, he closed his eyes and mumbled an invocation that it would be when she had grown taller, her bones longer, her face more defined. And as he imagined this child of his own flesh ageing, he brought his face down to hers so that he might mumble a sound of his great choking love.

'Please, Daddy. Stay with me.'

He sat down on her bed and stroked the hair away from her temples. 'There's no room for me. Your bed's too small.'

'Please, Daddy. Don't leave me.'

With some cushions taken from the sofa downstairs, he made a small and uncomfortable rectangle on the floor beside Becca's bed. She peered over the side of her bed at her father down below, his knees drawn up. Her eyes grew heavy and she slept at last.

Eileen Campbell had another stroke in 1981. Leonard was at her side as she passed away. Becca was nearly four and Julia only sixteen months, so the death, when it came, was a borderline event for Jane, who had her hands full. She felt as though Eileen, Leonard confessing his virginity, even

86

Leonard in the lecture hall were like an insubstantial vision of the past, a faintly familiar but opaque haunting that if she hadn't lived it, she would find faintly unbelievable.

In November of that year, as Julia approached her second birthday, they moved to a three-bedroom house in Claygate. When Becca finally went to school, in September 1982, Jane looked forward to some time alone with her second daughter – the one who asked so little of her. But Becca wouldn't skip off into the playground without a fight. She cried every morning of her reception year. Jane and Miss Linaker, Becca's teacher, became adept at straightening the little fingers that gripped her mother's arm, dress and hair. Miss Linaker was sympathetic at first, but as March rolled around, Jane felt the weight of her judgement. That Becca's inability to settle must be her fault. And as she watched all the other children skip off into the morning sunshine, she knew she was right.

At the end of the spring term, Jane and Leonard were summoned to a meeting with Miss Linaker and the headmistress, Mrs Hollinghurst, a small, round woman with salt-and-pepper hair pulled back into a tight bun. The kind of hair arrangement designed to make the rest of the face suffer. Her office was small and brown with a desk that was too large for her and the confines of the room. She stood up and smiled at Leonard, revealing teeth that were yellow from nicotine.

'Mr Campbell,' she said. 'We met last year.'

Leonard shook her hand quickly, impatient for the meeting to begin.

'At the introductory morning for last year's leavers. You delivered a very motivational speech on the merits of hard work and endeavour.'

Jane had Julia nestled on her hip and swayed uncomfortably by his side.

Mrs Hollinghurst searched Leonard for more, the tips of her upper incisors on her bottom lip, like an eager rabbit, but finding there was none, indicated the chairs just behind them. 'Please. Sit down.'

'Thank you,' Jane said gratefully, settling Julia on her lap and turning to smile at Miss Linaker, who remained just behind Mrs Hollinghurst, ready for her cue.

'Thank you both for coming.' Mrs Hollinghurst looked at Jane for the first time. 'As you know, Rebecca has taken a long time to settle here.'

Jane kissed Julia's crown. It smelled of baby shampoo, fresh air, tractability.

'Yes, we are aware of her tears in the morning,' Leonard said carefully.

'Mr Campbell, her distress is not confined to the morning. She spends most of the day alone in the playground. She shuns the company of others and has recently become aggressive in the classroom.'

'Aggressive?'

'We understand she threatened one of the other children. Told him that if he didn't move from her space on the carpet, she'd "kick his head off".'

Leonard took a deep breath. 'Mrs Hollinghurst, I understand this may be a cause of some concern to you and your staff.' He acknowledged Miss Linaker by dipping his forehead briefly in her direction. 'But I don't believe an idle threat or the infantile tears of a five-year-old warrant this' – he looked around at all the brown – 'summit. I've had to arrange cover at a very busy time of year to be here this morning and I'm afraid I can't see what you'd like me to say apart from the obvious. My wife and I will talk to Rebecca this evening.'

The ardour had gone from Mrs Hollinghurst's eyes. Even her teeth had retracted to consider their next move. 'Mr Campbell, I am merely highlighting to you that we – as a school and staff – consider Rebecca to be a most *unusual* child.'

'And we understand that,' Jane said, lifting Julia so she could plant her feet on Jane's thighs. 'But why are we not also talking about how we can help Becca to feel more comfortable, happier in school? Are there any children in her class she gets on well with?'

'Becca spends most of her time alone—'

'Miss Linaker, allow me—' But Mrs Hollinghurst was halted by the sound of a sob breaking from Jane.

Leonard followed her gaze. 'Jane, what's wrong?'

'She's alone all day. This is why she has to be pulled from me. And I let them do it.'

Leonard put his arm around Jane's shoulders. 'Mrs Hollinghurst, thank you for letting us know. My wife and I need time to discuss the matters you've raised.'

'She's different, Leonard. You heard it yourself. No friends.'

'She didn't say "no friends" exactly.'

'Becca spends all day alone. That's what I heard. I don't know what conversation you were listening to.'

'And I understand that that's distressing to hear. It upsets me too, but I think we need to remain calm.'

They were in the kitchen. Leonard had planned to drop Jane and Julia home before returning to school, but his wife's tears had delayed that.

'That's easy for you to say. You don't have to suffer your child being prised from you every morning.'

'I just think this has been blown up out of all proportion. That woman, Hollinghurst, she's a notorious—'

'A notorious what? Busybody? Flirt? There's nothing you can say about her that will make me doubt the truth of what she's saying. That Becca's . . .'

'What? What *is* Becca? Aside from a shy, reticent little girl?'

'She's fragile. And needy. She needs so much.'

'What do you need, Jane? Tell me and I'll do it. Do you want to change schools?'

'I want to take her to see someone. A doctor.'

He looked at his watch as he stood up. 'As you wish.'

Dr Pattison was in his late fifties. His thighs were too big for his navy trousers; his waistcoat, made from a similar material at a later date, a shade darker.

'Mrs Campbell. What can I do for you?'

'It's about my daughter.'

'She looks well enough,' he said, leaning across to press one of his large thumbs into Julia's cheek.

'No, my other daughter. Rebecca.'

'Where is she?'

'She's at school, Doctor.'

'She can't be that poorly,' he said, lowering his glasses.

'It's not about being poorly. She's not getting on well at school. Not making friends. My husband thinks she's just shy, but . . .'

Dr Pattison leaned back. 'Is she sleeping well?'

'Well, that's half the problem. She wakes in the night with these dreams. They're so vivid she talks about them for days afterwards.'

'I see. And have you tried putting her to bed earlier?'

'I'm not sure that's really the issue. I think she might need to see someone. A professional who's had experience with children like Becca. I've been doing a bit of reading and it seems—'

'I'm going to stop you there,' he said, holding his hand up, the fingernails long and yellow. 'If I had a pound for every patient who tells me they've "done a bit of reading" . . .'

'But I have and it seems there is evidence to suggest some children have difficulties socially, that they're born with this inability to—'

'Mrs Campbell. Allow me to reassure you. There is nothing wrong with your daughter that a good night's sleep won't resolve. A good talking-to and a few early nights. She'll be fine.'

Chapter 9

Leonard was careful not to say, 'I told you so,' when Jane relayed her conversation with Dr Pattison. He knew she was disappointed, that she felt admonished by their GP's vigorous dismissal of her concerns, but what was disappointing to her was a relief to him. Becca was different, he knew that. But then so was he. And yet he'd been successful, got married – albeit late – and become a father. Becca would make her own way in life. A medical diagnosis, even if one could be constructed to suit her unique character, would only hinder that.

He loved his wife and daughters with absolute clarity. And he'd wanted more. When Julia had been about eight months – as he watched Jane spooning porridge into her small mouth while Becca chewed through the last of her toast – he'd decided to raise it with Jane.

'Darling.'

Julia's mouth opened only when the spoon was brought near. Jane looked up. 'Yes?'

'I've been thinking.' Leonard was seated at the head of the table, reading his newspaper. He dipped the right side of it to reveal himself. 'Shall we have another?'

'Oh, for goodness' sake, you can see how busy I am. Can't you make one for yourself?'

Not for the first time in their marriage, he felt wrong-footed. 'I don't understand.'

Jane looked at his cup.

'Oh,' he laughed. 'No.' He put the newspaper down, but as he did so, Becca swallowed the last of her toast and began emitting a low whine that would quickly gather pace and drown out all other noise.

'Becca—'

'What's the matter?' Leonard turned to her, always a step behind Jane, who would, he assumed, know exactly what was wrong with her.

'I want more.' Becca opened her mouth to reveal a tongue at odds with her demand. It lay large and sated amid the chewed fragments of toast.

'Becca, close your mouth, please,' Leonard said, looking – at the same time – for direction from Jane.

'Or you could make her some more while I feed Julia?'

'Yes. I can do that,' he said, standing up and walking towards the stove. 'Where is it?'

'Where's what?' With a small spoon she drew a no-nonsense lump of porridge up the side of the bowl.

'The toast.'

'The toast.' She turned, spoon in mid-air. 'Leonard, you mean the bread.'

'Yes, of course. Sorry. The bread.'

'The breadbin,' she said, opening her mouth to encourage Julia to do the same. She spooned the porridge in, scraping what squeezed back out from her soft cheeks and redelivering it in one deft movement.

'When I said another, I was referring to—'

'I want honey.'

'*Please*. I'd like honey, *please*.'

Becca took the word and made it plaintive. She bawled it across the table, lowering her forehead in piteous supplication.

'Leonard. I think your daughter would like honey.'

He looked at Jane.

'You don't know where the honey is, do you?'

Becca picked her head up to look at her mother.

'Am I being accused of something? In my own house?' He put his hands on his hips.

Jane put the spoon back in the bowl.

'Because I won't stand for it. Of course I know where the honey is. Here it is!' he said, grabbing the bottle of Fairy Liquid from behind the taps. He brought the bottle down to Becca's eye level and proffered it to her nose. 'This is from a particularly special hive I have out in the garden. Don't worry about that green colour – I think some of the bees had a nasty cold at the time. Oh, hang on. I think I've caught it,' and drawing his head back as if to sneeze, he saw Becca's eyes widen in delight. When the sneeze came, it was so theatrical and loud that Julia jumped, but Becca was spellbound, watching as her father brought his fingers up to his nose, where suddenly, inexplicably, Fairy Liquid dripped – like snot – onto the table.

Her guffaw was so overpowering she grabbed her stomach in an attempt to hold on as her body rocked in hilarity. Jane, who'd never seen Becca laugh so deeply, couldn't help but join her. Leonard, who was too happy to laugh, went to pick Julia up.

'What were you trying to say earlier?'

'Oh,' he said, shy after the success of his joke. 'I wanted to talk about us having another one of these.' He lifted Julia in example.

'Oh.'

'When Julia's a bit older.'

'Leonard, I don't know. Can we talk about it later?'

'Of course.'

Jane went to take Julia.

'No, I'll hold her while you make Becca's toast.'

'You really don't know where the honey is, do you?'

'No idea.'

Leonard was a happily married man. That's what he would tell people, if they ever asked. But they didn't. They took his married status for granted in the same way he did. He went off to work comforted by the rest he'd had and the history that was in front of him. He never noticed that his wife was becoming disenchanted with her load.

Becca's tears eventually dried up at the end of her second year, but she continued to walk away from Jane with her shoulders slumped. Jane stopped telling Leonard about their painful partings at the gate, at how she'd noticed that their daughter simply accepted her loneliness and isolation. She couldn't go back to Dr Pattison – he'd only dismiss her. So Jane resorted to hope. Hope that something might change or shift, a new teacher or pupil who might make all the difference.

By the time Julia started school the following year, Jane and Leonard had stopped talking about a third child. She had used her youth as a shield, told him they had plenty of time, but as the years passed, she realised her reluctance had nothing to do with age. She just didn't want another baby. She couldn't go back to the beginning again. Her understanding became a certainty the first morning she walked away from the school gates having dropped off Julia. Julia – who had walked across the playground calmly and happily, who didn't look back once for her mother. It was this action that convinced Jane of the appalling unpredictability of having children: how one might want you so much they'd happily crawl back inside, whereas another quietly and peacefully walks away, looking forward to the adventure of her own life. Jane resolved that morning, as she let herself into a quiet house and began washing up the breakfast dishes, that she had to carve out a life for herself. She could maintain a peaceful order, look after Leonard and the children, but she needed to do something for herself too. She'd read again. Perhaps she could resume the distance learning she'd started and never finished when pregnant with Becca.

So certain was she that she turned off the tap, dried her hands on a tea towel, grabbed her keys and a cardigan, and let herself out of the front door.

She walked the short distance to Claygate High School where Leonard had applied after they moved house.

'I'd like to speak to Mr Campbell, please.'

The school receptionist, who'd never met Jane before, peered more closely over her glasses.

'Is he expecting you?'

'No. He's not.'

'Well, in that case, I'm very sorry, madam, but you'll have to make an appointment. Our deputy heads are very busy people – particularly at the beginning of term.' She picked up her pen and asked Jane, 'What is it regarding, please?'

'It's about having another baby.' Jane, in that moment of decision, felt consoled by the pen. She had to have her decision committed to paper.

The receptionist looked up very slowly. 'What baby?'

'*Another* baby. I don't want to have any more. Could you let him know, please?'

The receptionist took a deep breath and looked around her. She was alone in her little office. 'I see. Can I have your name, please, madam?'

'Yes. It's Jane. Jane Campbell. I'm his wife.'

She put down her pen.

'You're Mr Campbell's wife? Mrs Campbell, why on earth didn't you say? Of course you can see him. I'll find out where he is.' She wheeled her chair backwards to peer at a sheet of paper pinned to the noticeboard on her right.

'There's no need. Will you just give him my message, please?'

'Yes, Mrs Campbell.' The receptionist looked smaller, more vulnerable, stranded as she was in the middle of the room. She leaned forward and pressed her heels into the floor quickly and rhythmically in an effort to wheel herself back to the desk, but Jane was already walking away, letting herself out of the heavy double doors and into a day that didn't involve any more children.

Chapter 10

On a cold, wet morning in 1987, Jane discovered her elderly neighbour's dead body slumped on the floor of his small kitchen at the back of the house. Mr Wilson's daughter-in-law had given the Campbells her telephone number for precisely this eventuality, but still nothing could have prepared Jane for the sight of his diminished figure, surrendered and alone.

Jane had the presence of mind to check for a pulse, but before she could probe for a beat under his ear, his cold, rigid skin answered her question. He'd been dead for several hours. She turned round and forced herself to walk away from him. His body. She fought to maintain a normal pace to the front door. A run would have unleashed a dangerous dog to her heels. It would have been upon her before she could pull down the latch. As she stepped onto the path, she closed the door firmly behind her, protecting the secret of death within. She had to steady herself with one hand against her own door as she struggled to insert the key. She went straight upstairs to the study at the front of the house, where Leonard was working on some papers.

'He's dead.'

Leonard's pen stopped, but he didn't raise his head.

Instead, he asked patiently, as though addressing a pupil who has failed to mention the year a reform act came into being, 'Who is dead?'

'Mr Wilson. I've just been in to check on him. He's in the kitchen.'

Leonard put his pen down calmly but then quickly brought his hand to his mouth. 'We must telephone the police. And his daughter.'

'His daughter-in-law.'

'Yes. Quite. Do you have her telephone number?'

'Downstairs. In the book.'

As they came down the stairs, quickly and with purpose, Becca emerged from the front room. 'What's wrong?'

Jane set about finding the phone book she'd just told Leonard to find.

'What are you looking for?' Becca pulled on Jane's sleeve.

'The phone book.'

'Why? What's happened?' she asked her father.

'I'm afraid it's Mr Wilson next door. We think he may have passed away.'

'He has, Leonard. There's no "think" about it,' Jane said as she stood up, pushing back her hair, which had fallen forward.

They didn't notice Becca's brow furrow or her slow walk up the stairs to her bedroom. By the time Jane had dialled the number for Mr Wilson's daughter-in-law, Becca was sobbing for a man she barely knew. She only knew that he had been alive and now he wasn't. As she cried, she hoped someone would come upstairs and sit beside her, place an arm across her shoulder – heavy and reassuring – and pull her back. But nobody did. Downstairs, her mother had begun, falteringly, with Leonard by her side, to relay the message that Mr Wilson was dead.

'Yes, of course. When do you think you might get here?'

'I see. Oh, right. Well, of course, it's up to you. But I must phone the police now . . . Thank you. Goodbye.'

'What did she say?'

'She said she has a hair appointment. That she'll come afterwards.'

When Mr Wilson's daughter-in-law finally knocked on the Campbells' front door, the police had already been and gone.

'Mrs Wilson.'

'Marion. Sorry I'm so late. I'd been ages trying to get that bleeding appointment, and then wouldn't you know, just as I'm going in—'

'I'm afraid the police have already gone. They couldn't wait any longer.'

'Ah God,' Marion said, looking over the wall at the house next door. 'Can I come in?' she said, looking up. 'Before I go . . . you know.' Her eyes shifted left.

'Yes, of course,' Jane said, stepping back. 'I'm sorry. Come in. Can I make you a cup of tea?'

Marion turned at the sight of the gilt-edged mirror above the telephone table and began pulling at her hair.

'Lovely. Milk and two sugars,' she said to herself, not noticing how her action obstructed Jane.

'Excuse me,' Jane said, forced to walk between Marion and her reflection. As the kettle boiled, she placed a teapot, two cups and saucers and the sugar bowl on the tray she kept on its side with the chopping boards. She considered getting out the bone-china milk jug her aunt had bought her as part of a wedding present, but as she stepped closer to the living room where Marion had gone to sit with Julia, she heard Marion ask her daughter what she was reading.

'*The Famous Five*,' Julia answered quickly.

'I didn't read much when I was a kid. Too busy running around playing kiss-chase with the boys.' Jane heard the snap, snap of a lighter and the slow, meditative inhalation of a philosopher pausing for thought. Jane opened the fridge and pulled a bottle of milk from the door.

'I was just saying to your girl here I never read much when I was young. Do you have an ashtray I could use?' Marion said, as Jane carried in the tray.

'I'm afraid not. Nobody smokes in this house.'

'Ah, sorry,' Marion said, waving her hand across the smoke that trailed towards Julia at the other end of the sofa.

'I'll get you a dish from the kitchen.'

'Thanks,' she said, moving forwards so she could sit up straight near the coffee table.

'Yes, Julia loves to read,' Jane said, as she came back into the room with the lid from a jam jar. 'Julia, why don't you go upstairs to your bedroom? Mrs Wilson and I need to have a little chat.'

'Call me Marion. Please.'

'Julia. Now, please. Go upstairs and see where Becca's got to.'

'You've got another one, have you? A little sister?' she said, turning to Julia.

'No. No, Becca's my older daughter. Julia is the baby,' she said, giving Julia a smile. 'Julia, come on. Upstairs, please.'

Marion's eyes followed Julia as she stood up and walked out.

'Julia and Becca are still very young. And you know, what with poor Mr Wilson. I'd like to spare them the details.'

'She's pretty.'

'Do you have children?' Jane asked, pouring the tea.

'Two boys. Jonathan and Robbie. Robbie's about the same age as your one. He's eight.'

'Julia's just turned seven.'

'How about your other girl?'

'She'll be ten in June.'

'Same age as my Jonathan, then. They'll get on like a house on fire.'

'Get on?'

'When we move in.'

'Oh! I see. Sorry, I didn't realise.'

'Yes,' Marion said, placing her cigarette in the lid. She picked up her cup and began slurping at the hot tea. 'Andrew and I have been wanting to move somewhere nicer for a while now.'

'Where are you at the moment?'

'In Stockwell. Do you know the Studley Estate?'

'No, I'm afraid I don't.'

Marion laughed and put her cup back on its saucer. 'It's a hellhole. Just behind the Tube station. We've got a two-bedroom flat. Been in it for years. The boys don't mind sharing, but we'd like a bit more space. And Andrew is an only child. So it'll all go to him. To us.'

'I see. Right. Well, I'd better give you the telephone numbers the police asked me to pass on to you. The first one is the coroner's office.' Jane passed Marion a sheet of paper torn from a spiral notebook. 'I'm sure they'll be able to advise you of the next steps.'

'Will you come with me?' Marion said. Her mouth narrowed with the effort of asking.

'Where to?'

'Next door. I've never seen a dead body before.'

'Oh no, Marion, he's not there. They've taken him away.'

'How's that?'

'I let the police in and said we should wait for you, but they insisted he be removed. They gave me those telephone numbers to give to you.'

'I see.' Marion's cigarette had long burned down to the filter, but she picked it up and sucked on it anyway.

'Marion, can I ask . . . ? Does your husband . . . Does Mr Wilson know his father has died?'

'He knows. But he never had a good relationship with him. A lot of bitterness in his childhood, you know.'

Jane nodded her head and, as she looked down at her lap, took the opportunity to check her watch. She needed to go upstairs and look in on the girls. On Becca.

'I'm sorry to hear that. And sorry, of course, for your loss. If there's anything I can do . . . ?' Jane said, standing up.

Marion followed her up with her eyes and drank the remaining tea in her cup. 'Thank you. I'll go home and phone these numbers. Actually, there is something you could do for me. What school do your girls go to?'

'St Matthew's.'

'St Matthew's. Have you got a pen?'

'Yes, of course.' Jane walked out to the telephone table, where she pulled open a drawer and rummaged for the biro she'd used that morning to write down the telephone numbers.

'Sorry,' she shouted back to Marion in the living room, 'I can never find a pen in this house,' and was just about to run up the stairs to Leonard's study when she heard Marion reply.

'Don't worry. I found one here on the coffee table.'

Jane walked back into the living room to see Marion scribbling the name of the school above the number of the coroner's office.

Chapter 11

Jane went alone to the funeral the following Thursday. There were very few mourners, around eight in total. Jane spotted Marion's blonde hair immediately; she was leaning against the wall of the chapel, smoking a cigarette. Beside her stood a tall, dark-haired man with his hands in his pockets. He was looking down at the gravel, shifting his weight from one foot to the other. In front of them stood two boys, both in suits, their dark pomaded hair shining like vinyl set to play atop their white heads. They were looking up at the sky, at an aeroplane cutting through the blue, noisy in its easy ascent.

'Hello, Marion.'

Marion stepped away from the wall. She dropped her cigarette onto the gravel and crunched it underfoot.

'Hi,' she said slowly, exhaling the last of the smoke. To her husband, she said, 'This is your dad's neighbour. I'm sorry but I've forgotten your name.'

'I'm Jane.' She extended her hand towards the man, who paused for an uncomfortable second before shaking it lightly.

'Andrew.'

'Nice to meet you, Andrew. I'm sorry for your loss.'

He nodded and held his hand out to his wife. Marion

extracted a packet of cigarettes from her handbag and put them down on his outstretched palm.

'And these must be your sons,' Jane said, smiling at the children before her.

'That's right. This is Jonathan.' Marion indicated the taller one. 'And this is my youngest, Robbie. This lady lives next door to your granddad. She found his body.'

Andrew looked up quickly, squinting at the smoke he was now producing.

'You found my dad?'

'Yes. I'm afraid I did.'

'Where was he?' he asked, offering Jane a cigarette.

'No, thank you. In the kitchen. He was in the kitchen.'

'Died of a heart attack,' Marion said.

Andrew nodded his head as though he were hearing it for the first time.

'I see. Presumably it would have been quite quick. What I mean by that,' Jane stammered, 'is that I hope he didn't suffer.'

'He got off lightly, then, didn't he?' Andrew put his free hand on Marion's shoulder and began steering her towards the entrance to the chapel. The boys followed in quiet procession, the younger looking up at the sky, hoping for more aeroplanes.

The service was brief. After a short eulogy from the vicar and a quiet speech from Mr Wilson's sister, it was over. Jane got up quickly and made her way to the back of the chapel. She was looking for Marion, but instead she found Andrew, already outside and smoking.

'I'm sorry I can't stay, but I have to collect my daughters from school.'

'Stay? What for?'

'For the burial.'

'Oh, don't worry about that. We'll see the old bastard put away. Thanks for coming.'

'It was the least I could do. And once again, my condolences.'

'Yeah. Thanks.'

'Marion mentioned you might move into your father's house?'

'Did she now?' he asked, inclining his head.

'I'm sorry. I didn't mean to speak out of turn.'

'She told you we'll be moving in?'

'Perhaps I misheard. It's none of my business.'

'Bloody woman,' he muttered to his shoes.

'I must go,' she said, stepping backwards. 'Goodbye.'

But Andrew hadn't heard her. He'd already gone back inside the chapel, looking for his wife's head.

Chapter 12

They moved in on a Wednesday. Jane noticed the white van parked across the driveway. It was around eleven and she was ironing in the front room. Standing the iron up on its end, she approached the bay window cautiously, but saw that the man leaning out of the driver's side window as he reversed was not Andrew. He was shorter, stocky with a shaved head. He turned the engine off and got out, but instead of walking towards the front door, he turned in her direction. She dropped the net curtain and stood back, returning to the iron in an effort to convince the room that she was too busy for snooping, but as she released more steam onto Leonard's shirt, she heard the doorbell.

'Morning.'

'Hello.'

'I'm sorry to bother you, but I wondered if it would be all right if I park my van across your driveway? Just for a couple of hours. We need to get the big lorry on the drive, you see.'

'Do you mean next door?'

'That's right.'

'Are you moving in?'

'Me? No. My cousin is, though. His dad lived here before him.'

'Oh, I see. Yes, I met Andrew at Mr Wilson's funeral.'

The skinhead smiled and nodded. 'Yeah. So is that OK?' His smile was open, wide and capable of great violence.

'Yes. Yes, of course. My husband won't be home until after six o'clock.'

'We'll be long gone by then. At least, I hope we will!'

Andrew appeared half an hour later – in the driver's seat of a much larger vehicle. He pulled onto the driveway and, turning off the engine, sat perfectly still for a minute before lighting a cigarette. He got down from the lorry and stood in front of the house, smoking and apparently reluctant to go inside. The skinhead who'd knocked on Jane's door walked over to join him, and the two men spoke without making eye contact. Andrew pointed to the Campbell house with his cigarette and asked the skinhead something.

Marion knocked on the door after lunch. Her blonde hair was pulled back and covered by a headscarf. She looked like she'd been for a run: her cheeks were red, and her eyes shining with barely repressed elation.

'Marion. Hello. I see you're moving in next door.'

'We are,' she said. 'I'm going to collect Jonathan and Robbie now. They've been with my mother-in-law all day.'

'Well, welcome to the road,' Jane said, at a loss for something warmer. 'Is there anything I can do for you?'

'A boiled kettle would be grand. The council are going to get the water on this afternoon sometime, but until then we've got nothing and the boys are gasping for a drink.'

Jane looked at her watch. 'Yes, of course. I'll do it now. Do you have cups? And milk and sugar?'

'Got it all. Just need hot water. Are you in a rush?' Marion asked, stepping into the hallway as Jane disappeared quickly to the kitchen.

'Not exactly,' Jane shouted over the sound of the water rushing from the tap to the kettle. 'I've got to collect my daughters at three. But this shouldn't take long.'

'You can head off if you like,' Marion said in the doorway. 'I'll pull the door behind me and leave your kettle on the doorstep.'

'That won't be necessary,' Jane said.

'Suit yourself.' Marion used Jane's refusal as an invitation to peer at her kitchen. 'How long have you been here, then?' she said, examining the floral wallpaper above the tiles. It was yellow and tired.

'Over six years.'

'And do you like it round here?'

'It's OK. I grew up in Hinchley Wood, so I know the area quite well.'

Marion peered into one of the pots on the stove. 'Smells good,' she said, before pulling out a chair and sitting herself down at the table.

'How about you? Do I detect an Irish accent?'

'You do. I'm from Dublin.'

'What made you come over here?'

'My mam and dad came over when I was thirteen.'

'And are they in Stockwell too?'

'They're both dead. Which is preferable if you ask me.'

'I'm sorry.' She pulled the lead from the hot kettle and turned to Marion. 'Probably easier if you take it,' she said.

'Thanks a million,' Marion said. She bent her knees to pick it up and held it out in front of her, allowing the steam to lead the way to the front door.

'Let me get that for you,' Jane said from behind her, but Marion had already opened the front door and was walking down the path.

Chapter 13

Becca couldn't hide her interest as they walked past on their way home from school that afternoon.

'How old are their children?' Becca asked, once she was settled at the kitchen table, watching her mother chopping vegetables for dinner.

'One of them is your age, I think,' Jane said.

'Boy or girl?'

'Boy. Jonathan.'

'And the other one?'

'Also a boy. Robbie. He's a year older than Julia,' she said, thinking about her younger daughter, who had taken in the arrival of the Wilsons as the logical next event in a story that had begun with the death of an old man. She needed no reassurance or additional information. Life for Julia was always in the present tense.

Becca wanted to go and knock for Jonathan as soon as possible. Jane was surprised: she'd had no warning that Becca would want to make friends, and she knew that denying her daughter would only bring down a torrent of noisy disappointment. And this time she'd be overheard. It struck Jane that the process of growing up, or watching a child grow up, really meant a steady awareness of the number of people watching. As Becca got older, Jane saw there was more of an audience. And she felt alone in her understanding of how they would judge her.

'Give them a chance to settle in, Becca. They only moved in today.'

'Will they go to our school?' she asked.

'So their mother seems to think.' Jane had begun trimming the fat from some chuck steak. She was making a beef casserole that would see them through to Friday.

'Will he be in my class?'

'Becca, I have no idea. Now, don't you have homework or reading to do? Your sister's already upstairs doing hers.'

Becca stepped closer to her mother. Jane put down the knife and stood still. She could sense Becca standing directly behind her and knew her daughter wanted her to turn round. Her muscles tense, she felt Becca's hands slide under her arms and connect across the soft lump of her stomach. Where those hands had begun. And then the gentle prod of Becca's nose in her spine. 'I'll make friends, Mummy, don't worry. I'll be less trouble to you then.' And without knowing or understanding it, as though Becca had just performed the Heimlich manoeuvre, Jane coughed up a hard ball of emotion. It was somewhere between sob and cry. And in that moment, as she faced away from her daughter, she knew Becca was vulnerable. And Jane felt the pain of failure before the calamity came.

Chapter 14

When Mrs Grieg introduced the new boy to the class, Becca felt as though he might belong to her. She could see that he was fragile, his brown freckles and red lips vivid against pale skin.

She put her hand up to speak.

'Rebecca? What is it?' Mrs Grieg asked her.

'Jonathan lives next door to me. In Mr Wilson's old house. Mr Wilson *died*.'

'Yeah,' Jonathan said to his new teacher. 'My granddad died and they put him in a coffin and buried him in the ground.'

'I see. And, Jonathan, would you like to sit next to Rebecca? She could be your neighbour in class just as she is on your road?'

Jonathan nodded, transitioning from death to companionship with childish ease. Becca moved her chair along, leaving just enough room for Mrs Grieg to position another under the desk. She tucked the stray strands that had fallen around her face behind her ear and chanced a timid smile at Jonathan. She was pleased with herself.

Jonathan didn't say anything for the remainder of the morning. At break time he followed Becca out to the playground, happy to do whatever she did. But Becca didn't do anything at break time. She didn't have any friends. None of the girls wanted to include her, and the boys were unwilling for a girl to join their kicking and shoving. So Jonathan saw, that first morning of his first day in his new school, that Becca was accustomed to being on her own.

A boy called Neil jogged over to them. His arms were pumping gently at his side, and without looking at either of them, he stopped abruptly and turned on his right foot. He looked down at the grey pavement and said to no one in particular, 'Do you want to play?'

Jonathan dug his hands into his trouser pockets, as though the answer might lie deep in the seams, shrugged his shoulders and walked away from Becca to join the other boys. She was shocked by the sudden withdrawal but managed to swallow the pain and smile at Neil, who was now looking directly at her.

'Just boys, OK?' he said, by way of explanation.

But she understood the game a bit better now. She had to pretend she was happy even when she wasn't. She had to show she didn't care even if her heart was breaking. Because if she grabbed – as she wanted to do with Jonathan – he'd only retreat further away.

One of the boys kicked the ball to Jonathan, waiting for him to return the kick before running round the imagined boundary of the football pitch. As he moved, he noticed Becca step back to the edge of the playground and find a bench, where she sat down to wait. When Mrs Grieg came outside to ring the bell, Jonathan jogged back to Becca.

'What now?' he asked, out of breath.

'Follow me.'

Jonathan spent the day by Becca's side. She showed him

where to hang up his coat, which shelf contained the pots of pencils and where his tray was. She felt happy in a way that she tried to articulate to Jane when she came to collect her at 3 p.m.

'I helped Jonathan today and I think we're going to be friends.'

'Jonathan Wilson?'

'Yeah.' But in Becca's mind he'd already travelled far from being a Wilson. He was the boy who'd decided not to play another game of football at lunchtime and had played with her instead.

Becca had experienced vivid dreams for as long as she could remember. As she got older, instead of crying out for her parents, she began writing them down. Sometimes – if they were particularly frightening – she'd get out of bed and switch her bedside-table lamp on so she could write the details down. But most of the time she saved the written account for the morning, often embellishing the vision for her own enjoyment. She had no way of knowing that other children didn't experience the night in the same way she did. But Becca got into the habit of sharing her dreams with Jonathan. It wasn't long before he was asking for them every morning.

'And then what?'

'It started on a normal road. Like our road. And I walked along the pavement, going somewhere.'

'To school?'

'I don't think so. But I'm not sure. Anyway, I was walking along and then suddenly there was a great big wall in front of me.'

'How high?'

'Really high. Too high for me to reach the top.'

'And how wide?'

'It stretched across the pavement and the road. I couldn't get round it. And I couldn't climb it.'

Jonathan nodded his head.

'And it was really bright and colourful,' she said, turning to him, her eyes full of the thickly painted bricks. 'But I couldn't see what the picture was, because it was too high and wide for me to see.'

'So what did you do?'

'I walked up to it and started banging my head against it.'

Jonathan stopped walking and turned to her, the wall arresting his movement as it had Becca's. He looked at her forehead as she turned to meet his interest. 'And what happened?'

'I kept banging and banging,' she said, bobbing her head forwards and back in the manner of a grey woodpecker, 'and eventually a hole started to open up.'

Jonathan's mouth gaped. 'And then what?'

'And then I lifted my foot up and managed to crawl through the hole and onto the other side.'

Robbie and Julia – uninterested – caught up with them and walked on ahead.

'What was on the other side?'

'Warm, slippery ground. Like jelly or jam everywhere. I tried walking but kept falling over. I didn't care, though, because nobody was there and nobody could get in. Everyone was still on the other side of the wall.'

Jonathan was preoccupied by Becca's dream for the rest of the day. In class and at break time, he asked questions. How thick was the wall? How wide was the hole she made? Becca answered like a politician expecting a tough interview; she was unsurprised by the interest and at ease answering the questions.

'The ground on the other side was red, did you say?'

'No. It was slippery like jam but not red. I think it might have been grey, actually.'

'Grey. OK.' Jonathan looked around for some paper.

The following morning, when Jane led him into the kitchen to wait for Julia to come downstairs, Jonathan pulled a piece of folded A4 paper out of his bag and handed it to Becca.

'It's your dream. I've drawn it.'

Becca opened the sheet of paper and saw a cross-section of the brick wall in grey confident strokes, parallel to the margin and creased by the central fold. On one side was the hard pavement and the other the sticky, uneven ground.

'Where's the hole?'

'I couldn't get it in. I need to draw the wall head on for that.'

'Could you do it for me?'

Jonathan nodded and took the piece of paper just as Jane walked back into the kitchen. 'Julia's not feeling very well this morning. You three go on to school or you'll be late.'

That afternoon, as Mrs Grieg told the class to pack their things away and put their coats on, Jonathan handed Becca another piece of paper. Folded in exactly the same way. On the way home, in silence, Becca opened it up and looked at the perspective. This time, the paper was the wall, divided into four quadrants, but right in the middle was the hole she'd made with her head. And through the hole, barely perceptible, was the peaked, sticky ground. The peaks were like crests drawn as a child's impression of the choppy sea. It was the only thing juvenile about the picture. Jonathan dipped his head as he walked alongside her.

'I like this one. It's much better,' she said.

'OK.' He reached out for the piece of paper.

'Can't I keep it?' she said, gripping more tightly. 'It is my dream.'

'I'll make you another one.'

'Why can't I have this one?'

'Because I need this one to make the copy. And you said it's perfect.'

'I didn't say it was perfect. I said it was better.'

'What would make it perfect?'

'Me. If you put me in it. It's my place.'

'OK. What side? Pavement or sticky?'

'Sticky side.'

As Jonathan's interest in Becca's dreams increased, so too did Julia and Robbie's frustration at the slow pace of their walk to school. They no longer waited for their older siblings, despite Jane's injunction that they all stay together.

'I had another one last night.'

'What happened?'

'I found a new staircase in our house.'

'Up or down?'

'Down.'

'And what happened?'

'I went to get something out of the cupboard under the stairs. I can't remember what I was looking for. Maybe my school bag or shoes?'

Jonathan nodded.

'And then I saw a small brown door. I'd never seen it before. So I pushed it open.'

'Was it a rectangle? Like a normal door?'

'It was square. Because it was so small.'

'OK. Carry on.'

'And I pushed it, and when it opened, I saw some steps underneath it, so I walked down them. And it was really cold and dark down there. But . . .'

'But what?'

'I could see the shimmer of water down there. I knew there was water.'

'What did you do?'

'I carried on walking until I got to the bottom. My feet touched normal ground, but when I walked a bit further—'

'How much further?'

'Like ten steps.' Becca looked down at her feet moving across the pavement. 'No, maybe five. Yeah, five steps away was clear blue water, lit up from underneath, and you could just step into it. And it was so warm.'

'Did you jump in?'

'I stepped in. Just walked off the hard ground into the soft water!' She turned to look at Jonathan, triumphant in her vision.

He met her look with the hard concentration of an artist reaching for the end of an idea. 'And that was it? You just swam around in the water?'

'No. It pulled me away under the houses. It was swim-along water.'

'Swim-along water,' he said to himself.

At lunchtime, Jonathan took his notepad and pencil to a quiet corner of the playground. He didn't have to invite Becca, who always looked for him, to sit down and recite her dream again as he sketched. As she spoke, the dream became more textured and vivid to her; the floor at the bottom of the stairs, the one that led to the swim-along water, was thick, black carpet in vivid contrast to the bright blue of the water. Jonathan sketched and noted in the margin, his grey pencil straining to keep pace with the developing hue of Becca's dream.

'What about me? Where am I?'

'Where do you want to go?'

'At the end of the drawing. Just as I float away.'

Jonathan grabbed at Becca's dreams because they were so new and unseen. He enjoyed the process of outlining something dim and just beyond the boundary of realisation. With his pencil he gave life to a vision that had never existed before.

Jane nodded to Marion most afternoons as she waited for the gates to open, ready to claim her children. Marion was often late, red-faced and craning at the back of the crowd for a glimpse of her dark-haired boys. They were very measured in their reception of her, walking slowly to where they knew she would be, not wishing to betray their relief that she had come for them. Sometimes, inevitably, Jane found herself walking home with Marion, their four children trotting out in front like mismatched horses.

Marion chatted easily, indiscriminately, never quite look-ing at Jane, never really listening to her. She looked ahead and shared to her left, passing the time and houses until she reached her own. One afternoon in early July, Jane felt Marion's eyes suddenly on her, scrutinising the flesh on her upper arm.

'Good man, is he?'

'Yes. Leonard's a good husband,' Jane said, giving Marion something.

Marion looked ahead at the children, all four of whom had stopped at a pedestrian crossing. And as the gap between the two generations closed, she said, 'Andrew's not.'

Jane's lips relaxed into a flat line across her face as she made a judgement on the distance between them and the children. She knew they were travelling too fast, but she felt reckless.

'In what way?'

Marion turned to Jane and smiled at her interest. 'He's naughty.' Her cheeks coloured at the disclosure. 'Do you know what I mean?'

But they'd reached the children and Jane didn't know what she meant. Becca, sensing the unearthing of something between the two women, stuck close to Jane for the remainder of the walk home. She didn't understand that as she waited for speech, she was stifling it further. That nothing could thrive in her stranglehold.

The following afternoon, on the walk home from school, Jane asked Marion in for a cup of tea.

'What, now?' Marion asked, looking at her watch.

'Only if you can,' Jane said, embarrassed. She had hoped that their brief intimacy the previous afternoon would be sufficient subtext for the invitation, but it appeared Marion had forgotten all about it.

'I haven't got my ciggies. Do you mind if I nip home first and get them?'

'No, of course not. The boys can come in with me now,' she said, stopping at the edge of her driveway.

'OK. I'll be along in a minute.'

Jane spread her arms like a trustworthy shepherd and herded the children up the sloping driveway towards the front door. But ten minutes later, Marion's cup of tea was going cold on the kitchen table. She walked in on the children in the lounge; they were ranged forward on the sofa, eating the biscuits she'd given them and watching television.

'Jonathan, do you know what could have held your mum up?'

'She's probably getting on with a few jobs. Shall I go and get her?'

'No, I'll go over. You stay here.'

She put on her sandals, catching sight of her face in the mirror as she did so. She pushed her hair back and smoothed it down, seeing herself for the first time in weeks. There was a soft beauty to her cheeks, and her eyes were shining with the sudden imperative to knock on the Wilsons' door.

She stepped down onto the path and craned her neck to get a look at their door, searching for a sign that Marion was on her way, but it was resolutely shut. As she approached, she heard voices. Her right arm floated up to make contact with the wood, but she held it down in favour of her ear, pressing the side of her head to the door.

'Why not?' she heard Marion say.

'Because it's out of order.'

'*She* offered!'

'She offered to make you a cup of tea. Not mind your kids while you put your feet up.'

'Would you ever leave me alone? It's always something with you.'

'You were so keen to leave Stockwell, but you don't know how to behave around nice people. Jane's a nice woman. Her husband's a head teacher or something.'

'Her husband is in the early stages of rigor mortis.' She heard the bellow of Andrew's laughter before the gentle ticking of Marion's. Their hilarity was so sudden, so precise it was painful.

Jane heard feet shuffle closer to the door and then Marion's voice return to normal as she shouted to Andrew, 'Just going over now.' She knew a decision was urgent. And for the second time in the space of six months – knowing she couldn't pretend not to have heard the mockery – she turned her back on the Wilson house and ran for it. She had just opened her own front door when she heard Marion's slam. The gap was slender – the margin by which she escaped as narrow as the door that had separated her from their contempt for her marriage – and in her eagerness to avoid being seen, Jane never stopped to consider that it was Marion, who had taken her kindness and thrown it over her shoulder, who should be ashamed.

Marion pushed Jane's front door open, confident it would be on the latch. That Jane would let her back in. She went straight through to the kitchen, where she knew a cup of tea would be waiting. Her certainty angered Jane, who was standing by the table, not having had time to sit down, fuming at Marion's mockery.

'I was about to send out a search party.'

'Sorry,' Marion said, fishing a packet of cigarettes out of her back pocket. 'Andrew's home, so we got chatting and, you know . . . he's a terrible bastard when he wants to be.' Marion smiled and put a cigarette between her lips, closing her eyes in concentration as she lit up.

'What do you mean?'

'Oh, nothing,' she said, waving the smoke and the topic away. But then as the air cleared, she pointed her cigarette at Jane. 'What about your feller? How long have yous been married?'

'Eleven years.' Jane took a sip. 'Since 1976.'

'The year before us. We're ten years this month. Same age as Jonathan.' Marion got up to tap her cigarette into the sink.

'Oh, let me get you something for that,' Jane said, reaching into the cupboard under the sink for the lid she'd used when Marion first came over.

'So Jonathan rather forced matters, did he?'

'You mean was I up the pole? I certainly was. I come from a long line of fertile Irish women. They're all farmers on my mother's side, from out in Navan, County Meath. Hips built for babies. I fell for my two very quickly.'

'Yes,' Jane said, looking down at her own knees, pushed together. She could hear the volume on the television in the lounge had been turned up.

'Was it the same for you? Did you fall for Rebecca early?'

'Becca. Yes, quite soon into our marriage.'

'How did you meet?'

'Oh. Well, Leonard was at my school.'

'He must have been a few years above you?'

Jane swallowed. 'He was my teacher. My history teacher.'

Marion threw her head back and exhaled the smoke straight up, like a flare. 'Are you serious?'

'Yes,' Jane said, sitting up straight. 'Leonard is a very gifted teacher and we fell in love.'

'Oh my God,' Marion said, shaking her head.

Jane saw how Marion might parcel up this story for Andrew later that night. How they'd get into bed and laugh into each other's faces, mocking Leonard's age and her innocence.

'There was nothing untoward about our relationship.'

'Oh, I'm sure. I'm not criticising or anything. I'm just thinking back to some of the teachers I had, and Jesus, I'd have sooner eaten my own face than allow one of them to get near it.'

'So what about you? How did you and Andrew meet?'

'He was a friend of my brother Jonny's. He helped us out after my mam and dad died. And then, you know, he had his wicked way with me and before I knew it, well, you know how it goes. We had to get married.'

'Where does your brother live?'

'All over the place.'

'I'm sorry?'

'He's a drunk. Like my da before him. You see, that also runs in my family – the men are terrible drinkers. And my brother is no different.'

Marion was comfortable in her own skin: she smoked and talked with such ease, not caring what impression Jane formed of her life or choices. So comfortable was she in her own skin, Jane felt herself squirm within her own.

Later that evening, as Jane headed to bed, she looked in on Leonard, who was sitting at his desk with his head bent low over a textbook. He was making small, precise notes in a notebook to his right. He looked up as she came to the door.

'Are you coming to bed?'

'Yes, in a little while.'

'You work too hard,' she said, reaching out to place her hand on his shoulder. He turned his head to look at her.

'I won't be long,' he said, allowing his pen to fall to the paper as he lifted his hand to cover hers.

Jane pulled away and walked to the bathroom, where she lifted her dress and hooking her thumbs into the waistband of her knickers, pulled them down before sitting on the toilet. As the urine flowed out of her into the bowl, she considered what next. Leonard would come to bed thinking she wanted sex. As she stood up to flush the toilet, she caught sight of a few drops of blood, spreading like smoke clouds in the water. She picked up her knickers and saw the early smear of her period. Balling them up, she dropped them in the laundry basket and brushed her teeth. She thought of the colours: the deep red of the first day's bleed and the white foam of a clean before bed, and wondered at how Marion's day had concluded.

Jane was reading her book when Leonard came to bed ten minutes later. She watched him untuck his shirt and begin unbuttoning it. He moved his shoulders forward as he pulled it from his body, revealing the thick, greying hair that grew like moss on his chest. When he bent over to push his trousers down, Jane saw his soft, saggy tummy tip like an upended mushroom towards the floor. He folded his trousers onto a hanger and replaced them in the wardrobe for more of the same tomorrow. He got into bed and immediately lifted his pelvis to the covers so he could pull his underpants off. Jane knew she had to tell him about her period, but he had prepared himself for sex with the same quiet, determined professionalism he used for a lesson with his sixth formers. She didn't know how to introduce the topic of her menstrual blood. To a man so cerebral. And dead.

'What's the matter? Don't you want to?'

And she heard their laughter again. Behind the door.

'Jane?' He said her name softly now.

'Turn off the light, please.' And in the darkness she tugged the tampon from inside her and dropped it in the wastepaper basket by the side of the bed. She drew her nightgown up over her hips and, crisscrossing her arms, pulled it over her head in imitation of a stretch. As she felt her nipples wake up, she turned towards Leonard, who – she knew – would want to make love in the same position they'd been using since the first night of their marriage.

She pivoted on her right elbow so that her left leg could lift and cock itself over Leonard's body. She was on top of him before he had time to speak. His hands lifted instinctively to hold her in place, reaching up to touch his wife's breasts as she lowered herself onto him. The sigh she heard from Leonard's lips encouraged her to hold his head and kiss his lips, but as she did so, she heard Marion and Andrew's laughter, as if they were in the room watching her body move on top of his, sniggering at his aged frame, his sighs of pleasure, the dying grunts of a man too old to enjoy such physical gratification.

She whispered in his ear, 'Fuck me.' He dropped his hands, his body paralysed by the naming of the thing. So she pressed on: 'I want you to fuck me. Hard.' The room was silent now. And she knew that in her attempt to banish Marion and Andrew's mockery of her marriage, she'd ambushed Leonard. He pushed her gently from him and reached for the lamp on his bedside. And with the light came the violence. The red. Their white sheets daubed with blood. But Jane didn't look for his disgust. She simply stared at the ceiling and waited for him to say something.

'What's all this?'

'My period,' Jane said, and closed her eyes.

'What you said then. I don't like that . . . that kind of talk.'

She turned onto her side, showing him her long, smooth spine.

'What's got into you?' His voice was louder now.

She plucked her nightdress from the floor and sat up so she could put it on over her head. 'I wanted *you* to get into me,' she said recklessly.

'I'm going to read a little more,' he said, swinging his legs out of bed. 'In the study. I won't be able to sleep like this.' He gestured at the red patches.

She reached out to touch the blood that had already soaked through the cotton fibres of the sheet as her husband left the room.

Chapter 15

As the boys grew older, Marion dipped in and out of her parental responsibility as she would a mascara tube. Some afternoons she'd turn up at the school gate and walk the boys home with Jane and her girls, pausing for a chat on Jane's doorstep; other times she'd merely wave if the families happened to pass on their way; and then some days she didn't bother to pick her sons up at all.

Andrew left for work early in the mornings – just after seven. He was collected by the skinhead in the van who had appeared the morning he and Marion moved in. His wife rarely emerged before midday, but when she did, her hair was set smooth like a mould, her black lashes thick with mascara, her lips flaming with red.

Leonard was oblivious to the Wilsons. The van collected Andrew before he left for work and returned around four o'clock, long before Leonard pulled onto the driveway in search of his study and the quiet of the evening. He knew nothing of the couple next door, their sons or their contempt for him as a man.

In the spring of 1989, at around eight o'clock in the evening, there was a knock at the door. Jane had just sat down with a paperback she'd picked up in a charity shop. It wasn't very good, the plot too light and coincidental. She thought of Leonard upstairs in his study reading a new book on Disraeli and put her own one down.

Quiet at first, the knock became more insistent as she walked towards the bay window. Pulling back the net curtain, she saw it was Andrew. He turned towards the light and their faces were suddenly too close. She dropped the curtain and went to open the door.

'Andrew. Is everything OK?'

'It's Robbie. I'm worried about him.'

'What's happened?'

'He's got a really high temperature. He was complaining about his throat earlier and now he's just lying there not saying anything. I don't know what to do.'

'Have you phoned the doctor?'

'I don't know if we have one. Marion was supposed to see to all that, but I don't know where she is. I can't get hold of her.'

'OK. Don't worry – I'll come over. Let me grab my keys and tell Leonard.'

Jane ran upstairs. Leonard was slumped on the desk, his head on the glossy cover of his new book.

'Leonard.' Jane shook his shoulders. 'Leonard. Wake up.'

He lifted his head; a faint line of dried saliva had chalked its way down his chin. 'What's happened?'

'It's Robbie.'

'Who's Robbie?'

'The boy next door,' Jane whispered, conscious of Andrew waiting for her.

'Right.'

'He's not well. I'm going to pop over there now and see if I can help.'

'Yes. Indeed.'

Jane ran down the stairs and joined Andrew on the path. He was standing with his back to her, smoking a cigarette. As he heard the front door shut quietly behind him, he dropped the cigarette to the path and crushed it beneath his boot. They walked in silence to his house, and as he let her in, she inhaled the sudden violence of central heating on too hot. The air was unbearable and bodily, full of warmth that didn't belong to her.

'Why is it so hot in here?'

'I've got the heating on. Thought I should try and sweat the fever out.'

'No. You need to turn it off. Where is he?'

'Upstairs. In his bedroom.'

Jane slipped her shoes off and ran upstairs. She knew Robbie would be in the box room, the one Leonard used as his study, because she could smell the fetid air. He was underneath the blankets, his head sunk in the pillow, and looked as though he was about to go under. With an urgency and understanding that only a mother knows, she pulled at the covers and put her cool hands on his forehead. He was delirious, his mouth glued by thick saliva. It began opening at Jane's touch, as though her fingers were tubers that might feed him. She pushed the damp hair back, pressing her hand down, cool and in control, at the hairline.

Andrew stood at the door, watching Jane and his son in horror of his own failing.

'Get me a cold flannel, please. We need to cool him down as quickly as possible.' Andrew disappeared before she'd finished her sentence, bumping into Jonathan on the narrow landing. He had come out of his room when he heard Jane's voice.

Jane pushed the back of her hand down into the soft mattress and slid it under Robbie's hot neck. Once the nape of his neck was on the inside of her forearm, she began pulling his heavy head up from the pillow. She looked up and saw Jonathan standing where Andrew had been.

'Jonathan, help me, will you? Grab his shoulders and help me hold him.'

Jonathan walked into the room and put his hands on his brother's shoulder blades, holding him upright as his head lolled in feverish indifference.

'Try and support his head. We need to get his pyjamas off. He's too hot.' She unbuttoned his top, her fingers working quickly and efficiently, then slid her right hand up his spine and under Jonathan's hands, which were in place, supporting from the outside. 'I'll hold him. You take his top off.'

By the time Andrew returned with a bowl of cool water and a flannel, Jane had laid Robbie on top of the duvet and was using the back of her hands to try and cool his temples.

'What do you think?' he asked.

'Can you open a window?'

'Yeah. Out of the way, Jon,' Andrew said, moving quickly towards the window.

'It doesn't open, Dad. Granddad nailed it shut.'

'Shit. Go get my tools downstairs.'

'I don't know where they are.'

'Under the stairs. Go!'

Jonathan ran down the stairs.

In the silence, Andrew turned to the window and ran his hands through his hair. 'Fucking thing,' he muttered.

'I can't find them!' Jonathan shouted from downstairs.

Jane was about to suggest they move Robbie to another bedroom when she saw Andrew take a step back and lift his right foot to the wooden casement. His back tensed as he delivered a powerful kick to the mechanism. He held on to the wall and pivoted on his standing foot so that the next kick might be administered with even greater lateral force. The glass shattered before the wood splintered. The window buckled under his fury at his father's DIY, his son's insufferable body temperature and the absence of a wife who should have been sitting in Jane's place.

Andrew came and stood before her and Robbie, his chest rising and falling with the effort of waiting for her to speak again. 'What now?'

He was a man of action. He wanted instructions. All she had to do was say the words and he'd comply. It made her feel powerful and singled out.

'We need to call the doctor. You stay here and I'll go home and call the out-of-hours service,' she said.

'And if he doesn't come?' The still-flexing muscles of his upper arms ready to make the next thing happen.

'Then we phone an ambulance. He needs medical attention.'

As Jane stood, Andrew moved back to allow her to get past. He picked up the bowl of water and held it still as Jane dropped the flannel into it.

'Wring that out and dab his face, neck and chest. Have you got any paracetamol?'

'I don't know. I'll look in the bathroom.'

'Don't worry. I've got some at home. I'll bring it back with me after I've called the doctor.'

Andrew looked down into the water. For a moment Jane thought he was going to cry. And still possessed by the authority with which he'd endowed her, she touched his arm quickly and firmly. 'He'll be fine. Go and sit with him. I'll be back in a few minutes.'

The doctor, when he arrived, was a tall Nigerian man. Jane opened the door and led him upstairs. Andrew stood up and squared his shoulders as the doctor dipped his head to walk gently into the room.

'Hello, sir,' he said quietly, and before Andrew could make any answer, he dropped to his knees beside Robbie and put his hand on his forehead. 'What can I do for you, young man? Your mother is very worried about you.'

Jane was leaning against the door frame, her arms folded across her chest. She smiled gently, reassuringly at Andrew as the mistake lingered in the air. Andrew was chewing the inside of his cheeks; the mistake had been made long before the doctor arrived.

'Where does it hurt?' he asked the room, scanning the wall in front of him for information.

Andrew's shoulders fell as he joined the doctor on the carpet at the bedside. 'It was his throat, Doctor. He kept telling me it hurt when he swallowed. But now he won't swallow anything at all. And his temperature . . .' He looked up at Jane in desperation.

'OK,' the doctor said, running his fingers down the side of Robbie's face and bringing them to rest on the swollen glands beneath his ears.

'What's your name, young man?'

'Robbie,' Andrew said.

'Robbie.' He sat back on his haunches and began rummaging in his bag. He extracted a smooth, flat wooden stick and torch, and levering Robbie's jaw open with this thumbs, depressed his tongue and shone the light at the back of his throat.

'Tonsillitis,' he said, turning to Jane, who was no longer leaning but standing with her arms by her side.

'What does that mean?' Andrew asked.

The doctor stood up, waving the wooden stick in his right hand as though he'd just finished an ice lolly. 'His tonsils have become infected, causing the body's temperature to rise. I will write you a prescription for some antibiotics. He needs a dose four times a day until the course is finished. Do you have a bin?'

'Here, give that to me,' Andrew said, taking the stick. 'Thank you, Doctor. Thank you very much.'

'That's OK. But, please, make sure you wash hands thoroughly.'

'And the fever?' Jane asked from the hallway as the doctor made his way out of the room. 'Should we just keep giving him paracetamol?'

'Every four hours until the temperature comes down. The antibiotics will work quickly.'

'But, Doctor' – Jane twisted her left wrist into view – 'it's very late now. Will we have to wait until morning?'

Andrew stood up behind the doctor, his eyes full of her question.

'You can take this prescription to your nearest accident and emergency department. They will dispense your medication.'

Jane looked down at the illegible scrawl on the green paper. As she tried to read it, the doctor pushed past her and made his way down the stairs. Andrew followed him, while Jane went back into Robbie's bedroom, content to be a subordinate again.

When Andrew returned, he was putting on his jacket. 'Do

you mind staying here while I head down to the hospital?'

'No, of course not,' she said, pulling Robbie's desk chair over to his bedside. 'I'll stay with him.'

'Thank you.'

'No problem.'

Despite the paracetamol, Robbie's temperature remained dangerously high. Jane found a large paperback book of dinosaurs on his desk and began fanning the boy's face. As she watched the damp fronds of hair move reluctantly, she thought of her own girls. And how she would feel if another woman had been called to care for them. It was the question there had been no time to ask but the only question that circled the air that evening, waiting to land.

It was close to eleven when Jane heard the sound of Andrew's key in the lock.

'Did you manage to get them?' she asked Andrew, who was clutching a small white paper bag. His cheeks were red, his hair scruffy on his head. He looked like he'd been briefly possessed by the outside and had come back to tell her about it. Jane looked at his left hand, gripping the paper bag. His fingers were slender and strong, the kind that would stroke before they grabbed.

'You look tired,' he said. The medicine and late hour had made him benevolent.

'Don't worry about me. We should probably get the first dose into him now.'

'Yeah. Let's do that.'

They sat close together on the bed, the sick child making their physical proximity necessary. Jane reached under Robbie and pulled him up gently. Andrew put his arm across his son's shoulders as he came off the mattress, his skin on Jane's briefly.

'That's it, Rob. It's gonna be OK. Just going to give you a bit of medicine.'

He held him in place as Jane fumbled with the bag and pulled the bottle of yellow liquid out of it. As she brought the spoon to his parted lips, she felt Andrew watching her. Assessing her skill as a mother. As a woman. She stood up and walked out of the room.

'I can't thank you enough,' he said, following her.

'Don't thank me. It's what anyone would do.' The question had landed.

'Not my wife. Not my useless fucking wife.'

It should have been shocking, but it wasn't.

'I'm sorry. I shouldn't swear like that.'

'It's OK. Please don't worry,' she said, looking him in the eye, afraid her eyes might drop to his chest. His arms. 'I must be getting back. Leonard will be wondering what's happened to me.'

'Yeah, sorry. Thank you.'

'No problem. Do let me know if you need anything else. I'll call in on you tomorrow morning and see how he is.'

'Thank you. You're a lifesaver.'

But as Jane walked down the stairs and let herself out quietly, she felt the opposite. Something unstoppable and dangerous had been unleashed that evening.

Jane didn't call on Robbie the following Monday morning because Jonathan told her all she needed to know when he came to see if Becca and Julia were ready for school.

'Jonathan. Come in,' she said, stepping back and allowing him to enter the hallway. 'How's Robbie?'

'He's OK.'

'Has his temperature come down?'

138

Jonathan shrugged his shoulders as he sat down at the kitchen table. Becca sat opposite, her eyes dipped to the last of the milk in her cereal bowl.

'I'd better pop over and see for myself,' she said, as Becca raised the bowl to her lips.

'No. Don't. Please, Mrs Campbell.'

'Why not? What's wrong?'

'My mum. They're over there arguing.'

'What about?' She shouldn't have asked, but the question was out and yapping for the truth before she could pull it back in. Jonathan didn't seem to mind.

'My dad's angry with her for going away. He tried phoning my aunt before he came over here, but she wasn't there.'

'I see.'

Becca slipped her hand into Jane's. 'Is Robbie going to die?'

'What?' she said, looking down at Becca's soft brown head.

'Is Robbie going to die? Julia said when you have a really high temperature, your heart can explode.'

Jonathan rolled his eyes and pulled Becca's free hand. 'Come on, we're going to be late.'

Chapter 16

Alone in the house, Jane tried to get on with chores. She walked upstairs slowly and began pulling clothes from the laundry basket in her bedroom, sorting the whites from the darks and waiting to see the larger pile emerge. But as she walked down the stairs, the washing tight to her chest, she saw the outline and hue of a blonde head behind the glass of the front door. And for the first time in her life, she considered hiding away. Taking her pile of dirty laundry and finding a corner of the house where she wasn't needed. Or expected.

Marion's eyes were heavily made up, the black eyeliner sunk deep in the swollen pink tissue. In the act of opening the door, Jane had taken one arm from her dirty laundry. A pair of her knickers, off-white and loose, fell to the doormat. Marion followed it with her eyes. Jane bent to pick it up, placing her chin protectively on the private load.

'Marion. Is everything all right?'

'Can I come in?'

'Of course. I was just about to put these on.'

'I won't keep you,' Marion said, following Jane into the kitchen. Her movements were heavy, deliberate. Jane bundled her load into the washing machine and pulled a chair back for Marion.

'Thank you.'

'Marion, what's the matter?' Jane saw the bones at the top of her spine protrude sharply and suddenly as Marion tipped forwards and began crying quietly onto the back of her right hand. With her nose nestled between her little and ring fingers, the snot worked its way down and glued them together. A web of her own making, Jane thought, as she remembered the laughter behind the front door that afternoon.

'Marion, talk to me. What's wrong?'

'I can't take living with him anymore. Oh God. And you know Robbie was ill last night?'

'Yes, I know. Andrew came by and asked for my help. How is he this morning?'

'Better. Much better. I gave him some more of the antibiotics first thing.'

'Let me find you a tissue,' Jane said, reaching to pull two sheets from the box on the windowsill. 'Who's with him now?' Jane said, glancing up at the kitchen clock. It was twenty minutes past nine.

'Andrew. I told him I was popping out for some ciggies, but I just need a few minutes on my own, you know?'

Jane looked at Becca's cereal bowl on the table in front of her, the milk shallow in defeat. She did know.

'What happened? Where were you last night?'

Marion looked straight ahead of her, momentarily calmed by the white of the wall. Jane took a box of detergent out from the cupboard beneath the sink and poured some in the open drawer. As she selected a hot wash, she turned to look at the back of Marion's head; the hair had been blow-dried up and away from her scalp, creating a void – a dark forest floor of follicles and brown roots.

'Jonathan said Andrew tried phoning his aunt and, well, you weren't there?'

Marion began crying again as the washing machine filled with water, the hiss drowning out her noise. When she looked up, her face was inexpressibly ugly. 'I thought this was what I wanted.'

'What? Andrew?'

'No. The house. Surrey. Getting away from the estate.'

'And you're not happy?'

'I went home.'

'Back to Stockwell?'

'Stockwell is not my home. I went home home. Back to Ireland.'

'Last night?'

'On Friday night. Took the train to Holyhead and the boat to Dún Laoghaire.'

'I see.'

'Have you ever wanted to escape?' she asked.

'I'm not sure what you mean.'

'I thought moving here would fix things. Or help. I couldn't stay on the estate a minute longer, but here we are, on a nice road, and I know it's not enough.'

'What's not enough? Marion, it's none of my business, but are you and Andrew having problems?'

'We've always had problems. The only thing that's ever come easy to us is the sex.' Marion looked steadily at Jane, willing her to understand.

'Oh, Marion.' Jane searched for something to say. 'Marriage is a long business. Sometimes you just need a break from it all. Do you feel better for your trip home?'

'I was looking at flats on Saturday, near where I grew up. I have the paperwork to sign over there. I looked at the school I want to send the boys to.'

'But they've only just started at St Matthew's.'

Marion's eyes narrowed. 'It's so easy for you, isn't it? You grew up around here, married your teacher. You're settled. But I'm not.' She lowered her forehead to her hand as though she'd make up her mind to continue crying once her eyes were down and out of sight.

'Marion, it's not . . .' Jane didn't know what to say, so she turned – as she often did in times of need – to the kettle. 'I'm very settled. You're right.'

'I don't mean to start on you. You've been very kind to us, and it was nice of you to look after Robbie.'

'But we all make sacrifices. I told you when you were last here that Leonard was my teacher.'

'Yes.'

Jane put the kettle back on its stand but didn't turn it on. She returned to her seat opposite Marion. 'Well, you know, some might say I sacrificed my youth. I was married and pregnant in little over a year. And I didn't know what I'd given up until it was too late. So I think I know something of what you're feeling.' She looked to Marion for her cue to continue, but no sign was forthcoming. 'But to take the boys and uproot their lives again. It would be very hard on them, and what I'm saying is that this feeling will pass.'

'It won't. I wanted to go home that first morning we took the boat with my mam and dad and Jonny. And then when my parents died, I should have packed my bags and gone back, but I let Jonny talk me out of it. And now where is he? Drunk or dead somewhere.' She pulled a tissue from her pocket and held it open between her two hands. 'I can't seem to find my way back. Does that make any sense? I know the way – I took the train and the boat and it leads me to a place I remember and recognise, but it's not home. My boys are here, and when I return, I find Robbie's sick, Andrew's bloody mad, and Jonathan ... well, Jonathan's in a world of his own.'

'What about a family holiday? Could you go over for a week in the summer?'

'Andrew won't step foot in Ireland. He's always said that.'

'Why not?'

'Says I'll get ideas. That I'll try to talk him into moving there.'

'These things have a way of working themselves out,' Jane said, reaching for Marion's hands, still holding her tissue as though she were trying to read from it.

Marion looked up at Jane. At her clean white skin and short brown hair. She focused, with some effort, on the brown irises, so plain and unremarkable. And then she looked down at their hands, now joined by sympathy on one side and necessity on the other.

'I'm sure you're right.' Marion pulled her hand back and began twisting her wedding ring, and as she did so, Jane saw that two of the fingernails on her right hand were broken and slightly bloody.

And in that moment, Jane felt intensely grateful for Leonard. His balding head and sharp bones, his preference for one sexual position and love of the nineteenth century. His quiet and unending loyalty to his wife and daughters. And with this realisation she understood that she wanted this woman out of her house.

'Marion, I'm sorry, but I've got to get on. Would you like

me to have Jonathan this afternoon after school?'

Marion shook her head. 'No, you've done enough. Thank you.' She stood up to leave and walked slowly out of the kitchen, neither woman knowing they'd never see each other again.

Chapter 17

Jane was walking back from the shops when she saw the three of them huddled on the doorstep. She'd gone to buy lamb chops for dinner and had got stuck chatting to the butcher. It was only when she looked at her watch that she realised Becca and Julia would be almost home and, no doubt, waiting for her to let them in. But she hadn't anticipated Jonathan being with them.

'Hello, you three. Jonathan, everything OK?'

He shook his head and looked at Becca.

'His mum and dad are arguing. We heard them through the door. Can Jonathan have tea with us?'

'Yes.' Jane put her shopping bag down and fumbled in her handbag for the keys. 'Go on inside. You too, Jonathan. I'll be over in a bit.'

'Where are you going?' Becca asked from the hallway.

'Never mind that. Just go on inside.'

Jane walked over to the Wilsons' front door, not sure exactly what she was going to do once she got there. The silence on the other side of the door reinforced her impotence. But then she heard Marion's angry roar.

'You don't tell me where I can and can't go. Have you got that?'

'Most women would want to be at home when their kids are sick. But not you.'

'I didn't know that would happen.'

'No, you didn't know. Because you were too busy planning the next move. For fuck's sake, Marion, I'm here, aren't I? I did what you asked. I'm living in the house of a man I despised ... for you! And the boys. You're never fucking happy. That's your trouble.'

Jane stepped backwards from the doorstep and walked across the driveway that separated the two houses. She picked up her shopping bags, noticing as she did so that the lamb chops had bled through the butcher paper, pressing their heavy red stain against the thin plastic bag.

Jane grilled the chops and made mashed potatoes with peas for dinner. She called the children to the table just after five o'clock. Jonathan sat down, subdued, and not entirely convinced by the diversion of dinner. Becca took a seat beside him and began patting her mash with the flat of her knife.

'Becca, darling. Please don't play with your food.'

'I'm making it into a cuboid.'

Julia rolled her eyes as she stuck a fork into her chop and began cutting the meat away.

Jonathan sat with his hands by his sides, staring at the salt and pepper shakers in the middle of the table.

Jane looked at his plate and the chop she'd sacrificed to him. 'Come on, Jonathan. Please try to eat something,' she said, turning back to the sink and the kitchen window.

Jonathan ate nothing on his plate. Becca spent her time dividing her cuboid mash into eight sections and placing a pea on each one. Her chop was also untouched. Only Julia had actually eaten her dinner; she was holding the chop between her fingers and gnawing at the bone for remaining meat. There was a knock at the front door.

'Stay here, please,' she said to Jonathan, and went to open the door. Just as she expected, it was Andrew. He looked shrunken and tired, his pupils dilated by alcohol. Or perhaps pain. She couldn't be sure.

'I take it Jonathan's here?'

'Yes, he's in the kitchen. Would you like to come in and see him?'

'No. I mean yes, but I can't. Marion and I really need to talk.'

'Where's Robbie? Would you like me to have him?'

'He's watching a film at home. He's OK.'

'Andrew, it's none of my business, but I think you should know . . . Jonathan heard you arguing.'

He rubbed his forehead, the tips of his fingers yellowing under the pressure. As though he could force the impression from his frontal lobe and make it disappear. 'I know. We're having a few problems, that's all.'

'Are you sure you won't come in?'

'No, I can't. I just wanted to check on Jonathan.'

Jane nodded her head as she recalled Andrew's angry voice from a few hours earlier. The swear words he never used with her. She imagined his neck had been red and sinewy with rage – flesh that cheapens itself with exertion. Her eyes drifted down to his throat and saw – rising on the right side – thin rivulets of red, clawed in a downward motion by angry nails.

He put his hands up to his throat, conscious of where she was staring. As he pressed down on them, she saw that the scratches were deep and speckled by blood. He rubbed them thoughtfully, his mind already elsewhere. But where Jane

148

could never guess. Living in his father's old house, Marion's absence when her son was ill, the public humiliation of a marriage failing – it had all been too much for him. His wife's claw marks on his throat were the violent truth behind their union. But the real sundering. Anyone could see that would be hard won.

Chapter 18

Jonathan knocked on the Campbells' front door early the next morning. When Jane asked him in, it was as if he hadn't heard her.

'Jonathan, what's the matter?'

'My mum's gone to Ireland for a little while.'

'What do you mean?' Jane said, closing the door firmly. 'When?'

'Now. She's already gone. My dad said she's going to stay with relatives.'

'That sounds temporary. Sometimes mums and dads need to take some time to work things out.'

Jonathan shrugged his shoulders. 'Dad said she wants me and Robbie to go to school over there.'

'How's Robbie?'

'He's asleep.'

'Becca! Julia!' Jane shouted up the stairs. 'Jonathan's here. Come on, you'll be late.' She said this even though Jonathan was early. She was chivvying her children because it filled the silence.

*

Later that morning, at around eleven thirty, Andrew knocked on the door. He looked pale and disorientated, and the left side of his face still bore the imprint of the pillow he'd slept on. 'Andrew, come in. Jonathan told me.'

'Thanks.' He stepped into the hallway and, looking in the mirror, spotted the pillow marks on his face. He rubbed them and tried to pat down his hair. 'I've just had a sleep. I was up all night trying to work it out.'

'Jonathan said she's gone to Ireland?'

'I think so. That's where she was the night Robbie was ill. In Dublin, looking at flats and a school for the boys. After I moved here for her. Gave her everything she wanted.'

'Why don't you have a seat in the lounge? Can I get you a cup of tea or coffee?'

'No, thanks, nothing for me. I've got to get back, but I just wanted to ask if you wouldn't mind looking after the boys for me after school today?'

'Of course not.'

'Cheers.'

'Do you have an address?'

'Eh?'

'For Marion. Did she leave you an address?'

'No,' he said, rubbing his stubble. 'She hasn't got one yet. She mentioned her aunt or something. Christ, I can't re-member. What am I going to do? How could she have done this to us?'

'Andrew, I'm sorry. I don't know what to say. Marion did mention—'

'What did she say?'

'That she wanted to escape. To return to Ireland.'

'I was never enough for her.' He banged the top of his

temple with the heel of his hand, just above where his face bore the mark of his recent rest.

'Don't, Andrew.' Jane reached out and held his forearm. 'I'm sure she'll return. She probably just needs some time to think. Please try not to worry.'

He nodded in agreement, his eyes locked on her hand as if to experience her touch more deeply. 'Let's hope so. And for the record, I'm sorry about all of this. I bet you wish we'd never moved in, don't you?'

'Not at all,' she said, withdrawing her hand. 'Let me know if there's anything else I can do to help.'

The following Thursday, Andrew received a letter from Marion with a Dublin postmark.

'She wants a clean break from me. Says it was all a mistake marrying me.' He was sitting in the lounge with Jane, holding the envelope with the letter inside.

'But the boys? She can't mean she doesn't want to see the boys?'

'She says she's found a flat and that when she's more settled, she'll send for them.'

'Oh God, Andrew. I'm sorry.'

'Not as sorry as she'll be. If she thinks I'll let Jonathan and Robbie go over there, she's got another thing coming.'

'But they'll need to see their mother?'

'Will they?' He looked up, suddenly angry.

Jane sat back in her seat. 'I just mean … it's not good for children to get caught in the middle of something like this. Jonathan and Robbie will want to continue to see their mother.'

'Well, she can whistle for them.' He stood up, tall and

powerful. 'She's made her bed. Now she can lie in it.' And bumping into the coffee table, he walked out, slamming the front door behind him.

Part II:

Marion and Andrew

The gift of marriage brings husband and wife together in the delight and tenderness of sexual union and joyful commitment to the end of their lives.

The Marriage Service

Chapter 19

Marion was fifteen when her mother died in St Mary's Hospital in Paddington. The cancer in her womb, undetected and undeterred, had invaded other parts of her body. She passed away on 3 December 1975 with her husband and daughter by her side. Marion's older brother, Jonny, was nursing a hangover somewhere in north London.

Marion held her father's hand on the bus home to Kilburn, his fingers still functioning but unresponsive, and she knew he wouldn't outlive her mother for long.

'I'm sorry, Marion.'

'I'll look after you.'

'I can't.'

'Can't what?'

'I can't let you look after me. That was your mother's job, and God knows it killed her. You'll find your own way, Marion.' He patted her hand, his eyes dry but his lower lip wet and trembling as he spoke. 'And it'll be the right way.'

Marion knew, in his own way, he was right. And as she looked at him, the first sting came to her eyes, but the tears were not for her mother, whose body was still warm in the hospital morgue, but for her father's defeat. She saw he had decided to go home in his own way. And he wasn't taking her with him.

Aidan was found dead in nearby Queen's Park in the early hours of Saturday, 3 April 1976. He'd been missing for several days by the time the police knocked on Marion's door. Jonny hadn't yet returned from work – he was a barman at the Swan in Stockwell and often slept on floors in various digs until the morning presented itself and he made his way back up to north London.

Marion had been sitting at the kitchen table with a cup of tea and a cigarette preparing for a day of work herself. She was a shop girl in a bakery on Tottenham Court Road, where she made enough to buy food and groceries for her and her father.

Marion extinguished the cigarette she'd been smoking and opened the door. When she saw the two policemen, she prepared herself for words that would wind her.

'Miss Donnelly?'

'Yes.'

'Can we come in?'

'Yes.' She stood back and allowed them to walk, uncertainly at first, into the dark room.

'May we sit down?' the younger, slimmer man said when he saw the chairs round the small table.

Marion nodded and went to stand up against the cooker. She didn't want to sit with them.

The other police officer, the one who had yet to speak, sat down with a groan. He was heavier. More tired, it would appear.

The young one followed Marion's lead and remained standing. His colleague, low and expectant, looked between them trying to decide whether or not to feel uncomfortable. He leaned back and widened his legs, and with his head bent and his gaze upon his groin, he waited for his younger, more inexperienced colleague to get on with the job and tell this girl her daddy was dead.

'Miss Donnelly, I understand you've registered your father, a Mr Aidan Donnelly, as missing?'

'That's right. Have you found him?'

'We've had reports of a body found this morning,' he said, frowning slightly at his colleague, who'd now folded his arms across his chest, in quiet enjoyment of the performance. 'We'd like you to come and identify the body.'

Marion reached for her packet of cigarettes on the table and offered one to the young man, who shook his head. She lit the cigarette and, in the suck, pulled up enough confidence to ask, in the first flourish of smoke, 'Is it him, though?' She squinted as she waited for the answer.

The fat police officer made to stand up. 'Madam, it might be. It might not be. We find lots of dead Irish men. We just need you to identify your one.'

'Stan. Leave this to me.'

'Well, stop bloody flirting and let her know what's what,' he said, filling the room with a boom that might, in other circumstances, have shaken some laughter out of it. 'They found a bloke this morning. Drank himself to death. Does that sound like anyone you know?'

She hacked into her hand, the sound wet and urgent and unbelieving.

The young policeman walked round the table and stood in front of her. He didn't know where he could touch her or what contact he could make with the retching girl. But her wanted her to know that he was sorry.

'Miss Donnelly. Marion. Can I call you Marion?' he said, bending down so she could see his face. 'We don't know if it is him. Is there anyone you can ask to come with you?'

'My brother.' She managed to swallow and took a deep breath. 'I'll go and get my brother, Jonny.'

They left her then, alone. Deciding to find Jonny first, she took the Tube down to Stockwell, where she knocked on some of the doors she knew were friendly to her brother. And then travelled back up to north London with him to identify all that was left of Aidan Donnelly.

Chapter 20

Andrew was a friend of Jonny's. He lived on the Studley Estate, a sprawling expanse of concrete behind Stockwell Tube Station. His mum and auntie Li had flats in the same high-rise tower block, and their sons grew up close, like brothers. Steve, who was eighteen months older than Andrew, was stocky and, even at the age of twenty-one, was starting to thin on top. They got to know Jonny when he came to work in their local pub. Steve had left school at sixteen and, with help from his mum and her then boyfriend, bought a small van. When Andrew left school a year later, he joined Steve in his makeshift removals business. By the time they met Jonny behind the bar of the Swan, their business had started to grow and diversify as more and more tenants – destined for concrete boxes in south London – called on them to move in and move out.

Just three days after identifying his father's body, Jonny was back at work and serving customers as usual. Andrew was alone at the bar, waiting for Steve. 'Sorry to hear about your dad.'

'Thanks. Sad business all round.'

'How old was he?'

'Forty-three.'

'Jesus.'

'I know.'

'And what about your sister?'

Jonny began pulling a pint for Steve, who'd just walked in the door.

'She'll have to live with me, I suppose.'

'In Kilburn?'

'For the time being. I need to try and rent a place down here. I can't be trekking up and down every day, and we've no reason to be up there. It was just where my parents went, you know . . . like all the Irish fresh off the boat.'

'We know a bloke, don't we?' Andrew said to Steve, who, having just arrived, was more interested in the pint in front of him than the question.

'What's that?

'I was just saying we know someone who rents flats off the council and then sublets to people who wouldn't normally get on the list.'

'Yeah. Something like that.'

Andrew wrote a number on a notepad Jonny kept behind the bar. During his lunch break, Jonny walked across the road and into Stockwell Tube Station, where he used a payphone to call the number he'd been given. The man he spoke to, who didn't give him his name, arranged to meet him on the estate the following morning.

But Marion didn't want to move. The flat, the kitchen table, even the stove were all she had left of the life her parents had blindly cobbled together for her.

'You can't live here alone.'

'I bloody can,' she said, lighting a cigarette.

Jonny was sitting opposite her in the dark kitchen.

'You can't afford it, for one.'

'I'll get more hours at the bakery. I can manage.'

'Marion, you can't. And it's not right for you to be here on your own. Mam and Dad wouldn't have wanted it. What if somebody breaks in?'

'And what help would you be? You're away working every night. I'd be better off here where I know people than down in that shitehole.'

'I'm meeting yer man tomorrow. And you're coming with me.'

'Do I not get a say in any of this?'

'You're sixteen and you're my sister. So no.'

'Ground-floor flats always come up. People don't want them,' Steve said carelessly as he sipped his pint.

'What do you mean?' Jonny asked, as he replaced the clean glasses under the bar.

'Easier to break into,' Steve sniffed.

'Is that right?' Jonny turned to Andrew.

Andrew shrugged. 'Sometimes. But you'll be all right. Anyway, you can always get bars fitted.'

Jonny whistled.

'Look, don't worry about it. The main thing is the flat is down the road and your sister can live with you. When do you need us, then?'

Jonny took the Tube up to Kilburn and told his sister to pack up her things. He left no other explanation for Mrs Cooper other than an envelope with enough cash to cover the rest of the month. And so, in the space of six months, Marion lost her mother closely followed by her father, and in the act of moving she met the man that she would eventually marry.

Chapter 21

The council estate off Binfield Road was as depressing as it was far. The flat they were looking to rent was one of only six in a rare three-storey block. It stood in the middle of a green square, the blades of grass so sparse you could see the dog shit poking through.

A tall bearded man with black curly hair was waiting for them outside the entrance to the block, his gaze fixed on a group of five or six children playing on a burnt-out care-taker's hut that had collapsed to the ground. Its coarse surface presented opportunities to scale the different levels, leap the upturned nails and land on the charred felt. They were lost in their own fiction, renaming and reassigning the tokens of failure and neglect all around them.

Jonny and Marion approached quickly. Jonny extended his hand as soon as he was within striking distance. Marion held back and followed the man's gaze where she too took in the children.

'Jonny Donnelly. Thanks for meeting us. This is my sister, Marion.' Jonny pushed her forwards.

'Let's get inside,' the man said, holding open the door for them. It was strong and heavy, with three panels of fire-resistant glass separated by wired squares – which Marion found reassuringly arithmetical. The hallway within was cold and impersonal. As she waited for the man to unlock the apartment door, first the bottom Chubb and then the upper Yale, Marion took a deep breath. Locked in or locked out. She shifted her weight from one foot to the other in anticipation. The man stood back to allow her and Jonny to enter and as Jonny walked ahead, his shoulders higher, set and strong, she knew there were no other options open to her. This was what Jonny wanted and Jonny was all she had left.

The living room opened up to her right, the lino on the floor broken into sharp fragments. Two glass doors led to a balcony and small garden.

'Is that ours?' Marion asked.

'It belongs to everyone.'

Jonny walked on ahead, eager to claim the large bedroom at the end of the hall – the one with two windows in it. 'It's the right thing, Marion. We're on the ground floor here. I need to be ready if someone tries to break in.'

'There's a window in the smaller room. What do you suggest we do with that one? Will we brick it up?'

The man looked at his watch.

'We'll take it,' said Jonny.

'OK. You know about the toilet, don't you?'

'Yeah, that's fine.'

'What about the toilet?' Marion demanded.

'You can't use it. It's blocked up. I told your brother on the phone.'

'We'll get it sorted. Don't worry about that.'

'Jonny. What are you—'

'Listen, thanks a million. I've got that money for you.'

'Jonny Donnelly—'

165

'Leave this to me, would you?'

Marion walked out onto the balcony – exactly the same in dimension as the ones above her – except this one could be climbed over. Or into. She gazed at the green in front of her, skirted by tower blocks, walls of balconies strung with grey washing.

'Is pissing in a toilet a luxury we can't afford?' she asked when Jonny came to join her on the balcony.

'Relax. The guys I was telling you about – Andrew and Steve, their mams live in Strudwick Court. They'll let us use the crapper.'

'Jesus Christ, Jonny, is that your solution? What have I let you lead me to?'

'An affordable flat in a central London zone, that's what.'

'A piss-poor flat in a fucking war zone! Did you see what those kids were playing on? The burnt remains of God knows what. I should have stayed in Kilburn with Mam and Dad's people. I should never have let you talk me into this.'

'I'll get it fixed. Andrew knows all sorts of people. Stop worrying.'

Andrew and Steve drove their stuff down from Kilburn the next day. There wasn't much of it – almost all of the furniture belonged to Mrs Cooper, the landlady – but Marion had kept her mother's clothes. She'd folded her mother's best jacket carefully in her suitcase; it was too small for her and didn't button at the front, but it was the one she had worn to Mass every Sunday morning and Marion couldn't let it go. She'd tried it on after her mother died, along with the matching A-line woollen skirt. She had held the hoop of the waistband open before her feet, willing them to ignore the slim proportions and step in, but she saw that she had no hope of wearing it. She could hear her mother's tight voice: 'You take after the Donnellys, so you do. Hips built for heaving.'

Marion first met Andrew on a warm Tuesday morning. Jonny was still asleep on a mattress on the floor of his new bedroom. Marion had spent the night on a small two-seater sofa donated by the landlady at the Swan. She had slept on her side, with her arms folded in a gesture of impotent protest. There were no curtains and she woke surprised to see the sun shining brightly through the window, warming her face, lighting the room as it would any other. For the first time, she realised that a home didn't have to be a house. It didn't even have to contain parents. As if in confirmation of this fact, she heard a loud knock at the door.

Her shoes were by the sofa, where she'd kicked them off the night before. She'd fallen asleep too exhausted to eat, so when she reached for her shoes and slowly slipped her feet inside, first right and then left, she felt suddenly hot and light-headed. The knock came again, and this time its vibration registered in the flat as a final warning. She heard Jonny's bedroom door open and saw him emerge, in his underpants, squinting at the sunlight.

'What's the matter with you? Can't you hear the door or what?'

'I was on my way. They haven't given me a chance.'

Jonny was looking through the spyhole. 'It's Andrew. You open it. I'll go and put some trousers on.'

Marion did as she was told. Andrew – red from exertion – registered surprise at finding her on the other side of the door.

'Morning. I'm Andrew.'

'Marion. Nice to meet you. Have you got our stuff?'

167

'Yeah,' he said, looking around him. 'I mean, not here. It's in the van. There wasn't much of it.'

'No, I know. Will you come in?' Marion asked, opening the door wider, allowing the sunlight to flood the entranceway.

'We're just unloading it all. Is Jonny around?'

'Here I am. Hiya,' said Jonny, pulling a T-shirt down over his torso. 'What can I do?'

'We're just out here,' Andrew said, leading Jonny to the rear entrance of the block. As they walked away, Marion heard him say, again, 'There wasn't much stuff. Your landlady told me all the furniture's hers.'

When they returned, Steve was with them.

'This is my cousin,' Andrew said to Marion, by way of explanation.

Marion glanced at him briefly but didn't smile.

'I don't bite,' Steve said to her, but his mouth was wide and his teeth large. And unbidden, she had a memory of her mother telling her the story of Little Red Riding Hood's curiosity in the moment before she was eaten.

'As soon as I can find the kettle, I'll make yous all a cup of tea,' Marion said as the men came in and out.

Only Andrew caught the offered kindness and returned it to her with a smile. 'Milk and two sugars, please.'

She'd had little contact with boys in her life: her late child-hood and early adolescence had been so marked by anxiety for her parents that she'd never relaxed enough to consider how she might leave them before they left her. But from the moment she saw Andrew smiling at her, she knew he wanted to have sex with her. She understood, both intuitively and objectively, that any communion they might have would in-volve a physical joining. And as she watched him carry boxes containing her past life into her new home, she wondered how they'd do it. If he'd get on top of her like she'd been told by the other girls at school.

'Which one's yours?' Andrew asked her, standing in the hallway. She was in the kitchen, stirring sugar into his tea.

'I'm not having one.'

'Eh?'

'Tea. I'm not having one.'

'No, which room is yours? This box has your name on it.'

'Oh, sorry,' she said, smiling. 'Down the hall, the one on the right,' she said, walking behind him and watching his back arch with the weight of the box.

When he reached the closed door, he turned to her and stepped back. 'Could you get that for me?'

'Sorry,' she said, extending her arm and pushing down the handle.

'Thanks,' he said, putting the box down at the far end of the room, underneath the windowsill. The room was small but bright. 'Where's your bed?'

'My bed?'

'Yeah, there's no bed in the van. Where are you going to sleep?'

'I slept on the sofa.'

'You want to have a word with your brother about that. Jonny!' he shouted, filling the empty room with sound.

'Yeah?' Jonny's voice, like his movements, was powered by a bustling energy that moved him from room to room with urgency.

'Your sister. There's no bed here.'

'Ah, I know. We're going to buy one. As soon as we've got the money. I told you that,' he said, turning to Marion.

'She can't sleep on the sofa every night. Let me speak to Steve. He's got an old sofa bed he might be able to lend you.'

'Don't worry. Honestly. We can't take any more from you guys. We'll get a bed second hand from somewhere.'

'Steve!' Andrew shouted. Marion looked between Andrew and Jonny in the suspended silence that Steve continued to evade. 'I'll have a word with him. He's probably outside.'

When Andrew returned, Steve was beside him. 'Steve's going to ask his mum about the sofa bed,' Andrew said, turning to Steve. 'Isn't that right?'

'Yeah, yeah. She was thinking of selling it anyway. I'll go up and have a word with her.'

'Please don't go to any trouble,' Marion said, looking at Steve and attempting a smile.

'It's no trouble. He'll go and talk to her now,' said Andrew.

Theirs was a relationship that began with obligation. Marion felt as though she owed him something – for moving her stuff, sourcing a bed, smiling at her. And he enjoyed the feeling of benevolence, of mounting credit, of anticipating what this young girl might give him.

Marion was grateful when the sofa bed entered the flat, having been carried down twelve flights of stairs, across the green, into the small entrance hall and then along the corridor to her bedroom. She followed behind, noticing how Andrew's T-shirt clung to his sweating back as he instructed Steve to tilt so they could get it through the door. They placed it in the middle of the room and straightened up. Andrew turned, sensing her behind him. 'Where do you want it, then?'

'Over by the window. Under the windowsill,' she said, as though the location required clarifying.

Steve bent down to push the cardboard box to one side, ready to do her bidding, but Andrew remained motionless. 'That's not a good idea.' He frowned at the offending window.

'The cold air will go straight to your head.' He turned to look directly at her forehead and then up a bit.

She felt thrilled by the attention, the concern for her head and how it would fare exposed to the elements. She folded her arms across her chest and looked down at her breasts — how the action lifted and pushed them together. When she looked up, she saw Andrew had followed her gaze, that his eyes were still on her breasts, while Steve stood waiting for a decision from his cousin on what next.

Chapter 22

It was early evening and Jonny was working. Marion was wiping down the shelves in the kitchen when she heard the knock at the door. The front door to the house in Kilburn had been managed by Mrs Cooper. And nobody ever called for them in the evening, so it wasn't a problem. She decided to look through the spyhole and, even though she could see it was Andrew, shouted, 'Who is it?' The volume of her voice surprised her. She didn't know she had so much sound within her.

'It's Andrew. Steve's cousin.'

And then, because she needed a little more time to make up her mind about how she felt about him being on the other side of the door, she said, 'What do you want?'

'I just came to say hello. Can you let me in?'

Marion took a deep breath and opened the door. There was nothing and no one behind her. He stepped inside, but Marion didn't move. She only stepped back when she felt his shoulder press up against her as he slid along the wall in order to get himself behind the door and close it.

'I wondered if you'd like to come to the cinema with me.'

'Now?' Marion looked down at her slippers.

'No, I was thinking Saturday night. There's a film I'd like to see and I hoped you might want to come with me.'

'Have you asked Jonny?'

'Don't get me wrong – I like Jonny, but I'm not up for a night at the pictures with him.' Marion stared at him blankly. 'You know, he's not my type,' Andrew winked.

'Oh,' she smiled, and forced a laugh. 'Oh yes. No, I mean, have you asked him if I can go? With you, like.'

'Yeah. I've just been down at the pub. He's happy for me to take you as long as I bring you home sober and in one piece.' He smiled and winked again.

Marion, prompted by the wink, laughed for real this time.

'So what do you think?'

'Where will we go?'

'I was thinking the Classic, up Brixton way. Haven't been there for a while.'

'I've never been.'

'You're in for a treat. I'll come round here after we've had our lunch. Say six o'clock.'

'OK.'

'See you then.'

'See you then.'

They had very little to say to one another. South London was too busy for them: the buses manoeuvring slowly into Stockwell Bus Garage, the drunks slumped and shouting from outside the supermarket. As they rounded the corner onto Clapham Road, the station yawned for them. 'Are we taking the Tube?'

'Nah, let's walk. It's not far.'

They waited at the pedestrian crossing, forced by the traffic to stand before the Swan on the corner opposite.

Andrew noticed that Marion was looking at the pub. 'Do you fancy a quick one? Jonny'll be in there.'

'No, thank you.'

'Come on. We've got time.'

Marion thought of her father, who'd willingly walked into the pubs of Kilburn, knowing he'd leave a piece of himself at the bar each time.

'I'm after telling you no.'

'All right, all right.'

Marion felt the vibration of disaster as a lorry thundered past. She waited on the island beside Andrew for the opportunity to cross. It would be so easy to step out and surprise the next driver, to watch the panic as he tried to steer away from her and slow the force of his heavy vehicle. As Marion contemplated oblivion, Andrew led her across the road so that they could both stand before the double doors, the warmth and noise radiating from within. He looked at her.

'I thought we were going to the cinema,' she said quietly. 'That's what you told me.'

'And we are. I've just got to go and give something to Steve, that's all. Come in with me.'

'I'll wait for you out here. I don't want to go inside.'

'Suit yourself.' Andrew shrugged and went through the doors. She turned round in disbelief, as if the busy streets of Stockwell might have witnessed what just happened. But all she saw was the wide mouth of the Tube, asking her where she wanted to go. It was always a decision in London, always a question of where you want to go and never where you've been. Or even if you like where you are. She walked back to the crossing and pressed the button. Once she was across the road, she checked to see if Andrew was coming, but there was no sign of him. So she went into the supermarket and bought herself a Dime bar, which she chewed slowly as she walked back to the estate.

And for the first time since she moved in, Marion felt grateful for the flat. As she put her key into the lock, she felt sudden pleasure for the silence and emptiness on the other side of the door. She had a little cubbyhole in busy London where she could go and lock herself away. A place where she could run her hands through her hair, pull her tights off and boil the kettle. And as she did all these things, she thought of her mother. And longed for her with an intensity that took her breath away. She gasped at the fresh understanding of an established fact. But Marion had never really grieved for her mother – or her father. She had looked ahead and swallowed. And when her father died, she knew there was no time for the lump that swelled in her throat. Smoke a cigarette, suck in your breath and move on. The Irish way. But her strategy had led her to this hopeless place, standing alone in a kitchen that didn't really belong to her.

And as the outline of her mother's face began to present itself, Marion closed her eyes and looked harder. Her chin, small and square with a dimple in its centre, covered lightly with white fur as if it contained a secret, the lines that led up to her lips, and there it was, her mother's mouth. She gulped as she saw it: the bottom lip fuller than the top and always slightly wet, moistened by her tongue. She never stuck it out, just pulled her bottom lip up so it could get a wash of saliva from within. Marion banged her fist on the worktop and opened her eyes. She had to get this. She had to commit the image to paper and pluck her mother from the nothingness. But before she could locate a pen, she heard steps in the entranceway and then a loud knock.

'What's the matter with you?' he said loudly, his face red, as she opened the door.

'I told you I didn't want to go to the pub.'

'And you also told me you'd wait outside! I came out and you were gone.'

Marion thought of the Dime bar she'd eaten on the way home. The time she'd spent in the kitchen. 'How long did you look for me?'

'A while. I went into the Tube station, thought you might be standing around in there.'

Marion thought of her mother, the outline blurry again. 'I've lost it.'

'Lost what? Let me in, will you?' he said, forcing her backwards as he stepped across the threshold.

'Nothing. Never mind.'

'What's wrong?' he asked, standing too close.

She smelled the alcohol on him. 'You've been drinking. You weren't looking for me.'

'I had one. That's all.' He bent his knees so that his face was in front of hers and took hold of her elbows. 'I really wanted to see you tonight. Take you out.'

She dropped her head.

'Hey, hey. Come on. Don't be like that.' He lifted her chin with his right hand, his thumb pulling her lower lip down, and lingered as the moisture of her mouth transferred itself to his thumb pad. In those few brief seconds, there was still time to stop the kiss. She could have stepped back, asked him if he wanted a cup of tea or even shown him the door. But Andrew was master of the space. He was indisputably there and about to kiss her. And when it came, it was as if his thumb were a placeholder. He merely moved it so he could take her mouth with his.

With his knees still bent, he reached under her cardigan and grabbed for her breast. She inhaled sharply, but that made his kiss harder. More urgent. He pushed her against the closed front door and forced his tongue between her lips. And as he did, she knew she had to make a decision: to meet his force with her own or soften and let him in. His body was heavy, but as he unclasped her bra and ran his hands round to cup both her breasts, she felt a sudden rush of pleasure at her own daring. It felt freeing to be in someone else's hands. As if he could reshape her. He went down on his knees and began nuzzling her groin, lifting her skirt slowly. She put her hands on his shoulders and pushed him gently backwards.

'Not here,' she said, breathless with her own tacit consent.

He stood up and took her hand, leading Marion to her bedroom, where he sat down in the middle of the sofa bed he'd got for her and motioned to the seat next to him. She closed the curtains and turned on the light.

'No, leave it off.'

She did as he asked and walked over to him.

'Take your knickers off.'

She followed his instructions slowly and deliberately, and found that she enjoyed the thrill of capitulation. She wanted him to take control. To be taken care of.

'Put your knee here and the other one over here,' he whispered, patting the other side of him. She understood it would mean pulling up her skirt. She put her right knee down first and then lifted the left into place. In the darkness of that Saturday evening, with no family to save her, Marion lowered herself to Andrew Wilson.

Chapter 23

He didn't stay the night. He didn't linger long after he came inside her. Marion wasn't expecting him to – so stunned had she been by their rhythmic rocking, by the way their pelvises had come together as if they knew one another. His face had contorted at the end as he held her, the abundance of her breasts too much for him. Marion felt pity for his uncontrolled surrender to the moment, his deep pleasure so intense it made him weak.

She lifted her left knee, and as she brought it back to rejoin the right, Andrew moved to stand up. He tucked himself away and said to Marion, who was still kneeling on the sofa and had her back to him, 'Can I use your toilet?'

'It's just across the hallway.'

When she heard the toilet door close, she put her hand between her legs. Her body was wet and open in a way she hadn't known was possible. It was speaking a new language – as if it had always known this function would one day be required. She put her right foot down on the floor and, as she stood up and pulled her skirt back into place, felt Andrew's semen follow it down the inside of her thighs.

Andrew walked back into her bedroom and turned on the

light. Marion squinted as she looked at him standing with his hands in his pockets.

'I'm sorry about that.'

'About what?'

'Not taking you out tonight. The mix-up outside the pub. I will take you out, though. Next time.'

'Right so.'

'But I think I'd better go now. Before Jonny gets back.'

'OK.'

'Marion?'

'Yeah?'

'You won't tell him about this, will you? You know – you and me here. Alone.'

She remembered his face. The urgent rocking. 'No. I won't.'

'Thanks,' he said, stepping closer. He bent his knees and kissed her on the cheek. His lips made a barely perceptible impression on her cheek.

After he left, she went to run herself a bath. There was a thin smear of blood in her knickers. Bright red and un-explained. And then she felt inside herself again, trying to put her fingers on the throbbing. When they came away bloodied, she understood Andrew had done it.

By the time Jonny came home from work, she was in bed. She heard him opening and closing the cupboard doors in the kitchen, and then the pressured release of a can being opened. She considered getting out of bed and tiptoeing down the hallway to where he'd be, sitting down in their only armchair, the can resting on his knee with his eyes closed. She thought about the words she might use to tell him about Andrew, to piece the truth together and lay it out before him. But the thing she wanted to make tangible had already happened. And if she brought it back to life, she'd expose herself to Jonny's reaction: his judgement and disapproval. So she lay on her back and looked up at the ceiling and waited for her brother to go to bed. When he was asleep and the flat was silent, she closed her eyes and joined in the darkness.

Marion woke early the following morning and had another quick bath. She rinsed her hair with the measuring jug she kept beside the taps and got dressed quickly. Jonny slept on as she let herself – quietly – out of the flat and walked with steady determination to a far corner of the estate that led on to Larkhall Lane. She crossed the road and joined other people, mostly women, making their way into the Church of St Francis for the 9 a.m. Mass.

She didn't believe the water she dipped her fingers in was endowed with any power beyond the deep cold conferred by the stone basin. She didn't believe in her own inadequacy as she kneeled before the altar, and she didn't feel the presence of any deity within her breast as she invoked Holy Mary Mother of God to pray for her. But she wanted a piece of her mother on the morning after she lost her virginity. She wanted to grab at the rituals of Irish devotion and sandbag prayers around herself, shoring up the boundaries before the deluge that would come now that she'd let Andrew in.

And for that hour it worked. As the 'Our Father' came to an end, she looked around her and prepared to offer the sign of peace. The woman to her right had a young baby pressed against her chest, his sleeping head resting on her shoulder. She turned her body to Marion and, supporting the sleeping child with her left hand, extended her right to Marion and smiled as she said, 'Peace be with you.'

'And you,' Marion said as she shook the woman's hand. And the touch of a soft hand, with fingers that held hers, however briefly, made her smile with unexpected pleasure. 'How old is he?'

'Three months,' the woman whispered.

Marion detected an accent she couldn't place. And just as she was about to ask, she felt someone tap her left shoulder. Marion turned to find a small old man standing beside her. He was wearing a grey suit worn to a sheen, waiting with his hand outstretched.

'Peace be with you,' he said.

'Peace be with you,' Marion said with impatience, eager to turn back to the young woman, but when she did, she saw that she'd already stepped out to the aisle and had joined the queue of people shuffling forwards for Communion. By the time Marion edged out, she was several heads back. She watched as the young woman raised her chin and allowed the priest to place the Eucharist on her tongue. Her son slept on, oblivious to the body of Christ.

As the priest informed them the Mass was over and instructed all before him to love and serve the Lord, Marion turned to the woman in a more open repeat of their earlier handshake. 'I'm Marion. You're not from round here, are you?'

'No. My husband and I come from Scotland. A place called Dunbarton. Have you ever heard of it?'

'No, I've never been.'

'Where are you from?' she asked, but her eyes drifted down to Marion's side as the old man who'd been impatient to bestow peace earlier in the Mass now wanted to push past her.

'Sorry,' Marion said to the top of his head, pressing herself back into the pew so he could get past. He smiled at her breasts and told them, 'The Mass is over, don't you know?'

'I'm from Kilburn, but my ma and dad came over from Dublin.'

The two women walked down the steps and out onto Larkhall Lane, where the priest was waiting to shake their hands.

'Thank you, Father. Lovely service.'

'Bless you, my child. And this one too,' he said, placing his hand on the baby's head.

'Thank you, Father,' Marion said dutifully as she stepped down to the pavement.

'I don't think I've seen you here before. Are you new to St Francis's?'

'I am, Father. We moved here last week.'

'And who is "we"? Is that you and your husband?'

'My brother, Father.' The priest looked at her, waiting for more. 'He was working until very late last night.'

'Well, be sure to tell your brother we're here for him as well. We all need God's peace and love,' he said with sudden seriousness, as Marion kept her eye on her new friend, willing her to wait for her.

'I didn't catch your name,' Marion said quickly as she joined the woman on the pavement.

'Samantha. But call me Sam. And this here is Daniel.'

'It's nice to meet someone round here. Do you live on the estate?'

'Yes. We're in Barton Court over there.' Sam indicated with her free hand. 'We have a little flat on the first floor. And you? Did you say you live with your brother?'

'We're in Marshall Court. On the ground floor.'

'And you're with your brother?'

'Yes. My parents have passed.'

'I'm sorry.'

'I lived with them up in Kilburn, but we've moved down here now for Jonny's work.'

Daniel lifted his little head and began making sucking noises. 'This one's going to need a feed soon. I'd better head back.'

'I'll come with you. I'm going that way myself.'

Marion kept stealing glances at Sam as she walked. She was wearing a knee-length floral dress that buttoned up at the front. Her beige shoes were simple and soft, spread wide by feet that had few other shoes. She was somewhere between slim and no-longer slender, her body waiting for the flesh to settle again. She walked with Daniel pressed to her, her right hand securing his eager head as she shushed his more urgent cries. Marion looked at the purple skin beneath her eyes, at the bags that told their own version of motherhood.

'Are you very tired?'

'It's OK. Not as bad as you might think.'

But Marion hadn't thought. In the hours since Andrew came inside her, she hadn't considered the possibility that they might have made a baby. A thing that would grow inside her and demand feeding at all hours of the night. And at the thought of having made a human being with someone she hardly knew, she began to laugh.

'What's funny?' Sam turned her body to Marion.

'Oh, nothing. I was just thinking how mad it is that anyone can just make one of those. You know, a baby.'

'It's easier than you might think,' Sam said, cradling Daniel lower in her arm and patting his bottom in time to her steps. 'So do you have a young man yourself?'

'Yes, a friend of my brother's.'

'What's his name?'

'Andrew.'

'And does he live round here?'

'Strudwick Court.'

'Andrew Wilson? The Wilsons?'

'I think so, yeah. He has a cousin called Steve.'

'Everyone knows the Wilsons.'

'We've only been out the once.'

Sam was looking down at Daniel. She lifted her right hand to stroke the hair on his head and said, tenderly, 'That's all it takes.'

When Marion returned to the flat, Andrew was already there. He was standing in the kitchen with Jonny, who was in a pair of shorts and the misshapen grey T-shirt he slept in.

'Here she is!' Andrew said brightly. 'I came looking for you and Jonny said you'd gone to church. I never took you for a religious girl.'

'I like to go to Mass.' Marion felt defensive. She turned to Jonny. 'Have you only just got up?'

'It was a late one. Don't have a go at me.'

'Have you had any breakfast?'

'Not yet.'

'Shall I do you some eggs?'

'Yeah.'

'Go on and sit down,' she said, opening the cupboard above the work surface Andrew was leaning against. The nearness of him – his hands and arms and the parts of his body she'd encountered the night before – stirred her up inside and she felt self-conscious as she fumbled with the frying pan. He didn't move an inch, making it clear that he wanted her close again. With her back to him, as she poured oil into the pan, she said, 'And I suppose you'd like some too?'

He waited until Jonny had left the kitchen before going to

stand close behind her. He pushed her hard against the stove so that she had to reach out to stop herself falling onto the pan. 'I'll have whatever you've got,' he breathed into her neck.

And in that moment, as she steadied herself against the brute force of his desire, she didn't know if she was frightened or aroused. But as she cracked the first egg against the pan and watched the messy albumin whiten round the yolk, she realised the answer lay in the hot fat. That she was both.

Chapter 24

Andrew's visits became more frequent, vacillating between the chaste drop-in when Jonny was home and the more illicit appearances in the evening, when he knew Marion would be alone. She knew it would have been better had they gone out properly, announced their relationship in a series of dates, but being alone and naked was too easy and immediately satisfying. They pulled at the sofa cushions, unfolding the mattress before they pulled at each other's clothes. It had become important to make love horizontally, to get fully naked and enjoy the freedom of an empty flat. He never mentioned condoms or the Pill, and Marion never asked about things she considered the domain of married women. It would have interrupted the accepted routine, the thrusting that had become part of who they were and how they were with one another. She knew her acquiescence was consent, she knew the opening of her legs was a gateway to a baby, and yet she didn't know if she wanted to stop it. She'd seen women on the estate with babies. A few of them – like Sam – had husbands, some had boyfriends, and many had no one beyond the child they'd created.

But their relationship – a thing that was never announced

– simply came into being. It assumed a form that had begun to touch upon Jonny. Andrew knew that Jonny, who had at first been wrong-footed by his kindness – moving their stuff, the sofa bed – now began to see that it wasn't for him. And Andrew, in apology for having sex with his sister, began going to the pub for his postcoital pint, presenting himself before Jonny and Steve.

'Here he is,' Steve said, darkly, as Andrew approached the bar one muggy evening in August.

'All right, lads. A pint of the usual, please, Jonny.' Andrew began digging in his jeans pocket for change.

'Where you been?'

Andrew met his cousin's gaze. 'About.'

Steve chuckled to himself as he sipped his drink.

'There you go,' Jonny said, wiping the bottom of the glass with his hand.

'Cheers,' Andrew said, pushing the coins across the bar.

'Well, aren't you going to tell him?' Steve said.

Andrew took a slow drink and stared at Steve. 'Tell him what?'

'About number forty-three.'

'What are you talking about?'

'The lesbians in the flat above me and Mum. They're being evicted next week. Selling a load of stuff. I thought you were going to tell Jonny,' he said, indicating Jonny, who was only half listening.

'Oh yeah. Jon, did you hear that? Family above my aunt's flat – do you want me to take a look? See if they've got anything you might find useful.'

'I need to hold off on buying stuff for a little while. Money's in short supply at the moment.'

'Don't worry about that. You can always pay me back later.'

'Or his sister can,' Steve mumbled into his pint.

Marion told Jonny before Andrew. She was sitting in the kitchen one bright morning in October with a cup of hot water before her. Her face was pale and drawn.

'What's the matter with you?' he asked, sitting down and peering over at the steaming fluid that filled her cup.

'I'm pregnant.'

'You're what?'

'You heard me. I'm pregnant.'

'Jesus Christ.' He stood up and walked over to the window. 'Are you sure?'

'I'm sure.'

'It's Andrew's, I suppose?'

She closed her eyes, the steam from the hot water reaching up and warming her face.

He turned round, expecting an answer. But all he saw was the crown of her lowered head, the white circle of scalp exposed by flat hair. He felt a sudden impulse to put his hand on her head and draw her to him. He went to her, squatted down on his haunches and, holding the edge of the table to balance himself, asked her quietly, 'Is this what you want?'

She looked at the tips of his fingers as they whitened with the effort of holding on. 'You mean the baby?'

He shook his head. 'Andrew. Is he what you want?'

'I want something of my own, Jonny.'

'What do you mean?' He got up and sat in the chair opposite her.

'This baby,' she said, putting her hand on her stomach. 'It'll be mine. Not used, not borrowed, not damaged. It'll be mine.'

'And Andrew's?'

'I know that.'

'What'll you do?'

'I don't know.'

'Is Andrew going to take care of you? And the baby?'

'He doesn't know.'

'Jesus. Don't you think you'd better tell him?'

'Give me a chance, Jonny. I've only just told you.'

'He needs to know. If he's the father, he needs to know.'

'Mother of God, what do you think of me? Of course he's the father!'

'Don't upset yourself.' Jonny reached for her hand. Marion looked up in surprise. He'd never held or stroked a part of her before and yet, in the space of just a few minutes, her body had become accessible and available to him.

'I should have looked after you better.' It was a truth too staggering to bear. She heard it in his voice and in the words that followed. 'I'm sorry, Marion.'

And then, craning with disbelief, she looked for his face. His head was bent low to the table, but nothing could hide his tears. Marion watched with panic. He didn't want her to be with Andrew. But it was too late. The egg had been cracked.

Chapter 25

Life took on a new normality following the upheaval of Marion's announcement. Jonny remained in the flat, supervising its transformation as a new double mattress, bed frame and a three-seater sofa in the lounge marked Andrew's slow and insistent incursion. When Marion was twelve weeks, she was ushered into a lift that stank powerfully of piss, up to the fifth floor to meet Lorraine Wilson.

Andrew's mother was a small, softly spoken woman in her mid-forties with grey hair cut close to her head. Her every movement was muted, cut off prematurely. She sat on the edge of the armchair instead of squarely on the cushions; her sentences trailed off at the end; she mumbled even as her listener leaned forwards to hear. It was as though she lived in constant fear of going too far, appearing too loud, being too much. Andrew guarded her peace carefully, softening his own voice to a whisper as soon as they entered the flat. He tiptoed around her, placing a hand on her back as she lowered herself quietly into an armchair. She smiled at Marion with great effort and asked her how long she'd lived on the estate.

'Since the end of May.'

Lorraine nodded at this information, as though Marion

were confirming something she'd always suspected. 'Marshall Court, isn't it?'

'That's right. Number seven.'

Another nod. Andrew got up and went into the kitchen to collect the tea his mother had made.

'Andrew's been very helpful. Moving our stuff for us and helping buy furniture. That kind of thing.'

'He's a good boy,' she smiled kindly.

Andrew brought in three cups, gripping the handles of two together in his right hand and the third in his left. He kneeled down beside his mother's armchair and held out the single cup. As she received it, Marion noticed the long fingernails. They had been carefully shaped and painted. There was no wedding ring.

Andrew took a seat next to Marion and put their cups on the carpet in front of them. He picked up Marion's hand and tried to lace his fingers through hers. 'We've come over because we've got something to tell you.'

'Oh yes?'

'We're going to have a baby.' He smiled shyly. 'Marion's going to have a baby.'

Lorraine lifted the corners of her mouth in an attempt to smile. 'When's it due?'

'In April. Is that right?' he said, turning to Marion.

'Baby's due in May, not April.'

'I see,' mumbled Lorraine.

'Are you pleased, Mum? You're going to be a granny.'

'Of course I'm pleased. Come here.' And Andrew, kneeling down in front of her once again, waited for his mother to put her arms around his neck and pull him to her. 'Well done, son,' she said, before looking up at Marion. 'You too, dear. Congratulations.'

'Thank you.'

'Have you told Steve?'

'Yeah, Steve knows.'

'And Auntie Li?'

'I don't think so.'

'Oh, go on up and tell her. She'll be so happy for you.'

Marion and Andrew took the stairs up to the seventh floor and knocked on another door. Steve opened it – half asleep with only a pair of navy underpants on.

'What is it?' he asked, rubbing his eye. When he lowered his hand, he saw Marion behind Andrew and tried to cover himself. 'Hang on. Let me get some clothes on.'

'Come in,' Andrew said, ushering Marion into a warmer, more sharply decorated flat. The carpet in the lounge was a deep red, and the leather sofas – sitting heavily upon it   were dark brown. Marion took a deep breath and looked behind her, but Andrew had already shut the door. He shouted for his aunt.

'Coming! Give me a moment,' came a voice from one of the bedrooms.

'Take a seat. She'll be out soon.'

'Is Li your mother's sister?'

'Yeah. Lillian, but we all call her Li. She's four years older than my mum.'

'And has she always lived on top of her?'

'Not always. Sit down.'

Marion lowered herself into the leather and waited for Andrew to answer her. 'We moved here when I was about three.'

'Just the two of you?'

'Yeah.'

Marion looked at the smooth polished glass of the coffee

table, its four corners bitten in place by gold columns. In its reflection she saw the spiky fractals of an elaborate chandelier above it. She realised, as she waited for Andrew to speak again, that she would like to see it fall and shatter.

'What happened to your dad?'

'He's not around,' Andrew sniffed.

'Why not? What happened to him?'

'It's not important.'

'Of course it's important.'

'I can't go into it now. It'll upset Li if I start talking about him.'

Li walked into the room with open arms, her small, skinny body raised high on stilettos. She walked up to Marion with sway and purpose, smiling at the knowledge that eyes were upon her. Marion stood, as if drawn by a magnet, and waited for Li's force to pull her in.

'Congratulations, darling,' she said, embracing Marion with her fingertips. Her black curly hair was abundant and suffused by cigarette smoke. As Marion held Li's shoulder blades, the swirl of her hair infiltrating her nostrils, she felt bewildered. Who were these people that welcomed her? The north side of Dublin, Dún Laoghaire dock, even Mrs Cooper's rooms in Kilburn – they were like breadcrumbs. She'd always been able to conceive of the path that led back home, but this dark flat, accessed by a complex matrix of lift buttons and door numbers, defeated all that. She held Li's gaze a heartbeat too long as she pictured herself running for the front door. But where would she go?

'Sit down, Maria. Do you mind if I smoke?'

'It's Marion. No, go ahead.'

'Sorry, darling. Andrew, go and tell Steve to get his arse out here and to bring my fags while he's at it.' Andrew walked away as Li pushed her hair back over her shoulders, as though taming an eager dog. 'Now tell me all about it. Steve's already told me, but I want to hear it from the horse's mouth.' She smiled, revealing her yellow teeth. 'He says you haven't been together long?'

'That's right.' Marion shifted uncomfortably in her seat. 'Me and my brother. We only moved to the estate a few months ago.'

'And the boys helped move your boxes, eh?'

'They were very good,' Marion said. She couldn't take her eyes off Li's teeth. She imagined trying to walk on them, slipping on the plaque as she would algae on a rock.

'Was it you and your brother who took the sofa bed?'

'Yes, that's right.' And then because Li continued to smile at her in expectation, she said, 'Thank you.'

'Oh, darling' – Li waved her hand with casual benevolence – 'whatever you need. Andrew's like a son to me.'

'He said you and his mother are very close.'

At that moment Steve walked in, dressed but without socks on. He didn't look at Marion, didn't say hello, just handed his mother a packet of cigarettes and went to walk back out again.

'Ain't you going to say hello, then?'

'Hello,' he said, frowning at his mother.

'Not to me, you big bastard. Say hello to Andrew's girl-friend here.'

'Hello.' He nodded at Marion and turned round.

'Where're you going?'

'Down to the lock-up. Got a few things to sort out.'

'Is Andrew going?'

'Yeah.'

'Right, well, we can get to know each other, in that case,' she said, turning back to Marion.

Marion's first thought was not where or what Andrew was doing with Steve; it was how to get out of the concrete labyrinth once she was on her own. She decided she'd take the stairs and just keep going down until the ground was firm and there was a doorway to the outside. She planned all this as Li took advantage of a deep inhalation to really look at the Irish girl before her.

'Don't worry about Andrew. He won't be long.'

'That's OK. I can't stay for very long myself. My brother needs me.'

'Oh, shush. You'll stay for lunch, won't you? Baby needs you to eat, you know?'

'I don't think I can. I need to prepare something for Jonny.'

'Jonny can fend for himself. Stay here and chat with me a while.'

Marion sat in her seat and allowed her cheek to be kissed by Andrew as he prepared to head out with Steve. His cousin waited in the hallway, offering no goodbye to his mother or Marion.

'He doesn't say much, does he?' Marion said.

'Who? Andrew?'

'Steve. I don't think he's said two words in the time I've known him.'

'Don't worry about him. He's the strong, silent type.' She smiled, conspiratorial, her head tilted forwards for more questions. But Marion's eyes had dropped to the glass table as she imagined again how a heavy rock to the centre would shatter it.

'What happened to Andrew's father?'

'Eh?'

'His da. He said he and Lorraine moved to this block when he was very young. I just wondered what happened to him.'

'Nothing happened to him, unfortunately.' Li's sucks were shorter now, the skin round her eyes creased at the acrid inhalation. 'He's still alive. Still a fucking cunt.'

The words were so violent, so loaded with sharp fragments, Marion closed her mouth against them.

'He used to beat my sister up. Very badly. And you've seen her – she wouldn't say boo to a goose.'

'What happened?'

'Well, she had to get out of there. He'd moved on to Andrew by the time she got her act together. She came to stay with me until she could get registered for a flat of her own.'

'And where is he now?'

'Oh, living it up in a big house in Surrey. He comes from money.'

'Does he still see Andrew?'

'God, no. Hasn't since he was a toddler. He came round here once or twice looking for them. The last time was about five years ago. Kept saying he wants to leave everything to Andrew when he dies. The bloke I was seeing chased him away with a carving knife.' Li was matter-of-fact about events, as though the incident having passed into words could now be handled safely. The accepted denouement of that day protected them all from it.

'I need to go. It was lovely to meet you.'

'Oh, stay. I was going to make you a sandwich.'

'No, I can't,' and in order to finally be free of all the red and brown, Marion put her hand on her stomach and said, 'I need to lie down. I'm feeling a bit tired.'

'Course you are, dear. Listen, don't mention any of this

stuff about his dad to Andrew. He don't like talking about it and I don't blame him. Is that OK?'

'No problem.'

Andrew's role in her life became more established as her stomach grew. He insisted Marion give up work at the bakery and began appearing at odd times of the day and night, sometimes spending the night, at others preferring to return to Lorraine's flat. He left small bundles of cash on Marion's bedside table so she could buy things for the baby.

'How am I going to fit a cot in this room?'

'We're going to move your stuff into Jonny's room. This'll be where the baby sleeps.'

'And what does Jonny have to say about that?'

'He understands. He's looking for a new place now.'

'Jonny's my brother. We can't just kick him out.'

'We're not kicking him out. He wants to go. Listen, it makes sense for me to move in when the baby comes. And we can't all live in this small room. Besides, Jonny won't want to live with us.'

'I don't know. I feel uneasy about not having him around,' Marion said, rubbing her stomach. It was early March and she was seven months pregnant.

'Listen, we're going to be a family. You'll have this baby, and once the little fella's out, we'll get married. OK?'

'Is that a proposal?'

'Mum wants us to get married. And I think she's right. Do you want me to get down on one knee?'

'Don't be a bloody eejit.'

But Andrew got down on both knees and positioned himself before Marion's distended bellybutton. 'Listen to me, son. I've just asked your mum to marry me. What do you say? Is that a good idea?'

'Get out of that,' Marion said, laughing despite herself.

Andrew turned his head to press his ear against the taut skin. 'What's that?'

'What?'

'He says you should say yes. That you're the luckiest girl in the world. And could his daddy have a bacon sandwich.'

'You're some mighty gobshite, Wilson.'

Marion's first pregnancy felt like a long soak in a lukewarm bath: Jonny and Andrew generally left her alone to rest and grow the child, interrupting the peace with occasional requests for meals, mostly cooked breakfasts after a long night in the pub. Andrew was careful and caring for her in a way he never was again.

Marion continued going to Mass every Sunday, if only to see Sam and continue the ritual of their weekly cup of tea. One sunny morning at the beginning of May, as the sun shone strong and bright on her face, she felt her baby kick against her bladder. They were still a few minutes from Sam's flat.

'Jesus, this one. He's determined to kick the last drop of tea out of me.'

'Can you wait until we get back?'

'Sure I'll have to. If I squat down now, you'd never get me back up again.' And at the thought of the water within her, she remembered the cold water without, the stuff she'd dipped her fingers in as she walked out of the church.

'Did you have Daniel baptised at St Francis's?'

'No. My mother wouldn't have stood for it. We went home to Dunbarton.' Daniel's eyes were closing as his mother pushed him along, as though he was content the details of his christening were accurate and could now surrender to sleep. 'What will you do?' she asked, turning her head to find Marion's eyes.

'I want to have the baby baptised. My ma and da would want that.'

'But you're not—'

'Not yet. Andrew wants to get married after the baby's born. He wants us to be a family.'

'And will you get married there as well?'

'I think so.'

But Andrew didn't like the sound of a church wedding when Marion mentioned it to him that evening in the kitchen.

'Why not? That's where everybody gets married at home.'

'But we're not in Ireland now. This is England, and I don't want some priest telling me what I can and can't do.'

'You've already done what you can't do as far as the priest is concerned. Why worry about what else he has to say?'

'I didn't see you complaining. Or telling me God or Jesus wouldn't like it.'

'This has got nothing to do with God and Jesus.'

'So what are we arguing about, then?'

'About the right thing. I want to get this child baptised. God knows we haven't done things in the right order, but I know my mother would want it.'

'And my mum wants nothing to do with God.'

Andrew leaned up against the work surface and crossed one ankle over the other. 'Because of my dad. They were married in a church, went every Sunday and he still beat her up. And me.'

'I know.'

'How do you know?'

'Li told me.'

'Right. So you know he was a cruel prick? That he'd started to hit me – a three-year-old! Fucking sick bastard.'

'I know it. I know it all.' She reached out to touch his face. Stubble had grown along his jawbone. She found herself stroking it downwards, distracted by the hard bristles that prevented access to the softer skin.

'Listen, I'm not letting a priest anywhere near my kid, and if you want to be Mrs Wilson, you won't either.'

Andrew and Jonny set off for the Swan just before seven o'clock. Marion decided against a bath: her body was too heavy and uncomfortable. She went into the lounge and sat back in the armchair. Andrew had bought her a matching footstool, but putting her feet up forced her coccyx into the soft void between back cushion and top seat. She put her hands down and levered herself up to a seated position. Sitting on the edge of the armchair, she looked around her: at the bare walls and cold stone floor. Andrew and Jonny had pulled up the broken lino, but they hadn't got round to carpeting it yet. She thought of Li's deep red carpet and the brown sofas that floated on top of them and felt suddenly sick. The bile rose in her throat, and forcing herself to a stand, she lumbered – as quickly as she could – to the toilet, where she got down on her knees and tried to bring up the cup of black tea she'd just drunk.

Afterwards, she walked into the kitchen and stood before the window that overlooked the estate. Reminded of the evening she'd tried to sketch her mother's face, she rummaged in a drawer for a pen and paper, and sat down at the table, determined to do what Andrew had interrupted back in June.

But it wasn't her mother's features she sought to produce. At the first curve of the temple and the gentle strokes of the hair, abundant in Bic blue, she began to discern the sphere of her baby's head. Just as she'd wanted to pull her mother from the blur of death, this evening – the night of her son's birth – she wanted to make the features she'd imagined tangible. And then, as if her body were taking pity on her efforts, her womb gave up the plug that had held in her baby's bath water.

'Holy Jesus,' she said, looking down at the puddle between her knees. She was reminded of the first time she had sex with Andrew in the room across the hallway. Fluid had drained out of her then. She grabbed a tea towel hanging from the oven door and threw it on the puddle.

The pain was like a visitation from the dead. It was something her mother had experienced and her own mother before her. And yet here it was, urgent and new, insistent and imminent. It was a secret she'd take to her own grave: the pain of breathing new life. The pursuit of that life over your own. And one day this baby would have to decide what to do with her body.

She pushed herself up from the table and opened the front door. She didn't know who she could call for help: Jonny had told her to have nothing to do with the other flats in the block. She didn't fancy walking up to the pub and presenting herself at the bar, her body so physically distorted by the sex she'd had and the pain she was in. She went back inside the flat but left the door ajar. Locating her slippers under the kitchen table, she sat on one of the chairs and managed to slip her bare feet inside, then grabbed her keys and went outside, pulling the door closed behind her.

She knew she must return to the labyrinth of Strudwick Court. That only Andrew's mother or aunt could offer any help at this hour. *Got to go Lo or Li*, she thought to herself, managing a little chuckle despite the contractions. Tired by the time she arrived, she called the lift, but presented with the dimly lit piss-filled box, she decided to take the stairs. As she walked up, she lost track of what floor she was on. She knew Lorraine was on the fifth, but she didn't know what her door number was. She searched the doors – two on each floor – for a number that made sense, but she couldn't find one. Meanwhile, the baby inside her, who cared nothing for her confusion, kicked at the contracting muscles. She decided to knock at the first door on the next floor, but an angry African voice responded, 'What do you want?' She smelled the unfamiliar cooking and decided to walk on. She knocked at the next door, but receiving no answer, stumbled up another flight of stairs. When she got there, she had to sit down and wait for the roll of another contraction before she could compose herself to knock on the next door. This one was opened by a small child, of around six or seven years. He had blond hair and sharp eyes.

'Can you get your mammy for me?' Marion asked, bent double.

'What?'

'Your mammy—'

But the door was wrestled open by an angry woman whose black hair was pulled back into a high ponytail. 'What 'ave I told you about opening—'

'Please help me. I'm having a baby.'

'Christ. Move back,' she shouted at her son. 'That's it. Come in and sit down.'

'I'm OK. Do you know Lorraine Wilson?'

'Yeah, I know Lorraine. She lives on the floor above. Kevin, run up and get Lorraine. Tell her . . . What's your name?'

'Marion. Tell her Marion wants her.'

'Go on, then! Don't just stand there gawping.'

But Kevin returned two minutes later. 'She's not in. There's no one there.'

'Try Li. She lives two floors above. She might be there,' the woman said.

Kevin ran off, pleased with the urgency of his errand. Within a few minutes Marion heard the imperative tones and clack-slap of Li's slippers float down the concrete stairs towards the open door.

'Where is she?'

'In here,' Kevin said proudly, presenting the pregnant woman he'd discovered.

'Oh my God. You're in labour?'

Marion could only nod.

'Does Andrew know?'

She shook her head.

'Is he out with Steve? In the pub?'

'Yes,' she breathed.

'I'll go and get him. You wait here. Sue'll look after you.'

When Li burst into the pub with the news that his sister was in labour, Jonny threw down the tea towel he was holding and ran with Andrew across the road and down Binfield Road to Marshall Court. They didn't give Li a chance to tell them she wasn't in the flat. She met them on the way back, Jonny frantic that he couldn't find Marion.

'Where the hell is she?'

'At Sue's. Number thirty-two. She was trying to find Lorraine and knocked on the wrong door.'

Jonny pushed past Andrew and, taking several steps at a time, knocked loudly at number 32. Kevin opened the door quickly, but before he could get the words out, they heard Marion's deep moan from the lounge.

'Marion. Are you OK? Come on, up you come. That's it. We'll get you to the hospital. Andrew, get the other side.' And with her arms held up, her head slumped in surrender to the unending pain, Marion allowed herself to be dragged – like one crucified – from the wrong flat.

Her baby was born a few hours later in St Thomas's Hospital. Marion remembered very little of the actual labour, only that her brother and Andrew left her to the care of the midwife, who – for those brief hours – understood what her body was capable of better than she did. Marion allowed herself to be instructed; it meant she could look up at the ceiling and concentrate on the pain. It felt as though she were breaking, that her limbs would eventually come away from her pelvis and within the broken fragments they'd find a crying baby. But he didn't cry. When they pulled him out and showed him to her, his face was perfectly still and blue, and for a confusing moment, Marion thought it was because of the Bic biro. The midwife lay him down on the bed between Marion's legs and rubbed him vigorously, encouraging a cough and then crying to emerge into the room.

By the time Andrew and Jonny were readmitted to the room, Marion was sitting up in bed with a cup of tea. Jonathan was sleeping in a transparent cot beside her.

'Well done,' Jonny said, stroking Marion's hair and kissing her gently on the cheek.

She felt tears on her face and wondered if they were Jonny's, but when they dripped onto her chest, she knew her own eyes were producing them. The sleeping baby beside her was another big step on the path from her old life. From

Elizabeth and Aidan Donnelly and Ireland. A big crumb that would weigh her down. She knew now, as she looked at Andrew looking at his son, that finding her way home again would be impossible.

Jonny sat on the bed beside her, nodding at her sobs as though he understood why she was crying. 'He's a good boy,' he managed to say.

'Yeah.'

'And you'll be a great mam.'

She looked up at him and saw the sorrow crease his face. Elizabeth should have been there and he couldn't stay. 'You and Andrew need to be on your own now.'

'No, Jonny.'

'It's the right thing, Marion. Yous are a family now. And I've got a room in the pub until I can find something more permanent.'

'Don't leave me,' she whispered.

Andrew looked up for the first time. 'Come on,' he said, approaching the bed. 'I'll look after you. We're a family. Just like Jonny said.'

'I'll be close by. And anyway, I want to see my little nephew. What's he called?'

'Jonathan Aidan,' Marion said quickly.

'Is he?' said Andrew.

'Yes. After my brother and my da. It's what I want.'

'OK. But he's Wilson, isn't he?'

'Yes, he's a Wilson.'

Chapter 26

Marion and Andrew were married six weeks later – on Tuesday, 28 June 1977 – in Lambeth Registry Office. Jonny took the afternoon off work and served as witness. The party returned to a small reception in Li's flat. It consisted of a shop-bought cake and lager donated from the pub. Marion stayed for an hour and then asked Andrew to take them home – Jonathan needed a feed and a bath before bed.

Their life as the Wilsons had begun and it was a quiet one. It suited Marion, once Jonny had moved out, to keep her small family to herself. Jonathan began to grow, and as he did, Marion saw that she too could relax and expand in her environment. She was a married woman with a young son and for a while she felt almost happy. Li and Lorraine were always happy to look after Jonathan if she needed to go out, and Li often called round in the mornings after Andrew had gone to work for a cigarette and a cup of tea. And one morning, despite not having smoked for over a year, after a particularly tiring night in which Jonathan, his gums red and hot with emerging teeth, had cried for most it, she pulled a cigarette from Li's packet and waited for her to catch on and light it.

It was never a friendship, but she had grown to rely on

Li's presence. She liked the way her eyes drifted down as she spoke and opened wide again as she inhaled.

Lorraine never came to see them. She'd been in the night Kevin hammered on her door, but fear prevented her from opening it. She made it clear to Andrew that he and Marion were always welcome but she had no plans to leave her own flat and travel across the green to Marshall Court.

'What's the matter with her?' Marion asked Andrew one evening while she was preparing dinner. Jonathan was in his high chair, playing with a wooden spoon and a measuring jug.

'Nothing. She just doesn't like coming out, that's all.'

'Because of what happened with your da?' The steam from the potatoes and attending to Jonathan distracted Marion. It dulled her sensitivity to Andrew's defensiveness.

'My mum's been through a lot, all right?'

'I know, but come on. You'd think she'd want to come and see her grandson in his own home once in a while.'

Andrew stood up abruptly. 'What the fuck's the matter with you?'

Her first look was to Jonathan. As though he were the one who'd just sworn at her. 'What's the matter with *me*?'

'She's been through a lot in her life. My dad almost killed her. And you think she should just get over it all and walk over here because it's more convenient for you?'

'He's not going to do anything to her now, is he? Living it up in Surrey! I tell you what, loneliness will kill her before your da.'

'Watch your mouth.'

'And you watch yours!'

He took a step towards her, his right fist clenched by his side.

'You fucking try, Andrew Wilson. I'll have this fork in your eyeball before you take your next breath.'

With his thumb, he wiped the small ball of saliva that had appeared at the corner of his mouth. And then quietly, as if he had something more important to do, he said, 'Fuck this,' and walked out through the front door, slamming it hard behind him.

Marion stood in the middle of the kitchen and tried to locate the feeling that suddenly assailed her. She looked at Jonathan, who was blowing raspberries, a long string of drool extending down to the plastic tray beneath him, and she knew she was afraid.

Andrew and Steve's business – removals and general handy-men with a van – went from strength to strength. They were out most days, all over south London, and when there were no removals jobs, they shifted scrap metal and did a bit of waste disposal. They were always busy. Andrew delivered a set amount of cash to Marion at the end of every day, before he went to have a bath and clean up ready for dinner. The flat became warmer and more homely: Andrew had carpeted the front room and sourced various pieces of furniture to fit the spaces left by Jonny's departure. Marriage and a baby son had provided a framework for him and he enjoyed his role as provider.

Marion, with no mother and only Li and Sam for com-pany, found her feet quickly. She fed Jonathan at around seven in the morning and then put him down for another short sleep. In that time, she'd have a bath and put on a bit of make-up. Li might drop in around nine thirty for a cup of tea and a cigarette, and by ten she was ready to put Jonathan in the pushchair and go out to the shops on the

Clapham Road. She'd buy meat and vegetables for dinner and put them in the basket beneath Jonathan, lifting his chubby legs so she could wedge the shopping under him. She knew what she had to do, and Andrew gave her the means to do it.

But at the beginning of 1978, Marion began to suspect she was pregnant again. She felt a sinking nausea when Li offered her a cigarette in the morning. She tried to smoke through it, as though a cigarette and the illusion of normality would shake a foetus not determined enough to hold on. But by the end of the January, her period was very late and her revulsion at Li's smoking was complete.

'What's the matter with you? Why are you making that face?'

'It's the smoke. It makes me feel sick.'

'You're not pregnant again, are you?'

'I think so.'

'Bloody hell. How old is Jon?'

'Jonathan. Seven months.'

'You don't wait around, do you?'

'What do you mean?'

'It'll be a small gap,' she began, counting on her fingers. 'Sixteen months. You're gonna have your work cut out.'

'We'll manage.'

'But you don't have to manage.'

'What are you saying?'

'I'm saying . . . after this one, go along to the doctor's and get yourself on the Pill. You take it every day and then you can't get pregnant.'

'And they just hand these pills out, do they?'

'Yeah. You're a married woman. Why wouldn't they?'

'I don't know.'

Li laughed as she exhaled. 'You're in England now. The Pope doesn't give a shit what you do.'

Robert Andrew Wilson was born on 3 September 1978. Not even a second pregnancy and a toddler still in nappies could shake Marion's stubborn contentment. She gripped tightly to a sense of what she had to do, and part of that – as she got her first year of marriage under her belt – was not to ask too many questions of Andrew. His business flourished and the cash was abundant, but she was no longer convinced it was just from removals and driving a van around south London. He came home late at night and left early in the morning, always with thick bundles of cash on him. If she opened his bedside-table drawer, she'd find an array of gold jewellery – watches, necklaces, sovereign rings – that she knew didn't belong to him. A few days later, they'd be gone, replaced by different pieces of similar value and number.

She began asking for more money. At first, she cited the boys as the reason – Jonathan needed new trainers; the push-chair was broken – but she realised Andrew didn't care what she spent the money on. He was rarely round to inspect the new things she bought, so she began spending it on herself. At first, it was a pair of shoes or a new dress, and then she had her hair cut short and highlighted. And one morning, when Robbie was at nursery and Jonathan at school, she went to a beauty salon and had her nails manicured, selecting a colour that reminded her of that first meeting with Lorraine. She began to feel good, to feel wealthy, if not entirely cared for. But it was always a disappointment to come back to the estate, and when she pushed the door to Marshall Court open, she felt the grey concrete mocking her pretensions.

The money flowed up to Strudwick Court too. Andrew

had arranged for new carpets throughout his mother's flat. The walls of the lounge had been freshly wallpapered the year after Robbie's birth. And once Robbie started school, Marion got into the habit of taking them to see their grandmother in the afternoons: she had lost her fear of the block of flats and now allowed the boys to fight over pushing the button to call the lift. Lorraine looked after them for a few hours and gave them their tea, an arrangement that suited Marion, though she'd long given up hope that one day Lorraine might offer to collect them herself.

Marion saw very little of her brother in those years. He dropped by twice a year, often a few weeks after one of the boys had a birthday, and would stay for an hour or so. He'd fish in his pocket for some cash as he was leaving, muttering, 'Happy birthday, now,' to his excited nephews.

On Robbie's sixth birthday, Marion, alarmed by how pale and thin Jonny looked, asked him where he was working. They were sitting in the kitchen of the flat, now transformed by white goods and new, fitted cupboards.

'I'm working on a school up in Thornton Heath. Knocking down part of it and extending across some playing fields.'

'You look thin. What happened to the Jolly Sailor?'

'Had a row with yer man and that was that.'

'Let me make you something. What do you want?'

'Nothing. I've no appetite. Listen, I better go.'

'Ah, stay. Andrew will be home later – you haven't seen him in years.'

'No, don't worry – tell him I said hello.'

'Jonny, stay and talk to him. He has loads of work – I'm sure he could give you something.'

'I don't need any work. I'm just after telling you about the school.'

'I'm worried about you. Please stay.'

'Are you happy?'

'What kind of question is that?'

'It was my job to look after you.'

'And you did.'

'So he's a good man? He's good to you?'

'What's got into you?'

Jonny looked at her, his eyes yellow and tired. 'I mean I wish we didn't live in this place, but that's nothing new.

'Look after yourself, right? I mean that. Look after yourself. Don't leave it to anybody else.'

'What are you talking about?'

'I'll see you, right? Bye, boys!' he shouted as he walked towards the front door.

It was an unexpectedly swift farewell, one that was in motion before Marion could fully participate. Jonny closed the front door behind him, not knowing that the next time he came looking for his sister, it would be at a different door in a very different place.

Chapter 27

In 1985, two events occurred in quick succession, both of which convinced Marion she had to leave the estate. The first one was during the summer holidays. The boys were playing out on the green with the other children, while Marion watched them from the kitchen window as she did the washing-up. Jonathan came over to stand just below the open window and asked if he could go and play video games at one of the boys' flats. Marion knew the mother of the boy and agreed, telling Jonathan to take Robbie with him and to be back in time for tea.

But ten minutes later, she heard knocking at the door. Robbie was crying, his face chewed up by the effort of speaking and understanding at the same time. Jonathan was behind him, quiet and impassive, his hand resting on his brother's shoulder.

'What happened?' In the distance, Marion heard the approach of sirens. 'Christ.'

'In Sandham Court—'

'Get in here.' She pulled a sobbing Robbie and Jonathan, still attached by a need to protect his little brother, inside and slammed the door shut behind them. 'What's happened? Tell me right now. Jonathan?'

'They were fighting. And then one of them had a knife.'

'Fucking Jesus!' She began lifting Robbie's top, looking for a wound, for blood, for any sign that someone had messed with one of her babies.

'It's not us, Mum. Calm down.'

'Who had a knife? Are you hurt?' she said, peering closely at Jonathan as though any violence would replay itself against the black screen of his pupils.

'No, Mum. Listen. We're fine. It was a gang and they just started fighting. We were waiting for the lift and one of them pulled out a knife really near Robbie.'

'Oh my Christ. What did you do?'

'I grabbed him and we ran.'

'Good boy. Oh, good boy,' she said, falling to her knees and pulling both of her sons to her.

By the time the police were knocking on doors, news had gone round the estate that a fifteen-year-old boy was in a critical condition in hospital. Marion phoned Li and asked her to come over.

'How much did they see?'

'Jonathan said they saw the knife being pulled, but that was it. He grabbed Robbie and they ran home.'

'Are they OK?'

'Jonathan is, but Robbie's very shaken up. He's lying down,' Marion said, turning in the direction of the lounge. Robbie was laid out on the sofa, his head propped up by cushions, watching television.

'Did Jon see the boy who did it?'

'Jonathan. He saw the knife. I don't know if he saw the boy who pulled it out.'

'Whatever. It doesn't matter. He needs to say nothing. You do nothing.'

'Li, the boy nearly bled to death.'

'It doesn't matter. It wasn't your boy, and if you say anything to the police, it could well be one of them next time. You say nothing. Do you understand?'

'Yes.'

Li, concerned by Marion, managed to get a message to Andrew. He came home early that evening, agitated and ready, not for the near miss his sons had experienced but for the impending assault of his wife, whose desperation to leave the estate was becoming increasingly unmanageable.

'He'd have bled out in the stairwell if the ambulance hadn't got to him. Like a stuck pig!' They were in the lounge, standing up as they shouted at one another. The boys had gone to bed.

'But nothing happened, did it?'

'Jonathan said it was *this* close,' she said with her forefinger and thumb an inch apart, her nails filed to a point.

'It was never going to be for them. You don't understand – you haven't grown up on this estate like I have – but it's gangs. They're not interested in knifing a six-year-old.'

'And I don't want *them* growing up in this godforsaken place. Robbie couldn't stop crying; Jonathan's gone to bed as pale as the sheet. I can't live here anymore, Andrew!'

'Listen to me. No one's going to hurt them. I wouldn't let anyone hurt them.'

'You weren't there this afternoon! And neither was I. Jesus, Andrew, the feller who did it is probably walking free right now. I've got Li telling me to keep my mouth shut in case they come after the boys. I don't know how much more of this I can take.'

'She's right.' He sat down and held his hand out to her. 'Come here.'

Marion sat beside him with her arms folded across her chest. Andrew pulled at one of them and tried to hold her hand. 'Li's right. You can't say anything to the police. On this estate, you deal with your own problems. And today, I know you can't get your head round this yet, but today was not for us. It's a problem for someone else. So we move on and mind our own business. Look at me.'

She turned to face him.

'You keep your mouth shut. Do you understand?'

She stood up and walked towards the window.

'Because if you don't, it'll be Jon and Rob they hurt, not you and me.'

'Andrew, I've never asked for anything from you—'

'That's not true. You ask me for money all the time, but go on.'

'I'd give up the money, the clothes, everything. Just get us out of this place. Can you do that?' She turned to face him.

'I know it's not perfect.'

'I'm not joking. If you don't look into it, I will.'

'What are you talking about?'

'I'll take them to Ireland.' She scanned the room, her gaze held momentarily by the space above Andrew's head. 'I'll stay with my auntie Brida. She'll have us. Artane's rough but nothing like this.'

He followed her eyes, saw how they moved restlessly around the room, and in order to pinion them to his face, he jumped up and grabbed her throat, pushing her backwards. He held her up against the wall and began shouting as her eyes widened in concentration.

'You're not taking my sons anywhere. Do you hear me?'

She wanted to nod, but he'd disabled any movement of her head.

'I'm not having them grow up in Ireland.'

She gurgled her agreement. The saliva spilled over her lower lip and drooled lightly onto his hand. He released her and turned away as Marion collapsed to the floor like a cat, curving her back as she tried to remember how to breathe.

He sat down on the sofa and watched her retch. 'Look, I don't want to stay here for ever either. But for now, we're near my mum and Steve.'

'I couldn't give a fuck about Steve,' she managed to cough.

'Don't push me, Marion.'

'I'm not scared of you,' she said, dipping her lower back so she could face him.

'I don't want you to be scared of me.'

'You think you can throw me around. That you can play the tough guy with me.'

'Leave off. I said I'm sorry.'

'You did not say you were sorry.'

'I just don't like you talking about taking my kids away. That's not right, Marion.'

'I'm not interested in what you like.' She sat back against the wall, her long legs open wide before her. 'I want you to get us out of here.' She reached her hand up to the windowsill in order to pull herself up to standing. 'I'm not going to stop,' she said, limping slowly out of the room. 'You can beat me until I'm black and blue, but I'm not going to stop until you get us out of here.'

*

Marion's injunction to Andrew hardened overnight and became her own rallying cry. The following morning, she took the boys up to Lorraine's flat and asked her to look after them for a few hours. She had a few errands to run and she didn't want them playing outside after the events of the day before. Lorraine, who was meek in everything, accepted the delivery of her grandsons and set about making their breakfast while Marion bid them a hurried farewell. She made her way to Stockwell Tube Station, where she took the Northern line up to Holborn. She had to ask a passer-by for directions to the Aldwych, but as she skirted the corner from Kingsway, she found St Catherine's House and went inside.

Andrew's birth certificate bore the names of his parents: George William Wilson and Lorraine Steadham. Under 'usual address', Marion found what she was looking for: an address in Claygate, Surrey. She made a note of it and gathered her things together. At Holborn Tube Station, she queued up at the ticket office to ask what train would take her to Claygate.

Do it quickly, she said to herself as she boarded a train at Waterloo. She knew Lorraine would tell Andrew about her long absence and that she'd have some explaining to do, but as Clapham Junction came into view, Marion knew she'd gone further in a morning than Andrew ever would. Her own mother had been brave enough to take the boat, and here she was, taking the train, into a middle-class heartland full of people who knew bricks and newspapers, coffees and Conservatives. They didn't carry knives; their skin wasn't thinly sewn over bones vibrating with violence. Her journey to Claygate felt necessary – it was her sons' right and she wasn't going to be cowed. She thought of Lorraine, closeted behind her front door, confined to her little box, accepting of every burden, and as the trees flew past, she rejected it all. Do it quickly.

At Claygate Station, an attendant pointed her in the direction of the road she was looking for. Marion, who'd spent the morning in Central London, felt the expanse as a burden. Everything was further apart and her feet began to hurt. The wide pavements and solid houses, set back with generous front gardens, represented the frontier of a new world. It didn't matter that her only link to that world was a violent man she'd never met who'd beaten his wife and young son. She came from a long line of uncomfortable truths. She wanted to cross another boundary with her sons, to settle them in a better place with better people.

It took her ten minutes to walk along the road and find the brown stable door of her father-in-law's house. The house that would one day become home. She knocked on the top half and waited. A minute passed before she heard an uncertain voice: 'Who is it?'

'My name's Marion. I'm married to your son, Andrew.'

She heard the shuffling of footsteps and a key in the lock. The top half of the door was pulled back to reveal a small man with a pale head. Marion saw that his hair was thin and grey on top but thicker, with darker curls that put her in mind of Andrew's, round the side. He squinted into the sun and put his hand above his eyes like a visor in order to peer at Marion more closely.

'Who did you say you are?'

'I'm married to your boy. Remember him?'

'Of course I do.'

'I've come to introduce myself. And to tell you that you've got two grandsons. Can I come in?'

Mr Wilson looked down, as though he were searching for

words of apology, but he released a catch that allowed him to open the bottom half. He stepped back and held both halves open for Marion to step down into the hallway.

'Come on in.'

He directed her into the lounge. It was stuffy and dry, shot through by thin, fetid air. Marion put her hand over her mouth and looked around. There was no sofa, only three armchairs, one of which had a newspaper stuffed down the side of it, the cushion still depressed. Marion imagined reaching out to touch it, what it would smell like and felt as though she might be sick.

'Mr Wilson, I'm not going to stay long.'

'Call me George. Let me make you a cup of tea. I've just made one for myself so the water's still hot.'

'Grand. Thank you.'

'Please. Sit down.'

Marion pulled her handbag up onto her knees and began digging around inside. 'I wanted to show you some photos,' she said. 'That's Jonathan there – he's my eldest – and next to him is Robbie. He's seven next month.'

George looked up cautiously. 'Does Andrew know you're here?'

'No.'

He handed back the photo. 'I'm not sure this is a good idea.'

'Listen, George, I don't know what went on between yous all those years ago, but I know my boys have a right to know where they've come from. Who they are. My own mother and father passed a while ago. You and Lorraine are the only grandparents they have.'

'Lorraine. She still alive, is she?'

'She is. She's looking after Jonathan and Robbie right now.'

'I was a different man back then. I suppose they've told you I hurt them?'

Marion nodded.

'I drank, you see.'

'So I hear.'

'Where are you from?'

'Dublin originally. My family came over when I was thirteen.'

'I don't drink anymore.'

'Good for you.'

'Haven't touched the stuff for fifteen years.'

'There you go. It just goes to show it's never too late.'

'Oh, it's too late. That's for sure.'

Marion stayed for an hour but stood up to leave when George offered her another cup of tea. As she approached the front door, George shuffled on ahead and pulled the top half back.

'You're not expecting me to jump over that thing, are you?'

He coughed a smoker's laugh. 'It was here when we moved in and I've always liked it. You can frame the sunset, like a picture.'

Marion stood next to him for a moment and looked out onto the residential road. 'That's quite a picture,' she said. George patted her hand. 'It's all his, you know.'

'What is?'

And as if he were gifting the houses opposite, and not his own, he said, 'This house. I've left it to Andrew in my will. I have no other family. It'll be my way of saying sorry. Do you think he'll ever forgive me?'

Marion reached down to pull the bottom half back. 'No, George, I don't think so. But I do. And my boys will.'

*

The second incident occurred a month later, when Robbie turned seven. He'd asked for a pair of Reebok trainers, a gift Andrew had given Marion the cash to fulfil. But that afternoon, as he played on the estate with his brother and friends, some older boys had approached Robbie and, without touching him, threatened to cut his throat. They produced no knife, but the verbal threat was enough, especially after the violence they'd witnessed a few weeks ago. Jonathan told Robbie to take his trainers off, and as the thieves walked away calmly, Jonathan and Robbie ran frantically back to Marshall Court.

Marion felt as though her boys were closer this time. That the arc of the slashing knife had widened and their skin would be next. Using the phone she'd had recently installed, she called Andrew at the lock-up and screamed at him to come home.

He looked down at his younger son, standing in the hallway in his socks. Marion stood beside him, her hands on her hips.

'What's happened?'

'Look at your son's feet,' she said with quiet rage.

'I'm looking. What's wrong?'

'Some fucking bastard stole his new trainers today. That's what.'

'You're joking.'

'Do I look like I'm joking? Now do you see?'

'Calm down,' he said, kneeling before Robbie. 'Tell me what happened. What did they do?'

But it was Jonathan who spoke from the doorway of the boys' bedroom. 'They said they'd cut his throat if he didn't hand them over.'

'They said that to you?'

'To all of us.'

'And what did you do?'

'We gave them the trainers.'

Andrew hung his head. 'Son, on this estate, you have to stand up for yourself.'

'Are you fucking mad? He was going to cut your son's throat and you're disappointed he didn't lay himself out for the knife?'

'Did you see a knife?'

'No,' Jonathan said quietly.

'Who was it, son?'

Jonathan shrugged. 'I'm not sure.'

'Who were they with?'

'Dean,' Robbie supplied.

'Dean who?'

'From Rushby Court,' Jonathan conceded. 'He was with them but didn't do anything.'

'Right. You stay here and be good for your mum. I'm going out for a bit.'

'Where are you going?' asked Marion.

'To sort this out. No one robs from my sons. And until they're old enough to make sure of that themselves, I'll have to do it.'

'Andrew—'

'Just get them to bed. You wanted me to sort this out and that's what I'm going to do.'

Andrew was gone all evening. He returned in the early hours of the morning, stealing into bed beside his wife. She was aware of the mattress sagging beneath her and then the bursts of digested beer that filled the room with each gentle exhalation as he started to snore.

Marion took the boys to Larkhall Park while Andrew slept

in the following morning. She dropped them off at Lorraine's afterwards and went up the stairs to Li's flat, where she knocked quietly. Steve opened the door. He was dressed in shorts and T-shirt, his eyes red and puffy.

'Is Li here?'

'Brixton. Gone to do a bit of shopping.'

'Can I come in?'

'If you must,' he said, stepping back.

Marion walked into the lounge, but Steve didn't follow her. He went into the kitchen, where she heard him opening drawers and cupboards. She entered as he pulled two slices of white bread from the bread bin and put them in the toaster.

'Were you out with Andrew last night?'

He looked up at her and smiled. 'You'll have to ask him that.'

'I will. But I want to hear it from you. What did you do last night?'

'Like I said. You'll have to ask him.'

'Did you go after the boy that took Robbie's trainers?'

'We sort our own problems out on this estate. We don't go to the police. We don't run away.'

'What's that supposed to mean?'

'You Irish. You're different to us. Something's difficult so you run away. Get drunk. Blame it on others.'

'What do you know about the Irish?'

He stood up and walked towards her. 'That they're sticky.'

Marion stared back at him, their eyes level in new understanding. The toast popped up and tried to pull Steve back to the business of his breakfast.

'Tell Li I was here. That I'm looking for her.'

Steve laughed at her. 'He won't always be this nice to you, you know. And when he isn't' – he smiled again, his jaw opening just wide enough to let the words out – 'I'll be there to pick up the pieces.'

Marion ran down the steps and out onto the estate. With every step she winced: here or there but never anywhere. Never anywhere she wanted to be. Always visiting, shifting, settling. She looked behind her at Strudwick Court, at the little window that contained Steve and all his malice towards her, and then without moving her body, turned her head back towards Marshall Court and a life she'd never chosen. She took a deep breath and looked up at the sky. As the clouds moved across the blue, offended by the concrete fingers that reached towards them, she felt a painful stretch in her throat. She knew that a wrong step would cast her into the scattered turds, the piss-stained lift, a beating from her husband. She could tell Andrew about Steve and hope for some reassurance, but in the end, what could he ever give her? A character summary of his cousin, an outline of his personality that would somehow account for his hostile attitude towards her? She knew Steve was right, that he'd identified a truth she was dimly aware of herself: Andrew's love, if you could call it that, was already waning. He had grown tired of her and her incessant demands to move, and one day, he would stop being nice to her. She thought of Lorraine holed up in her flat and understood, for the first time, why that might be necessary when your husband has turned on you.

She let herself into the flat and crept along to the bedroom where Andrew was still sleeping off the night before. She stepped out of her clothes and, leaving a little pile on the carpet, climbed into bed, naked, beside her husband.

Chapter 28

Andrew and Steve had beaten a man in Rushby Court to within an inch of his life. That was what Li told her, with some satisfaction, later that same day.

'Course, I don't know for sure it was them. But the word on the estate this morning is that it was his son who took Robbie's trainers.'

'When did it happen?'

'Yesterday – around eight o'clock, I think. Two blokes called for him, dragged him out to the stairwell and beat the living daylights out of him.'

'Oh Jesus,' Marion said, lowering her forehead to the table. She remembered Andrew's hands on her that morning, how he'd pulled her naked body towards his.

'Hey, hey,' Li said, reaching out to touch the crown of her head. She stroked downwards, once, twice and then took her hand back. 'We look after our own. That's what they were doing – protecting Robbie. No one'll touch him now. You'll see.'

'And do you think that's right, Li? To nearly kill a man because *his son* did something wrong.'

'No, I don't think it's right. But don't kid yourself. His son was involved and he needs to be taught a lesson.'

'I can't do this,' she said, standing up.

'There's nothing for you to do,' Li said, stubbing out her cigarette and standing up to put her hands on Marion's shoulders. 'Andrew's taken care of it. And he'll take care of you. You've got nothing to worry about.'

But at the end of September Marion decided it was time for another visit to Claygate. And this time she took the boys with her. George was pleased to see her when he opened the door. He took the boys in as one might a glass of water after a long thirst: in an effort to disguise the extent of his longing, he worked hard to maintain eye contact with Marion, but the shifting of his eyes told its own story. He was greedy for his grandsons.

'Come on in. Please. I'm afraid I haven't tidied up. I didn't know you were coming.'

'I know. I'm sorry, George. I must take your telephone number so I can phone ahead next time.'

'Next time. Oh yes. Next time, we'll arrange it.'

Jonathan stepped down into the hallway first and, walking over to the stairs, stood by the bottom step so he could look up at the point at which they twisted away from him. He'd never lived in a home with stairs inside, carpeted and soft, exclusively for his own use. Robbie joined him at the bottom and together they looked up and left, like a pair of meerkats.

'You'd think they'd never been inside a house before. Boys, say hello to your granddad. This is your da's dad.'

George looked down at his slippered feet and searched for something he could give them. These boys who'd grown from a son he'd tried – in another life – to cut down. It was too much to apologise for. They'd never understand the depth of his sorrow or the urgency of his need to atone. Instead, he said, 'You can go upstairs if you want to.'

'Ah no, George. Boys, go on in the lounge and sit down. And don't touch anything.'

'I don't have anything for you. I mean, I have some bread and butter. Would you like me to nip out to the shops? I could buy some cake? What do they like?'

'Don't worry about us. I'll have a cup of tea and then we could take them for a walk. Is there a park near here?'

'Yes, there are some swings a few roads away that are popular with the mums round here. I'll put the kettle on.'

'Go way out of that. You go on in there and talk to your grandsons. I'll make the tea.'

The work surface was busy with crumbs, medication and old teabags that had been squeezed and forgotten on teaspoons. Marion lifted the loaf of bread from the chopping board and put it in the bread bin. She looked around the sink for a cloth but couldn't find one, so using her right hand as a scoop, she swept the crumbs into her waiting left hand and deposited everything in the sink. Then she filled the kettle and put it on to boil. She was just opening the cupboard to look for the teabags when she heard a knock at the door.

'I'll get it,' Marion said, but realised – as she approached it – she had no idea how to open it.

'Just undo the top latch! Both panels are together,' George shouted from the lounge.

Marion opened the door, remembering as she looked up at the small, neat figure of Jane Campbell that the hallway was lower than the doorstep. 'Can I help you?'

'Oh, I'm sorry. I was looking for Mr Wilson. I'm his neighbour.'

'George! There's somebody here for you.'

George shuffled out to the hallway. 'Hello, Jane.'

'Morning. I'm just about to head out to the shops with the girls. I wondered if you need anything.'

'No, I'm OK, thank you. I have my daughter-in-law here.'

'Oh, I see.' Jane smiled at Marion. 'I didn't realise you had a son,' she said to George, but continued looking at Marion.

'I'm married to his son. We've got two boys together.'

'I see. Well, very nice to meet you. I'll leave you alone in that case.'

They had planned to go for a walk after tea, but Marion could see George was too tired. 'I think you need to go to bed,' she said as he tried to pull himself from his armchair. 'You don't look well.'

He coughed, using his upturned fist to mark the rhythm in his sternum. 'It's this chest infection. I can't shake it. Will the boys be very disappointed?' he whispered.

They looked over at Jonathan and Robbie, slumped in the armchairs watching the television.

'Don't worry about them. How about we come back in a week or two? When you're feeling better?'

'Yes, please, Marion. I'd like that.'

Marion waited for Andrew to come home that evening, knowing that when he did, the boys would tell them they'd been to see their grandfather. But her courage wavered as she waited for him to find her in the kitchen. She stood up and walked back towards the windowsill where she kept the knife block.

'What's this about going to see their granddad? Your dad?'

'Andrew, you know my da's dead.'

'I know that. I mean to his grave or something—'

'George Wilson. That's who we went to see today.'

His arms hung limply at his sides. 'With the boys? You went to him behind my back?'

'For the second time, yes.'

'You want to be fucking joking.' He walked towards her, his right hand curling into a fist.

'I'm not joking. And don't take another step towards me, do you hear?'

'You've got some nerve,' he said, his face flushing red.

'I tell you what I've got,' she said, reaching behind her for a knife. 'I've got to get my boys out of here. I told you that.'

'And you think this is the way to do it? By going to see my dad. A man you know nothing about. Nothing about what he did to me and my mum.'

'I know he's sick, Andrew—'

'Too fucking right.'

'Really sick. You know, physically. And that he wants to give you his house. A great big house.'

'I don't want anything from him.'

'But I do! I want that house and all that it'll give us. And I'm not too proud to go and see him and wait for him to die.'

He relaxed his fist and sat down. 'Jesus, Marion. What do you want from me? I can't go and see him.' With his arm resting on the back of the chair, he ran his fingers through his hair. 'My mum hasn't come out of her flat for years. And all because of what he did. Do you know what he did?'

'Yes.'

'Because I don't think you do. I don't think if you really knew—'

'He's spent. It's all gone. He's an old man with a lot of money. He can't do anything to you anymore.'

'I'd fucking kill him. Smash him to pieces—'

'There's no need.' She put the knife down and went to kneel in front of him. 'Andrew' – she took his hand – 'it's over. He can't hurt you or Lorraine ever again.'

'I couldn't protect her. I was too small. And now look at her,' he said, pointing uselessly at the window, his lower lip trembling.

'Listen to me. I'm not excusing what he did. And neither is he. He knows what he did was wrong. What I'm saying is, he wants to make amends. And give you and your family something.'

'He's seen the boys, has he?'

'Today.'

'What did he say?'

'It's not what he said. It's how he is. He couldn't take his eyes off them.'

He shook his head. 'It's not happening, Marion. I can't just pretend he didn't ruin me and my mum's life.'

'You don't have to do anything. I'll go. With the boys. He's not well, Andrew. I've seen the medication.'

'I want nothing to do with him.'

'But on my own. What if you just left it to me?'

'No. Steve and Li won't like it.'

'Don't be worrying about those two. This is about you and me. And our boys.'

Three weeks later, Marion returned to Surrey with Jonathan and Robbie. They stopped at a supermarket on the way and bought cakes and a loaf of fresh bread and milk. After tea, they walked to the park, where the boys played on the roundabout; they were so loud and ambitious for its rotation that other children were deterred from joining them. Marion lit a cigarette and sat down on a nearby bench. George joined her and together they watched the boys.

'It's great to see them playing together. Thank you for bringing them to see me.'

'That's OK. I want them to get out and see there's life outside of the estate.'

'This is the Studley Estate?'

'That's right.'

'I know Lillian – Lorraine's sister – has a flat there.'

'And Lorraine a couple of floors below her.'

'Yes, I know. I've tried in the past to get in touch, but I'm too old now.'

'You'd have a job, George. She doesn't open the door to anyone. Doesn't go out.'

'I ruined her.'

Marion smoked beside him, watching a small, overweight mother place her toddler at the top of the slide. She opened her arms in encouragement, willing the child to let go. 'Don't be so hard on yourself.'

'Eh?'

'We all make our own way in life. And Lorraine's is to hide away.'

'She hides away because of what I did to her.'

'So why don't you make it up?'

'The damage is done. There's a reason Andrew's never come near me. He hates me. I wouldn't know where to begin.'

'You could begin with his sons.'

George nodded and looked down at the cigarette butts on the hard grey ground. 'I'm not sure how much time I have left for that. For getting to know them, I mean.'

'Are you sick?' Marion asked abruptly.

'Heart disease.' He gave her a wry smile. 'I haven't looked after myself, as you might imagine. Living on my own all these years. Not that I'm blaming anyone – it's all my own fault.'

Marion watched Robbie, who, with one foot on the ground, pushed hard to propel the roundabout while Jonathan held on, resisting the pull of the centrifugal force. 'I'm sorry to hear that, George,' Marion said, reaching into her handbag for her packet of cigarettes. 'Would you like one?'

They went home and had more tea. Marion made some sandwiches while the boys watched TV in the lounge. George sat in his armchair and read the paper. Just after three o'clock, as George's eyes started to close, Marion stood up and announced they'd better head home.

At the front door, George kissed her cheek and thanked her for bringing the boys to see him. 'It's more than I deserve.'

As they walked away, Marion waited for the sound of the front door closing. And as soon as it did, she turned her steps towards the house next door.

'Where are you going?' Jonathan asked from the pavement.

'Just wait there, will you?'

Jane answered the door and smiled. 'Oh, hello again. Is everything OK?'

'Yes, fine, thank you. I just wanted to leave my name and telephone number with you. You know, in case you need to get in touch with us.'

'Oh yes, let me just find my address book.' Jane turned her back on Marion as she pulled the drawer of the telephone table out. 'Please, come in,' she said, looking up and tucking her hair behind her ear as she searched the drawer.

'I won't, thank you. The boys are waiting for me.'

'Oh, right. Here it is,' she said, handing Marion a small black leather book, opened to 'W'. 'Will you just write your name and address in there? Here's a pen.'

'Thank you,' Marion said. 'Please God you'll never need to contact us, but you never know.'

Part III:

Becca and Jonathan

It is given as the foundation of family life in which children are born and nurtured.

The Marriage Service

Chapter 29

In 1988, the year before Marion left, Becca started at the same girls' school Jane had attended. She was aware of how her parents had met – she knew her mother had been a pupil of her father's – but it was only when she was seated at one of the desks in a fusty classroom in the old block that she began to question the nature of their coming together. Her teachers were *old*. She decided to ask her parents about it, the evening that followed her first day at secondary school. They were in the kitchen, Jane was peeling potatoes by the sink, the bulk of her attention claimed by a hardback open on the work surface. She had used a small potato to pin down the lighter half. Leonard was sitting at the table reading the newspaper.

'How's my big girl?' he asked brightly as she walked into the room.

'Tired,' she said, pulling a chair out beside him. He leaned over to move the briefcase he'd deposited there.

'It is tiring, isn't it? That's why they have the young ones start a couple of days early. Before the rest of the school returns.'

'Did they do that when you taught at my school?'

Jane rinsed a potato under the tap and dropped it into the pot.

Leonard scratched his cheekbone. 'I can't remember. I never taught the lower school.'

'So you never taught eleven-year-olds?'

Leonard put down the paper. 'I don't think I did. Why do you ask?'

'But then how did you meet Mummy?'

Jane picked a large potato from the bag and turned the peeler so that she could gouge a green spot from the flesh with its sharp end.

'Mummy wasn't in her first year when we met,' Leonard laughed.

'I was eighteen, darling.'

'Well, not quite,' Leonard corrected.

'The point is,' she said, looking from the potato to Leonard, 'I was an adult. Pretty much.'

She remembered Jamie's hand tight around her wrist, attempting to pull her from the foyer. 'I wanted to be with Daddy and I was old enough to make that decision.'

'I don't want to marry any of my teachers.'

'Oh, Becca,' Jane laughed, and crouched down in front of her daughter so she could take her hands in hers. 'You don't have to marry your teachers. I didn't *have* to marry Daddy. I wanted to.' She twisted her neck so that Leonard might respond, but squatted down on her haunches, she was unable to complete the turn. 'Isn't that right?'

'Oh, everybody wanted to, Becca. I had a class of twelve clamouring for my hand. But Mummy was the prettiest, cleverest girl by far.'

'Leonard—'

He coughed. 'No, that's right. We chose to get married,

but Mummy was a lot older than you are now. And we're both jolly glad we did now that we have you and Julia.'

Becca became accustomed to life at secondary school. And with the absence of Jonathan, who'd gone to the boys' comprehensive several miles away, she found she was better able to seek out her own company. The library was large and dark enough to swallow her solitude and turn it into apparent diligence and endeavour.

In her second year, she had an English teacher called Mr Dobson. He rarely shaved, and his jackets were shabby and covered in lint, hanging off his shoulders in apology for his meagre frame. He looked as though he rolled out of bed in the morning and in his despair just about found the strength to pull a suit from the hanger and dress himself. Had a narrator emerged from behind him as he walked from his car to the school building and explained that Mr Dobson had had no breakfast or his socks were the same as yesterday's, nobody – colleagues and pupils alike – would have been surprised.

He looked unfit to lead a group of thirty girls in academic exploration of a text, but when he spoke, Becca got the sense of his other life – the hours he spent writing – and began to see that, for him, teaching was about survival, subsistence so he could inhabit his imagination each evening.

He began a topic on short stories by handing out copies of 'Billennium' by J.G. Ballard.

'This is called a short story,' he said to the back of the room. 'It's a form favoured by—'

Becca put up her hand.

'Yes' – he ran his hand through his greasy hair – 'er . . .'

'Becca, sir.'

'Yes, sorry. Becca.'

'Where can I read more of these?'

'Let's just concentrate on this one for the time being.'

Becca didn't see the other girls rolling their eyes at her. Her enthusiasm for the short story was just another example of her strangeness, and yet it was precisely the *otherness* of the short story that appealed to Becca. The self-contained story that began with little ceremony and worked its way to a conclusion that became suddenly – almost painfully – logical delighted her anew each time.

They were asked to write their own. Two to three thousand words on a topic of their choice. Becca, with a spontaneity she would eventually come to recognise as the gift of the writer, turned to the back of her exercise book and began immediately. The task, written up on the board, was a crude invitation to something sublime within her.

She wrote about a roach fish that believed itself happy as it swam along the bottom of a river. But as it grew fat and contented on the riverbed, it began to wonder what led the other fish to rise to the surface. So one day it followed, and when it saw the morsel of food hanging in the water, it understood why they'd all abandoned the bottom. In the act of opening its mouth – of enjoying the first rush of experience – it found itself pulled from the water, flying through the air in a swift arc of terror.

'What're you doing?'

Becca looked up. She was in the library and Danielle Simpson was standing before her. 'Just writing my short story.'

'You've already done it? Oh my God, Becks.'

Becca put down her pen.

'Listen,' Danielle said, sitting down. 'You know my mum's ill, don't you?' She sat on the corner of a chair, ready to spring.

'No, I didn't know.'

'Well, she is. And it's been really hard for me to find time to study. I don't know how I'm going to get this homework done.'

'You could come and sit here with me. I won't disturb you.'

'I've got to go and have my lunch. Haven't had any yet.'

'Neither have—'

'But you've written that so quickly. Do you think you could do one for me? Pretty please? Just this once?'

Becca looked down at her story and felt her stomach growl. 'I don't think I can. I was going to go and get lunch too.'

'Why don't I have this one and you can write another one later? Come to lunch with us if you like? Tracey and the others are waiting outside the canteen.'

She knew, even as Danielle ripped the pages from the back of her exercise book, that she should have stayed in the library, but she followed her out and into the canteen because, just like her roach fish, she longed – sometimes inexplicably – to join the light and play that bubbled at the surface.

Danielle never read the story. She copied it quickly and without examination into her own exercise book and handed it in the following week. But Becca, though she was sorry to see her writing passed off as someone else's, saw her story as payment for entry to another world. She was absorbed by Danielle's group, permitted to join them at lunch and break times, to sit with them during registration and on the bus home in the afternoon.

Mr Dobson marked the short stories on a Sunday evening two weeks after setting the homework. He'd drawn the curtains on a damp and disappointing day and turned on the lamps in his lounge, put on some Joni Mitchell and poured himself a large glass of red wine. His preferred seat for marking was a deep beanbag. The glass of wine and pile of green exercise books stood, like two sentinels, on the small TV stand to his right, and he worked his way through both, his deep impression among the beans making any frivolous trips to the kitchen or outside for a cigarette unlikely.

But he stood up when he read Danielle's story. The words – so obviously not her own – copied in Danielle's large, looping, self-consciously neat handwriting struck him as obscene. He was so affronted he drained his glass of wine and tipped left onto his waiting hand so that he might push himself up into a squat. Folding the exercise book on itself, he opened the back door and stepped outside. It was like peering through a dirty oven door at something perfectly risen.

The following morning, he put a note in Danielle's form tutor's pigeonhole and asked for her to be sent to his classroom immediately after registration. He beckoned to Danielle as the last stragglers from his form pulled belongings from their lockers at the back of the room.

'Miss Simpson. Have a seat, please.'

'Sir? I've got chemistry.'

'Sit down.'

'Where?'

'Right here,' he said, pointing to a row of chairs in front of his desk.

'Sir.'

'I want to talk to you about your short story.'

'Did you like it, sir?'

'Yes, very much,' Mr Dobson said, sitting down at his desk and crossing his ankles. 'I thought it was excellent.'

'Thank you.'

'How did you come up with it?'

'Eh?'

'The idea. How did you come up with it?'

'I just thought of it.'

'So it just came to you?'

'Something like that.'

'And the idea of the fish fattening itself on the riverbed, never seeking the enjoyments of the surface. I take it that's a metaphor?'

'Er. Yeah.'

'What for?'

'For the homework.'

'No, what was the metaphor meant to signify?'

'Nothing. It's just something I thought up.'

'Right. And what's the significance of the ending?'

'Just that. It's an ending.'

'I see. And, Miss Simpson, if I may, I have one more question for you. What is a roach?'

'It's something you use to . . . Er, you find it in the sea.'

'You don't know, do you?'

'Yeah, I do. I've just forgotten, that's all.'

'It's a fish. It's the fish at the centre of your story.'

'Yeah, that's it.'

'Miss Simpson, you did not write this story. Of that I am certain. And the pages ripped out of the back of Rebecca Campbell's exercise book would suggest she wrote it and, for whatever reason, allowed you to plagiarise her work. When you go to chemistry, kindly inform Miss Campbell I'd like to see her at break time, please.'

When Becca knocked on Mr Dobson's classroom door, she was preparing her defence. Danielle had pleaded with her to say that it was a joint venture, that they'd worked on it together, but Becca knew from the resigned look on Mr Dobson's face that there was no point. He saw it all.

'I'm sorry, sir.'

'Becca,' he said, standing up and walking towards her. 'I have very little to say to you except this. Your short story was extraordinary. Do you understand what I mean by that?'

'Yes, I—'

'No, you don't. But tell me, what was the significance of the roach?'

'I just liked the idea.'

'The idea of what?'

'Of all that water, all those other fish. And he finds it easier to stay by himself.'

'That's what I mean when I say extraordinary. I don't think anybody else could have written it. And certainly not that cretin Simpson.'

'Sir.'

'If you remember anything from this incident, Becca, let it be this: never give yourself away so cheaply again.'

'Yes, sir.'

'Now go.'

Chapter 30

Jane awaited the Wilson boys' knock on her door every morning. In the weeks and months following Marion's departure, she stepped into the role of surrogate mother, checking they had their lunch, done their homework, brushed their hair if necessary and straightened their uniforms in the same way she did with her own daughters. It was an offering to Andrew, who set off for work early each morning, and a kindness to Marion, a woman who'd come to her for help and finding no friendly ear, had decided she had no option but to abandon her family for good. But most of all it was an act of love for Becca, who came alive in Jonathan's presence. She saw her daughter's eagerness for the boy, how they pored over drawings and notebooks together. Becca, who had never so much as been invited to play at another child's house, had a friend. Someone as interested in her as she was in him. And so she continued to mother the boys in an attempt to give something precious to her daughter.

In the wake of their loss, Jonathan grew closer to the Campbells through Becca, but Robbie, a school year above Julia, found he had nothing in common with a girl who was not only younger than him but far more studious. In fact,

Julia's devotion to books and learning in general – while it made her a favourite of her father and her teachers – was off-putting to most children her age. Her classmates regarded her as aloof, superior and unpleasant to be around. She cared very little for friendships and didn't work to foster one with Robbie, who began making trouble for himself.

He was never late, because Jane ensured they set off at the same time together each morning, but he was inattentive in class, rude to teachers who pointed out his lack of concentration and rough in the playground. He saw any physical play as an opportunity to pound too hard, to pull where he shouldn't and punch in retreat. His mother's sudden and unexplained departure from his life had wounded him so deeply he didn't know where he bled from or how extensive the bruising. He just understood, in the way he sought to hurt others, that he'd been very seriously injured. So seriously he need not worry about the consequences of his own actions, for he surely couldn't survive his whole life without ever seeing his mother again.

The teachers had been informed of the circumstances. They digested the details in chunks they could process: the mother wasn't dead; she'd abandoned the family to return to Ireland; the father was struggling to bring them up on his own; the mother of the Campbell girls was helping and should be contacted in an emergency.

But for Robbie their understanding was an outrage. It was something he wanted to pinch and bite and suck from them. The details still left him stranded and alone in the playground – the other boys, now wary, kept their distance more each day – and always, always hopeful that his mother would be outside the gates at three o'clock. It was like a terrible wound on a much-used joint. No matter how quickly it scabbed over, he'd just as quickly forget and, straining to see her, would break it open again.

Robbie understood that he was in pain, but he couldn't understand how it wasn't shared by his father or brother. They both went about their lives as though nothing had happened. The only tangible differences – apart from the devastating absence of his mother's voice and face and body – were that the house was always untidy, his bed was never made, and his breakfast bowl was still festering in the sink – exactly where he'd left it – after school and for the rest of the evening. He took it out the following morning and rinsed it under the tap before filling it with cornflakes again. It wasn't that he didn't understand he'd now have to do these things for himself – make the bed, wash up after himself; it was that he fought against them. Because the moment he began doing what his mother used to do for him was the moment he accepted she was gone for ever. And he couldn't do that.

It was Julia who noticed that Jane was doing more and more for the Wilsons. On days when Andrew knew he wouldn't be home for tea, Jane cooked for all four children, leaving a serving of whatever she'd made for Leonard sitting in a bowl above a saucepan of simmering water. If Andrew telephoned to say he was delayed, she'd oversee the boys' preparations for bed and once Leonard was home, would take them next door and sit up until Andrew came home. By June of that year, she had a ready supply of pyjamas for the boys and spare toothbrushes in the cup in the bathroom.

'When is Mrs Wilson coming back?' Julia asked one morning as she returned her toothbrush to the cup.

'I don't know, darling. Nobody knows.'

'She's been gone a long time.'

'I know. It's very difficult.'

'Why's it so difficult? Can't they find her?'

'Andrew knows where she is, but sometimes when mums and dads no longer get on, they decide to stay separated. And I think that's what has happened here.'

'But how long are you going to have to look after Jonathan and Robbie?'

Jane had been holding her cupped hand under the running tap, rinsing the toothpaste and saliva that flowed down the basin's sides with water. She stood up, straightening her spine, and dried her hand on her skirt.

'Until they're a bit older. I'm going to be a kind of child-minder to them.'

Julia dried her hands on a towel.

'Is that OK?'

'I don't know.'

'Do you not want them here?'

'Not really.'

'But, darling, imagine if I suddenly left you alone.' Jane licked her lower lip, aware she couldn't have begun a sentence like that within Becca's earshot. 'Wouldn't you want somebody to help Daddy?'

'Where would you go?'

'Nowhere. I just want you to understand that you're very lucky to have me and Daddy, and some children are not so fortunate. Shouldn't we help them?'

'Not any more. We've helped them enough. It's time for them to stand on their own two feet.'

'Where did you hear that phrase?'

'From Daddy. He said it last night when you took them home.'

'Well, Daddy should try to be more compassionate.

Perhaps you could tell him that next time. Now, go and get your uniform on – the boys will be here soon and you won't be ready.'

Chapter 31

In the years that followed Marion's departure, Jonathan and Robbie grew into the unmistakable forms of young men, their widening shoulders and chests making a mockery of their school uniforms. They no longer needed so much of Jane's attention, but she saw that Jonathan wanted to stay close to her family. He continued to return to their house after school to sit with Becca at the kitchen table and do his homework while Jane prepared dinner. She was happy for their closeness to continue. His influence on Becca was a good one: she appeared more confident, positive and spoke with the expectation of being listened to. Jane could see her daughter had found some stability that didn't involve her, so the muddled truth was not that Jane was helping the Wilsons but that Jonathan had helped Becca plant her feet hip-width apart and look around herself a bit more.

But one October night when Becca was around fourteen, she woke to the sound of her father's voice, raised and angry, downstairs. Leonard never shouted; he was emphatic and precise, carefully stringing his sentences together so that he might reach his listener and prod them into agreement. But that night was different. She got out of bed and tiptoed to the top of the stairs, where the sound flew and ricocheted inside the chasm of the stairwell.

'I don't understand this, Jane. It's not like we need the money. He's taking advantage of you and us.'

'His wife left him. His sons are our daughters' friends. What are we supposed to do? Just leave them to forage for food every night?'

'They're his responsibility! Just as you and the girls are mine. And frankly I need you to focus on us a little more. Is that too much to ask?'

'That's all I ever do! All of your washing; every evening meal you've ever eaten has been cooked by me. You have your study, silence and complete freedom to get on with whatever it is you want to do.'

'There was a time when what I enjoyed interested you too.'

'That was a long time ago, Leonard. I haven't got time to read nineteenth-century novels anymore. That's a luxury I can't afford.'

'A luxury! You spend all your time running after a common thug. And all because his disgusting wife abandoned her family. Are you about to do the same?'

'How could you? I've been a good wife to you. Despite what it cost me.'

'What it *cost* you? What have I cost you?' There was a new, menacing edge to her father's voice.

'I was a girl. Just a girl when we married.'

Becca sat down on the top step and edged down one and then two. Her nightie had been pushed up by the downward motion so that she sat like a bride with a train behind her. She put her head between the banisters and waited for the silence to deliver something.

'I'm sorry I've been such a disappointment to you.'

'Don't be so dramatic, Leonard.'

'I believe you regret our marriage. Our life together.'

'No, no. Leonard, I'm sorry. That was wrong of me. I'm sorry.'

'I need you now, Jane. A vacancy has come up in a school in Wimbledon. It's a headship. But I need to know you're behind me. I can't go for it without your support.'

'I'll talk to Andrew tomorrow. I'll tell him the boys can still come here after school, but he's got to find someone else – maybe his aunt in Stockwell – if he's going to work in the evenings.'

But Li never came to babysit. Leonard began working longer hours at school, preparing for his interview, and into this void stepped Andrew. He began turning up at five in the afternoon, always in a good mood – relaxed and interested – asking his sons how their day had been before turning to Jane and asking her if there was anything he could do. Sometimes she gave him potatoes to peel or poured him a drink. It became a strange sort of ritual that the children grew to accept. Andrew, despite being unable to get home any earlier than 8 p.m. for the previous six months, was suddenly back in Claygate every day at teatime.

He was pleased to sit down and be looked after by a woman. He sank into one of the chairs round the kitchen table, heavy with his day and the journey he'd just had. He shared tales of the Rotherhithe Tunnel, idiots in their BMWs and lane closures on the A3 with anyone who'd listen. Jane busied herself about him, murmuring and agreeing as she prepared dinner.

'I'm so relieved I'll never have that pleasure.'

'What? Of driving?'

'I've never learned.'

'How come? You grew up around here, didn't you?'

'Yes, but I was so young when Leonard and I met, and he already had a car and drove, so—'

'Do you want to learn?' It was such a direct question, she felt wrong-footed.

'Oh no. No. I walk to the shops, and if we go anywhere, well, Leonard drives.'

'That's not what I asked,' he said quietly.

'Oh, I don't know,' she said, bending down to look in the cupboard beneath the sink, but all she could see were bottles of detergent, bleach and some scourers.

'Do you want to learn?'

'Perhaps. One day.' She had no idea why she'd opened the cupboard.

'Well, let me teach you, then.'

'Andrew, no. In your van?' She stood up and pushed the hair that had fallen forward onto her face back into place.

'Why not? I've been driving since I was seventeen. I'll get you on the road in a few weeks. You'll be nipping here, there and everywhere.'

'I couldn't. And Leonard. He wouldn't like it.'

'He wouldn't like you learning or wouldn't like me teaching you?'

'No, I didn't mean that. He just wouldn't see the need, that's all.'

'Let me talk to Leonard.'

'No, Andrew. Don't do that. Listen, maybe one afternoon, before he gets home from work, you could show me how it all works. But—'

'Say no more. It'll be our little secret.'

She pictured him then, driving along Streatham High

Road, accelerating into the gaps, nudging his way – relent-
lessly – home. He was a good driver. She could see that.

'I think my dad fancies your mum,' Jonathan whispered to
Becca one afternoon as they awaited Andrew's knock on the
door.

'In what way?'

'Well, he's always over here.'

'To collect you.'

'Do you really think I need collecting?'

'They're friends. He's just being friendly.'

'But what if they are?'

'What if they are what?'

'Having sex. You know' – Jonathan lowered his head and
his voice to the table so that the words emerged wrapped in
steamy, stagnant breath – 'fucking.'

Becca smelled it before she understood it. 'My mum
wouldn't do that.'

'Ssshhhhh!'

'But she wouldn't.'

'Of course she would. She must have done to have you and
Julia.'

'Stop it, Jonathan.'

'What? I'm just telling the truth.'

'That's not truth! Even if my mum and dad have sex, that
doesn't mean she has it with your dad.'

'Suit yourself. But I think they are. And if they're not, they
will. My dad always gets his way.'

Becca lowered her head to her homework and tried to turn
her nose from the foul vapour that still swirled round her
pencil. And when her mother led Andrew into the kitch-
en at ten minutes past five, Becca was alive to the routined

movements, the glass of cold beer set down on the table, the familiar drop and sigh as he sat down in a chair just behind Jane. She looked up and watched Andrew with a new intensity; she saw how his eyes kept drifting to her mother's bottom, wrapped up like a gift with her apron tied across her tailbone. She spied a connection that Jonathan had crudely tried to alert her to. But it wasn't fucking. It was his eyes on her mother's body. It was the opaque and unintelligible desire he had for her bum. Her arse. What was it? Her mother's body took on new meaning that afternoon in the kitchen as she realised another man might covet it. A man who no longer had his wife's. She felt Jonathan's eyes on her as she watched his father watch her mother. She stood up, too quickly, and interrupted the silent circuit.

Jane turned round. 'Becca? What is it?'

'Your apron,' Becca said, standing between her mother and Andrew. 'It's loose. I'll just retie it for you.'

'Oh, thank you, darling.'

Becca and Jonathan watched from her bedroom window as Jane climbed up into the driver's side of Andrew's van. In her seat, she suddenly reigned over the steering wheel and gearstick. She held on to the steering wheel as she leaned out with her right arm to pull the door shut. As she clicked her seatbelt into place, she saw Andrew had shifted into the middle seat, so close to her thigh she could feel the coarse texture of his jeans through the thin cotton of her dress.

'Don't worry about your seatbelt. We'll put it on if we go on the road.'

'I shouldn't have worn a dress,' she said as she looked at the pedals.

'It's pretty.' He tapped her knee gently with his fingers as he told her to turn the key in the ignition. The tips of his fingers felt roughened, calloused in a way that made her want to hold them to her face.

'Like this?'

'That's it. You've got it.'

The van shuddered with a tired growl.

'Now, with your left foot you press the clutch down.'

'That's this one?' She turned to him, extending her left leg so that her dress rode up against his denim.

'That's it. And now go into first.'

She pushed up the gearstick.

'No, that's third. Hang on,' and he put his right hand on top of hers and moved the gearstick towards him and then up. 'That's it and now, keeping your right foot on the brake ... No, the middle peddle. Yeah, that's it. With your foot on the brake, release the handbrake.'

'I don't have enough hands.'

'You don't have to keep your hand on the gearstick. It's in gear now. So use your left hand to release the handbrake. That's it. And now ... slowly. Slowly, lift your foot on the clutch. That's this one,' he said, tapping her naked thigh with his fingers again. But this time the contact was higher up. 'And put your right foot down on the gas.'

But Jane was flustered by the actions of her own hands and now Andrew's. She pulled her left foot up too quickly and the sudden loss of gas, to a van that was already struggling under new leadership, was enough to make it judder and stall before the end of the drive.

Becca and Jonathan stopped watching after the van stalled. They didn't see Andrew stroke her thigh so that the dress was eventually pushed up and out of the way, revealing knickers he never thought he'd see. When his fingers pushed them to one side so that he might touch inside her, Jane released a low growl of violent pleasure. She knew – in that moment – where the word 'fuck' came from. The word she'd whispered to Leonard in bed one night. It was never meant for whispering. It was a deep call for help before desire swallowed you.

Had Becca and Jonathan continued watching, they'd have seen Jane eventually climb down from the van like one who'd been poisoned. She walked unsteadily – trying to maintain a straight line – towards her own front door. In the hallway, she took a moment to look in the mirror, and what she found was more profoundly unsettling than the noises she'd made when Andrew had touched her. Her cheeks had heard the news her heart was thumping in triumph. But it was her eyes. As she stood and stared at herself, waiting for her daughter to descend the stairs, she saw the answer to her great question. The one that began the afternoon she read *Anna Karenina*, pregnant and already weighed down by her decision to marry Leonard. The need to have part of you awakened by the attentions of another. A desire so strong it makes you want to fall before a train. Or betray a loving husband. And in the confined space of a white van, her moment had come.

Chapter 32

In January 1992, Leonard took up his post as head teacher of the school in Wimbledon. His new role was all-encompassing; he took on more teaching in an effort to get to know the students and stayed late in the evenings so he could witness, first hand, all the school had to offer in terms of after-school clubs, drama performances and prize evenings. Both Becca and Julia became more used to the sound of their parents arguing downstairs.

'Julia told me he was here again this afternoon. Is it now a daily occurrence?'

'Leonard, he's collecting the boys. And showing his appreciation to me, that's all.'

'I don't like that man, and I don't want him here all the time.'

'He's not here all the time. It's half an hour at best while the boys finish their tea.'

'Half an hour every day is unacceptable. Have you considered what other people might make of your behaviour?'

'What exactly are you accusing me of?'

'Are you having some kind of sordid affair?'

'Of course not! Leonard, the children are here – all four of them – having their tea. How exactly do you imagine we're having an affair?'

'He's here too much.'

'Have you ever considered that I like the company? That I never bloody see you anymore! You're either at school or in your study. I'm perfectly invisible to you.'

'Keep your voice down.'

Neither Becca nor Julia had any inclination to eavesdrop further. They were beginning to understand more than they wanted to about the state of their parents' marriage.

But during the February half-term, things went from bad to worse. Becca was in the kitchen one morning writing a five-hundred-word story for English that had to include a desert island. She'd just completed her description of falling – terrified – from the storm-damaged fuselage of an aeroplane and counted the words. There were only two hundred left to her. Her notebook was dotted with the pinpricks of her pencil and numbers in the margin – all of which testified to an anxiety greater than the isolation of finding herself on a desert island – when she heard a knock at the door. Her mother and Julia were out shopping, and her father was upstairs at his work.

She opened it.

On the other side was a tall, tired man with long hair speckled with grey. His eyebrows were raised as though the expectation lay on his side of the threshold.

'How are ye?' he asked quickly.

Becca stared at him.

'Is your mammy or daddy home?'

Becca leaned back, keeping her eyes on him, and shouted up the stairs, 'Dad!'

'What is it?' came the irritated sound of Leonard.

'Someone's at the door!'

'Who is it?'

'Who are you?' Becca said, turning to the man.

'I'm looking for me sister. Her name is Marion. Have you seen her anywhere?'

'Do you mean Mrs Wilson?'

'I do, yeah. Mrs Wilson. Where is she?'

'She left.'

'Left to go where?' He took a step closer.

'I don't know. But she left Jonathan and Robbie.'

'You know my nephews?'

'Yes. My mum helps Mr Wilson look after them.'

As she was speaking, Becca heard the hurried footsteps of her father coming down the stairs. He opened the door wider and pulled Becca back by her shoulder. 'How do you do? I'm Leonard Campbell. Won't you come in?'

'I don't want to cause you any bother. I'm just looking for me sister, Marion. Your daughter here seems to think she's gone away.'

'Please come in.'

Becca joined them quietly at the table and picked up her pencil, remembering how overwritten her beginning was and how she had no hope of cramming a middle and an end into two hundred words.

Jonny spoke first. 'I haven't heard from Marion in a long time. And I've just called round next door – at their house – and there's no one there. So I thought I'd try the neighbours.'

Leonard, who was standing at the sink filling the kettle, turned to Jonny. 'I'm sorry to be the bearer of bad news, but it would appear Mrs Wilson left her husband and sons a few years ago. We understand, from your brother-in-law, that she has gone back to Ireland, where she intends to remain.'

'Did she say whereabouts? In Dublin?'

'I'm afraid I'm not familiar with the details. My wife may be,' Leonard said, looking down at Becca's poised pencil.

'Where's your wife, if you don't mind me asking? I'd like to talk to her.'

'She's taken our younger daughter out to buy some shoes. I'd happily pass on your details and get her to give you a phone call?'

'I haven't exactly got a fixed address at the moment, you see,' Jonny said, bringing his right hand – swollen and red – up to his stubble and stroking the hair downwards thoughtfully. Leonard looked at him and took a deep breath in through his nostrils, and sure enough, there was a scent of stale alcohol in the air.

'Do you take milk and sugar, Mr . . . ?'

'Donnelly. And yes, milk and two sugars, please.'

Leonard nodded, as though he had no choice but to sanction Jonny's choices, and turned back to the work surface.

'What are you doing there?' Jonny asked Becca, who'd begun writing again.

'I have to write a story for English.'

'What's it about?'

'About being stuck on a desert island.'

Leonard handed Jonny his tea.

'All that water and not a drop to drink,' he said, as he slurped at the hot liquid.

Leonard made himself a cup of instant coffee and sat down beside Becca. It was clear from the way he looked over her shoulder at what she was writing that he could think of nothing to say.

'What's he been like? Andrew?'

'I'm sorry?'

'What's he been like to my sister? A good husband?'

'Well, Mr Donnelly, I'm sure I don't know. It really is none of our business—'

'I mean has she been happy? Has he treated her right?'

'I have no idea. I can't say I've paid much attention.'

'But if she's left him and gone back to Ireland as you say, she can't have been happy.'

'Well, yes, quite. But that's not something I would expect my wife and I to concern ourselves with.' He spoke with a faltering smile, one designed to convey his unease at having to be so blunt.

'I'm not asking for much here. She's a stubborn old goat, my sister, but if she's left her boys, then something must have happened, you know?'

Leonard repeated the words to himself, as if he were hearing them for the first time. He'd only ever approached the issue of Jane and Andrew as it presented itself to him. He'd never considered why Andrew was suddenly so interested in his wife and what had caused Marion to be so immediately and entirely absent from the situation. He felt alone and isolated in his understanding, and as he looked down at what Becca was writing, it suddenly occurred to him that Jane was no longer beside him. The realisation was too sharp and immediate for words. And because he couldn't speak, he decided to pretend to read Becca's story.

Jonny finished his tea and made a show of waiting for Jane, but Leonard couldn't tolerate his presence in the house any longer.

'I'm afraid my wife may not return for some time and I

have a lot to do this afternoon. Might I suggest you return another time?'

'Will you tell her and Andrew I was looking for them?'

Her and Andrew.

'Yes, of course.'

'Good luck with the story,' he said to Becca's bent head. 'Do you get off the island in the end?'

'Yes,' she said, without looking up.

'How?'

'I swim out to the horizon and jump off the other side.'

'Good for you. Wish I could do that. Say hello to Jonathan and Robbie for me.'

The argument that night was more ferocious than previous ones. Becca and Julia sat on the landing – they couldn't risk being discovered on the stairs. Their father's anguish was new and frightening.

'Where is she, Jane? Have you ever wondered where she's gone?'

'To Ireland. She sent him a letter!'

'Did you see the letter? Has there in fact been any trace of that woman since she mysteriously *left him*?'

'She came over here and told me how unhappy she was. That she'd like to take the boys and move back to Ireland. And that's what she's done.'

'That's *not* what she's done. The boys are still here and she isn't.'

'What are you saying, Leonard? That he's killed her?'

'What if he has? What do we really know about these people?'

'I know I've heard enough. And that poor man has been

through enough. I'm trying to help him and care for Becca's one and only friend!'

Becca sat up straight, surprised by how her name was currency in an exchange that was quickly getting out of control.

'So this is about Becca, is it? It's got nothing to do with desire . . . with your desire for that man!'

'What are you talking about?'

'Are you having sex with him? Tell me. I demand to know the truth.'

'How could you?'

'I'm a reasonable man, but this is too much. I must know – have you been unfaithful?'

'For the last time, no. I can't take any more of this, Leonard. I thought I could keep it together, but I can't.'

'The answer is obvious. You must stop having anything to do with that family. They're tearing our own apart.'

'I enjoy helping them. I like Andrew . . . Hear me out, Leonard! I'm not saying I'm in love with him or that I lust after him. I'm just saying I think he's a good person, a good father and I want to help him. And Becca, you can't deny Becca is a happier child with Jonathan around. Why can't you put your petty suspicions to one side?'

'Because something's not right. You mark my words, Jane, something's not right.'

'So you say.'

But there were no more words after that. Leonard, for all his intelligence and self-control, was unable to face down his wife's willingness to minister to next door. It never occurred to him that the stubbornness he was witnessing was the very same quality that had caused Jane to defy her parents fifteen years earlier. He'd asked her to mark his words, but he took

her at her own. He chose to believe her because the alterna-
tive was too unbearable.

The following morning, after the girls had gone to school
and she'd cleared away the breakfast things, Jane decided to
go and knock on Andrew's door. The van stood cold and inert
on the driveway.

He opened the door quickly. 'Come in,' he said, stepping
back.

'I can't stay long.' She walked briskly past and heard the
door close as she took her place before the bay window in the
lounge, a mirror image of her own.

'No more driving lessons,' she said the moment he entered
the room.

'OK.'

'Don't do that.'

'Do what?' he said, laughing.

'Laugh at me. How dare you laugh at me? I'm a married
woman.'

'I didn't hear any complaints at the time, Jane.'

'Don't twist my words. I'm not here to complain. I'm here
to tell you that what we did, what *happened*,' she said, drawing
herself up, 'must never happen again. Do you understand?'

'Where's this come from?' he said, moving closer.

'Stay where you are. Just listen to me. I like you, Andrew.
As you know, I've grown very fond of you and the boys, and
I'm happy to help with after-school care – it's the least I can
do given all that happened. With Marion and everything.
But . . .' she hesitated as she looked at the net curtains, their
damp, unwashed odour in her nostrils, 'you and me. That
can't happen again.'

'Jane, I'm not going—'

'Do you understand?'

'I understand, but I—'

'Good. I'll show myself out.'

He reached out for her as she walked past. He didn't know that her speed was because she felt tears coming. That they were coursing down her face even as she pulled his front door shut. She let herself back into her own quiet house. The empty quiet. She'd wanted it. Craved it so much she'd been prepared to announce her decision not to have any more children to the school secretary instead of Leonard. But now it closed around her, in whispered mockery of all she wanted. She sat on the bottom step and wept for the husband who loved her. For the daughters who needed her to remain constant and unchanging. But in truth she cried for the red she'd seen. The brief glimpse of something hot and vital and searing. It had bubbled up and spilled over and now, because it was wrong – because Andrew wasn't her husband and Leonard was – now she had no choice but to let the fissure close. And she knew the healing would be painful.

Chapter 33

However well meaning Mr Dobson's advice in the second year had been, Becca's generosity towards Danielle Simpson continued into the fourth year. It meant she was accepted by a group of girls — an outlier, riding alone on the fringe of things, but still belonging to a group and less alone.

Danielle and another girl called Matilda had been locked in a near-constant battle for supremacy since the first year. Becca's lowly position meant she didn't have to choose sides when the arguments turned nasty, as they did from time to time. She delivered notes if called upon, but was careful to keep her counsel until peace had been restored. It was exhausting, but it felt like a price worth paying. Until she became collateral damage.

Towards the end of the summer term, Matilda turned up at morning registration with her hair pulled self-consciously across the side of her face. She walked quickly to her seat and sat down beside Danielle, who was waving a ruler in Becca's direction to underline some point she'd been making. Danielle knew from Matilda's silence and heavy drop in the seat that something had happened. She turned to her and Matilda brought the short and insubstantial curtain of her hair forward so that they could closet themselves behind it and have a private conversation.

'Let me see,' Danielle whispered, and Matilda, with a flourish she'd been waiting to perform, lifted her hair to reveal two little earrings in the cartilage of her right ear. 'Oh my God. It's amazing.'

'Ssshhh,' Matilda admonished, but it was the first time she'd smiled since entering the classroom.

'What is it?' Becca asked, though she'd seen and heard everything.

'Nothing.' Matilda shrugged her shoulders. 'Beth took me to have it done.'

Matilda's older sister, Beth, was in the sixth form. She had several piercings, including one in her nose and another in her belly button, and had, apparently, had sex with at least four different boys since losing her virginity the year before. Matilda had also found cannabis in her bedroom.

'Did it hurt?' Becca asked.

'Not really.' Matilda was sanguine, but as she spoke, she reached up to touch her ear and the obvious tenderness that glowed red beneath her fingertips.

'I want one.' Danielle spoke quickly.

'Why?' Becca asked, but her question went unanswered. This was a high-level discussion about cartilage and the levels of deception required to make it happen. Their form tutor entered the room and ordered the class to be quiet.

That evening, Jonathan and Becca were up in her bedroom sharing the news of the day. Matilda and Danielle, in a joint declaration and show of unity, had decreed that all members of the group should obtain some kind of piercing.

'But your ears are already pierced.' Jonathan, who was

sitting cross-legged, craned his head to examine her earlobes. Becca pulled her hair back and up onto the top of her head, revealing the bright white curve of her neck. Jonathan found it difficult to focus on the man-made holes when the natural strait of her body was so perfect. So flawless.

'I know. But Danielle wants us to get another one.'

'Danielle wants you to get another piercing so she doesn't get in trouble for her own?'

'It's not her own. Matilda's the one who had it done.'

'You're going to pierce the cartilage of your ear because someone called Danielle, working on the say-so of a girl called Matilda, told you to?'

'Yes.'

'And has it occurred to you to tell her to go fuck herself?'

'Jonathan,' Becca wailed, sinking back against her headboard.

'This is totally fucking stupid. You don't want another piercing, and your mum and dad will go nuts if you have one, but you're acting on the orders of some div called Danielle.'

'Will you help me?'

'No.'

'Fine. I'll do it myself, then.'

Though shaky and shallow, her breaths were enough to mist the mirror in regular beats, clouding the glass with a determination that dissipated almost immediately. Becca had a clothes peg fastened to the top of her ear and an ice pack to her lobe. She had taken a needle from the messy drawer in the kitchen and dropped it in a mug of boiling water. The water had cooled enough for her to reach for it, and now she stood poised before the bathroom mirror, working up the courage to push it through her flesh. She thought of

Matilda's performance the morning after her piercing, how she'd sat down in her seat with such expectation of praise. She thought of how delighted Danielle would be and she pushed, pushed and pushed again.

The following morning, she walked into the form room, looking for Danielle or Matilda. Danielle was standing by the lockers, her face red and blotchy with tears, surrounded by three hangers-on. Matilda was nowhere to be seen.

'What's the matter?' Becca asked as she put her bag down on the nearest table.

'It's Matilda,' one of the girls said, turning to Becca briefly but keeping her eye on Danielle. She was within touching distance and didn't want to give up her place. 'Danielle's mum rang Matilda's mum last night and told her about the piercing. Matilda's grounded and so is Beth. They're both blaming Danielle.'

Becca pulled her hair down, the light strands too much for the throbbing heat of her ear to support. 'So Danielle hasn't done it?'

The girl turned back again. 'No. Like I said, she's grounded.'

Becca sat down in her seat and waited for their form tutor to enter the room and take the register. She wanted to go home and take out the earring she'd used to keep the hole open. She wanted to go back to the day before and respect her skin's resistance to the incision. She wanted to go back to Jonathan, who had understood the situation from the beginning. Who'd told her to tell Danielle to go fuck herself. And with Danielle sobbing behind her because she'd been grounded, saved by her parents from a painful and unnecessary piercing, she saw he'd been right.

She stood up, her fingers wide and ready to pull back the hangers-on so that she could approach the crying girl. Not to stroke or peer, doe-eyed at someone's sorrow. No, she wanted to get nose to nose, so close Danielle would smell the toothpaste she'd used that morning as she shouted – angry and suddenly free – at the girl who'd always kept her at arm's length, ordered her to pierce her ear, who'd ripped her story from the back of her exercise book, 'Why don't you go fuck yourself?'

Her words were like the launching of a bowling ball. The shock rolled around the room, the unexpected force scattering Danielle and her friends first, before ricocheting towards the front of the room, where her form tutor was standing, the register clamped to her chest, her mouth wide in sudden expectation of the heavy weight coming towards her.

She was sent to the deputy head's office and her parents were called. Danielle was also summoned, and the two of them sat before Mrs Evanshaw's desk, the accounts tumbling out, in Danielle's case the truth rinsed but not spun, the words emerging heavy with her own innocence. But Becca didn't lie. She didn't have it in her. The piercing had been secretive and clandestine, but had her mother knocked on the bathroom door and asked her what she was doing, she'd have told her. And perhaps saved herself a lot of pain.

When the school secretary knocked on the door and said Mrs Campbell was outside, Becca started crying. But it wasn't because her ear was throbbing with the discomfort of early infection or because she anticipated the admonishment of her parents. It was because her mother was there. In a confusing world of thinly maintained friendships, where allegiances separated on a knife edge, where she'd so often been alone but had never quite understood why, her mother had arrived. And her mother was there for her.

Jane lifted Becca's hair gently and nodded at the piercing.

As if it was everything she'd expected. She dropped her bag from her shoulder and kneeled down in front of her daughter, cupping Becca's face in her hands. Because she knew why she'd done it. She knew, without looking, who that girl sitting in the other chair was. Another Brenda Barrow, a girl more worldly-wise than her own daughter, who'd tried to pull her towards a painful adulthood.

'Mrs Campbell. Please sit down. I'll have my secretary bring you a chair.'

But Jane didn't answer. Becca fell against her mother's shoulder and began sobbing. It had all been too much. Too difficult. She couldn't do it anymore. And Jane wouldn't make her. Without speaking, they both understood that Becca wouldn't attend another day. They'd find another solution.

'I didn't make her do anything,' Danielle shouted as Jane pulled Becca to a stand.

'I'm taking my daughter home,' Jane said, as much to Danielle as to Mrs Evanshaw.

They called in at the doctor's surgery on their way home. The receptionist, who knew Jane and the family well, told them to take a seat in the waiting room – there'd been a cancellation and the doctor would see them in ten minutes. They sat side by side, unspeaking until Becca reached for her mother's hand.

'I'm sorry,' she whispered.

Jane swallowed. 'You have nothing to be sorry for.'

'I shouldn't have done it.'

'No. You shouldn't. But sometimes we only understand something is wrong when we actually do it. And live to regret it.'

'Do you regret me?'

'Becca, no. Of course not.' She turned in her seat. 'I just

mean in life, you know, things you do. Small things. Becca, you and Julia, well, you're the thing – not thing – *people* I'm most proud of. Sometimes I think you're too pure for this world.'

'Danielle Simpson doesn't.'

'Let me tell you about Danielle Simpson,' Jane said, swallowing the grim taste of bile at the back of her throat. 'She's not worth a hair on your head.'

She turned back to face the posters on the wall opposite and narrowed her eyes as though she were considering a vaccination. 'I'm keeping you close for a while. Until you're stronger. OK?'

Becca nodded.

When they got home, Jane settled Becca on the sofa with a blanket and a glass of water while she went out to the chemist's to collect the antibiotics. By the time she got back, Becca had put on *Far From the Madding Crowd*, recorded from the television the previous year, and together, with Becca's feet propped up on her lap, they gave themselves up to Julie Christie and Terence Stamp.

Becca had already had two doses of her medication by the time Julia knocked on her bedroom door that evening. She was sitting up in bed, writing quickly in her notebook, her lips moving silently.

'Mum told me what happened.'

Becca looked at the pages and put down her pen. She began rubbing her thumbs together.

'What are you doing?'

'Just a little story I thought of.'

Julia sat on the edge of the bed and looked at Becca's ear, now taped up with a plaster.

'Have you got cream on it?'

'Eh? Oh yes, underneath,' she said, raising her fingers to her ear.

'I wish you'd told me. You could have come and hung around with me.'

'I should be able to make my own friends.'

'The Simpsons are like a pack of wolves. Her little brother, Tony, is in my year . . .'

'I don't think you'd have done something like this. Something this stupid.'

'No. But we're different, that's all.'

'I can't go back there. Danielle and Matilda will tear me limb from limb.'

'Mum and Dad are talking about it now. I heard Dad say he'd find you a tutor.'

'A tutor? How would that work?'

Julia shrugged. 'Don't know. But I came up here to tell you that if you do go back, I'll wait for you in the playground at break times so you're not alone anymore.'

Julia's kindness to her sister was unnecessary. Jane was adamant Becca would not return to her school, and with just a year to go before her GCSEs, it was decided that Becca would go to school with her father every day. He had the caretaker move a desk into his secretary's office, and from there Becca was attended by subject teachers, who were happy to be paid a private tutor rate during their free periods. Leonard managed to cobble together a timetable and materials that would allow Becca to sit her exams at the end of the fifth year.

Chapter 34

Jonathan's school was single sex up to the sixth form. While the gender split of the sixth form was still predominantly male, each year they had a small number of female applicants join. And in 1993, Becca was one of them.

The art rooms in Jonathan's school were up in the rafters. Sixth formers were permitted to climb the dark stairs and walk along the narrow corridor that transected the vault of the chapel and led to the oldest part of the school building. Up there, amid the dust and high ceilings, they were allowed to work on their art, collect materials or just eat lunch. Becca thought it was nothing short of miraculous: a place where one could be alone but not lonely. She followed Jonathan up there every lunchtime, knowing as they ascended that they would separate – silently – in order to continue with their work and come back together, later, when the bell rang and it was time to return to the busy school. Becca would spend the time writing: essays and coursework first and then – if she had time – short stories. Sometimes as Jonathan neared completion on a particular art piece, she'd include whatever it was in her story, writing it into her fiction with a light and deft touch.

It was their custom to go straight up to her room as soon as they got back to Claygate, their friendship so thick and established that Jane never thought to question what they were doing up there.

'So why is position important?' Becca was sitting cross-legged on her bed, leaning back against the headboard. Jonathan was mirroring her at the opposite end of the bed, forcing his weight into the soft mattress.

'I'm just interested in how it works, how it changes the body.' He reached down for his art case. 'You sitting like that, for example,' he said, pulling two large sheets of paper, and a much smaller one that looked like it had been torn from a notepad, from the bag. 'When you lean backwards, your tits get pushed up. They're more visible and prominent.'

'Don't call them that.'

'What? Tits?'

'Yes. They're "breasts". Or "boobs" if you're really stuck.'

'What's wrong with "tits"?'

'It's too close to "teats". And I'm not an animal.'

'We're all animals, Becca.'

'What's that?' Becca asked, reaching for the small piece of paper.

'Don't worry about that one. I'll show you in a minute. This is what I wanted you to see.' He held up a sketch of a naked woman lying on her side. Her hip rose up like a gentle peak in a graph and then fell away before climbing again, in gentle increments, across her ribs. Her head was resting on her arm, but there was no face. Her breasts were large and soft; the left one had collapsed on the right in the effort of staying upright.

'Who's that?'

'It's not anyone. I drew her on her side because I liked the way her jugs drop towards the bed.'

'Are you joking?'

'You didn't say anything about "jugs".'

'What's that little one?'

'Oh. This,' he said, looking down at the torn scrap of paper. 'It's a drawing of me when I was a baby.'

'Who did it?'

'My mum.'

'Your mum? As in Marion?'

'I only have one mum,' he said, passing the picture to her.

'It's really . . . I don't know. It's not quite there, is it? Like it's almost a baby but not.'

'She told me she did it the night I was born. Before she had me.'

'She was sketching this as she was in labour?'

'I think so.'

Becca looked at the image again. Marion's strokes were loud and urgent. *Not unlike a real baby*, Becca thought momentarily.

She looked at the other sketch. It was a woman on her back with her legs apart, her vagina open and exposed. 'That's so gross. You can't show this to Miss Whittaker.'

'No, this one's for me,' he said, putting it back in his art bag. 'But I want to draw the second in the series. I need a naked woman sitting back on her haunches. You know, like they do in Japan. I've read about it. It's called the *seiza* position. Can you do it?'

'What? Like this?' Becca said, getting off the bed and folding her legs underneath her. Her back looked unnaturally straight, primed to please.

'Yeah, that's it. Will you pose for me?'

'Naked?'

'Yeah. I wouldn't put your face in. Just like this one. No one will know it's you.'

'If you draw me, you put my face in it.'

'Is that a yes?'

'I don't know.'

'I promise I won't get a boner.'

Since puberty she'd been careful not to be seen naked by anyone, protecting the secret of her new hair and budding breasts. But she'd grown up trusting her innermost dreams to Jonathan's pencil and she was curious to see how her body might be reflected back to her.

Becca was wearing a dressing gown and nothing else when they began the following week. Once in position, she moved the dressing gown down past her shoulders, revealing her breasts slowly, self-consciously. Jonathan propped her desk chair against the door.

He spent a long time sketching the cat's cradle of Becca's collarbone. His gaze was fixated on it, so much so that he encouraged her to move her shoulders forwards to create the deep, triangular pools either side of her throat. It forced her small breasts forwards, but Jonathan wasn't looking at them. Not yet, at least. She saw where his eyes were most attracted, how he was dedicated to getting her throat just right. Sometimes, frustrated, he sketched faster and then rubbed out vigorously, in vicious punishment for his own mistake. And when he was pleased with something, his hand slowed right down as though a small line of smoke had appeared between the lead and the paper, and just a few gentle, well-timed breaths would serve to kindle the flame.

Becca, whose thighs were not used to sitting in such a position, began to shift after a period of five, sometimes ten minutes.

'What's the matter?'

'I'm getting pins and needles.'

'Can you stay still for a bit longer?'

'Can't I just sit on my bum? Are you doing my legs yet?'

'No, still on your throat.'

'So can I change position?'

'If you sit on your bum, it changes everything. Your neck and shoulders slump down.'

Becca took a deep breath and tried to ignore the tingling in her legs. She folded her hands in her lap, covering her pubic hair by pushing down into her thighs and lengthening her trunk.

'I can't,' she said, collapsing to one side.

He dropped the pad and then threw the pencil to land on top of it.

'Fucking useless.'

'I'm doing my best.'

'Not you. Sorry – it's me. I can't get it right.'

'What are you trying to do?' she asked, and, forgetting she was naked, approached Jonathan on all fours.

'It's your throat. I want to get the curve of your voice box. This bit,' he said, using his thumb and forefinger to articulate the length of his own.

'Use mine,' she said, grabbing his hand. And with his thumb and forefinger on her throat, touching the thing he was trying to bring to life, Becca swallowed, awakening them both to the naked reality of their situation: Becca with no clothes on, Jonathan with his hand upon her skin. He pulled back and looked at her properly for the first time, saw her breasts, her hips and felt the stirring he'd promised wouldn't happen.

'What's the matter?'

'I'd better go.'

'But your picture?'

'Your legs are hurting. We'll do a bit more tomorrow. I think I heard my dad downstairs.'

'Jonathan. What have I done?' She was sitting back again, her head and neck taunting him in their near perfection.

Jonathan didn't come over the following evening, or the one after that. Jane tried to ask her what had happened, but Becca – even if she could explain the sketching endeavour – could never account for Jonathan's sudden withdrawal.

When he did finally return, it was with his father the following Monday. Jane called to Becca, who rushed down the stairs to find Andrew standing with his hand on the back of Jonathan's neck.

'I'm not sure what's happened here,' Andrew began, looking tentatively at Jane, 'but I think you two should make it up.'

'Yes,' Jane said, licking her lips. 'It's such a shame. You get on so well.'

'Nothing's happened,' Jonathan mumbled to himself.

'Becca?' Jane asked.

Her daughter was midway down the stairs, poised to spring back and return to her room. She shrugged her shoulders at her mother and said to Jonathan, 'Do you want to come up?'

He felt his father pinch the skin over his right shoulder and slap him on the back. 'There you go. Go upstairs and play nicely.'

Jonathan trudged up the stairs behind Becca. 'I'm sorry,' he said as soon as she closed the door.

'What did I do?'

He sat down heavily at the end of her bed and put his head in his hands.

'What's the matter?'

'I just . . . When I was touching your throat the other day, I got—'

'What?'

'You know.' He looked up at her hopefully.

She continued watching him, her back against the bed's headboard.

'I don't know.'

'I got a boner. I got hard.'

'Oh.' Becca lay back and stretched her legs out towards him. 'Is that bad?'

'Well, no, but . . .'

'But what?'

'Well, I don't know what it means. I mean, obviously I know what it means.'

'Do you think you want to have sex with me?'

'Yes.'

'Why?'

'Because I love your body. Your throat, your neck and chest. They're beautiful.'

All Jonathan could see was the sharp triangle of Becca's chin pointing up at the ceiling. He couldn't see the smile on her face or the elation that vibrated in her muscles. She stretched her arms and legs out in luxurious pleasure, elongating her body and delighting in its physicality and Jonathan's eyes upon her. He got up on his knees, lowered his weight onto her. As his head lined up with hers, he saw the smile.

She was at the limit of her stretch, her muscles relaxed back in time with her exhausted breath. With the fingers of his left hand, he traced her collarbone. She moved her shoulder forwards, creating the pool for his fingers.

He kissed her gently, with the restraint of a novice. It wasn't his first kiss, but it was the first one he'd ever initiated. Becca, who'd never so much as held a boy's hand before, tried to close her eyes. She tried, but the effort was too much; she wanted to keep them open and see Jonathan's face, newly punctured by stubble, so close to her own. As he lowered his weight, what she knew must be his erection came to rest against the top of her thigh. It was somehow at odds with the circumspect approach – as if the bloodrush of his desire was tearing him away from himself, the hardness mocking his indulgent exploration of her neck.

'You need to open your mouth.'

'Like this?'

Jonathan used his tongue to introduce his body to hers. It was the first physical exchange they'd ever had. This girl who had given him her innermost thoughts and dreams now waited for him to enter her in some way. Becca felt the soft wetness as a gift, an overabundance that made her body relax in a way that surprised her. She felt tension she didn't even know was there release itself, and as it did, Jonathan's pressure on her frame increased and he reached down to touch her. Those same hands she'd watched sketching her dreams when they were younger, and then attempting to do the same with her body were now taking a more direct approach. And the relaxation tipped over into arousal.

Julia became curious when Becca began closing her bedroom door more frequently and for longer periods. She didn't want to join them, but she did want to know what had changed. Why they were suddenly so guarded about their time together.

She took the opportunity one night during the week, just as she heard Becca getting into bed, to knock on the door and ask to come in.

'I just thought I'd come and say good night.' The room was dark. Becca had already arranged her hair behind her on the pillow.

'You never come in to say good night.' Becca sat up and turned on the small lamp on her bedside table. The dim light was enough to snap Julia in the act of stepping towards her sister's bed.

'What are you and Jonathan up to every day in here?' she asked, sitting down on the edge of the bed.

'Oh, you know.'

'No. I don't.'

'Why do you want to know?'

'Because I'm worried about you.'

'You're worried about me? Let's not forget who's the older sister here.'

'Just because you're my big sister doesn't mean I can't worry for you.'

'Julia. I'm fine. But I'm tired. Good night.'

'Are you having sex?'

'Yes. Lots of it. Now good night.'

'Boys view sex differently to us. They see it in purely physical terms, but for girls it's much more emotional.'

'I'll try to be less emotional about it.'

'I'm just not sure Jonathan is the right person for you.'

'We've known each other a long time. And anyway, I was joking. We're not having sex.'

'Yet.'

'I'm old enough to make up my own mind, thank you very much.'

'I just wanted to say that if you ever need any help or advice, I'm here for you. That's all.'

'Thank you. Good night.'

During the summer holidays, Becca and Jonathan made the most of the long days and took to exploring parks, farmland and wooded areas in search of privacy. Jonathan's erection appeared as soon as they started kissing; it was like an impatient younger sibling, ever present and nagging, reminding them of where their kiss – suddenly so urgent and necessary – was headed.

One evening at the end of August, as the dusk became dark, they managed to find a large willow tree on the edge of a golf course.

'Is it time?' she asked, drawing back and looking down at his lap.

'Now? You want to do it here?'

'Why not?'

'I don't think I want to do it outside. Or on a golf course.'

'What's the golf course got to do with it?'

'It's a bit green and middle class, isn't it?'

'So's everything round here. What's *not* middle class in Surrey?'

'I just mean probably every sixth former in a five-mile radius has come here with a bottle of Beaujolais and fucked for the first time. It's just so *obvious*.'

'Your hard-on's going.'

'Plus I want to sketch you afterwards. Becks, this is our

experience,' he said, kneeling up on the twigs and reaching out for her hair. 'I want us to be imaginative,' he said, allowing the thin strands to slip through his fingers.

'I could lie down on a bed of leaves and twigs, and you could have knocked your ball into the woods and crawled in on your hands and knees to retrieve it, and—'

'That's really crass. Come on, Becks, we can do better than this. I want you for the first time with nothing and no one else around. I want us to journey somewhere different, cut off, inaccessible to everyone else. Do you understand what I'm saying?'

Her dreams were peopled by such places. 'We can't do it at my house. My mum is always home.'

'What about when we go back to school?'

'In school?'

'No, not *in* school. You could bunk off and so could I. Just one day. My dad will be out at work.'

'My mum might see us.'

'You set off for school as you usually would, and then when you get to the bottom of the road, just take a left and come back on yourself down the alley. I'll let you in through our back gate.'

'I don't know. What if your dad comes home early or the school phones my mum?'

'I'll fake a note from your mum telling them you have a dentist's appointment in the morning. That way, they won't be expecting you until the afternoon.'

'And your dad?'

'My dad never comes home early. We'll have the whole morning together – we'll have enough time to, you know, and then I can get a draft outline of you finished.'

*

287

The night before she lost her virginity, Becca went to speak to her sister. Julia was sitting at her desk, writing something on a lined A4 notepad.

'What are you doing?'

Julia looked up and then immediately returned to her paper. 'Just making some notes on hyperbole in *Romeo and Juliet*.'

'What's "hyperbole"?' Becca said, closing the door quietly behind her. She didn't want to wake her father, who had gone to bed early.

'It's when you overstate something,' Julia said, holding the quivering sheet of paper over the waiting spikes of the ring binder. She snapped them shut, wincing mercilessly. 'Like "the brightness of her cheek would shame those stars" – that kind of thing.'

'But what's hyperbole about that?'

'Why is that hyperbolic? Because stars can't feel shame for one thing, and even if they could be outshone, it wouldn't be by a woman's cheek. So it's an exaggeration of Romeo's love for Juliet.'

'You should be a teacher.'

'I'm thinking about it.'

'Julia?'

'Yes.'

'Can I ask you something?'

'Yep, let me just put this in my bag.' Becca watched her sister's busy hands as she bent over the rucksack, holding it open so that her folder might slide in easily.

'Have you had sex before?'

Julia straightened up. She reached towards her desk for *Romeo and Juliet*, and placing it gently beside the folder in her bag, she said, 'Someone in my class asked me to do it with him. A boy called Eric.'

'And did you?'

She shook her head. 'He's really skinny. And always smells of milk. I'm too young, anyway. There's a greater chance of cervical cancer in girls who have sex early.'

'But what about the cheek embarrassing the stars?'

'Shaming the stars. What's that got to do with it?'

'I just mean if you love someone so much . . . you know, think they're as beautiful as the stars, wouldn't you just forget about everything else? Cancer and smelling of milk and all that kind of thing.'

'I don't love him. Not at all. So how can I forget about all those things? Do you love Jonathan?'

'Yes,' she whispered. 'I know I do.'

Julia nodded to acknowledge Becca's words as she gathered up the remaining pen and highlighter pens.

'There,' was all she could think to say as she stared at her empty desk.

The morning they chose was the last Friday before the October half-term – selected because they assumed their form tutor would be less likely to chase up absence after a week away from school.

Becca hadn't been inside Jonathan's house for many years. There had been no need – he was always at hers, in the care of her mother after school. All the curtains were still drawn; the rooms were dark and messy: clothes were strewn in the hallway and in the bedrooms. From the landing, Becca could see into Andrew's bedroom. The wardrobe doors hung open, and the drawers were midway out, with small garments spilling over the sides. On top of the chest of drawers – pushed up against the chimney breast – were bottles of perfume and lotions.

'Are they your mum's?'

'What?'

'The bottles of perfume.'

'Yeah.'

Becca walked into the bedroom once shared by Andrew and Marion. She felt the floorboards creak beneath the carpet, a muffled reminder that they'd been there all along, sharing the burden of carpet and hair and dead skin cells that had floated down and settled into the fibres. It had held up the shifting weight of two people arguing, circling one another with their claims and complaints, their supine load in sleep and sex and the unfathomable lightness of a separation. She reached out to touch the garments pushed to the far right-hand side of the wardrobe.

'Is this your mum's jacket?' she said, pulling a navy blazer that had fallen from the hanger and onto the shoes below.

'That was my nan's. My mum kept it after she died.'

'Do you think she'll ever come home?' Becca pulled an empty hanger from the rail and replaced the jacket carefully.

Jonathan shrugged his shoulders. 'Maybe. I don't know. Come on, this is my room.'

By contrast, Jonathan's bedroom was neat and tidy. It was the second largest, and his window looked out on the back garden. He pulled the curtains closed and began taking off his clothes. Becca had never seen him entirely naked – the sketching in her room hadn't required it, and they'd had to be so careful when they were out. He jumped into bed and pulled the duvet up over him. She followed his example but without haste. When she was naked, Jonathan lifted the duvet and invited her in.

They kissed gently, their naked bodies still separated by a few insulating inches. When Jonathan pulled her hip towards him, she took a deep breath in through her nose. The smell and taste of him invaded her senses with such force that she opened her eyes. And when she did, when she saw the tiny pores of his delicate skin, the eyelashes resting at the fringe of his closed lids, she felt the pounding of pleasure. It was warm and spherical and beat beneath her ribs, somewhere between her heart and lungs. She knew that if she took her hand from Jonathan's body and put it to her own, she'd feel its throb. She didn't know what it was, but she knew it was telling her to stop resisting, to let go.

When Jonathan pulled away from her to open his beside drawer, she lay on her back and closed her eyes. She had thought, in preparing for that morning, that it would feel like piercing her ear again – holding out a piece of flesh because she believed the right thing lay on the other side of the puncture – but it was nothing like that. It was a surrendering, yes, but one she wanted to make. She never doubted, as he moved inside her, that she was giving him something, that she was allowing him to enter a special place.

Jonathan sketched her lying on her side in his bed. He sat cross-legged on the carpet beside her, his penis hanging loose and lethargic as he drew. He pulled the duvet from her body so that he might have more of her for his pencil. Becca lay with her head on her outstretched arm. 'This is more comfortable,' she said, and he smiled as he continued down her ribcage.

An hour passed and Becca fell asleep. When she woke, her arm was numb from the weight of her head. She sat up and pulled her arm back to her. Jonathan was sitting at the end of the bed – still naked – his back to her.

'Have you finished?' she asked, pinching her arm to encourage the blood back again.

'Yeah,' he said without turning round. His shoulders were slumped forward, the tip of his pencil just visible as she leaned to the right.

'Can I see?'

'Hang on. Nearly finished.'

He turned round and held the image up to her. Her body was rendered faithfully, clearly in grey strokes. But her face. There was no face. Only the circular outline that should contain her features.

'I'm not in it.'

'What do you mean? That's you.'

'But my face. Why haven't you drawn my nose or my eyes?'

'I told you why. Then everyone will know you've posed naked for me.'

'I don't care about that. It's my body – I should be in it.'

'OK,' Jonathan nodded. 'But we both need to get back to school for afternoon registration. I can do it later.'

But that afternoon when Becca arrived home, her father's coat and bag were in the hallway.

'Dad?' she shouted.

'Up here,' came her mother's voice.

'What's going on?'

'We'll be down in a minute.'

But it was only Jane who came down. Becca was sitting in the kitchen with her bag unopened on the table before her.

'What's the matter with Dad? Why's he home early?'

'He's not feeling very well. It's been a very tiring half-term.'

'So he's just tired?'

'We don't know. He's going to see the doctor on Monday.'

'Can I go up?'

'Yes, but if he's asleep, come back down.'

The room was dark. As Becca tiptoed round to her father's side of the bed, she thought about how many times her parents had done what she and Jonathan had done that morning. She peered closely at her father's fifty-seven-year-old face, looking for clues to his exhaustion. She noticed how thin and yellow his skin had become, how deeply his head had sunk into the pillow. She was afraid for him.

Her mother was reading as she prepared dinner. In the intervening years she had dispensed with potatoes as a paperweight and bought herself a wooden book stand with a sprung clip to hold the book open in the right place.

'He looks really tired.'

'Yes,' she said, emptying a tin of kidney beans into a sieve and running cold water over them. 'He's working too hard.'

'And what about you?'

'What about me?'

'You haven't exactly made it easy for him, have you?'

Jane turned to look squarely at Becca. 'What's that supposed to mean?'

'All that business with Andrew. Daddy never wanted him here.'

'There's a lot you don't understand, Becca.'

Becca watched her mother move from sink to table to work surface. Suddenly she stopped and threw the sieve into the sink, scattering the deep red of the kidney beans against the sides. 'How dare you say such things to me? Who do you think you are?'

'I'm his daughter. And he's upstairs, tired and sick. You ignored him for all those years and now look!'

'I was childminding! I did it to help the boys. And now what? It's my fault Daddy isn't well?'

'You did it to help yourself.'

'I'm not going to discuss this with you. What you've said to me is unforgivable. I'd like you to go to your room, please.'

Chapter 35

Leonard went back to school after half-term, but he was physically exhausted, and though his doctor had advised him to come home each day at three o'clock so he could rest, he didn't improve – his skin was yellow with an uncomfortable sheen on it. It hung from his cheekbones, and he looked painfully frail and weak. Jane accompanied him to the GP for the second time in December and succeeded in obtaining a referral to see a specialist at Kingston Hospital, where, in January 1994, he was diagnosed with pancreatic cancer. The yellow tinge of his skin was caused by a tumour blocking bile from flowing into the small intestine. The oncologist was optimistic that they still had time to operate and try to remove the tumour.

Leonard's poor health and sudden vulnerability changed Jane. Becca witnessed her mother take charge of her father's health in a way that reasserted, firmly and finally, the roles in the house. She put Leonard to bed and cooked for him, washed him, talked to him and began reading passages from his favourite history books. When Becca came home from school, she would go and sit on the end of her parents' bed and listen to her mother reading.

'Disraeli referred to Gladstone as "that unprincipled maniac ... extraordinary mixture of envy, vindictiveness, hypocrisy and superstition".' She heard a coughing sound and looked over at her father. He was laughing up at the ceiling, and Jane, turning at the sound, began laughing as well. 'Do you remember that?'

He nodded.

'Gladstone and the Reform Act of 1884 ... Wasn't that the "one man, one vote" system?'

'Yes. You were such a dedicated student,' he whispered sadly.

Leonard underwent surgery in March. His surgeon declared the operation a success, but Leonard never returned to work. His body was so decimated by the illness, the operation and then the long process of convalescence that nobody expected his strength to return. Least of all him. And the strange truth that settled on the family was that nobody really wanted his strength to return. His cancer kept Andrew Wilson out and brought his daughters and wife close. It was an unlooked-for side effect but one for which the family, including Jane, seemed grateful.

The following September, Becca and Jonathan, an established couple in the eyes of everyone who knew them, continued into the upper sixth together. Jonathan was intent on an art foundation course, preferably in London so he could live at home and stay near Becca and his brother.

Robbie was in his final year of secondary school and had promised his father he'd try to get at least five decent grades at GCSE. It was a struggle for him and everyone else: his teachers had given up on him; the other boys viewed him as some sort of illicit drug – something to be approached recreationally and with caution. And Robbie couldn't see the point of working hard beyond keeping his father on side. Andrew had become increasingly firm on the point: sometimes shouting, shoving and more often than not threatening to send him back to the estate, where he could live with his granny. The last threat was always enough to remind Robbie he had to get his head down and study. He thought of his grandmother's flat – its stale, unopened air – sustained by the presence of Li and Steve two floors above. It wasn't that the thought filled him with horror, but the person he really loved, really cared for now his mother was gone was Jonathan. He was the only person who could possibly understand the loss he'd suffered, and if he were sent away to Stockwell, to languish in a tower block, he knew that Jonathan – busy with his art and Becca – would forget about him. So he got on and approached the teachers of subjects he thought he had a chance of passing and asked them to help him. Most of them were kind, some were positively euphoric, and one – his geography teacher – stroked his nicotine-stained beard and told Robbie to 'Go get yourself a job, son. School's not for you.'

Robbie, like his mother many years before, set his teeth together and focused his every effort on getting what he wanted. And what he wanted was to prove the old fucker wrong. So he sought out Julia, a year below him and just beginning her GCSE courses, and asked if he could study alongside her. Julia, self-sufficient and contained, allowed Robbie to sit beside her in the school library and learn from her example: he began copying her quick pencil, ready highlighting, paper-clipped sheets, folders and attention. He felt as though he'd achieved something at the end of every session by her side and began photocopying the pages of her books so he could continue studying into the night.

Leonard's strength never recovered because the tumour in his pancreas did. It came back, and so too did the jaundice. In June 1995, his oncologist told Jane and Leonard that the cancer was terminal.

Leonard swallowed and Jane instinctively grabbed for his hand. They were sitting side by side in front of the doctor's desk. Her hold was firm and hard, as though he were already beginning to disappear.

'How long?'

'It's not always helpful to think in terms of how long, but—'

'If you'll excuse me, Doctor, I'll be the judge of what's helpful. I'd like to know how much longer I have with my husband.'

'Mr Campbell? Are you happy for me to answer your wife's question?'

But Leonard couldn't lift his head. The diagnosis was exactly what he'd expected, what he'd thought his doctor was going to say, and yet when it came, when the words were finally in the room, he felt shocked and appalled by what was going to happen to him. He was going to die. And he couldn't lift his head to see his wife's face. He couldn't turn to the girl he'd fallen in love with all those years ago, when he'd been too old for her, and see the pain he knew he was causing. He'd been her teacher and then her husband, and soon he would be neither. He put his hand to his forehead and rubbed his temples. Jane still held his left hand as though it belonged to her.

'I can see this is a terrible shock to you both. It never gets any easier telling patients—'

'How long, Doctor?'

'In my opinion, a few months. Perhaps the autumn. It's very difficult to say.'

Leonard stood up. 'I need to use the toilet. Please excuse me.'

'Yes, it's just down the hall there on the right. When you come back, we can discuss our options for palliative care.'

But Jane couldn't bring herself to say anything to the oncologist as she helped Leonard out of the door. There was no 'our' in palliative care. It was for Leonard. She had been for Leonard, and soon she would never be again.

Becca took the news harder than Julia. They'd been under no illusions that while the surgery might have extended his life by a small margin, the cancer he had was an aggressive one and his continual decline spoke only of an end that was coming. The end of her father's life was all she could think about. As Jonathan waited for his A-level results, eager to find out where he'd go to study his art foundation course, Becca planned only to remain at home with her mother and sister. She had no interest in going to university and had withdrawn her UCAS application earlier in the year.

Jane rarely left Leonard's side. She read *Hard Times* and *Great Expectations* to him, holding his hand and trying different voices for the characters. Leonard, whose eyes were mostly half closed, would remind her that she'd used the same voice for Herbert Pocket as she'd used for Pip. She became more affectionate to him, joking that he was like Mr Todd in *A Handful of Dust*, keeping her beside him with endless reading of Dickens. She stroked his face to underline the humour, combing his thin hair with her fingertips and sometimes whispering to him as he fell asleep.

In September, Jonathan, who'd achieved all 'A's, went to

study art at Central St Martins. Robbie, transformed by Julia's example and a year of hard studying, left school with grades that astonished his teachers. He got 'A's in geography, history and English, and 'B's in all other subjects except food technology. He decided to follow in Jonathan's footsteps and enrolled in the sixth form to do his A levels.

But by the beginning of October, Leonard was about to die. Jane, always with him now, raised the topic of a hospice to him. 'I'd stay by your side,' she reassured him.

'At home, Jane. With you.'

She was lying behind him, Leonard beneath the duvet, her on top. She had her left arm around him; her right arm was redundant and curled up over her head like a flag.

'Are you sure this is what you want?'

'That man . . .'

'What man?'

'You know.'

'Oh, Leonard, please. Let's not talk about him.'

'I don't want to know. I don't need to know.'

'OK, but—'

'Please. Don't. I was much too old for you. I robbed you of your girlhood. Your parents knew it.'

'No, that's not true. They grew to like you and I chose you. I wanted to be with you. Remember?'

'I remember loving you.'

He'd never spoken to her in this way. In nineteen years he'd never relaxed enough to speak to her in sentences that sagged under the weight of their honesty.

'And I've loved you.'

'But not in the way you wanted to be loved. I always knew that.'

'I think this is the morphine speaking.'

'It's me speaking for the morphine. Could I have a drink of water?'

Jane leaned over him and picked up the plastic bottle of water with a straw sticking out of it. She brought it close to his lips, her chest resting against his left shoulder as he drank.

As she put it back on the bedside table, he began speaking again, this time more clearly. As though all he'd needed were to lubricate his throat.

'I've been a disappointment to you.'

'No, absolutely not. You haven't.' She pulled his left shoulder gently towards her bosom. He smiled.

'Yes, I have. I could never bring myself to do the things you wanted. In bed.'

'Leonard, please.' She relinquished his shoulder and lay back on the bed, her arms by her side, defeated by all her husband understood and had kept from her. The truth of their marriage was spilling out between them just as they felt the necessity of the bond. It was ruffling the sheets, dampening the pillows, and yet still they remained near one another. There was nowhere else to go.

'Don't upset yourself,' he continued, looking straight ahead of him at the wall. 'I know that I've been the lucky one. Would you pull me onto my back, please?'

Jane put her right hand on his shoulder and her left on his hip, now protruding sharply through his cotton pyjama bottoms. She rotated him backwards so that they were both able to lie, side by side, staring up at the ceiling.

'I've been lucky because I've had you by my side,' he said, reaching for her hand. 'And you've remained mine. And given me two daughters, one of whom, like me, has always wanted to remain by your side.' They both smiled at the ceiling, as though Becca's face could be traced in the Artex.

'But you're young yet. I want you to be happy. To continue living your life. Do you understand what I'm saying to you?'

'Yes.'

'But not him.'

'Leonard—'

'Please. Listen to me. I don't wish to say his name. You know to whom I'm referring. I've never liked the thought of him near you or our daughters. Please, Jane, not him.'

And in the peace of that afternoon, when the hum of their marriage drowned out all other noises, Jane made a promise to her dying husband. A necessary promise, and one she knew she'd never be able to keep.

Chapter 36

Leonard's death, when it came, was brutal and resolute. The moments of quiet, the drop and blur of morphine were poor preparation for the raw ravages of a life departing. Jane stayed close throughout, touching him with her voice, her face, her fingers, but the rattle was beyond her. It was beyond Leonard, taking him to a place for which he wasn't ready. It pulled at his failed and depleted body, ignoring the wife who now tried to hold him back.

He died on 13 October, a year after his daughter had lost her virginity to the boy next door, a year after he'd come home from school – exhausted and unwell – and thrown himself on his wife's care. The cancer had travelled quickly and, in kneading their family back together, had taken a quick and unflinching bite before anybody could stop it.

The silence that followed his death baffled Becca. There had been so much to say before, so much heavy noise in the house. The sound of water dripping back into the basin as Jane gave Leonard a bed bath, his quiet groan as she moved him onto his back and then onto his side in an effort to evade bedsores; the whispers, the tears, the gentle laughter – they were loud and Becca heard them all, so the resolute silence that followed felt like a new country. A place where the sound of her mother sneezing was loud and empty. The water dripping from the kitchen tap a terrible attempt to reproduce the old ways. Becca wasn't sure how she'd got there – she felt locked in one of her dreams, except this time she wanted out.

Julia had found her own way out because she never came fully in. She tried hard to maintain an outer core of strength, convincing herself she was doing it for her mother and sister. But on her own, with the door closed, she allowed herself to cry for the passing of a man who had been a part of her, a model for her own life. Every day she got up early to study. She was determined to follow in Leonard's footsteps, so she focused her attention – very minutely – on her new A-level courses and a place at Oxford.

Jane drew herself up for Leonard's funeral. In the days after his removal, she selected his best navy-blue suit, the one he'd worn for his interview at Wimbledon, and a white cotton shirt. It was only when she placed it down on the ironing board that she realised her care and effort for Leonard were about to come to an end. That once the shirt was crease-free and smooth, she would hand it over to people whose job it was to dress her husband's corpse. She allowed the tears to fall. They dropped onto the cotton and she ironed over them, releasing the steam that rose up to touch her wet face, and she felt it was all one: the tears, the steam, the hot pressure on the wrinkled garment. And she saw that it would soon be over.

Leonard's funeral service was held on Friday, 28 October at St George's Church, Esher. He was buried in Long Ditton Cemetery. Two weeks later, his school held a memorial service, which Jane, Becca and Julia attended. When she got home, Jane took off her shoes and coat, and trudged upstairs. In her bedroom, she stepped out of her skirt, tights, blouse and cardigan, and, leaving them in a heap on the floor, got into bed and fell asleep for three hours. When she woke up, her throat was sore and her chest had begun to ache. She stayed in the bed Leonard had died in and allowed the flu to close in over her. Her poor health, though temporary, served to highlight what a heavy undertaking death was. And as she coughed at the phlegm that remained stubbornly at the back of her throat, she felt – for moments at a time – what a precipice Leonard had been on. His age and poor health had been too heavy a weight; they'd all known he was going to tip over. But she was still young. At thirty-six years of age, she had another life before her. She could ease her aching lungs back to health and wash the sheets. She could take a shower and look at her face again.

As Becca poked her head round the door to ask if she wanted anything, she knew she had to step back from the edge.

Andrew bought a large bouquet of flowers and left them with Becca on the Wednesday following Leonard's death. It was a kind gesture met with mute acceptance from Becca, who took them from him without saying a word.

'I'm so sorry about your dad.'

She looked down at the red roses, sniffing at her own sorrow and ignoring the confident perfume of the colour beneath her.

'Jonathan told me.' Andrew brought a hand up to his nose, rubbing it and looking around him for something to beat at the silence with. 'Listen, tell your mum if there's anything I can do, I'd like to help in any way I can.'

Becca nodded and stepped back to close the door, but Andrew's foot was suddenly in the way.

'I know what it's like, you know. To not have a dad.'

She looked at him, bewildered.

'I mean, he was alive, but I never saw him. I just mean' – he rubbed his nose again – 'I know it's hard, but at least you know your dad loved you. I'm sorry – ignore me. Tell your mum I called round, please.'

Becca closed the door and walked down the hallway and into the back garden, where she lifted the lid of the outside bin as though it were one half of a set of cymbals. She threw the roses in and closed the lid with a bang.

Jonathan came to see her every evening on his way home from college. He showed her what he'd been working on and what artists he was studying as part of his written assessments, but Becca found it very hard to be interested.

'Why don't you come and meet me for lunch one day?'

'Where?'

'At St Martins. We could go and have a sandwich somewhere. I think you need to get out of this house.'

'I need to stay with my mum.'

'Well, when she's better, then. Come on, Becks – you hardly speak; you don't go anywhere, speak to anyone. Your dad wouldn't have wanted this.'

'I'm not turning into a recluse, don't worry. I just want to stay with my mum a bit longer. Until I know.'

'Know what?'

'Don't worry.'

'No, what? Tell me.'

'If she's going to get together with Andrew.'

'Oh.'

'What's that supposed to mean?'

'I'd just . . .'

'You'd just what?'

'I'd just forgotten about it, that's all.'

'You'd forgotten about it? You were the one who first put the idea in my head.'

'That was a long time ago.'

'Well, he was round here only last week with flowers for her.'

'He's just trying to be nice. It's the normal thing to do when someone dies.'

'And when someone's trying to worm his way in here.'

'I know you're upset, but don't take it out on my dad. He's trying to be nice.'

'Well, fuck him. And his fucking flowers.'

'There's no talking to you at the moment.'

'You just want to hear that I'm fine. That I'm coping. But my dad is gone now and she's all I've got left.'

Chapter 37

So much of marriage is stuff, Jane thought the morning she attempted to clear Leonard's desk. His cassette tapes were arranged neatly in a plastic case, his recorder still holding an Elgar symphony by the spools, reluctant to let go of Leonard's last choice. She was wiping uselessly at his desk, the back of his chair when Julia returned from her run.

'What are you doing?' she asked, pausing briefly at the door before going to the bathroom.

'Just giving this room a bit of a clean. It needs it. Daddy never dusted.'

'What can I do?' she asked, pulling her sweaty top off and throwing it in the laundry basket.

'Take those tapes downstairs, will you? Leave them by the door. The charity shop might want them.'

When Julia returned to her father's study, she began lifting the books in clumps of five from the shelves, holding them tight and together in the manner of an accordion player so that she could upend the pile at the last minute and build towers on the landing.

'I'll just wipe the shelves. We'll put them back later,' Jane said.

Julia nodded.

'You might want them when you go to university.'

'Yes.'

Leonard's belongings were shifted, temporarily displaced and then returned by women who didn't know how to accept he'd never use them again. But the tapes stayed on the telephone table, a victim of Jane's determination that something should go now that her husband had died. And as the first layer of thin dust fell lightly around them and began to settle, Jane saw that she had to make a decision.

Andrew called round one Saturday morning at the beginning of December. His hair was damp and his shirt so new it still bore the folded quadrants of the packaging.

'I'm just about to go to B&Q. The sealant round the shower tray needs doing and I suddenly thought I could seal in your bath if you want me to. You know, that bit near the taps.'

'Oh yes. But don't worry about that,' Jane said, stepping back. 'Do you want to come in?'

'No, I'd better get on. I'll be over later this afternoon if that's OK – do yours after I've done mine?'

'That's great. See you then,' she said, closing the door.

He returned just after four. Becca had emerged from her bedroom when she heard his voice in the hallway and then slunk back behind her door when she heard his heavy tread on the stairs. He went into the bathroom and turned on the radio, which was always tuned to Radio 4. She heard the crackle and hiss of retuning before he settled on some pop music she didn't recognise and then the contented whistling of someone who wants only sound to work.

'I've brought you a cup of tea,' Jane shouted above the music as she reached the landing.

'Lovely. Just stick it over there.'

'Is that what came off?' she asked, gesturing to the pile of blackened sealant.

'Yeah,' Andrew laughed. 'Pretty old.'

'Leonard wasn't much of a handyman.'

The song on the radio sounded louder in the silence that followed.

'I've been meaning to ask you a question, actually.'

'Oh yes?'

'Well, tell me if this is a bad idea or if you already have plans, but I was wondering what you're doing for Christmas.'

'Oh. I don't know. I think just a very quiet one here with the girls.'

'Well, that's what I was thinking. Christmas has been very quiet for us too, since, well, since Marion left. And I thought we could just have a quiet one together?'

'Here, you mean?'

'Or at mine. I don't mind.'

'I don't know.'

'I know Jonathan would love to spend it with Becca this year. And you know it might take everyone's mind off things.'

'Let me talk to the girls. See what they think.'

Jane raised the topic with her daughters the following evening after dinner. She was still sitting at the table, nursing the final few sips of red wine in her glass. Becca was standing by the bin, scraping away the remains of her chicken.

'Becca? Are you happy for me to invite the Wilsons over for Christmas this year?'

'I was planning to go over to Jonathan's in the evening anyway.'

'So it would be OK, then? To have them here during the day?'

'I didn't say that.'

'Becca, what difference does it make?' Julia asked from the sink, elbow-deep in the hot, foamy water.

'It makes a lot of difference. He's always here, fixing this, dropping off that. Can't we have one day when it's just us? Just the three of us?'

'Look around you,' Julia countered. 'It's always the three of us. Why don't you think of Mum? Or someone other than yourself for a change?'

'That's enough, Julia. Becca's entitled to her opinion.'

Julia pulled her arms from the water and dried them on a tea towel. 'We all miss Daddy. I do. Mum does,' she said, pointing to Jane, who had just pushed her chair back from the table so she could cross her legs. 'But he would want us to move on. He would want us all to be happy.'

Becca noticed how her mother looked down at her lap when Julia said this. She dropped the plate and cutlery into the bin in one smooth gesture.

'What the hell are you doing?'

'You think Andrew here on Christmas Day would make Daddy happy?'

'I'm saying we need to move on. That's all.'

'And I'm saying Daddy couldn't stand Andrew.' Becca looked across at her mother.

Jane stood up. 'Becca—'

'I'm right, aren't I? He hated him being here. He never approved of you looking after the boys.'

'It was a simple question, Becca, that's all. I take it from your response that you don't want them here, and I understand.

I'll let Andrew know in the morning.' Jane picked up her almost-empty wine glass and left the room.

Becca turned back to the bin and pushed her sleeve up so she could reach in to pull out the plate.

'You're so spoiled.'

She found the knife first and pushed past Julia to drop it into the sink.

'And needy,' Julia said, as Becca returned to the bin.

With a deeper rummage, she grabbed the plate, but as she turned to take it over to the sink, Julia blocked her way. 'I've always supported you and tried to help you. But it's time you got your act together and started thinking about what Mum needs.'

'Is that right?'

Julia grabbed the plate from Becca's grip and dropped it in the sink.

'That's right,' she said, walking out of the kitchen.

Jane pulled her cardigan on and let herself out of the house. She hesitated before Andrew's door, knocking slowly and quietly.

'It's too soon,' she said, when he invited her in. 'Becca and Julia are arguing about it now.'

'What's there to argue about?'

'Julia doesn't mind, but Becca—'

'She's not my biggest fan, is she?'

'It's difficult. Leonard's passing is still so recent. We need to give her time.'

'And you?'

'What about me?'

'How much time do you need?'

'Andrew—'

'I've waited, Jane. And I'll go on waiting, but I want to know if there's, you know . . .'

'What?'

'Something at the end of it,' he said, stepping towards her. With his fingers he pulled her forearms towards him. She allowed her body to go, for her nose to find his chest. She heard the vibration of his words: 'Just let me look after you.'

She knew that he was waiting for her to look up. That a simple extension of her upper spine would call down his kiss, his breath, and then their conversation, their delicate dance around her dead husband would fall away.

He used his hands to reach under her ears and tilt back her face. With his right thumb, he caressed her cheekbone. 'I want you. You know that.'

'Andrew—'

'I think it's time we stopped talking,' he said, kissing her gently on the mouth.

'But the boys,' she mumbled as he began pulling the cardigan down from her shoulders, restricting the movement of her arms.

'They're out. Won't be back for another hour.'

'Are you sure?'

'Positive,' he said, pulling her towards the sofa.

Andrew brought two bottles of expensive red with him. Jane placed the roasted turkey in the centre of the table and handed him the carving knife and fork. He pushed his chair back and cut into the breast, hesitantly at first and then with greater force as the slices of white flesh, capped with crispy yellow skin, began to fall from the bird.

Andrew topped his and Jane's glass up at every opportunity, offering wine to Becca, Jonathan and then, on Jane's say-so, to Julia and finally Robbie. Becca had drunk wine before, but never of this quality, and as she sipped, she felt her cheeks flush and her face loosen in a way that felt pleasant and freeing. She looked across at Jonathan and saw how relaxed he had become, laughing at his dad's jokes and offering his cracker to Julia, who had failed to secure a paper crown. She lifted her foot, nosing up his shin with her toes. He looked over at her and smiled.

'Who's for some Christmas pudding?' Jane said, standing up.

'Not for me, thanks,' Jonathan said, looking over at Becca.

'Do you mind if we head upstairs for a while? I'm a bit full.' Becca put her hand on her stomach.

'No, of course not. Shall I save you some?'

'Yes, please,' Becca said, pushing her wine glass towards Andrew, who dutifully refilled it.

'I think Becca's about to pull Jonathan's cracker,' Julia laughed after they'd left the room.

'Julia,' Jane said sharply. 'None of that, please.'

'What? It was a joke.'

'Not a very funny one.'

'I'm sure they'll find plenty to laugh at once she's given it a good tug,' Robbie sniggered.

'That's enough,' Andrew said, unable to shake the smile that threatened his face. And Jane, who sat beside him, felt his smile even though she couldn't see it. She felt the warmth and relaxation that radiated from his body and his happiness. Because it was happiness. They were together, their children coupled upstairs and laughing downstairs, and they had a new idea to explore.

*

When they closed the door, Becca began pulling at Jonathan's belt. The wine had made her possessive and impatient for Jonathan's body, his white skin and dark hair, the nakedness she had come to know yet still gasped at. She left him where he was, his back against the door, and lay down on the bed, lifting her hips so she could pull her skirt up and knickers down. He watched her get ready for him, her knees bent and legs apart as though awaiting a medical examination. He pulled his jeans and underpants off, standing on one leg as he did so, using Becca as a focal point to keep his balance.

They made love quickly, dimly aware of the noises downstairs, the scrape of the chairs and movements between rooms. Afterwards, Jonathan dressed and tiptoed back downstairs to get his art bag.

'What were they doing?' Becca asked as soon as he returned. She was still naked under the covers.

'Julia and Rob have gone next door.'

'And my mum?'

'They've gone into the lounge.'

'Have they closed the door?'

'Why do you care?'

'I just want to know.'

'The door is open and your mum is opening a Christmas present.'

'OK.'

'Except it's not OK, is it? What you really want to know is if they're naked. Like you are now.'

'You think I'm not being fair.'

'I think we should live and let live. We're together – why begrudge them their togetherness?'

She looked at his lips; they were dry and tinged red by the

wine. She liked how coarse they felt on her own. 'Not today. Please, I don't want to argue about them.'

'Well, that suits me. I wanted to show you something anyway.'

'What is it?' she asked, smoothing out the duvet in front of her.

'That picture my mum drew. I've decided to use it,' he said, pulling an A3 sheet from his bag. The baby's head and face had been rendered in the centre of the paper, the strokes self-consciously blue and broken. Round the outside of the head he'd drawn – in charcoal – a pair of wrinkled hands, spotted with age and decay, cradling the baby's head. The nails were long and ridged.

'It's beautiful. And sort of terrifying.'

'Isn't it?' Jonathan agreed. 'The hands are too old to grip this young life.'

'They're going to drop it.'

'But can't grasp it in order to drop it.'

'It reminds me of Beckett.'

'What's that?'

'Samuel Beckett. In *Waiting for Godot*, Pozzo says something about giving birth over a grave. How the light shines for a moment and then it's gone.'

'I need to write that down,' he said, reaching for a pen. 'So the hands are night and the baby is light?'

'It's more the idea that there isn't much space between being a baby and being an old person.'

'So you think narrow the space between the hands and the head?'

'Yeah.'

'That's brilliant,' he said, leaning across the duvet to kiss her. 'You know what this makes you?'

'What?'

'My muse.'

'We work well together,' she said smiling. But Jonathan was too busy scribbling on his picture to do anything but nod.

Jane and Andrew, content to have the kitchen to themselves, piled the dishes beside the sink and put the oven trays to soak. They filled their glasses once again, and Jane, with a box of Quality Street tucked under her arm, led the way to the lounge.

The Christmas tree was a small artificial one Andrew had dug out of the loft. Jane, Becca and Julia had opened their gifts to each other that morning, but as she took a seat on the sofa, she saw there was a neatly wrapped, perfectly square package under the branches.

'What's this?'

'Well,' he said, kneeling before her so he could take the Quality Street from her lap and place it on the carpet by her feet, 'it's just a very small thing. That might lead to a bigger thing.'

'That's rather intriguing.'

'Here,' he said, handing it to her. 'Open it.'

It was an Ella Fitzgerald CD. All her greatest hits in one compilation album.

'Andrew.'

'I know, I know. We said we wouldn't buy presents, but I saw the tapes by the front door and I thought, well, if you like listening to Ella on tape, you'll love the quality of a CD.'

'But I don't have a CD player.'

'So now for the bigger thing,' he said, reaching behind the curtain for a large cardboard box that hadn't been wrapped.

'Andrew, it's too much. I feel awful now. I haven't got any-thing for you.'

'I thought I could listen to it over here with you. In the evenings. So really, it's as much for me as it is for you.'

She looked down at his hopeful face. From this angle, she could peer closely at the thin red lines on his cheeks, the burst capillaries that spoke of his fondness for a drink. An in-clination for excess buried beneath the epidermis. And what she couldn't tell him was that the charm of Ella Fitzgerald was bound up in Leonard going upstairs to fetch his crappy cassette player. He didn't care the format was dated or there was no stereo permanently situated in the lounge. When he went up to his study to 'get the music', he was reaching for something he knew would give her pleasure. The recollection – too sharp and sudden – made her cry.

'What's the matter?'

Unable to stop the tears, her face bunched up in its efforts not to produce any sound.

'I'm sorry. I just thought you'd like it. I'll take it back.'

'No. No. It's just a memory. I'm fine. I *do* like it. Her, I mean.'

'Let me connect it up. We don't have to listen to anything tonight.'

But the following morning, when Julia got up to go for her run, she noticed the tapes by the front door had gone. A perfect rectangle of exposed polished wood amid the dust was all that was left to attest to their ever having been there.

Chapter 38

When Jonathan returned to college in January, his tutor left a message in his pigeonhole asking him to drop by before he went home for the day. Philippa Banks was a woman in her late forties, tall and thin and – on the surface – more conservative than Jonathan had expected to find in an art teacher. She wore a black jacket and a dusty pink shirt over jeans. On her left hand was a large three-stone engagement ring and small, functional watch with a brown leather strap. Her jeans were torn with flecks of paint around the crotch and knees, but her boots were pristine and expensive. Her hair was piled on her head and clipped into place with hundreds of kirby grips, but her make-up was neat and her eyeliner immaculately applied. Philippa asked Jonathan to sit down and then closed the door. Her office was small, so her return to her desk chair required her to walk uncomfortably close to Jonathan before she could slide back into place.

'How are you getting on?'

'OK, I think. I'm about to finish the Hockney stuff.'

'Oh yes, don't worry … I haven't asked you in here to discuss that. No, what I wanted to talk to you about is Japan.'

'Japan.'

'In your personal statement you mentioned an interest in Japanese art and culture. You said' – she looked down at a photocopied sheet of paper clipped to a page in her notebook – 'you were "exploring female posturing in particular".'

'That was for my A-level coursework.'

'And are you still interested?'

'In Japanese art? Yes.'

'Listen, Jonathan, I've caught you unawares, I can tell. The reason I'm reminding you of all this is because Tokyo University of the Arts are interested in setting up an exchange programme with one or two art colleges here in London. We're looking to send three, maybe four students to study in Tokyo and they would send a similar number here. If successful, we'd formalise the arrangement and broaden its scope.' She smiled at Jonathan. 'So what do you think?'

He nodded his head in an effort to fill the silence. 'That's great.'

'Jonathan, I'm asking whether you'd be interested in filling one of those spaces.'

'Me?'

'Yes. Would you like to go and study in Japan?'

His first thought was for his mother in Ireland. How would she ever find him if he were in Tokyo? But Philippa's smile and diamonds and paint under her fingernails were so much more tangible than the face that had slipped away six years ago. His second thought was for Becca, his friend and now girlfriend, who had holed herself up behind a wall of her own making.

'Can I think about it?'

Chapter 39

Becca's response, when he mentioned Philippa's offer a week later, surprised him. They were sitting on the floor of his bedroom.

'I wanted you, not him.'

'What do you mean?'

'She always used you as a justification for having you and Robbie here so much. That you were a friend to me when I didn't have anyone else. Even when my dad was so dead against it.'

'And?'

'And now you're leaving. You were for me and now you're going.'

'I don't understand. Why are you so ... so static all of a sudden? You could come with me, you know.'

'How would that work?'

'I don't know. You could save up, ask your mum for money. Just come and hang out. I'd sketch you; you could write a novel. Don't you want to just *live* again?'

'I need to stay here. For her.'

He shuffled closer and peered into her eyes. 'Becks, remember the art rooms? How we'd separate when we got there but always come back together? We can do that somewhere else. Somewhere far away.'

'He'd love that.'

'Are you on about my dad? Again? Yes, they're together. We suspected it for a long time and now it's happening. What's wrong with that?'

'Because there's something not right about him. My dad knew it and I know it.'

'Fuck you, Becca.'

She nodded.

'I love you, but I can't just stop and stand still like you. I have to live my life.'

'I wish I could do the same.'

'So do it.'

'I have this feeling. I'm not expecting you to understand . . .'

'Go on.'

'I need to hold on to her.' There was so much more that she wanted to say: that in the process of holding on to her mother, she felt as though she were losing herself. That she felt slowly crossed out – as though the events that had begun the day she let him inside her were the beginning of her own obliteration. The same day her father had started dying. But she stopped herself because she knew from the way he held his arms out to her that he'd decided to go.

He left on a wet, grey afternoon in April. Becca watched him climb into the passenger side of his dad's van and drive away. He raised a hand to her, more surrender than wave, as she stared back at him from the lounge window. Her vision blurred with tears in the seconds after the van disappeared, when she knew he really wasn't coming back. She lowered the net curtain and walked towards the door, but she felt clumsy and shaken by the farewell and hadn't noticed the tall wooden CD stand that stood like an arrogant skyscraper next to the television. She walked into it with force; the pain was red-hot and outrageous. It hurt when so much else hurt. When her heart, her fucking heart was already breaking. She picked up the tower and threw it across the room, the CDs tumbling from their slots as it fell. The violence satisfied an instinct that throbbed inside her. She knew it was wrong, even as she pulled the player from its leads, but she couldn't stop. She launched it at the same wall and enjoyed, for a brief second, the dull thud of its defeat against the wallpaper.

Becca was upstairs in her bedroom when Jane came home.

'Becca!'

'Up here,' Becca shouted.

'What on earth?' She ran upstairs and opened her door. Becca was sitting on her bed with a bag of frozen peas resting across the metatarsals of her right foot. 'Have you seen downstairs? Did they hurt you?' she shouted, her voice rising at the sight of the peas.

'No. Mum—'

'Have you called the police? How did they get in? I must phone Andrew—'

'It was me.'

Jane's hands dropped. She looked small and helpless before the truth, so candidly delivered.

'What?'

'I stubbed my toe.'

'Yes, I see that. But what about the CDs and the stereo? They're all over the carpet.'

'I got angry.'

'Oh my God.' Jane leaned back against the wall, squatting down with relief and then incomprehension. 'You did all that because you hurt your toe?'

But as she spoke, they heard a knock at the door.

'Andrew.'

'Don't let him in,' Becca cried.

'What? Becca, this is getting out of hand. How am I going to explain downstairs?'

'Don't explain anything. Just tell him to go away. Or to fuck the fuck off.'

Jane pulled herself up at the second knock. 'I can't take any more of this, Becca. Stay here. I'll be back in a minute.'

She heard her mother open the door and then Andrew's voice.

'He got off OK. Bloody nightmare parking, though.'

'Andrew, I can't talk now. I'll pop over to you in a bit.'

'What's the matter? Is it Becca?'

'It's nothing.'

'What's she done?'

'Please, Andrew. Let me deal with this. I'll speak to you later?'

Jane paused at Becca's open door on the way to her own bedroom. She didn't have the strength to go inside. 'Is it broken?' she asked, looking at the peas from the hallway.

'I don't know.'

'Well, is it swollen?' she asked, walking over to Becca's bed and sitting down beside her. But instead of looking at her toe, she began stroking her daughter's hair. The way she used to when Becca woke, frightened by one of her dreams, in the middle of the night. 'I know you loved him.'

She felt the fine strands shift beneath her hand as Becca

nodded at her simple sentence. 'And that you'll miss him. But I'm here. You're not alone.'

And Becca, with a sudden desire to be a little girl again, put her arms around her mother's waist and pulled her close. The peas slid from the top of her foot and Jane was able to see that her toes weren't swollen.

Many of the CD cases were cracked, and the tower didn't stand alone anymore. When Andrew came over the following evening, he noticed immediately that it was propped against the wall.

'What's happened here?' He turned to the CD player and pressed the 'eject' button. They stood in silence as the motor whirred but no disc tray appeared. 'Is it broken?'

'We had a little accident,' Jane said quietly.

He drew himself up and stood tall. 'What kind of accident?'

'I walked into the tower and knocked it over.'

'Is that right?'

'Yes,' Jane said, sitting down on the sofa.

'And I suppose the tower fell into the player and broke it?'

'It must have done.'

'And it's got nothing to do with Becca?'

'Andrew. I've told you what happened.'

'That's bullshit, Jane. And you know it.'

'Don't speak to me like that,' she said, standing up. 'Not in my own house. I've told you what happened and that's it. I'm not obliged to offer you any other explanations.'

'No, you don't owe me nothing. Never mind I bought you all this. That I look after you, seal the bath, get things out of the loft and anything else you want done around here.'

'And for that I should be grateful? For that I should put up with this? An inquisition in my own home! I'm sorry about

325

the CDs and the player. I will gladly refund you every penny.'

'I don't want your money. I just want you. I want you and me to be happy. Can't you see that?'

'Yes, I can.' Jane lowered her voice. 'But you need to understand that Becca's different. She's complicated but pure and good. And sometimes I think I'm the only person who's ever understood her.'

Chapter 40

Becca stopped writing and began to gain weight. Her inertia was greedy, hungry for calories – it prompted her to wander downstairs to the kitchen at all hours of the night and day. She ate whole packets of biscuits, dry crackers, toast thick with peanut butter. Her thirst was unquenchable; it needed sugar and carbonation. She drank bottles of Coca-Cola, and when they were finished, emptied the fridge of whatever juice she could find. She felt her waist widen and took a perverse joy in standing before the mirror naked. Her bones were sinking beneath the new, abundant softness. She strained to lift her neck and force her shoulders forward so that she might see her clavicle and remember Jonathan's restless eyes and agitated strokes as he worked to commit her to paper. She stepped towards the mirror and relaxed her shoulders to look more closely at her stomach. It was long and almost rectangular now; like a baking tray full of cake batter before it goes in the oven. It had spilled over her pelvis, falling gently towards her thighs.

For the first few weeks Jonathan sent postcards to Becca. On the reverse was artwork by famous Japanese artists, often containing elegant geishas, their eyes pulled sharp and wide to express their disregard for the exchange programme they found themselves enmeshed in.

His sentences were meant for her – they contained reflections on life in Japan, the people, customs and even the food – but there was nothing for her specifically. At first, Becca wondered if it was because the postcard was so public, that perhaps the presence of an envelope would change things. As the weeks passed and the postcards dwindled in frequency, she found she couldn't bring herself to reply. And out of her malaise she remembered the first dream she ever shared with Jonathan: the one with the hole in the wall and the sticky place on the other side. It struck her then that Jonathan had always seen her through the hole. She'd had to guide him to draw it wide enough for her to appear on the other side, and then, years later, she'd guided him towards her in order for his art to flourish. But with distance the hole had decreased to a tiny pinprick of light by which he might remember her. And Becca, still devastated by her father's death and the spectre of her mother's relationship with Andrew, was content to be forgotten.

Jonathan never returned to the UK. He stopped writing to Becca, but she heard about him through her mother and Andrew, who had become – by September 1997, less than two years after her father's death – her mother's almost constant companion.

Jonathan had managed to apply for and transfer to a full degree course at the university in Tokyo. In the same year, Robbie started at Lancaster University, where he went to study media studies, and the following year, Andrew drove Julia, all her belongings packed in the back of his van, to the same college Leonard had attended in Oxford, where she'd secured a place to read history. Their family had dwindled, and now that it was just the two of them, Becca knew Andrew would continue his attempts to have Jane all for himself.

Becca had also begun to assume a kind of observant normalcy. She got a job in Waitrose, initially on the shop floor, restocking shelves and affixing special-offer labels to the shelves, but quickly progressed to the tills, where she was happier. She enjoyed the efficiency of scanning through items, slowing as the customer struggled to pack and then increasing in speed as she ushered the final few from her conveyor belt. She would use that lull to strike up conversation, ask somebody how their day had been or ring the bell if an item hadn't scanned properly. She liked how clearly laid out her work was, and after three months' service, she earned her staff discount of fifteen per cent off – something Jane was grateful for. Leonard's pension had passed over to her, as well as a lump sum for his death in service. They had no mortgage, but Jane, cautious by nature, knew that what money she had saved up had to be preserved. With only two mouths to feed and Becca's small wage from the supermarket, they weren't exactly frugal, but nothing was wasted.

After Julia went to Oxford, Andrew – who regularly spent the night at Jane's – raised the topic of moving in together. It was after dinner and Becca had already eaten and disappeared upstairs. She never missed an opportunity to disappear when Andrew was in the house.

'I think it might be a bit soon for that.'

'How is it too soon? Your kids are all grown and so are mine.'

'Yes, but I still have one of mine at home.'

'Well, maybe me moving in will help with that.'

'And how on earth would it work? Me to you or you to me?'

'I'd keep my place and move in here. I've never liked it very much – moving into it was all Marion's idea.' The mention of his wife's name stalled the conversation. Jane stood up and, putting her plate on top of Andrew's, carried them over to the sink. 'What's the matter?'

'You haven't mentioned her for such a long time.'

'That's because it was a long time ago.'

'I don't know, Andrew. That's the honest answer. I feel I need to maintain some stability for Becca. She's lost her father and then Jonathan and now Julia. I'm all she has left.'

Andrew looked down at the table and shook his head. He had a double chin and soft, saggy skin where once his face had been slim and cruel.

'What?'

'You say she needs stability, but has it ever occurred to you that maybe what she needs is shaking up?'

Jane squirted washing-up liquid across the plates and watched the grease dissolve under the hot spray of water.

'I'm not going to shake my daughter up.'

'That's not what I'm saying. But if you always make it easy for them, then of course they're going to stick around.' He stood up and approached her at the sink, cupping her elbows and turning her round to face him. 'It was the same with Robbie. I gave him two options: study for your GCSEs or go back to live on the estate with my mum. I rocked the boat for him. And I think that's what you've got to do with Becca. She's too comfortable here.'

Jane stared into his broad chest and raised her hands to his shoulders, as though she wanted to hang from him for a little while. He held her close and whispered, 'Come on, come back to mine tonight.'

She nodded and turned off the tap.

Chapter 41

As long as Becca remained at home, Jane wouldn't coun-
tenance them living together. It was something that
frustrated Andrew, but by 2001, he had grown to accept the
arrangement.

Jonathan had moved to southern Japan, where he'd taken
on the role of director of a small contemporary art gallery in
Matsuyama city. Within months of settling in Matsuyama,
he began seeing his assistant, an ambitious woman eighteen
months younger than him, called Minako. She had a small,
well-located apartment in Dōgo, which Jonathan quickly
moved into. Together they began showcasing provocative
artwork with special exhibitions in the evening at which they
served a variety of gin and played cutting-edge hip-hop. It
was a successful formula in a city flooded with US and UK
expats all searching for the right blend of alcohol, art and
music. By May 2001, they were viewing larger premises near
Matsuyama Castle and Minako had convinced Jonathan to
showcase some of his own art on the opening night.

Jonathan phoned Andrew early one morning just as his
father was going to bed and asked him to come to Japan for
the opening night.

'When is it?'

'We think we're looking at September now. Possibly the first or second week. I'll know more soon. We haven't signed the lease yet, but I'm pretty sure it will go through.'

'Sounds like it's all working out for you, son.'

'It is. I'd like you to come and see it.'

'I don't know. It's a long way.'

'Bring Jane.'

'I'll see what she says.'

'So that's a yes?'

'It's a we'll see.'

Jane was more positive than Andrew had anticipated. She remembered Jonathan's postcards from years before, where the stamp had spoken of a land far removed from her own. But she was clear from the beginning: Becca had to come.

'I thought this might be an opportunity for you and me to spend some time together. You know, proper time. In a hotel room on our own.'

'This is exactly the kind of opportunity that Becca needs. Her life has narrowed so considerably since she lost Leonard, and what with Julia and Jonathan both off on their separate adventures, I think she needs this.'

'But Jonathan and Minako? That's not going to be easy, is it?'

'That was a long time ago. I think she'd enjoy seeing him again. Let's not forget they were friends for a long time before anything else happened.'

'That reminds me of another couple I know.'

'Were we ever friends?'

'Friends with benefits,' he said, winking.

'Let me talk to Becca.'

It was a long twelve hours for all three of them, but for Becca it was an opportunity to watch the progress of the flight on the screen in front of her and consider how far she'd travelled from Jonathan since he'd begun his foundation course in London. She stared at the little animation of her plane caught between London and Osaka, like a bird on a wire, hovering above Russia, apparently unmoving but with a ground speed of five hundred and fifty miles per hour, and wondered if she might find an answer in Japan. In Jonathan. She knew he had a girlfriend – her mother had told her all about Minako – and the thought of his having moved on didn't perturb her, but she wondered if his example, of having removed himself from one life in order to successfully build another, might be the prompt she needed to get on and live her own again.

Kansai Airport was a blur of Japanese symbols and deceptively legible signs that, once decoded, still made no sense. She followed her mother, who held on to Andrew as he, towering above the Japanese, fought his way through the neat lines of people. Their airline representative ushered them through immigration and towards the gate for their internal flight to Matsuyama.

Matsuyama Airport was much smaller but no less clean. It hummed to its own order, and Andrew, who had given up trying to make sense of the signs, allowed himself to be swept along by the Japanese passengers, who walked calmly towards baggage reclaim and the arrivals hall. On the other side of the automatic doors was Jonathan, his hair longer and his face damp from the humidity of getting out of his car and walking into the airport.

'Welcome to Japan,' he said with his arms out wide, as

Andrew pushed the trolley towards him.

'Hello, son,' he said, his voice suddenly husky. He put his hands on Jonathan's shoulders and held him in place for a minute. 'What's all this?' he said, lifting the ends of his brown hair, which now hung down the back of his neck.

But Jonathan, misunderstanding him, said, 'Oh, this is Minako,' and from behind Jonathan emerged a small woman with shoulder-length black hair, her fringe cut uncompromisingly above her eyebrows.

'Nice to meet you,' Andrew said, bending at the waist, enunciating every word horribly.

'Jane, thanks so much for making the journey.' Jonathan held his arms out to her and looked sideways at Becca, who stood back. He smiled at her as he hugged Jane.

'And you,' he said, stepping back so he was in line with Becca. 'I've missed you. Thanks for coming.'

'It's lovely to be here.' They continued smiling at each other until Becca said, 'Do I not get a hug?'

'Come here,' he said, and pulled her to him, but before she could say anything, Andrew was thrusting Minako at Becca and Jane.

'And this is Minako.'

'Mina-chan, please meet my dad's girlfriend, Jane, and her daughter Becca.'

Becca and Jane stood side by side, straitened by the description.

Jane had the presence of mind to smile and break the tension. She held out her hand to Minako. 'It's very nice to meet you.'

'Come this way, guys,' Jonathan said, ushering them through the arrivals lounge. 'We'll get your things in the car and get going. Mina-chan's been cooking, and we've laid out futons for you. So you can have a sleep if you want one, or we can take you to Dōgo Onsen—'

'Son, Jane and I have booked a hotel,' but as he was speaking, the doors opened and unleashed the dank, oppressive humidity of Japan in the summer. 'Christ,' Andrew said, looking at his son as though there was something Jonathan could do about it.

'I know.'

'We call it "*mushi mushi*",' Minako said, smiling at Becca, who pulled her suitcase while trying to move the now sticky hair from out of her eyes.

In the car, Andrew explained that he'd booked rooms for the three of them in a nearby hotel.

'It's called a ree-oh-kan, I think,' Jane said from the back seat.

Jonathan was driving, and Andrew sat beside him in the passenger seat. Minako, with her slender waist and small frame, had positioned herself between Becca and Jane.

'Ah yes, a ryokan. Traditional Japanese inn.'

'Yes, that's it,' Jane said, turning her body to Minako but keeping her face near the air-conditioning vent.

'You didn't need to do that, Dad. We can put you up.'

'I know, but we want to give you your space. You've got a lot coming up with the exhibition. When is it?'

'Tomorrow night. So we've got time to do something tonight. If you feel up to it.'

'The only thing I feel up to right now is my bed.'

'But we're looking forward to tomorrow night, and I'm sure, once we've had a shower and a sleep, we'll be right as rain,' Jane spoke to the space between the two men.

Becca sat with her body angled away from Minako and stared out of the window.

The following morning, Becca tapped lightly on Jane and Andrew's door, but hearing nothing, she went downstairs to the reception and out into the bright sunshine. She'd had the good sense to wear knee-length shorts and sandals and a loose-fitting cotton T-shirt, but within a few blocks she felt the sweat gather and fall down her spine, collecting at the top of her waistband. She continued walking until she came to a small convenience store, and feeling suddenly thirsty for water and air-conditioning, she stepped inside. All the buildings looked so temporary and flimsy in design, and yet once she was inside, she felt as though she'd crossed into another dimension, one brighter, colder and infinitely more civilised than the street outside. She bought a bottle of water and a triangle snack that appeared to promise rice and seaweed. She paid with a ten-thousand-yen note her mother had given her at the airport.

Becca took her snack and water, and crossed the road, where she saw a bench in the middle of a patch of green, under a tree. She opened her water and tasted something unexpectedly sweet. She unwrapped the snack and took a bite. The seaweed was crisp and salty, breaking easily under her teeth, and beneath was rice and the taste of concentrated salmon. Tired from the flight, hungry from a sleep that had ended too early, the onigiri tasted delicious. It was new and sustaining in a way she hadn't expected. She took another swig of the sweet water and chewed thoughtfully. She knew her mother would wake next to Andrew and that they'd probably start having sex as soon as consciousness of their privacy came to them, but for the first time in what felt like years, she didn't care. She understood why Jonathan had felt the need to travel so far. There was a place for her, and it turned out it was on the sticky side of the wall.

Chapter 42

Becca had arranged to meet her mother and Andrew downstairs in the lobby at 6 p.m. The exhibition was due to start at 7.30 p.m., and Jonathan had assured them it was a twenty-minute walk or a five-minute cab ride. Andrew was reluctant to walk, but Becca managed to convince Jane that she knew the way. She'd spent the day exploring Dōgo and had walked into Matsuyama town centre earlier, returning on the tram to have a shower and prepare herself for the evening. The temperature had also dropped, so the mugginess was less oppressive. Jane, lifted by Becca's eagerness and the time she'd spent alone with Andrew, was keen to acquiesce.

'If Jonathan's right about how long it will take us to walk, we've got plenty of time. We could even stop off for a drink if you like.'

Andrew considered this. 'And you've got a map, have you?'

Becca nodded to her mother. 'I've got a map, but I know the way.'

'Let's go, then,' Andrew said as he put his hand on the small of Jane's back.

*

The gallery was on a road that skirted Matsuyama Castle. It ascended gently to a place where you could take a cable car to the top of the castle. They were at the gallery by six thirty and could see Jonathan and Minako busily arranging furniture and speaking on the phone through the closed doors.

'Let's get a beer over there,' Andrew said, pointing to a small bar with the London Underground sign positioned on some outside decking. They crossed the road and sat down, Becca first and then Jane next to her. Andrew sat opposite and looked around him. 'I feel like someone's going to ask for my ticket any minute.'

'*Konbanwa.*' A young man wearing white espadrilles approached the table.

'English,' Andrew said. 'You speak?'

'Yes, of course. Good evening. Can I get you something to drink?'

'Er, erm ...'

'Would you like to see the menu?' he said, turning to Jane and Becca.

'I'll have a white wine, please,' Jane said, and turned to Becca. 'Darling, what would you like?'

'A gin and tonic, please.'

'Gin tonic. And you, sir?' The waiter returned to Andrew, who appeared to be searching for something unsayable.

'*Nama beeru*, please,' he said suddenly, so pleased with himself that Jane threw her head back and laughed.

Even Becca had to smile.

'Oh, well done, darling. What's that?'

'A *beeru*. It means beer. I looked it up in our travel guide.'

'Very clever. And there's me just ordering a white wine. I should have made more of an effort.'

*

Jane took Andrew's hand as they walked into the small gallery. The air conditioning, so welcome at all other times, felt too cold and icy for the evening and their thin clothes. Goose pimples appeared on Jane's upper arms and she realised, as she pressed her body to Andrew's, that she was excited to be away with him, to be his girlfriend and at the beginning of an evening that would culminate in a hotel room where they could be as naked as they liked.

Jonathan walked towards them, his arms open in a more polished performance of yesterday's greeting at the airport. He was wearing an olive-green linen suit with a white shirt buttoned up to the collar, waiting patiently for a tie.

'Welcome to the Toyoshima-Lambert. Toyoshima-san is just over there,' Jonathan said, turning his body but not pointing to anyone. 'He founded the gallery in our old premises over the river, and Frederick Lambert, his companion' – Jonathan coughed into his hand – 'made this new move possible.' Andrew looked over his son's shoulder to see the men he was referring to, but he could only see five or six Japanese men in dark suits standing round an oil painting of a nose. It was large and curved, the nostrils wide and monstrous. There was one European-looking man with salt-and-pepper hair who stood among the Japanese men.

'Is that Lambert there?' Andrew said, inclining his forehead towards the grey-haired man.

'Yes, that's him,' Jonathan said without looking, and steered the three of them over to a tall white cube that stood in the corner of the room. 'Minako, will you get everyone a drink?'

'Of course,' Minako said, going behind the cube and pulling from within it several bottles of gin and one kind of tonic. 'Gin and tonic?' she asked, smiling up at Andrew and Jane.

'Yeah, sure.'

She began pulling cut-glass tumblers from the inner shelves of the cube.

'Ice?'

'No, thank you,' said Jane, crossing her arms to try and hide her nipples. The lemon and lime had already been cut into wedges; Minako squeezed a lime wedge and deposited a small black straw into each glass. Becca took hers and sipped gratefully. It tasted sharper than the one she'd just had, but it made the room feel smaller and more manageable. She stepped away from her mother and began examining the walls.

'What's that over there?' she heard Andrew ask Jonathan behind her.

'My new collection.'

Becca turned round to see where he was pointing. The wall was covered in a bright white sheet.

'How's that?'

'It's being unveiled in about twenty minutes. Mr Toyoshima and Mr Lambert have been kind enough to suggest I use tonight's opening to showcase my new collection.'

Andrew nodded his head and turned to Jane. '*Unveiled*, eh?'

Jane reached out for Jonathan's hand. 'Oh, Jonathan. You've really made a life for yourself here. We're so proud of you.'

'Thank you.' He bowed his head at the praise, and as if her use of the collective noun were too glaring to ignore, he said, 'I just wish Mum could have been here.'

'I know, son.'

'I've tried, you know.'

'Tried what?'

'Tried getting in touch. I found an email address for Uncle Jonny, but he said she never made contact with any of the family back in Ireland. Just disappeared.'

'Listen, of course your mum would've been proud. But let's not dwell on that. Tonight's your big night. And you've got to concentrate on that.'

At 8 p.m., Mr Toyoshima stood up in front of the white sheet and, in English, thanked everybody for coming.

'In Japanese, we say "*youkoso*",' he smiled at Jane, 'and it means "welcome". We like to say welcome to Jonathan-san's family, who have travelled here from England. We are very grateful for his hard work and his vision for this gallery. Jonathan-san, please!'

Amid clapping, Jonathan joined Mr Toyoshima in front of the sheet. Mr Toyoshima, whose cheeks were flushed red with gin, slapped him on the back and went to stand next to Frederick Lambert. Jonathan bowed deeply to both men and turned back to the room.

'I'd like to take this opportunity to thank Mr Toyoshima for placing his faith in me and to Mr Lambert for supporting, so fully, our endeavours here at the gallery. I'm confident we will fill this new space with artwork that is both powerful and compelling and, crucially, with people keen to view it. Galleries are sustained by two forces – the idea and the people drawn to that idea – and here, as director of the Toyoshima-Lambert, I seek to knit the two together in a most necessary marriage.'

Jane squeezed Andrew's hand as Jonathan continued.

'It is therefore my great honour,' he said, smiling at Minako, who had been standing in front of Becca, 'to reveal my latest collection, *yume*.' At Jonathan's smile, she went to stand beside the white sheet, her right hand poised to pull it down.

The sheet dropped and there on the wall were a combination of charcoal sketches and small- to medium-sized oil paintings on canvas. The group surged forward, but Becca stayed where she was, her eyes drawn to the images in the top right corner. She saw her naked self from years ago – small and slim – sitting in the *seiza* position. Except when she looked closer, she saw Jonathan had drawn her with short black hair and a hard fringe. The realisation he'd supplanted her head with Minako's was so sharp she felt it pierce the delicate triangle that formed between her lungs and the top of her diaphragm. Her breath, when it finally returned to the room, was shallow and hesitant. She looked to the drawing beside it and saw herself lying stretched and asleep, her head resting heavily on her left arm in a postcoital slump. But again, there was the despotic fringe falling in obedience to Jonathan's brush.

She stepped back as she felt herself jostled by those who'd already looked at the images on the other side of the display. They wanted some of what she'd seen. What she'd given Jonathan.

'What does "*yume*" mean?' she heard Andrew ask Jane.

'Dreams,' Becca answered as she stepped into the space vacated on the left. Even before she saw Jonathan's reworking of the wall with the hole in it, she knew what to expect. She knew the small figure on the other side of the wall would be Minako. Her eye shifted from one dream to the next until it was caught by the streak of azure in a picture in the bottom right-hand corner, striking because it was surrounded by so much black and grey, and there, floating in the swim-along water, was Minako.

She dropped her glass and heard it hit the stripped wood flooring before smashing into tiny pieces, the explosion of glass mirroring almost entirely the breaking of her own understanding. Her naked body, given as a gift to steady his pencil, the dreams she'd insisted – even as a child – that he place her in, he'd taken it all and given them to another woman.

Chapter 43

Becca was grateful for her own room in the hotel. She ran most of the way back to Dōgo so that by the time she walked into the air-conditioned lobby, she was sweating and flushed. She took her key and walked slowly, breathing through her nose, up the stairs and let herself in. The genkan and tatami mats gently reminded her to remove her shoes, and as she stepped up onto the soft rush straw and felt it creak beneath her, she felt calm enough to remember what she'd just seen. She sat down on her futon and replayed the moment she'd realised it was Minako who now occupied her dreams. But the violent shock, the pain of it, had been that transition from pleasure to pain, when she'd understood that yes, he'd remembered but he hadn't felt her worthy of her own dream. She lay face down on her futon and heard a knock at her door.

'Becca, let me in.'

Becca pushed herself up and opened the door to her mother.

'You have to take your shoes off.'

'Oh, sorry.' Jane stepped back down to the genkan and pulled off her sandals.

'What on earth's going on with you? Why did you run away like that? It was horribly embarrassing for Jonathan and Minako.'

'You wouldn't understand.'

'I think I do, Becca.'

Jane reached out a hand to stroke Becca's hair. 'Is it because there's so much of Minako in his artwork?'

Becca took a deep breath.

'Darling, she's his girlfriend. And I know you were once that to him, but we all have to move on. Look at me and Daddy. Of course I miss him, of course I think about him – every day, in fact – but we all have to move on. It doesn't mean I didn't love him. And Jonathan's fondness for Minako doesn't invalidate the way he felt about you.'

'Those pictures, they weren't his.'

'What do you mean? Whose are they, then?'

'I just feel as though everything's been taken from me. Daddy, Jonathan, you and now even my own dreams have been given to someone else.'

'I don't understand.'

'I said you wouldn't. Don't worry. Go back to Andrew.'

'Darling, I can't leave you like this.' Jane grabbed Becca's hand and held on to it tightly.

Becca pulled her mother's hand from hers, finger by finger. 'Yes, you can. And you will. Good night.'

They flew home the following Monday. Becca had said very little to her mother and nothing to Andrew since the night of the exhibition. Jonathan had tried to speak to her, but she wouldn't open the door of her room to him and so the three of them departed from Kansai Airport under a dismal cloud, one that only Becca understood. They arrived back at

Heathrow at 2 p.m. of the same day they left Japan – the long and unending day only adding to the general confusion and bewilderment of the whole trip. When they got home, Becca went up to her bedroom and fell on her bed, but the sound of Andrew's angry voice downstairs stopped her from falling asleep.

'You need to take that girl in hand.'

'It was very difficult for her. I don't think you understand how upsetting it can be to watch someone you love with another person.'

'I think we both know what that feels like.'

'That's not what I meant. Becca's had a terrible shock, one we don't fully understand. She mentioned something to do with dreams . . . I don't know.'

'I know that she's done nothing but hang around and get in the way of you and me.'

'How can you say that?'

'You know it's true. We were having a perfectly nice time before she threw a hissy fit in the gallery, embarrassing everyone. She could have caused real problems for Jonathan.'

'I think a little kindness would go a long way here. She's my daughter and she's always been—'

'What?'

'Attached. She's always been very attached to me. And I'm not sure I've ever been able to give her what she needs.'

'You've given her too much, Jane. That's why she's here, leeching off you.'

'That's my daughter you're talking about! How dare you?'

'I'm looking out for you. You and me, we can't live our lives as long as she's here, moping around upstairs, following us everywhere. You need to force her to stand on her own two feet!'

'And you need to mind your own business. She's my daughter and I'll do exactly what I feel is right.'

'And what am I? Some fucking mug?'

'Leave. Andrew, I want you to leave.'

'Don't worry. I'm going.'

News of the first plane crashing into the North Tower of the World Trade Center came through just before two in the afternoon of the following day. Jane was ironing in the kitchen when details of the breaking news came through on Radio 4. She put the iron down and rushed into the lounge to turn on the television. She scrolled through the channels until she found the news and then sat down on the sofa, horrified by what was being replayed.

'Becca!'

Becca appeared at the door to the lounge, her hair tousled by the deep sleep of jet lag. 'What is it?'

'Becca, you've got to see this.'

'What's happened ...? Oh my God.'

'It's New York. Oh, those poor people. I must just phone Julia.'

'Julia's in Oxford. She's nowhere near New York.'

'Yes, I know,' Jane said, jumping up and pulling open the drawer of the telephone table in the hallway, where she kept her mobile phone. She found Julia's number and dialled it from the landline.

'She's not answering. Should I leave a message?'

'She'll have a missed call from you, so you don't have to.'

'Right ... Oh, Julia, I meant to leave a missed call. I've just seen the terrible news from New York and I wanted to check you're OK. Please give me a call when you get this. Bye, darling.

'It's just the most hideous thing. And to think we were on a plane only yesterday,' she said, sitting down next to Becca.

'Headed for London.'

'But still, you see how it can happen.'

'I can see how it has happened to the people of New York, yes.'

'I should phone Jonathan. I wonder if Andrew's phoned Jonathan.'

'For Christ's sake, he's in Japan. Do you not understand where these towers are?'

'Oh, I know. You're right. It's just so awful. Blowing people up on planes. Flying them into buildings. What's the world coming to?'

'I can't watch this,' Becca said, standing up.

'No, it's awful,' Jane said, turning up the volume.

As Becca went to walk into the kitchen, she heard a knock at the front door and knew, from the dark shadow behind the glass, that it was Andrew.

'It's Andrew,' Jane shouted as she ran to get the door.

'Shame he wasn't in the World Trade Center this morning,' Becca mumbled as she pulled a container of milk from the fridge.

'I've just seen,' Andrew said from the doorstep. He looked tired and overcome. As though he'd walked directly from Manhattan.

'Oh, it's awful. Have you phoned Jonathan?'

'Yeah, he's OK.'

'Of course he's OK,' Becca said, carrying a bowl of cereal from the kitchen into the lounge. 'He's OK because he spent the night in a very tame city in Japan.'

'I've tried to get in touch with Julia,' Jane said as she closed the door behind Andrew.

'She'll be fine,' he said, reaching out a hand to squeeze her shoulder. Jane put her hand over it, holding his fingers still.

'I'm sorry, Jane. I should never have tried to interfere. And you have to do whatever you think is right.'

Jane nodded, her hand still holding his in place.

'And seeing all those people just now – you know some of them are jumping from the building? With no hope of surviving?'

'I know. It's dreadful.'

'It just brought it home to me. We shouldn't be fighting. Whatever you want to do is fine by me.'

'I'm sorry too. We're all tired from the flight and what happened.'

'Becca's part of your life and I accept that.'

'Thank you,' Jane said, and led him towards the kitchen, closing the lounge door as she went.

Chapter 44

Jonathan emailed Becca a week later.

Becca,
    I know you were upset by what you think you saw at the gallery. It wasn't my intention to steal from you. But the truth is, art cannot be owned (says the man who runs a gallery . . . ha!). Your dreams, your body, they were inspiration for something *other*, something different. Minako has helped me become a better artist. Those visions are better because of her. There's really no need to feel jealous. The last thing I wanted was to hurt you or for things to be awkward. Especially now your mum and my dad are finally giving things a go.
    Anyway, I hope we can stay in touch. I think you and Minako would get on really well if you ever came out to visit again.
    Love,
    Jonathan x

She couldn't reply. She couldn't get beyond his inability to understand what she was feeling. He thought she wanted to take Minako's place when in fact she simply wanted to take back her dreams and body. It wasn't jealousy, it was rage. So she ignored it and got on with her life, returning to work at the supermarket and taking on extra hours whenever she could. Julia continued to follow in her father's footsteps and enrolled at Roehampton University to begin her PGCE. She took a room on campus and began her first placement at a large comprehensive school nestled between Richmond and Ham. She came home occasionally – most often on a Sunday to wash her clothes and have a roast dinner with her mum and sister – but for the most part she disappeared into the busy life of a trainee teacher.

It was a cold November morning when Jane went outside and smelled excrement. She put her boots on and walked down the lawn looking for the mess that filled the air. Half-way down the garden, against the fence she shared not with Andrew but her other neighbour, she noticed that the mud looked softer and more sludgy than the rest of the area. She pressed her boot into the brown and smelled the foul stench. Leaving the soiled boots by the back door, she put on her everyday pumps and walked next door to number 63.

Mrs Conway, a widow in her mid-sixties, opened the door. She was still in her dressing gown and slippers.

'Good morning, Mrs Conway. I'm sorry to bother you, but I think we have a problem out the back. Have you been outside yet?' she said, looking down at Mrs Conway's slippered feet.

'No, dear. I was about to have a wash. What's the matter?'

'I think there's sewage in the back. The pipe might have broken or been damaged somehow. I'm not sure. Can I come and take a look?'

'Yes, of course. Come on in. Can I make you a cup of a tea?'

'No, no, don't worry about that. If it is broken, I'll have to get on to Thames Water.'

'Right you are,' Mrs Conway said, unlocking the back door for Jane. 'It's cold out there,' she warned.

'Yes, you go in the house, Mrs Conway. I'll be back in a minute.'

The problem was much worse in Mrs Conway's garden. The soft, smelly line of brown extended right across her lawn and disappeared under the next fence.

'It's as I thought,' she said to Mrs Conway, who was sitting at her kitchen table, spreading marmalade on a slice of burned toast. 'A pipe has burst and there's sewage everywhere.'

'Sewage? Where?'

'In the garden. I'd better go and phone Thames Water.'

'Let me know what they say, won't you?' she said, taking a loud bite of her toast.

Andrew came home as soon as he heard. He didn't so much as kiss Jane, just walked straight through to the rear of the house, throwing the back door open.

'Oh my God,' he said, running his hand through his hair.

'I've already phoned Thames Water.'

'You have?'

'Of course.'

'And what did they say?'

'They're sending someone over to inspect. He should be here before five.'

'Where does it end?' he said, stepping onto the lawn.

'It looks like it doesn't reach as far as your property, but it's right across Mrs Conway's. I mean, I don't know – I'm only going by the line I can see there.'

'Yeah. Jesus, that's bad.'

'Is it?'

'Well, of course it is!'

'I mean, I know it smells, but surely they'll be able to fix it.'

'They're going to have to dig the gardens up.'

'At least it's November. I'm sure they'll make it good, and the grass will have grown over by next year.'

'No, Jane, you don't understand. It's going to be a lot of upheaval. They're going to have to get their diggers back here.'

'Yes, I see. But hopefully it won't affect your side. Perhaps it stops here?'

'They'll want to replace the whole stretch of pipe. Shit.'

Jane laughed. 'Yes, exactly. A lot of shit.'

'It's not funny. You've got human waste in your garden.'

'I'm just trying to lift the mood, that's all.'

Andrew was there when the engineer arrived at a quarter to four in the afternoon. He inspected the area and took a sample from the soil. Andrew stayed with him, asking him questions in quick succession.

'What could have caused it?'

'It's difficult to say at this stage. A lot of these pipes are very old and sometimes they reach the end of their useful life earlier than expected.'

'Do you repair the pipe or replace it?'

'Oh, replace it. There's no point in repairing something like this. But I don't know – I've got to report back to head office and they make the call.'

'Are you going to do that now?'

'Now I need to go next door and keep going down the road until I can work out where it ends.'

'It doesn't look like it's gone into my garden.'

'Where's your garden?'

'Just next door. This side.' Andrew pointed behind him.

'Look, I don't know. We may well have to go into your garden as well.'

At five thirty, the engineer knocked on Jane's door. Andrew answered it.

'Oh, hello again. I just wanted to speak to Mrs Campbell. Is she there?'

'Yeah. Jane!'

Jane emerged from the kitchen, wiping her hands on her apron. 'Hi.'

'Just called round to say I've inspected the other properties on this side of the road and it looks like it extends through at least four of them. I've just been on the phone to my supervisor and we're going to have to replace the whole pipe.'

'Even mine?' Andrew asked.

'Remind me what number you are?' The engineer looked down at the Land Registry map attached to his clipboard.

'Number sixty-seven.'

'Oh yes, we'll need access to yours and the next one over. There's a natural break in the pipe at that point.'

'Well, it can't be helped,' Jane said. 'When will you start?'

'We're scheduling works to commence on Monday. I've got a little card here that I need to leave with you. It just details the nature of the works, why we have to do them, and there's a number you can phone there if you have any questions.'

'Thank you.'

'Yeah, thanks,' Andrew said, and stepped back to close the door.

*

When Becca got home from work the following evening, Jane was sitting at the kitchen table. She had several leaflets before her.

'What are they?' Becca asked, peering into the saucepan on the stove.

'They're things to do in the Cotswolds. Andrew wants to take us away for a long weekend.'

'Us?'

'Yes, you and me. Do you think you can take Monday and Tuesday off?'

'No. Why would I?'

'Wouldn't you like to get away and have a little break?'

'He wants to get away and have a little break with you, Mum. Not me.'

'That's not true. He was very specific – he said he wants you to come. Becca, he's really trying.'

'He is really trying.'

'That's not what I mean. And look at this – there's a model village we can go and see and lots of National Trust properties.'

'I don't want to go,' Becca said, and opened the cupboard to the right of the oven where the bowls were kept. She ladled out a generous spoonful of the chilli con carne and sat down at the table.

'Darling, I was about to make some rice. I was just waiting for you to get home.'

'Don't worry,' she said, reaching for the open packet of sliced bread on the table.

'Have a look at this arboretum. Don't you think the colours would be wonderful at this time of year?'

'You don't get it, do you? Andrew's only ever been interested in me to get to you. He's doing this because of Japan and the argument you had when we got back. He wants to show you that he *accepts* me. How very gracious of him.'

'He's doing this because he cares about you and me. Because Thames Water are going to dig up some disgusting waste in our back garden on Monday and he thinks it would be nice for us to be away in the countryside! Why is that so difficult for you to understand?'

'It's not difficult to understand. I just don't want to go.'

Jane stood up and went to walk out of the kitchen but then changed her mind. 'I don't know what I could have ever done for you, Becca.'

Becca stopped chewing and looked up at her. 'What's that supposed to mean?'

'Since you were a very tiny baby I've never felt I was enough for you. You pulled and pulled, always taking, always dragging and I can't take any more of it. I can't take the disappointment I've been to you.'

'You haven't been a disappointment to me.'

'I know I have. I know I let you and Daddy down. But there are things you don't understand. Things you can't understand about how a marriage works, and for all my failings, I loved your father very much. And I've missed him so. His kindness, his warmth, his intelligence.'

Becca said nothing. She continued looking at her mother.

'And I know you're wondering why Andrew, and sometimes I wonder myself, but I was very young when I married your father and became your mother. I never had time to be a young woman.'

'I'm sorry I stopped you from being a young woman.'

'You didn't, Becca. I chose you,' she said, sitting down again and taking her daughter's hand. 'But it was more than I could have known. It took more of me than I was prepared to give at the time. And Andrew has always felt like an indulgence I denied myself for so long.'

'He's a dangerous indulgence.'

'How can you say so?' she said, dropping Becca's hand.

'Daddy didn't like him. And I don't like him.'

'You haven't given him a chance. You've barely said a word to him since Daddy died.'

'That's because he moved in so quickly! Why don't you send him off to the Cotswolds on his own? We could hole up indoors together, like we used to. Watch *Far From the Madding Crowd* or *Pride and Prejudice*? That's worth another watch, isn't it?'

Jane took a deep breath. 'Becca, you know I'd love to do that. At any other time. And if I didn't think this was a way of undercutting Andrew's kindness.'

'He's trying to take you away from me.'

'Take me away! There's no taking me away. But you know, sometimes I do think you need to stand on your own two feet a little more.'

'Do you?' Becca said, turning back to her chilli. 'Well, don't worry – I plan to. You go off to the Cotswolds and I'll stay here amid the shit. Standing on my own two feet.'

Chapter 45

Jane set off with Andrew just after lunch on Sunday. She had given the details of the hotel in the Cotswolds together with the spare keys to Mrs Conway, who had agreed to grant access to Thames Water on Monday morning should they arrive after Becca had gone to work. Becca waved to her mother as they reversed out of the drive, and then raised her arms above her head and stretched her body out, smiling at the pleasure of her elongated limbs, at the luxury of having the house to herself. She thought of the vibrator she kept under her mattress and decided to leave that until tonight. She'd bought series three of *Sex and the City* on DVD at work the previous day in anticipation of just this moment.

She walked into the kitchen and made tea and toast with lashings of butter and jam. She settled herself on the sofa, her feet on the coffee table, and pressed 'play'.

At eight o'clock, Becca ordered a pizza and opened a bottle of white wine she'd also had the presence of mind to buy the previous day. She settled back onto the sofa and ate two-thirds of a large pizza and drank several glasses of wine. She went upstairs to her bedroom, pulling the curtains closed against a bright full moon. She took her clothes off in the half-darkness. Ordinarily she'd bolt her door and play some music in order to drown out the hum, but the silence of the empty house was too tempting and she decided to reach for her bunny with no other sounds discernible.

But as she turned it on, she noticed the buzz sounded strange. It had a scratchy, rhythmic undertone. She turned if off and was just about to unscrew the plastic casing and check the battery connection when she heard the same raspy, discordant sound. It was coming from her bedroom window. She got up and walked over to the window, pulled the curtain back and saw a dark figure bent over a shovel in Andrew's garden. He was taller, stockier than Andrew, his skinhead glinting in the moonlight. Becca was about to open the window and shout, thinking – absurdly – that he might be looking for the burst pipe when she remembered her naked-ness and kept quiet, continuing to watch him.

He continued digging until he reached soil soft enough for him to rummage with his fingers. Becca could make out the thin orange plastic of an old carrier bag. The figure reached into it as though it contained shopping. And just as suddenly he pulled something big, a giant vegetable, from the bag. It had long stems that allowed him to raise it high up into the air. Becca watched the thickness of his neck folds as he stood up straight and glared at the thing in front of his face. She watched, utterly enthralled, as a grimace forced his fat cheeks back, and it was only when she saw him recoil that she decided to look more closely at the object in front of him.

It was the remains of a human head.

Chapter 46

The scream was out of her before she could stop it. It rattled inside her chest and pushed its way up her throat. It hit the glass of her window and scattered around the room. She clamped her hand over her mouth, but it was too late. A few fragments of her fear had penetrated the glass and drifted down to the gardens, separated only by a fence. And Steve, who thought he was alone in the cold night air, turned from Marion's decomposed head to see the white outline of a naked girl in the first-floor window of the house next door.

He dropped the head and made to run for the back door. Becca stepped away from the window and looked around her. Her phone was downstairs, on the coffee table in the lounge. She began descending the stairs, and just as her own buzz had mirrored the sound of his digging, now her footsteps were in tune with his heavy tread as he made his way up the front path. The angry bang on the front door was too close, too violent for her to go any further. She knew she had to retreat, but how to phone the police? She remembered the landline extension in her mother's bedroom and ran back up the stairs. She closed the bedroom door just as the knock at the front door morphed into a heavy kicking – she knew the wood couldn't hold much longer. She looked around frantically for something heavy to put in his way while she phoned the police, but nothing appeared substantial enough to block his determined effort to get at her. She dragged her mother's dressing table across the door, her naked body weak and unequal to the task. She was dialling 999 as she heard the front door break from its hinges. She heard the words 'What service do you require?' as Steve thundered up the stairs towards her bedroom. She had only the time it would take him to work out she must be in one of the other two bedrooms before he'd be upon her.

She dropped the phone and ran to the window. She opened it as wide as it would go and, stepping onto the outside ledge, waited for what she knew must come. In the mirror of her mother's dressing table, like a hole in the wall, she caught sight of her naked body, terrified and alone, holding on to the window frame for dear life. As Steve forced his way into the room, she let go and allowed the darkness to pull her away.

Epilogue

Monday, 12 November 2001

Julia was met by two women at the entrance to the intensive-care ward.

'Is it Julia Campbell?'

'Yes. I'm here to see my sister. Who are you?'

The woman smiled and bent her head as she opened a leather wallet to reveal a warrant card. 'I'm DC Spence, and this is my colleague DC Roberts. We work on one of the Metropolitan Police murder teams. We're trying to get to the bottom of what happened last night.'

'Did someone push her?'

'We don't know what happened yet. But we do need to speak to all members of the family. I understand your mum is on her way here?' she asked Julia but looked to DC Roberts for the answer.

'Yes, she was away. With her boyfriend. Look, I really need to see my sister. Can I go inside?'

'Yes.' DC Spence knocked on the glass panel in the door, and a few seconds later they heard the release of the door.

364

She pushed it open and stepped back so Julia could go in.

'We'll wait here.'

Becca had sustained a very serious head injury. The consultant in charge of her care had decided to put her in an induced coma in an attempt to control the swelling of her brain. When Julia approached her bed, Becca's eyes were taped shut and her mouth open for the tube that breathed for her. Julia, usually so self-contained, bit her lower lip as she started to cry. She could see Becca was still falling, hovering between this world and the next.

She went to find a doctor. As she walked towards the secure doors of the ward, she saw Andrew through the glass panes that DC Spence had knocked on earlier. He had his hands behind his back as a uniformed officer handcuffed him. Jane stood to one side with her hand to her mouth.

Julia pressed the green button and released the door.

'What's going on?'

'They're arresting Andrew,' she said quietly. A matter of fact.

'What for?'

'Marion!' Jane's voice climbed to a shriek at the mention of her former neighbour.

'What's going on?' Julia asked DC Spence.

'It's best we don't discuss this here. When you've finished visiting your sister, I'd be grateful if you could join me at Kingston Police Station,' she said, handing Julia her card. 'And the same for you, Mrs Campbell. We'll need to speak to all family members.'

Jane gripped Julia's arm and attempted to follow her but kept turning back to look at Andrew and the police officer talking to him. Andrew was nodding. Jane opened her mouth to say something but then closed it resolutely. As though she'd had something pressing to voice but had forgotten it entirely.

'Mum, this way.'

'How can it be?'

But it was. And as she approached Becca's bed, she gasped at the sight of her broken daughter. Julia put her arm around her waist and pulled her into a chair.

'How could this have happened?'

'I don't know.'

'What do the doctors say?'

'I haven't seen one yet. I was about to go and find someone when I saw you.'

'She was fine yesterday. She waved at me from the front door and now this.'

'Was Andrew with you the whole time last night?'

Jane nodded.

'I think I need to go to the police station. You stay here with Becca, in case the doctor comes round.'

'Yes. Have you got your phone?'

'Yes.'

Becca regained consciousness on the last day of November, twelve days after her fall. Jane was in the room, was always beside her: intermittently holding her hand, walking round her bed and wondering how this nightmare had come to pass. It was made concrete by the machines, the jug of water on the table, the regular rounds by nurses, who sought to record the marginalia of her daughter's broken life. They didn't know, as they noted her temperature, that Becca used to pile dried lentils into a bowl and attempt to feed her dolls while Jane cooked beside her in the kitchen. Or that, as a little girl, she gripped her mother's hand tightly when they crossed the road and loosened as they stepped up onto the pavement, still willing the connection but no longer afraid of the cars. They didn't know – or understand – that Becca's body and brain were injured because of her own mother. Her own desire.

And as if to reassure her mother – the woman who'd suffered her constant need for attention – Becca's eyelids began flickering in response to the consultant's gradual reduction in barbiturates. Her fingers began to move with a control that was no longer reflexive. And this time it was Jane who gripped her daughter's hand. She held on tight and willed her to stay.

Becca's recovery was slow and halting. The loss of vision in her right eye was apparent very early on, and she suffered near-constant tremors on the right side of her face and in her hands and legs. But she could walk, at first managing just a few steps within the parallel bars of the physiotherapy suite and then later, in the hospital garden, greater distances with her cane. In the first few weeks, she would walk only with her mother on her left side. She turned her head intermittently to check Jane was still there.

When Andrew was given a life sentence for the murder and preventing the lawful and decent burial of Marion, Julia sent her mother a text message from outside the Old Bailey with the details and no more. She knew it was all Jane wanted: to know that Andrew would serve a long prison term. Jane thought of Leonard and how she'd been so attracted to his knowledge and learning and yet she hadn't learned from him. He'd known Andrew was wrong for her. And in his own way he'd tried to stop their inevitable coupling. A final act of love,

367

he'd tried to protect his wife and daughters from the evil he'd sensed next door.

Julia finished her PGCE in June 2002 and began applying for teaching jobs in Gloucestershire, where some of her friends from Oxford had moved. Julia, happy to peer in but always at an emotional remove, saw that Becca's recovery was well underway and that it was time for her to go and live her own life. And Jane, in a move redolent of Becca, put the house on the market and bought a two-bedroom ground-floor flat in Cheltenham so that she could care for Becca in close proximity to Julia.

In her darkest moments, she envied Marion her oblivion. Becca's injuries and impaired vision felt like a great punishment, a necessary mortification for having failed to heed her dying husband's warning. She knew that Becca had been tightly bound in the thick cords of her marriage from the very beginning. That its conclusion and her own attraction to Andrew had left Becca vulnerable. Her fall had been in motion long before her body dropped from the bedroom window.

And with knowledge came understanding. She felt her mind settle on a new truth: Becca's actions that night, her desperate attempt to escape Steve had saved them all. She alone had successfully exposed Andrew for what he really was.

They settled into their new life. Becca enrolled on a creative-writing course at the University of Gloucestershire, and with Becca out at seminars during the day, Jane began going to the library three or four times a week, where she'd pore over books and edit her reading list.

In November, Jane answered an advertisement for a sales assistant at her local bookshop. The role was just three mornings a week – one of which had to be a Saturday – and Jane smiled when they showed her the uniform: a green apron to be worn over her clothes. As if she needed protection from the splashes of truth the titles contained. And she was good at it: customers liked the way she listened carefully to them and went off in her quiet, unobtrusive way to find the perfect book, the way she spoke so knowingly about why a novel was worth reading. The manager kept her on after Christmas, and for the first time in her life, she found a job and a sense of purpose that belonged to her alone.

On sunny afternoons, no matter how low the temperature dropped, she walked to her favourite café, just a few doors down from the bookshop, and sat at one of the tables on the pavement with her face turned up towards the light. She closed her eyes so that the rays might warm her eyelids, and in this bright darkness she felt grief fall upon her like heavy wool on a warm summer's day. The idea of a person and the reality of a life together. She saw it all now.

Acknowledgements

To Alice Lutyens: an unrivalled agent and chief support. I'd be lost without you.

To Arzu Tahsin and Jennifer Kerslake: you believed in this book from the beginning and then made it happen. I am so grateful to you both.

To Jim Cowell, my most necessary husband. Thank you.

To Maddie and Thomas: this book, and everything I do, is powered by love of you.

To my mum: a loving mother, a strong woman and an absolute inspiration.

To my dad: for telling me I can run any race. And then beaming at me from the finish line.

To my brother Paul and sister Emma: for support, encouragement and banter that makes me forget myself and clutch my sides.

To Jennifer Cowell: for your incomparable sense of humour. You encourage me to see the world in a different way. And laugh at it.

To Bill Cowell: for key knowledge of the 1980s and marshalling readers.

To my oldest friend Nisha Bailey: for taking the time to go on an important research mission for this book.

To Keiko Ikematsu: for reading through the Japanese sections. どうもありがとうございました.

To Polly Evernden: my reading-twin, first editor and precious friend. You make my books better.

To Linda Rothera: for always giving of your time and expertise so generously. What would I do without you?

To Richard Ellis: for some key advice on footwear.

To my early readers: Alan and Laura Ashton, Helen and Jeremy Aves, Caroline Aird-Mash, Donna Dove, Louise Groves and Charlotte Morton.

To Louise Patke and Alice Thatcher: your friendship is a rare gift.

Finally, to the rest of the team at W&N: Loulou Clark, Rebecca Gray, Craig Lye, Theresa Howes and Maggy Park for all you do behind the scenes.